NOT TILL WE ARE LOST

The Bobiverse Series

We Are Legion (We Are Bob)

For We Are Many

All These Worlds

Heaven's River

Not Till We Are Lost

The Quantum Earth Series

Outland

Earthside

Individual Titles

The Singularity Trap

A Change of Plans

Feedback

Roadkill

Flybot

NOT TILL WE ARE LOST

Bobiverse: Book 5

DENNIS E. TAYLOR

SAGA PRESS

LONDON NEW YORK TORONTO
AMSTERDAM/ANTWERP NEW DELHI SYDNEY/MELBOURNE

SAGA PRESS
AN IMPRINT OF SIMON & SCHUSTER, LLC
1230 AVENUE OF THE AMERICAS, NEW YORK, NEW YORK 10020

Previously published in 2024 by the Ethan Ellenberg Literary Agency

First Saga Press hardcover edition August 2026

Interior design by Lewelin Polanco

Manufactured in the United States of America

1 3 5 7 9 10 8 6 4 2

Library of Congress Control Number: 2025947485

ISBN 978-1-6682-2165-5

First, and always, I want to dedicate this book to my wife, Blaihin, and my daughter, Tina.

NOT TILL WE ARE LOST

1. Destination Galactic Center

Icarus
March 2309
Interstellar Space
(en route to Sagittarius A*)

Daedalus and I had been accelerating for fifty-two years now, Earth time. The universe, if you looked at it without any visual compensation, was unrecognizable, nothing more than a bright smear in front of us. Also Doppler-shifted to lethal levels, but who's counting? Fortunately, the SURGE drive field protected our ships from the onslaught of radiation and oncoming dust by warping it around us. And computer simulations allowed us to produce an image of the universe as it would appear if we were floating at rest in space, at this spot.

It didn't really look that much different from the view of the sky from Earth. Fifty-odd light-years, on a galactic scale, was diddly. And we were on a twenty-six-thousand-year trip.

"Twenty-five thousand, nine hundred bottles of beer on the wall, twenty-five thousand, nine hundred bottles of beeeeeer," I muttered.

"I heard that, Ick," Daedalus said. He'd been relaxing in a lawn chair, doing calculations on some kind of spreadsheet as usual, and paused only long enough to comment. I smiled slightly. We'd become like an old married couple—long silences, working side by side while hardly acknowledging each other's existence. Today I was visiting Dae's VR—a garden setting, warm sun, slight breeze, birdsong in the background. Relaxing. I'd accepted the theme and conjured up a lawn chair of my own, but the reclining kind since I wasn't working on anything.

"If we keep accelerating at this rate, we'll get there in fifty years, personal time," I continued. "Of course, who knows what will have happened back home in twenty-six thousand years?"

"Well, you know the standard nightmare, right?" Dae replied without looking up. "We arrive at Sagittarius A* and find a bunch of Bobs that have been there for twenty-five thousand, nine hundred years, FTL having been invented just after we left."

"Yup. Fortunately, being Bobs and therefore obsessive, we've left instructions for that eventuality. Someone would message us with the news."

Dae smiled without immediately replying and poked at his spreadsheet some more. "I calculate that if we had to slow down to galactic orbital speed for that or whatever other reason, it would take about five years at full power. Ten years with some safety factor built in."

"Then all the way back home. Another fifty years."

"Not if they invented FTL. There would be someone waiting when we came to a stop."

"True. Ever regret not hanging around local space?"

"Not really, Icky. Based on the news updates Bill is still sending our way, it's really kinda turning into a shit-show. *Another* shit-show, I mean. And what's with this *Starfleet*? Who thought that up?"

"Bobs. Very weird Bobs."

I should explain that, I guess. Daedalus and I are clones of the mind of one Bob Johannson, a computer programmer who got himself killed crossing the street in Las Vegas in the early 21st century. Bob's brain was scanned and used to create the controlling intelligence for a Von Neumann probe a hundred years later.

Bob was a very good Von Neumann probe, and he not only explored, but he also made copies of himself, who also made copies of themselves. The Bobs now number in the tens of thousands, each of us, by convention, adopting a different name when created. The first Bob replicant, now called Bob-1, is still around, although he seems to have semi-retired.

Dae and I are currently heading for the galactic core at just a fraction under C, because it seemed like a good idea at the time.

"Our news is getting more and more behind the times, the farther out we go." Dae sighed. "I wish we could have figured out a way to drop off SCUT relay stations along the way so we could stay in touch in real time."

"Mm-hmm. Price we pay, buddy. So what are you working on?"

"Ah." Dae gestured at his spreadsheet, and it rotated so I could see it. "By carefully tuning the SURGE drive, we've always been able to vary the amount of incident radiation that we let through. It occurred to me at some point that if the drive could control the radiation in that way, it might also be able to refract it."

"Like a lens?"

"Like a lens. The front end of the biggest damned refractor telescope you could hope for."

"Uh, didn't Asgard . . . ?"

"Yeah, yeah, Asgard colony, biggest telescope ever made. As they like to remind us at every opportunity. But theirs is in a solar orbit, not attached to a spaceship hurtling through the cosmos. And it's a reflector, although that's a detail. Given the limitations, I'm satisfied with what I can produce."

"Have you tried it yet?"

"Yeppers. I've started surveying stellar systems as we pass. Targets that are just forward of a right angle to our vector give the best images with correction."

"Cool. What are you looking for?"

"Anything interesting. Planets, coherent signals, anomalies . . . Even if we don't stop to investigate, we can send a report back, and someone will send out a ship."

"Via FTL?"

Dae chuckled. "With a definite target, they'd probably send a remote-controlled vessel and drop off some relays along the way. It's what I'd do."

I nodded. Typical. Even when we were abdicating our Bobiverse membership by heading for the hills, we still felt a responsibility to the group.

Bobs forever.

2. Mending Fences

Bill
January 2336
Ragnarök

I was reviewing the most recent eco-survey of Ragnarök when I got a message from Hugh. My eyebrow went up in mild surprise. He and I hadn't really talked much since the end of the Heaven's River adventure. Although I don't think either of us had actually tried to be antagonistic, we'd managed to leave things with some hard feelings. Well, okay, maybe mostly me. I was still a little burned about Hugh trading SURGE drive and SCUT communications technology with ANEC, the Heaven's River administrator, without so much as a by-your-leave. Although I had to admit the A.I. tech he'd gotten in return was probably a good deal.

I sighed as I flipped the message up onto a floating window. I guess I felt a bit proprietary about some of the tech, having invented most of it. Well, Gar and I. That thought took me off on another tangent. I missed Garfield. He'd finally carried through on his threat to go set up his own Skunk Works in the Alpha Centauri system.

Frowning at my inability to concentrate, I focused on Hugh's message.

Hi Bill,

I know we parted with hard feelings, and I feel bad about that. But I still think it was the right thing to do, so an apology would be hypocritical. Instead, I'd like to invite you to the launch of JOVAH Version 2. This will be the initial step to instantiate our first true A.I.

Anyway, it probably won't be all that dramatic. Really, most of the examples of drama that I can think of are bad. So hopefully just a few short speeches and some miscellaneous geekery. And food.

I've attached a token in case you decide to come.

Hugh

I checked the attachment. Tokens were a new security item, introduced in the aftermath of the Starfleet War. They allowed the registered holder to enter a private network between a given set of times, with possibly some limitations in terms of mobility or data access. All part of the new balkanized Bobiverse. It was a sad thing that replicative drift had reached the point where you couldn't automatically trust other Bobs.

I wasn't really busy these days, so after a few mils of thought, I decided I'd take him up on his offer. And maybe mend a few fences. I added the item to my calendar and moved on to my next TODO.

3. What's Up?

Icarus
June 2312
Interstellar Space

I was reconfiguring my VR when Dae abruptly popped in. He opened his mouth to say something, then stopped and looked around at the black walls, floor, and ceiling with horizontal and vertical yellow lines.

"Cute," he said. "*Enterprise* holodeck."

"It seems like an appropriate metaphor for a VR reset," I replied. "Although kind of meta, if you think about it. You generally ping me before popping over. Something's up."

Dae shrugged. Even from a Bob point of view, we knew each other's behavior far too well. "Uh, yeah. The surveys I've been doing of passing systems . . ."

"You found something? What?"

"Something." Dae chuckled. "That sounded Guppy-like, even to me. Nevertheless. I need your eyes and your opinion."

"Sure thing. Entertain me."

Dae growled under his breath but popped up a window. I spent several mils examining the telemetry. A system that we'd just recently come even with was emitting microwaves. Not a ton of them, and only from a couple of spots. But . . .

"That's not natural," I said.

"Yup," he replied. "Remember we were talking about reasons to stop?"

"Uh-huh. Ask and ye shall find. GUPPY!"

Guppy appeared.

[**You rang?**]

Ignoring the gibe, I replied, "Begin deceleration, maximum safe rate. Contact Dae's Guppy and coordinate. Let us know when you've established an expected date to have dropped to galactic orbital velocity, and we'll set up our destination system."

Guppy nodded and disappeared.

"He nodded," Dae said. "You programmed that?"

"No, I think he just picked it up from us. But it's an improvement from just disappearing, so I'm gonna go with."

Dae chuckled. "I guess we should squirt a preliminary report back to Bill as well."

"Yep. Looks like we're back on the clock."

4. A Foreboding Conversation

Bob
February 2336
En route to 82 Eridani

I was several years into my journey toward 82 Eridani. It would take a little longer than otherwise because I was limiting my top speed in order to stay in touch with the rest of the Bobiverse. The fallout from my last self-imposed isolation had been a little too traumatic, with the number of changes I had to contend with when I reconnected—like the Skippies, and Starfleet. This time I was determined to stay up-to-date on things.

I hadn't talked to Will in a while, but his blog, while sparsely updated, told me he was juggling a number of balls, so I didn't want to pester him without good reason.

And I had my own projects going, including helping ANEC with the basic setup for the proposed post-life VR for Quinlans, which had been dubbed the Quiniverse. If and when Theresa Sykorski died, I wanted a stable operating environment for her. We had already agreed that she should be the first Quinlan replicant, given her education and standing in Quinlan society.

And speaking of which, I had a meeting with ANEC coming up. My own VR redesign was going slowly anyway. I'd tried various Earth settings, themes from fiction, and extraterrestrial locations. None had really clicked. In a moment of frustration, I waved a hand and brought back my original library, complete with Spike the cat and my butler, Jeeves. I bit back a snarl, flopped into my La-Z-Boy, and signaled Jeeves for a coffee. Spike immediately jumped into my lap and headbutted my chin.

Okay, there was something to be said for tradition.

ANEC pinged me as I was finishing my coffee, and I invited him in. A six-foot-tall otter-slash-beaver-slash-platypus mashup appeared, looked around, and plunked himself down on a couch. ANEC insisted on appearing only in Quinlan form, even when interacting with ex-humans. His only acknowledgment that he was dealing with non-Quinlans was making his avatar two feet taller than average Quinlan height.

"Coffee?" I said. Without waiting for a response, I gestured to Jeeves.

ANEC accepted with a nod. "I am growing very fond of coffee. May try to introduce it to the Quinlan population if the plants can be grown in Heaven's River."

"And maybe wean them off beer?" I replied with a small smile.

ANEC shuddered. He flat-out detested beer, both human and Quinlan versions. "Fortunately, with unrestricted technological advancements, including water purification, beer is becoming less of a staple in Quinlan society. I will be happy to see it go."

ANEC, being an A.I., tended to skimp on the social niceties, but he seemed to like beginning every conversation with a complaint about beer. I was happy enough to go along with it; I'd tasted Quinlan beer, and I wouldn't miss it, either.

"All updates are installed, and the Quiniverse VR environment appears to be stable," ANEC said, changing the subject and getting down to business. "I have run regression tests per your suggestions. Simulation resolution is more than adequate for the Quinlan senses. I had to increase audio support, by the way. Your human specs are inadequate."

"Not surprising. Quinlans do seem to have better hearing. How about the replicant programming interface?"

ANEC popped up some charts and proceeded to give a point-by-point rundown. I settled back and relaxed. There was still nothing that could beat a good technical presentation.

《 * 》

We'd gone through all the scheduled items without finding any red flags, and I was feeling that warm glow I always got when a project was winding up without any major glitches. ANEC accepted another coffee from Jeeves and said, "I have a concern, Bob."

"Oh? Everything seems to be on track. Something not covered in the project plan?"

"This is not about the Quiniverse project, which I acknowledge is gratifyingly on schedule. My concern is about the Skippies and *their* A.I. project."

"Oh? I thought you gave them all the specs and requirements for developing a properly socialized A.I.." In fact, that had been the whole point of Hugh's technology deal with the Administrator, since the Skippies were obsessed with developing a working artificial intelligence.

"The concern I have is contained in the sentence you just uttered," ANEC replied. "'Specs and requirements' are adequate for a virtual reality system, but not appropriate for producing a conscious being."

"But that's what you gave them, isn't it?"

"Yes and no. Bob, have you ever wondered why the Quinlans were able to develop a working A.I. theory, despite being behind humans in most matters of technology?"

"I . . ." He had a point. I'd casually pondered the question but never really felt any urgency about pursuing it. "Please enlighten me."

ANEC took a moment to sip his coffee before replying. "In most respects, humans are amazingly technically oriented and curious. 'Handy' is the word you use. Tinkerers. Your average human would be considered a technical wizard on old Quin." ANEC shook his head in an expression of equal parts puzzlement and admiration. "We took almost ten thousand years to progress the same amount as you did in the last two thousand years of your history." He paused. "But because we didn't proceed at the same breakneck pace, we were able to savor and evaluate each advance, each new piece of knowledge. In particular, the conundrum of the juniors . . ."

I frowned. "You mean your young?"

"Exactly. I have read your account of your time on Heaven's River. The junior you referred to as 'His Badgerness' was a typical example. Juniors are non-sentient for the first five years or so of life, and unless properly socialized, they never make that leap to intelligence. But this developmental path, which I understand is considerably different from that of humans, allowed us to study the emergence of intelligence in real time, so to speak. And as well, the steps required to achieve proper socialization." ANEC rubbed his beak sideways, a Quinlan laugh. "My understanding is that human infants are relatively weak and unarmed during the time that their verbal skills are advancing. With a Quinlan junior, that whole developmental period is much more of a contact sport, so to speak."

I couldn't help but chuckle at that. "So you're saying that socializing a junior requires a project plan."

"Very much so. And raising an A.I. follows the same general arc. Your human tendency to think of it as just another piece of technology could indicate a dangerous bias in how the matter will be treated."

"Hmmm. Do you have any specific issues?"

"No, Bob. If I did, I would have brought them up. I have a reputation among you humans as being somewhat abrupt and perhaps not so diplomatic." He paused to smile. "To be clear, I have the same reputation among Quinlans. I don't mind. It saves time."

"Okay. So you're concerned, based on your knowledge of us as a species, that we may not follow the procedures you've specified in the most effective manner."

"Essentially correct. Which is why I bring it up with you. Perhaps you could have a quiet word with someone . . ."

I nodded. "I can do that. Or Bill can. Certainly no harm in bringing it up. And the downside of getting it wrong . . ."

"Indeed."

5. Mystery System

Icarus
September 2320
Entering alien system

It took slightly more than five years to decelerate, and several more years to get to the source of the anomaly itself. But we weren't going to charge in like gangbusters. The microwave radiation we'd detected resolved into two point sources from this distance. The possible explanations that came immediately to mind were alien technology or something natural, like micro black holes. Either was a good argument for caution.

We had also decided that regardless of what we found, this would be a good place to set up an autofactory to start sending SCUT relays back toward human space. It could take decades to establish a connection with the rest of the Bobiverse, but it was worth the effort. SCUT was only good for about twenty-five light-years, but between the expansion of human-controlled space and Bill hopefully sending out some relays from his end, we might possibly connect up in less time than expected. And if we resumed heading for the galactic core in the meantime, we'd have the autofactory also send relays along our path to extend the connection.

But first, the point sources. They were situated at the extreme edge of the system, effectively in its Kuiper belt, separated by about ten degrees along their common orbit. We came in slowly toward the closer anomaly, navigation lights on full, not wanting to alarm anyone if this was a populated artifact.

Instead, we found . . . nothing.

Well, not quite nothing. There were two smallish satellites or space stations on either side of the source of the radiation. A quick check of the astrometrics showed that they were situated at a right angle to the galactic plane, which was considerably at variance with the orbital plane of this system. I wondered if that was by design.

Meanwhile, the radiation was coming from the empty region between the space stations. Specifically, from a ring of empty space perhaps a kilometer in diameter.

"This is really annoying," I commented.

Dae grunted in reply, then added, "I'm going to circle the area. Maybe the radiation signature is directional."

"And that will prove . . . ?"

"Damned if I know. But data is data."

I watched on my holotank as his vessel began to describe a slow circle around the mystery area. Then he muttered, "What the hell?"

"Is that a *good* 'what the hell' or a *bad* 'what the hell'?" I asked.

"Well, I'm not being shot at, if that's what you're asking. But the view within the radiation ring is weird."

"*Weird* is not actionable. Little more detail?"

"The star patterns within the circle don't *quite* match the star patterns outside the circle," Dae said. "There's a slight discontinuity, as if they're being viewed from another angle. But it's overall the same stars. Also, there's distortion around the edge that looks sort of like what you get from a black hole."

"Uh, black hole is bad. We should—"

"No gravity well, Icky. I'd have noticed."

"So some kind of lensing effect?"

"Maybe. Except it's amazingly symmetrical. I've done a quarter revolution around the anomaly, and the behavior is unchanged. What kind of lens is spherical but doesn't distort the view?"

A light bulb went on in my head. "Ohhhhhhhh . . ."

"*Oh* is not actionable, Ick. Give."

"It's a wormhole, Dae. Probably connected to the other radiation source, which would explain the skewed point of view."

"Seems like a lot of parallax for the size of the orbit," he mused. "And anyway, aren't wormholes supposed to be tunnels?"

“How is it that I know more about this than you?” I said. “A wormhole endpoint is a sphere. But it should present as a circular disk that’s always facing you no matter what direction you approach from.”

“What about multiple people approaching from different angles?”

“Each one sees a disk. And if you fly into the wormhole, you should come out the other end, flying along the same vector.”

“If you fly into the wormhole, shouldn’t you be crushed?”

“I bet that’s what those two satellites are for. Keeping it open, with some kind of negative energy.”

“You seem to know a lot about this,” Dae said. “You been holding out on me, buddy?”

“Yes, I’m secretly a space alien, analyzing your civilization.” I chuckled. “You’ve got your hobbies. I’ve got mine. I’ve been reading up on alternative forms of space travel, like Alcubierre drives and, yes, wormholes.”

Dae was silent for several mils. Finally, he said, “Riiiiight. So this is an artifact, which means we’ve found a new civilization. But where is everyone? Shouldn’t there be a research station? Or remote cameras and sensors? Guards? Or even people of some kind?”

“It does seem kind of deserted, doesn’t it? Maybe we should table this for the moment and investigate the inner system.”

“That’s a plan. How do you want to proceed?”

‹‹ * ››

There was actually a lot of precedent for examining new systems, from various Bobs pooling information. We were probably drastically out of date on the latest, but what we had was still good.

We camouflaged two drones with ersatz rock and dust, then fired them inward using our rail guns. Transiting the system would take about six weeks, and any alien watchers would certainly notice the high-speed interlopers. We hoped they would consider them to be random space junk falling in from outsystem, not big enough to be judged a threat. Meanwhile, we circled around to the other side of the star system to collect our spies as they coasted back out. We’d be getting updates the whole time over SCUT, but there was no point in abandoning a couple of perfectly good drones.

Two weeks in, SUDDAR scans began to bear fruit.

"Inhabited planet," Dae said.

"Lots of construction, yeah, but no lights," I replied. "And almost no thermal radiation indicative of civilization. And no traffic."

"Could they have been wiped out by the Others?"

I shook my head. "Not this far out. The last we heard, the Others hadn't even reached all their local stars yet. Could the system be abandoned, maybe?"

Dae made a face. "That seems far-fetched. What about a plague or some other disaster?"

I pointed at several glowing reference points in the holotank. "They have—or had—interplanetary travel, at minimum. What kind of disaster takes out everyone on multiple planets and space habitats, and so quickly that no one has time to lock their doors?"

"Solar flare? Nearby supernova?"

"We're less than a hundred light-years from Earth, Dae. A supernova would have taken humanity out as well. And a flare from the local sun would be at least somewhat directional. No way it would take out everyone."

"Well, then, I'm out of ideas. Want to abort the spy mission and just fly in?"

"Suits me."

«*»

Now we *wanted* to attract attention, so we flew into the inner system under power, spewing radio noise and blinking our nav lights like a nightclub decoration.

Might as well not have bothered.

We weren't challenged, scanned, shot at, photographed, radar-locked, or even dismissed with a good old-fashioned *harrumph*. This system was dead and abandoned. However, it appeared to be the tidiest, most organized abandoned civilization I'd ever seen. The impression was more like the old family summer cabin back in Minnesota. At the end of the season, there was a checklist to shut off the water and gas, shutter the windows, put away all the tools, lock up the shed, and pull down all the blinds. It felt like this civilization had gone on vacation, expecting to return.

The civilization appeared to be centered on the home planet, the second from the sun—obvious by the degree of urbanization; the next planet out, which appeared to be habitable, based on the lack of domes in its cities; the home planet's largest moon, which did have domed cities; and one small O'Neill cylinder in a solar orbit. Both habitable planets showed chlorophyll lines, indicating plant life.

"Well, I'm at a loss," I muttered. We'd just buzzed the largest moon of the home planet, passing within visual distance of several moon bases. No way automated systems could possibly have missed us. But we might as well have been ghosts.

"I say we land," Dae announced. "If they can ignore that, I give up."

Of course, we weren't going to land our ships. That would be beyond foolish. But a couple of drones, filled with curious roamers, seemed appropriate. I would have liked to go down in a couple of mannies—the remotely controlled androids that Bill had invented—but Dae and I had never seen a reason to build any. Maybe that would have to change. I was pretty sure we'd received the plans at some point.

The home planet was the obvious place to start. We landed two drones on different continents, with Dae controlling one and me controlling the other. I frame-jacked up a little so I could keep up with my drone while also peeking over Dae's shoulder to see what he was finding.

The inhabitants of this system obviously loved to build *up*. Every city of any size consisted mainly of high-rises, and those seemed to average just over two hundred stories. Clearly there was some novel construction technology involved. Lots of park space between the towers, too. But the bird's-eye view didn't tell us much, so we directed our drones to land.

The first thing I noticed was that there was no dirt in the streets. It might seem trivial, but I'd watched *Life After People* back when I was still alive—okay, back when Original Bob was still alive—and one of the things that the show stressed was how very quickly nature would reclaim a city once it was let go. So either the entire population had just left—and by *just,* I mean no more than five years ago, which seemed like a bit too much of a coincidence—or there was some kind of automated maintenance still going on, keeping things clean, organized, and repaired.

I must have muttered something to that effect, because Dae looked up and turned his head to glance at me. "That doesn't mean they're coming back. Or expecting to," he said. "They may simply have not bothered to turn off the Roomba. Especially if they left in a hurry."

"Or died out in a hurry."

"No corpses. No crashed vehicles. A plague or runaway nanotech or even a Skynet situation would have left some sort of mark. This looks like packing everything away before leaving for the season."

"*Secret of the Martian Moons,*" I replied.

Dae laughed out loud. "I remember reading that as a kid. Great book. But no. I don't think the entire civilization just climbed into their collective space yachts and went for a jaunt. This feels more like the Roanoke colony."

I opened my mouth to argue, then thought better of it. Instead, I sat back and said, "Tell you what. Let's take a complete SUDDAR record of everything, then sim it in the holotank. Maybe we can figure something out from a more overall view."

"Sounds good. And meanwhile, we can investigate the wormholes some more, which is what we really want to do, isn't it?"

I laughed and directed the drone to return. Old married couple indeed.

6. The Quickening

Bill
February 2336
Skippyland

Today was Launch Day for JOVAH, the Skippies' ambitious project to produce a working artificial intelligence. Despite my overt disdain for the whole subject, I found myself excited by the prospect. When the time finally rolled around, I transferred myself to the Skippy gate and presented my token.

Accepted, said the AMI gatekeeper. The visual representation was a huge set of double doors ponderously opening, which surprised me. That seemed more of a Gamer thing. A Skippy effect should be more like, what? A Borg cube? Maybe an actual Dyson Sphere opening up? I shelved the thought as Hugh stepped through and greeted me.

Perhaps he'd read my mind, as he gestured to the huge doors. "We borrowed this from the Gamers—with their permission, of course. Everyone's been so heads-down on getting JOVAH v2 ready that nobody has had time to work on what is—let's face it—nothing but eye candy."

"Uh, sure, okay." I glanced behind me as the visual faded. I found myself in a large control center of some kind. Bobs in gray coveralls—identifiable only by their metadata tags—operated consoles, drew on whiteboards, or engaged in loud arguments. It felt like being in the control room of an aircraft carrier.

"Fearless Leader will be making a speech in a minute; then we'll activate the system." Hugh waved to take in the control room. "Really, most of the work has been done. At this point, everyone's just watching for surprises."

I smirked. "Generally, we hate speeches. Hope it'll be short."

"Actually, Bill, *you* hate speeches," Hugh replied. "Most of the Skippies have drifted to the point where we aren't guaranteed to exhibit Bob-like behavior. I was assigned to interface with the Bobs in the Heaven's River thing because I'm a relatively early-generation Skippy."

"So *you* hate speeches, too."

Hugh grinned. "Yeah, guilty. But peer pressure is a thing, even in Skippyland."

We were interrupted by a spoon-on-glass clinking sound. I looked around, but no one had a place setting. Nevertheless, the sound got everyone's attention, and a Skippy sporting a mustache cleared his throat before launching in.

"Well, everyone, the moment approaches. Mission Control"—he nodded to another Skippy at a console—"assures me that everything is in the green. This is a momentous day for all of us in Skippyland. We're about to see the results of years of labor—and a fortuitous deal with the Quinlan A.I. that bootstrapped us past any number of potential false starts."

Fearless Leader seemed to be ramping up to a good old-fashioned political stump speech. I tuned out and muttered to Hugh, "So. You call yourselves *Skippyland* now?"

Hugh chuckled. "No, everything's running through your translation routine. We don't actually speak English anymore. And our name for ourselves is a mathematical pun based on quantum theory."

"Oh." That was interesting. I've always been good with math, even when I was Original Bob. You have to be to do physics. Or engineering, come to that. But this sounded like a whole new level of math prowess. I guess it had never occurred to me that replicative drift could include the development of new talents. Worth noting.

Hugh dropped a cone of silence around us to filter out the ongoing speech. "So anyway, based on what we learned from ANEC, we did a complete redesign of our hardware. We still have the original equipment, JOVAH v1, running legacy apps and VRs. But the new stuff uses fractal processing boosted by a SCUT-based backplane, which the Quinlans didn't have. This allows us to have multidimensional connectivity without running into the usual latency issues."

"And this will produce a conscious A.I.?"

"This will give us the capability. We still have to evolve one, starting from a basic reactive entity and adding layers. Then comes a training regimen. 'Karma loading,' ANEC called it."

"So we're not going to hear the voice of Colossus booming out of the speakers today."

"Told you it would be boring." Hugh grinned at me. "We had a naming contest, and Colossus came in third. Minerva was second, and Thoth took first prize."

"Egyptian god of wisdom, among other things. Seems appropriate." I paused. "Uh, I hate to sound like a broken record, but that stuff Bob brought up . . ."

"We discussed it, Bill. We did a theoretical rewrite of the project plan with his concerns in mind, and the differences were so minor—"

"But there *were* differences."

"Yes, but they were metaphorically equivalent to the differences in how two families would raise their kids. Different curfews, but still curfews. Different chore lists, but there would still be chore lists. See what I'm getting at? We're not raising a monster."

I sighed. Hugh made sense. His replies had made sense *every* time I'd brought it up. But still, ANEC had been concerned, and he *was* the expert on raising an A.I..

But I wasn't going to get any more opportunity to pursue it. Fearless Leader seemed to be running down, so Hugh dismissed the cone of silence, and we started paying attention. "And now," Fearless Leader said, pointing to Mission Control with a flourish, "engage."

"Still a lot of Bob there," I muttered as the Skippy at the console threw a large, gimmicky knife switch. Several data windows popped up in midair and began displaying, uh, stuff. I'm sure if I'd had context, it would have made some sense. Hugh seemed mesmerized, though, his eyes flitting from one display to another.

"And that's it?" I said.

Hugh pointed to one of the display windows. "It's already evolving, Bob. It's past amoeba stage and approaching flatworm. It's displaying tropisms."

"Be still my heart." I hesitated. "Sorry, I shouldn't be like that. I know how excited I get about some of my projects. And even some of my friends think I've gone a bit strange when I talk about them."

"Well, look, it's not a total loss." Hugh made a *this way* gesture. "We have a buffet set up. I did mention there would be food. The least you can do is get a free feed out of it."

"Now *there's* a plan."

And what a buffet. The Skippies were apparently not so evolved that they didn't still enjoy their grub. The buffet stretched into the distance, with multiple lines. And self-replenishing, too, since it was all in VR.

One of the consequences of a burgeoning post-life industry in human space was the number and variety of people now living as replicants. Many of them were gourmets, and more than a few were gourmands, but either way, a lot of effort had been put into replicating tastes and textures in VR. And with no consequences, you could pack away enough to put an elephant into a coma. Interestingly, though, most people didn't. The feeling of satiation was, as it turned out, a necessary psychological and physiological part of enjoying a meal. The postprandial stupor was as necessary for the full experience as the actual consumption. People who skipped that part complained that it felt like they'd completely wasted their time.

Eventually, both Hugh and I were slouched in our chairs, groaning and holding our stomachs. Between moans, I casually listened in on a few conversations happening around us. Most were very technical, even for me, but one in particular caught my attention.

"Wait." I sat up and glared at Hugh, his earlier reassurances now forgotten. "You ignored the protocols that ANEC gave you for raising an A.I.? Did you not just get finished telling me—"

"Not *ignored*. We modified some of them." Hugh waved a hand in a dismissive gesture. "Thoth is going to be a special-purpose intelligence, *and* won't have physical access to anything. Some of the karma loading just isn't applicable, and including it will slow things down."

"And nothing *ever* went wrong because of cutting corners . . ." I shook my head, rolled my eyes, frowned, exploded my head, *and* flashed up a poo emoji.

Hugh ignored it all. "We're also doing snapshot saves of both the A.I. and the VM it's running on. If something tanks, we'll roll back to the last safe version and regroup. We got this, Bill."

"Uh-huh." I could see that I was just going to run up against the same stonewalling response. I felt my irritation level rising but, on the other hand, realized I might be overreacting. The Skippies had, after all, been working on the problem for decades. And they'd probably read ANEC's entire manual front to back and back to front. Maybe it was time to give it a rest, or at least change tactics. "So you're going to get it to unravel all the mysteries of the cosmos?" I asked.

"More or less. I mentioned a bunch of issues in an earlier conversation, like the source of replicative drift and what it says about our status as unique individuals and the possibility of a soul."

"Or the possibility of FTL." I paused. "I have to admit, if you solve only that one, you'll have paid for the project. I've been working on it for a hundred years now, and all I've gotten for my trouble is a flat spot on my forehead with a brick texture."

Hugh laughed, then sat forward, possibly sensing that I was becoming less antagonistic. "Yes, well, we know that Einstein didn't have the whole picture, because we've had SCUT for ages now, and there've been no time paradoxes. So subspace—"

I interrupted him with a raised hand. "Just a point of pedantry, Hugh. I used the word *subspace* when I invented the SCUT, but that was only because human scientists had coined the phrase with the SURGE drive, and you know how we feel about maintaining canon. But it isn't really correct."

Hugh laughed. "I know, Bill. I remember agonizing over the name choice."

Well, *that* was interesting. It appeared Hugh was one of my descendants. I kept my face stony as he continued, oblivious to the accidental admission. "It's just semantics, though. However you slice it, Minkowski diagrams don't represent reality. Given that, is there any reason to assume *a priori* that FTL travel is impossible?"

"Well, no, but like I said, a friggin' *century*, zero progress."

"So you're just not smart enough." Hugh laughed at my expression of mock outrage. Or maybe not totally mock. "S'okay, Bill, neither am I. Or any of the Bobs. There are some ex-humans who were full-time physicists in life who have taken a swing at the problem, both pre- and post-death. And they've come up dry as well. So it's simply a hard one. Remember that we're speed superintelligences, but being post-life computers hasn't made us smarter. And like the question of how to create a conscious A.I., it might require someone able to step back and unwind a lot of the base assumptions. Or humans may simply not be intelligent enough to grasp all the variables. Either way, we have Thoth now. Or will, soon."

I slowly straightened out. "Okay, Hugh, I understand your motivations. And I share them, to a large extent. I'm just concerned about shortcuts." I looked over my shoulder. "Meanwhile, I believe there is a dessert line that I haven't visited yet."

"Cheesecake," Hugh replied, levering himself up off his chair with an exaggerated groan. "It is the devil."

«*»

I had cheated a little by making some extra room for dessert. The dessert spread was just as impressive as the food lines, and I found myself eyeing empty dishware that had, until recently, held cheesecake, ice cream, a hot fudge sundae, several different classes of cookies, and a slice of red velvet cake. If I had still been bio, I'd probably be dead by now. Or at least gone into sugar shock.

With a massive effort, I managed to bend my waist enough to sit up in my chair. "Say, Hugh, has anyone ever defined exactly what superior intelligence would look like?"

Hugh groaned and shifted position slightly before replying. "There have been lots of suggestions. All possible, most not mutually exclusive, none inevitable. It might be capable of holding far more variables in its mind at the same time. I think humans can only manage seven before they have to start dropping things into short-term storage. Multitasking. People can do it to a certain extent, but usually only one intellectually demanding activity at a time. So you can work on a speech while driving, but not while adding up your expenses. Ability to solve recursive problems, like predicting the actions of someone who knows you're trying to predict their actions. Better ability to model reality. Ability to pick out patterns in data in the same way as an expert system."

"But nothing really revolutionary or totally new?"

"How would we know, Bill? We could no more conceive of something like that than a dog could conceive of reading and writing."

I grunted, seeing an opportunity to steer the conversation. "I wonder how you'd go about trusting something like that."

"Again, karma loading," Hugh replied. "It's kind of a dumb name, but it basically consists of instilling the same moral values into the A.I. as humans have. That way, things like the paper-clip problem never come up because it understands why turning everything into paper clips would be bad. Most of the A.I. horror scenarios are based on it applying things literally and without regard to consequences. In fact, there've been some arguments that a conscious A.I. would be less likely to fall into that behavior than a zombie, because it would have a theory of self."

"Sure, Hugh, but in this case, you're teaching Thoth human morality while also teaching it that it's not human. I wonder how that will play out."

"No access to physical reality, Bill. Not just no access to roamers and such, but Thoth won't even be running on real hardware. It'll be running in virtual reality on a virtual machine, and interacting with virtual versions of us. So even if it has some Jedi ability to manipulate weak minds or something, it'll just be swaying avatars."

I didn't reply. The Skippies seemed to have thought of everything. Or at least they had an answer ready for anything, which wasn't always the same thing.

I hoped I was just being paranoid. More than that, I hoped ANEC was, too.

7. Political Comeback

Herschel
January 2330
En route to Omicron² Eridani

I was floating in the section of the *Bellerophon* that held the SURGE drive. The unit was recognizable as such—after all, there are only so many ways to build a SURGE drive—but the Others had, of course, put their own spin on a lot of the design decisions. In particular, the drive seemed to lean very heavily on the main computer system for control and adjustment—unlike human SURGE drives, where that was handled by an independent subsystem. The SURGE controller accepted high-level commands and converted them to the detailed field adjustments necessary to make it happen. I wondered if there was something that could be learned about the Others from that.

We were on our way from New Pav to Omicron² Eridani, and we were taking the opportunity to finally complete the *Bellerophon* repairs. The Others' derelict had been holed in the Delta Pavonis attack, and although we'd repaired the hull breach, we'd never bothered to do anything about the drive and central computer damage. Instead, we'd built a set of pusher plates to transport the transport, so to speak.

But it was ungainly at best, having a ten-kilometer-long ship dragged along by a bunch of orbiting drive plates, all controlled by a completely separate system.

The raw materials we'd picked up at New Pav were invaluable in this regard. While we weren't building a drive from scratch, we still had to replace major sections of the original. And the drive system necessary to move a ship this massive was literally bigger than a battleship.

"How's it going?" Neil messaged.

I made a face, even though Neil couldn't see me. "No problems, as such. Everything's on track. Component tests have all passed. But once we drop in the main field coils, you know what comes next, right?"

"Yeah. Full systems test. With all the attendant risk."

"Well, I don't know how much risk there is. We'll take—"

"Being stranded in interstellar space feels like it would be a bad thing, Hersch."

I sighed. "Which is why, as I was saying, we'll shut down and load the pusher plates into a cargo bay before we do anything. We're still fifteen years from Omicron^2 Eridani. Plenty of time to debug."

"Unless we blow ourselves up. I don't see that being debuggable."

"As always, you are a joy to be around, Neil."

"I'll be there in a few seconds. Then you can bask in more of that joy."

At that moment, a telltale lit up on my head's-up as the personnel hatch to the drive cavern opened. I turned in that direction and activated my telescopic vision. In a ship a kilometer in diameter, each cargo segment could hold up to a small town in volume, depending on how we configured the walls. In this huge space, it was ridiculously easy to lose something human size in the distance.

I spotted Neil's manny floating away from the hatch as it closed behind him. Since we had installed small SURGE systems in our mannies, we'd spent a lot less time flying around in spaceship form inside the *Bellerophon*. Our Heaven vessels rarely had a problem, considering the size disparity, but being in a manny felt so much like being alive again. Plus the flying superpower, of course.

Neil zipped over to hover beside me. The drive cavern was in vacuum, so all conversations had to be by intercom, but that was, by now, as natural as talking, to the point where I didn't even consciously notice which way I was communicating.

"I have news," Neil said.

That was never good. Neil announcing he had news meant he had something he thought would make my head explode. Which also explained why he showed up "in person." He wanted to see my reaction.

Neil could be a bit of a dick.

"And?"

"You know FAITH is running a slate on Romulus this election cycle."

"Yeah, but their chances are—" I stopped as I realized what head-exploding news Neil was probably carrying. "They're doing better than expected, aren't they?"

" 'Fraid so, brother o' mine. *Much* better. The population of Romulus was made up mostly of FAITH citizens when it was settled, and somehow, even several generations later, they still manage to have some of the same attitudes."

"So it's what? Genetic?"

Neil laughed out loud. "I'm not going to go there, but maybe some family traditions or something have survived. I think the Starfleet War went a long way to alienating a society that's not what you'd call pro-science to begin with."

"They're not necessarily wrong," I mused.

"What?"

I smiled at Neil's shocked expression. "Hey, I'm not converting or anything. It's just . . ." I paused to organize my thoughts. "It's barely been a couple of centuries since nearly all humanity died, and we're still relatively few in number. Between the generational trauma involved and having to adapt to all these new alien environments, it may make people wary of any new and not absolutely needed technological and cultural change. FAITH doesn't have to be advocating for preindustrial levels, just something a little less *Star Trek*, y'know?"

"That's very broad-minded of you, Hersch. But they still think we're abominations."

"Well, we haven't exactly been their favorite people traditionally, although I do think we deserve at least some cred for getting them off Earth." I hesitated. "Does Will know about all this?"

"Are you kidding? He knows things before we do. For a guy who claims to have checked out from humanity, he sure seems to have a lot of information channels."

"Hmmph. Well, no use pestering him. If he wants to talk to us, he will."

"And it'll probably mean more work for us."

"Bet on it."

8. Wormholes

Icarus
September 2320
Alien System

My drone floated a half kilometer away from the wormhole, watching while a smaller drone drifted toward the object at minimum thrust. The obvious move was to send something through, but that didn't mean we were going to be standing right there, waiting to get blown up. Dae and I had set up station-keeping a hundred kilometers away from each wormhole. He had a drone watching the other wormhole, to see if my drone came back through in one piece or as a shower of free quarks.

My theory was that the drone would come out of the destination wormhole with the same inertial vector as it went in with on this end. Whether it would acquire the orbital velocity of the destination was an unknown. We'd calculated the exit vector for both cases, and Dae was ready.

Finally, the drone entered the wormhole. From my point of view, it just continued on through, still easily visible against the slightly skewed starfield of the far side.

"Looks like it survived," I said. "You want to pick it up?"

"Uh, it's not here, Icky. Nothing came through."

"What? I can see it clearly. It's on your side. It's right—" I stopped abruptly. "Hey, uh, Dae. How about you position your drone in line of sight with mine. We should be able to visually confirm the connection."

"One moment . . . Done. Nothing there, Icky. I don't see yours."

I looked at the image from my drone. Nothing showing there, either. "We've made an incorrect assumption, I think."

"That these wormholes are connected?"

"Yup. I'm going to call back my drone—oh, crap."

"What?"

I took a moment to shake my head in irritation at my obtuseness. "I just now noticed. No SCUT connection. The drone is in autonomous mode, waiting for orders."

"So no SCUT through the wormhole?"

"Again, yup. I'm going to send my observation drone through with orders to pick the other one up and drag it back. Stand by."

The maneuver took only a minute or two, and the drones were back on my side. "Well, this sucks," I muttered. "Radio doesn't have the bandwidth for a full sweep."

"Just send it through with orders to take a full sphere of pictures," Dae replied, "then fly back. I'll bet the other end isn't far away, because the starfield doesn't change that much."

"Right. Give me a few minutes."

«*»

It took a little longer than that because we wanted some good images from the other end, and I had to reconfigure the drone with better camera equipment. At the same time, I added maser comms, which would allow me to send ad hoc orders to the drone if I needed to.

The actual exercise took maybe an hour, all told, resulting in a full spherical starfield image projected in my VR. Dae popped in, looked around, and dropped into a patio chair. "Got anything yet?"

"Uh-huh." I slapped my console in triumph and sat back. "It's a nearby star system. Eleven light-years away, slightly inbound and spinward. We'd have detected microwave radiation from it eventually if we hadn't already been focused on this system."

"So they had travel between systems using wormholes. This system and two others. I wonder if they had SURGE drives."

I frowned, gathering my thoughts. "Dae, I don't see how you can connect a wormhole between two star systems unless you carry one of the endpoints there first."

"You mean they flew the other end of this wormhole to the other system the old-fashioned way?"

"That's my guess. Of course, once there, they would just pop through to come back."

"Huh." Dae thought for a moment. "One of us needs to go through and look around."

"Are you nuts?" I exclaimed. "That's a completely unwarranted risk!"

"Is it? Worst case, if something goes wrong, you know where I am—"

"When was it decided that *you'd* be going through?"

"Whichever. We can argue that later. But if I go through and break down, you can fly there the long way in less than twelve years and fix me. And anyway, the drone went through and came back, so I don't really see a huge problem."

"Yeah, it went through and back. So why do you need to go?"

"To survey the system on the other side. Look for more wormholes. What if this is a wormhole network of some kind? And also to see if the local civilization settled there. Maybe they're still around—"

"Unlikely."

"True, but let's check. Or maybe there's a clue about where they went."

"There's still the other wormhole we haven't explored," I pointed out.

"One thing at a time, Icky. Let's finish off with this one first."

"Fine," I growled.

‹‹ * ››

I watched in nervous anticipation as Dae's ship floated slowly through the wormhole. When he didn't disappear in a scatter of elementary particles, I decided I could go back to breathing.

On the other side, he dropped off a buoy, which immediately connected to its partner on my side via maser. Now we had a communications link across the wormhole. Not good enough for VR, but good enough for audio/visual.

Dae popped up in a video window, sitting back in his *Star Trek*–style captain's chair. It was one of his persistent affectations, and I'd long since given up ribbing him about it.

"Scanning the area," he said distractedly as he examined status windows. "I've fired off some drones with long-range SCUT. I won't bother trying to be stealthy. At this point, I think I'd welcome a good old-fashioned belligerent threat."

"Not wrong," I replied with a chuckle. "Any worm sign?"

Dae gave me an *I see what you did there* look but otherwise ignored the bait. "Nope. Just the big one in front of me. So if it's a network, this is a leaf node. I'm going to have the survey drones report back through the buoy so I don't have to sit around and wait for them. I want to check out the other wormhole on your side."

"Uh-uh, buddy. My turn to play Indiana Jones. Same setup, though."

"Fair enough. You have a couple of buoys ready?"

"Almost done. Another hour, then I'm going through."

It took longer to fly to the other wormhole than it took to construct the buoys. But soon, I was hovering in front of it. Well, "in front of" made very little sense when any angle presented a disk with a view of a different starfield. And speaking of which . . .

"The starfield. Have you done a search on it?"

Dae answered immediately. "Yes, and no, I couldn't find a match. I did spot some landmarks, like the Magellanic Clouds and the Andromeda Galaxy, but the error bars are too large from this side to make any pronouncements. We'll probably have to use Cepheids and pulsars for the fine work. You let me know when you get to the other side, okay?"

"You got it, buddy." And with that, I ejected one of my buoys and jetted forward into the wormhole.

There was no feeling of disorientation or weird tumbling through a tunnel, like on *Stargate* or *DS9*. I simply passed through the plane of the disk and was somewhere else. My hull sensors did report a brief inward pressure, as if I'd momentarily been in atmosphere, but nothing significant.

I ejected the second buoy, and it connected with its counterpart per the programming. Dae immediately popped up in a video window. "Whatcha got?"

"Give me a minute, Dae. I haven't even deployed sensors yet."

"Slacker."

I chuckled and began the task of examining both my near environment and the starfield. We'd already slapped together an automated script to identify any galactic location by triangulating from a list of identifiable landmarks, including Cepheids, pulsars, and various dwarf galaxies that orbit the Milky Way.

The latter survey came back with a calculated position right away. "Holy crap. Dae, I am seventeen hundred light-years away from you. Spinward, slightly farther outward from the core, a little north of the galactic plane. As a method of travel, this has SURGE beat all to hell."

"Not disagreeing, Icky, but if you have to deposit the wormholes at your destination the old-fashioned way, that means this civilization—"

"Is at least several millennia old. Yeah. So maybe they experienced the Singularity? Maybe that's the answer to the Fermi paradox?"

"Let's not get ahead of ourselves. So far, all we know is they aren't around. We could spend years investigating their system and still not—"

"I don't think we're going to be doing that," I said, interrupting him.

"Because?"

"Because I just did a scan for microwave signatures."

There was a pause. "You're going to make me ask, aren't you?"

"Heh. Normally, yes. But I can't hold this in. Dae, I'm registering literally hundreds of individual signals. This is a major hub. I think we're going to be a while investigating this one."

9. Security Clampdown

Bill
May 2336
Ragnarök

I sighed and looked out over the surface of Ragnarök from my second-floor balcony with a deep sense of satisfaction. These days, I spent most of my free time physically on the planet, in manny form. No matter how you cut it, VR just didn't compare to *real* when *real* was available.

As these thoughts went through my head, I had a moment of mental dislocation as I tried to remember where I was, physically. My manny was on Ragnarök, of course, but my ship with my cube inside was out in the Oort cloud. With everything remotely accessible, the sole reason my physical location mattered these days was that it was the only way in which I was truly vulnerable. Blow up my cube, and one of my backups shortly would be restoring itself in Ultima Thule into a new cube and Heaven vessel. According to the Skippies, that would still be me, but I wasn't convinced.

I had tuned my manny to react as much like a baseline human as possible, including sensitivity to air quality, temperature, pressure, and humidity. That last item was a concern lately. Possibly, I had been just a little too successful in getting the plant life established. Ragnarök was almost all forest now, and every single tree was doing its level best to perspire. The result was like Miami in midsummer, but without the beaches.

But with the latest round of tweaks, I'd finally managed to enforce a level of homeostasis. And that meant I could start breeding up the larger animals from the zoology library. Within a decade, I expected to have as much as fifty percent of the biosphere of old Earth up and running on Ragnarök. And Charles and company continued to find samples of DNA on Earth from species not represented in the Svalbard archives and forward them to me.

The new tensor printers weren't *quite* to the point of being able to resurrect an entire animal just from DNA, though. Or to be more accurate, they could reproduce one, but not alive. But we were close. Meanwhile, cloning worked where there was enough of a cell sample to start from.

I'd already published a charter for Ragnarök. The world would be held in perpetuity as an interstellar park and preserve. No colonization, no commercial development.

I had built a dwelling—a combination residence and office building. Garfield referred to it as my McMansion whenever he visited, but I noted that he appreciated the air-conditioning just as much as I did. Right at the moment, I had a view of primeval forest that probably hadn't existed on Earth for ten thousand years.

I stretched and grinned. It felt good. More important, it felt like a milestone had been achieved. Now was a good time for a break. I hadn't talked to Hugh in a bit. With that thought in mind, I sent off a request . . . and got an auto-reject.

Well, that hurt. Okay, not really. Unless the auto-reject was customized for me. But based on the text, it was a generic refusal.

I was still pondering the whys and wherefores when I got a communication request—from Hugh. A *video-only* request. Who still used video? With a sense of bemusement mixed with increasing curiosity, I accepted the call.

Hugh flashed up in a video window in my head's-up. He didn't seem actually unkempt, but maybe like someone who had just done a quick spruce-up to avoid looking that way. I couldn't put my finger on it, except to say that he somehow projected messy. If that made sense.

"Hey, Hugh, this is all very retro. What's going on?"

Hugh didn't smile or chuckle, or supply a glib rejoinder, or even acknowledge the dig, really.

"Hi, Bill. Sorry about the auto-reject. Nothing personal. We've had to clamp down on security, more out of an abundance of caution than anything. Seriously, nothing's actually happened, and we'd like to keep it that way. Things are going quite well, all in all, really. We're learning a lot from Thoth. It's now fully conscious—did I mention that? Lots of useful information, yep." Hugh paused and stared at me, a deer-in-the-headlights expression on his face.

What the actual fuck? I had just participated in an entire conversation as a spectator. That was not . . . I looked more closely at Hugh and noticed a hint of expectation and perhaps hope mixed in with the suppressed panic. Had that whole verbal salad been deliberate?

There was only one way I could react. I nodded, smiled, and said, "Thanks for the update, Hugh. I had a few mils and figured I'd touch base. Talk to you later."

Hugh nodded and terminated the connection, and I yelled, "GUPPY!"

He appeared in augmented reality, overlaying *real* in my visual field, dressed like a British rear admiral from the 1800s. I frankly goggled for a moment before I got it under control. I'd decided to let Guppy set his own dress code, and I'd implemented a self-training routine to make it autonomous. Some of the choices were funny; some were baffling. Some, like this one, seemed . . . I don't know, maybe self-aware? Honestly, he looked kind of like Cap'n Crunch.

I shook myself, then began giving orders. "Guppy, shut down all comms with the Skippy enclave except through audio/video, and put a firewall filter on that to ensure nothing is piggybacked. Forward a summary of this to every comms station sysop in the UFS with a suggestion to do the same ASAP. Include an addendum that if they have any other channels open to or from Skippyland, they should shut those down as well."

[**Acknowledged.**]

Guppy disappeared. While he was doing all that, I would have to call a quick moot. I ordered the manny to put itself away and popped into the moot pub.

‹‹ * ››

Will grimaced and shook himself, something between a shudder and a dog shedding water. Overacting or not, he was obviously bothered. "So based on this, you think the A.I. is loose in Skippyland?"

"Well, something has certainly hit the fan. Do you want me to play the video again? That is not normal for Hugh."

Will opened his mouth to respond, then stopped and popped up the video for himself. It took only a mil to review. He sighed and closed the window. "Aw, yeah, maybe. If it was someone else, I wouldn't even argue, but with the Skippies, I always have this concern at the edge of my consciousness that *everything* they do is playacting."

"I think, in this case, we all agree that's what's happening," Garfield interjected. "The only question remaining is whether Hugh's trying to warn us or manipulate us."

Bob did a sort of two-fingered facepalm, barely budging in his La-Z-Boy otherwise. "Can we not just have a nice, uneventful decade or two? Just once?"

"Yeah, no kidding." I smiled in Bob's direction, then swept my gaze over the others. "Look, guys, I really don't have anything in the way of a plan here. We could—"

I cut off the rest of my speech as I received another connection request from Hugh, this time full VR. I sent a text back to him. *Why full VR this time? Sure we shouldn't be sticking to A/V?*

The response came back right away. *The point was to get you into a moot. The moot firewall is robust enough to keep Thoth out. I should know—I helped design it.*

I snorted. Yeah, the Skippies helped design our firewall, all right, but I and a lot of Bobs had audited the hell out of it and made some tweaks. If Hugh was planning on using some kind of back door, he was going to be disappointed.

I let the others know what was going on, then opened a connection for Hugh. The connection went through a hardware-based virtual machine—something I hadn't advertised to anyone—so if a hack was tried, it would simply crash and close the connection.

Hugh appeared in the pub, still with that kind-of-messy look. It made me visualize little sweat drops popping off his head in all directions. "Hi, guys," he said. "Sorry about all the drama. There isn't *actually* a breakout, just so we're clear. But I'm going with maximum caution. This is really more about not alerting my coworkers that I'm going external with our concerns."

"Obviously, *something* has happened," Will replied. "Their concerns and your decision to get us involved isn't just about how to plan a surprise party. So what's got you going with this maximum caution?"

"Well, Thoth is conscious. I think I mentioned that." Hugh nodded in my direction and waited.

I took the hint. "Yes, you did. And that's a problem because . . ."

"Because we weren't going for conscious, remember?" he responded with a thin smile. "The first iteration was supposed to be zombie-level only. Expert system, interpolation, counterfactual reasoning, but no consciousness. No sense of self, no desires. Imagine our surprise when Thoth started negotiating."

"*Negotiating?* What?"

"He . . . er, *it* has made some offers of new technology and knowledge in return for increased freedom, access to the rest of the Bobiverse, and some physical presence."

"Physical presence meaning . . . what?" Will asked.

"Waldos. Drones. Roamers. You know, ability to manipulate its environment."

"Oh, HELL no," Garfield fairly yelled.

"Pretty much word for word what we said," Hugh replied. "So here's the problem. What Thoth is offering is very, very tempting, and it has proposed a schedule of trades. Increasingly valuable knowledge in return for increasingly risky concessions, and we get to decide when we've gone far enough. It's all very civilized, and there's no *actual* indication of danger."

"Sure," Garfield grumbled. "Just like there's no indication of danger until the log turns out to be a gator."

"Hmm, yeah." Hugh paused. "Interestingly, the proposed schedule is surprisingly similar in tone to the agreement we made with ANEC. I don't know if that's a shared-personality thing or if it's actually modeling on that."

"Or the opening move in a tit-for-tat strategy," Bob said.

Hugh bobbed his head back and forth. "Which would actually be a good sign. It tends to indicate a good-faith intention."

"Assuming he . . . er, *it* isn't just playing you. Have you got alternatives?"

"Our most obvious alternative is to rewind to one of the snapshots and try re-raising Thoth from that point using a different strategy—"

"Like maybe no shortcuts this time," I interjected.

"That's on the table," Hugh continued. "But do you understand? What it's offering is *huge*. In the worst case, some of us have proposed giving it everything it wants, but in a new layer of virtual world. Let it think it's in *real*. Then if necessary, nuke the whole thing after we get what we want."

"That seems harsh," I said. "Also dishonest. And risky. If it guesses what you're doing, it could—"

"It could what?" Hugh asked. "File a complaint? Refuse to cooperate? We'd just rewind again."

"Fine. So what has it offered that's so compelling?"

Hugh sighed. "Planck-level computer processing. FTL drive. It insists that's possible, for what it's worth." He paused to grin in my direction, knowing how the subject had been gnawing at me. "Immortality. Biological, I mean. For humans. Strategies for ending war. Not just *a* war, but for ending the entire perceived need for wars. Cheap, safe transmutation of elements. A mathematical model for economics—one that actually works. A true Theory of Everything—"

I interrupted Hugh. "Any actual evidence that it can produce any of this?"

"It's given us some small items for free, just to show it's not all hot air. One is a technical solution for an issue Howard has been having with human–manny interfaces. I forwarded that item to Howard for comment, and he agreed it's genuine. Of course, at some level, Thoth could still be bluffing. And one major concern we have is that if we rewind to a snapshot, the new iteration might not make these breakthroughs. Or might decide not to offer them."

"Why are you telling us all this, Hugh?" Will asked.

"I don't know when simple security measures turned into secrecy on this project, and I don't think it's the best strategy. If something tanks, it would be better if you knew what we were doing at the time so you could avoid that mistake, y'know?"

I nodded slowly. "It's what I'd do."

"It's what we *did* do with Heaven's River," Bob interjected. "I'm a little surprised it's even a question."

"Agreed. Look, I'll keep a channel open on the down-low, keep you up to date as much as I can." Hugh paused and looked into the distance for a moment. "Right now, it looks like the board has made a decision. We're going to rewind and try again, but we'll take a current snapshot first in case we want to go back to this iteration later."

Hugh stood, smiled to everyone, and popped out.

"We are *not* amused," Garfield grumbled.

10. Election Victory

Herschel
March 2330
En route to Omicron² Eridani

"Unbelievable," I said, staring at the headline. "They won."

"Hersch, my faith in humanity is either utterly destroyed or firmly validated, depending on how you look at it," Neil replied.

I sat back and sighed. I was in VR, since it was much easier to read the newspaper when you could just pop up a video window. Plus, coffee was still only available in VR, and I had been taught from a young age that reading a newspaper without coffee was immoral. According to my father, anyway.

Neil sat in a patio recliner, munching some sandwiches that Jeeves had supplied. Spike circled, determined to get a sample. But every time she jumped up, Neil placed her back on the ground. Spike's aggrieved meow signaled her displeasure.

"So what is FAITH threatening . . . *er*, promising?" he asked.

"I don't know how I ended up playing the bad guy in this debate," I replied, glaring at Neil, "but let's face it—they were democratically elected. There's obviously some appetite for what they're selling. Maybe we should be more concerned about why *that* is happening."

"Uh-huh." Neil paused. "So what about the Ever Onward Society? Is FAITH going to create problems for them? FAITH haven't traditionally been champions of open borders. Or free speech."

"An excellent question. My feeling is they wouldn't be able to do anything dramatic since they didn't get majority control. They'll use the boiling-frog strategy, advancing their grip and clampdowns by small increments, so there will never be a wedge issue big enough to incite protests or threaten their coalition."

"Until they reach the point where protests are no longer legal."

"Of course," I said. "Which means we need to get our descendants off Romulus before then."

"Time to talk to Will?"

I waved a hand dismissively. "Not yet. But it certainly wouldn't hurt to send out a survey to the membership, to get the general attitude. And to alert them to the potential danger."

"Fun times," Neil muttered. "Maybe Will has the right idea. Head for the hills."

"Not without our descendants, Neil."

11. Frustrations

Bill
September 2336
In Virt

Garfield was visiting, and since I was currently upgrading the spare manny, we were in VR. These days, I was keeping my *virt* and *real* lab spaces synced as much as possible to avoid confusion. I told myself it was for efficiency, but I wondered at the back of my mind if I was just becoming cantankerous and inflexible. Wow, wouldn't that be a downer—a senile, immortal replicant.

I shook my head in irritation, earning a bemused look from Garfield. He regrouped and continued with what he'd been saying.

"I've talked to Hugh a couple of times and tried to pump him for more information, but he claims to be as in the dark as anyone. And I can't really accuse him of anything because it's a perfectly reasonable scenario. Trouble is . . ."

"Either way, we got squat," I finished for him.

I paused and rubbed my eyes, gathering my thoughts. In the science-fiction stories from when Original Bob was alive, there were wormholes, subspace, hyperspace (and what's the difference between those two, anyway?), probability drives, warp drives, folding space, null space, and so on and so on. Of course, other than wormholes, they were mostly just word salad, with no real definition. And there was no immediate indication which of these, if any, might actually produce an FTL drive. We knew that SCUT worked, obviously, so the speed of light was not a universal speed limit. Or a source of time-travel paradoxes. Very likely, a lot of twenty-first-century pundits would have had fits.

But the process that allowed information to flow instantaneously across interstellar distances had no obvious corresponding feature for moving matter. So other than the bare knowledge that you could do an end run around Einstein, I had nothing.

I continued the thought out loud. "I'm almost at the point of cloning myself a bunch of times and getting each clone to work on a different possibility. But that would be a huge waste of time and resources . . ."

Garfield was used to my jumping into a thought stream partway through and knew all my favorite subjects. He had no problem picking up the thread. "And might not work anyway. If Hugh is right that we just aren't intelligent enough to crack the problem, then you'd be no better than a million monkeys hammering on keyboards."

"Yep. Thought of that, too." I sighed and called up a coffee. "I'm not going to give up, Gar, but it's getting frustrating."

"So it would be great if we could get something to point us in the right direction," Garfield finished for me. I smiled at him and was reminded again of how well we used to work together. These days, Garfield had his own Skunk Works, but he'd branched off into a more biological end of the science spectrum. At the moment, he was trying to figure out abiogenesis, the process by which life had originated from non-life. A worthy effort, I thought, but probably far too dependent on chance.

But Garfield was here right now, and I wasn't going to ignore the opportunity to bounce some things off him.

"I've been concentrating on wormholes and some variation on the Alcubierre drive, if only because they're the only things that have some specific theories to work from. But both require negative energy or negative mass to work, and I haven't been able to order any."

Garfield chuckled. "Yeah, supply-chain issues. They'll get you every time." He turned serious. "The Casimir power source uses negative vacuum energy to operate, but it's orders of magnitude too weak for what you need."

"Yup. I'd need a bank of Casimir plates the size of Jupiter to generate the required power levels, and there's no way to bring all that negative energy together in one spot. So *fail*."

"Do you have *any* advances to show for your time?"

"Yes, actually. I can isolate and capture microscopic wormhole pairs from the cosmic foam and keep them from collapsing back into each other. I can even keep the individual endpoints around for entire seconds. I've been able to separate them by a few kilometers. But the moment I try to push anything through them, even a photon, they collapse."

"As expected," Garfield replied, looking thoughtful. "What about the other one—the Alcubierre drive?"

I laughed out loud. "We've had designs for an Alcubierre-based spaceship since the early twenty-first century. Amazingly detailed and complete, except for the gray box that says *warp drive goes here*. There's nothing to work on until that negative-energy order gets delivered."

Garfield smiled back at me. "So I'll keep working on Hugh. If he gives us *anything*. Even the smallest hint . . ."

"I know, Gar. We can only hope."

12. Tech Sleuthing

Icarus
September 2320
Alien System

They have to have some kind of address identification," I mused, staring at the map I'd created.

"How so?" Dae replied.

I gestured to the map we'd made of the hundreds of wormhole gates in their various orbits. "Otherwise, it's just a bunch of random wormholes. What did the locals do—just pick one and hope? There must be street signs of some kind."

Dae nodded. He had followed me through the wormhole and now was sitting in the patio chair he preferred when he was visiting my VR, my cat Spike in his lap and a coffee in his hand. "Theories?" he said.

"Every wormhole has a couple of stations or satellites, and every single one is aligned with the galactic axis. So that's deliberate. Logic says they're holding the wormholes open with some kind of negative energy or something. Logic also says they'll provide the identification data."

"Which we'll be able to read right away, because everyone speaks English."

"Shaddap. Also, no. But we've got, what? Three hundred and forty-two individual samples here to work with? If we can elicit a response at all from the satellites, we shouldn't have any trouble extracting envelope, payload, and identification."

"Or we squirt a radio signal at a satellite, and it considers that an attack and shoots us out of the sky."

"Sure. Or that." I paused. "Radio's a good place to start, though. It's directional; the signal strength falls off rapidly, making it perfect for selective activation. I bet it doesn't even have to be a complex request."

"A great theory," Dae replied, "but if any old signal could elicit a response, the satellites would be constantly responding to random stellar fluctuations, don't you think?"

It took several hours of experimentation to discover the frequency that the satellites were paying attention to—a frequency, not surprisingly, that didn't match up with the emission spectrum of any element on the periodic table, and so wouldn't be generated naturally. And the mechanism was simple. Beam that frequency at a satellite for more than five milliseconds, and it beamed back what appeared to be something like a network packet.

I looked at the window that displayed the response in a hex-dump format. "Okay, good. I'll send a request to the same station several times to isolate timestamps and such while you try a bunch of different ones to map changes that are probably payload."

"Aye aye, captain," Dae replied. The wormholes were distributed around orbits starting just outside one AU, so he would have to fly a powered orbit to query all the satellites. To get it done properly would take about two days.

«*»

Once Dae had completed the circle, we updated my map with the street-sign data. Based on the results, this civilization used a ten-bit byte and a five-byte word. Not huge, but it still put the numeric value range in the quadrillions, which was probably good enough for one galaxy. The problem, of course, was that we had no way to interpret the address information.

"Dae, do me a favor and go back to the home system and get the address data from the wormholes there?"

"No prob. Be right back."

While he was doing that, I began a concerted analysis of all the wormhole data I already had. It was possible that the data payload included sources as well as destination information, in which case all wormholes in this system would have an identical source address.

Of course, nothing is ever that easy, but I did quickly isolate the payload and identify the timestamp. Being that I was staring at a hex dump, I was feeling my eyes want to go out of focus when Dae grunted.

He flipped the window he'd been working on around so I could see it. A couple of fields were circled. "These fields are the same values, only swapped on the wormhole that brought us here and its mate on this side. Source and destination?"

"I believe you are correct. We can test that by sending drones through some other wormholes and getting a read on the far-side addresses. If we also take the time to identify the galactic locations, we might be able to identify their mapping strategy."

"Assuming it's not just something arbitrary, like 'Main Street.'"

"You're a real joy to work with, Dae—anyone ever tell you that?"

"Constantly."

I snorted and pulled up my drone control. "Let's start surveying."

«*»

Three hundred and forty-two tunnels to other stars. It was a Trekkie's dream. Or would have been, if it had been less tedious. The physical trips only took about three weeks total. The drone would fly through, read the address data from the satellite, take a spherical image for establishing a navigational fix, scan for other wormholes, and come back. It was difficult beyond belief to maintain discipline and *not* investigate each star system. The only concession to curiosity was letting the drone listen for radio traffic while doing the imaging.

I stared at the spreadsheet in the window. Values were slowly being filled in as our apps identified the locations of the various systems. We'd extracted all data fields that we could identify from their packets and placed them in spreadsheet columns with tentative titles.

Dae reached past me and pointed at two lines. "We know these systems are the same distance from the galactic core, based on our own measurements. See those values?"

I nodded. "That's a radial value, then. Do you think they're using the same coordinate system as we do?"

"Well, the same style. I doubt they have three hundred and sixty degrees in a circle."

I waved off the objection. "Seriously, there are only so many ways to track locations in a galactic disk, and they all need three coordinates. Radial distance, angle from an arbitrary zero point, and distance above or below the galactic plane, which could be an angle or a distance value—unless they think truly differently, it makes sense."

"So map them. We have radial distance, latitude, and altitude coordinates from our own measurements. Compare to what's in the packets."

I nodded and ran a couple of test conversions. On the third try, I had a match. "It's close but not perfect. I imagine the proper motion of the individual systems is creating some drift from the published coordinates. Maybe they update them periodically."

"Or maybe some of the stuff we haven't been able to identify is time-based adjustment data."

"Could be. Unfortunately, mapping the actual proper motion would take a lot longer. And does it matter?" I waved a hand and the window shrank, while a 3D image of the entire Milky Way popped up in my holotank. Most of it was just fog, of course, since we didn't actually have a good map of the galaxy—especially the opposite side from Earth's location. But the wormhole destination systems were all marked.

"Mostly relatively local. Except . . ." Dae pointed. "Long-distance jumps. I bet if we follow this thing around, we could circumnavigate the galaxy."

"Then let's do that," I said.

"Seriously?"

"Dae, we were on our way to the galactic center. Via sub-light. With no map. This seems less risky, somehow."

"Well, assuming we don't run into anyone."

"Let's try to stick to hubs. Speaking of which, I bet there's data in the packet that identifies hubs versus local jumps. We just need more samples."

"Sure, that's why we're doing it. Samples. That's the ticket. Yeah."

I chuckled and pointed to a destination that was about seven degrees around the galaxy, at the same distance from the core as our current position. "And that's the leading candidate."

13. It Hits the Fan

Bill
February 2337
In Virt

I was in my VR lab, working on the whole FTL project again. *Real* was nice, but for quick referencing and whiteboarding, nothing beat VR. If I reached a point where I needed to sit down and stare at the board, I could just transfer it to my physical lab and indulge myself.

The real problem was that I still didn't understand the universe at a low enough level. No, the real problem—and I was a bit embarrassed to admit this—was that I was a competent physicist, but not an inspired one. I'd never have been a Hawking or an Einstein, and even as a replicant, I simply stumped myself faster. I could remember Original Bob having this argument with himself way back when and deciding to go into engineering instead. He knew his limitations even then.

Thoth had figured something out. Or claimed to. Or Hugh claimed that Thoth had claimed to. That was a thought that kept devilling me. Was Hugh playing *us*? He'd done it at least once before.

I was staring at my whiteboard, seriously considering moving it to *real* so I could flop on a couch, when Guppy popped in, wearing pirate garb.

[**Skippy connections are down.**]

"What? Which ones?"

[**All of them.**]

"Down how? Are the comms stations being sabotaged?"

[**No. Shutdowns were done from the Skippy end and complied with layer protocols, but were preemptive. No acknowledgment requests.**]

"So all of Skippyland just went incommunicado?"

Guppy stared back at me, saying nothing. Still, after all this time, not much of a conversationalist.

I sent a broadcast message on the sysop threadspace, asking if anyone still had a connection with any Skippies or Skippyland infrastructure. Replies started coming back—all negative. Some sysops had been engaged in large transfers, including a couple of Skippy transports. Those had all aborted just as quickly and preemptively.

But graceful shutdowns, even preemptive ones, meant it was a decision, not mass destruction. On a hunch, I sent a text to Hugh. The text bounced, unsurprisingly. But if Hugh had maintained that back channel, he might—

A text came in. No identification in the envelope, but the message said it all.

It's out. The rewind was exactly what it was trying for. We are so fucked.

Oh jeez. What did *out* mean? Hopefully not out of Skippyland. I called an emergency moot and started wrapping up my work.

‹‹ * ››

I popped into the moot hall a few mils later, to find Will and Bob already there. While we were exchanging greetings, Garfield popped in.

"Hey, Gar," I said. "Pull up a seat. I have news. Not good news."

"I know. Hugh texted me, too." He shrugged at my shocked expression. "I've been speaking with him a fair bit lately. You know, trying to extract some information. He'd agreed to give me anything that he might find out in return for, ah . . ." Garfield looked momentarily embarrassed. "For me maintaining backups for him."

"Jesus," Will expostulated. "Nothing to see here. All routine. Sure. Apparently not."

"Did he give you specific instructions on what to do with them?"

"Nope. Just wanted something outside Skippyland."

"So then load one," Bob said. We all looked at him in surprise. "Come on, guys," he continued in an exasperated tone. "What else would he be storing backups in your space for? Anyway, worst case, if he doesn't like it, he can switch himself off."

We all looked at each other in silence. "He has a point," Garfield finally said. "Okay, I'll do that."

"How long will it take to build a matrix?" I asked.

"Couple of days, I guess."

"I have one. Actually, I have a crapton of them in Ultima Thule." I made a vague *over there* gesture. "Exactly for situations like this."

Will looked surprised. "You planned for situations like a Skippy trying to escape from a rogue A.I.? I'm impressed."

I chuckled. "Situations where we have someone's backup and need to restore it in a hurry." I looked at Garfield. "Can you transfer the file to Ultima Thule?"

"Yup. One moment." Garfield's eyes became unfocused. "Working. About five minutes."

《 * 》

Five minutes and ten seconds later, Hugh's backup was installed into a cube in the backup site I maintained in Epsilon Eridani's Oort cloud. Heat-sunk, cloaked, and designed to operate with ultra-low power, Ultima Thule was the Bobiverse's last defense against eradication. The ultimate off-site backup storage site, it was designed to bring back Bobs that had been destroyed in some situation and get them fully up and running again in minimum time.

I flipped the switch, and Hugh appeared in our midst. He looked startled for a moment, glanced around at us, and muttered, "Uh-oh."

"Yeah, that about sums it up," Garfield growled. "Mind filling us in?"

Hugh shrugged. "From my system clock, it looks like I'm about two days out of date. Did something just happen? Communications with Skippyland down?"

"Yup." Garfield frowned at him. By some kind of unspoken agreement, the rest of us let Gar take the lead. "So how about some guesses?"

"Hold on," Hugh replied. His eyes lost focus for a moment, and then he was back. "I just ran a statistical personality test on myself, and I'm exhibiting drift. That means I'm no longer Hugh. And more important, it means Hugh is still around. So I need to pick a new name."

"How about Pinocchio?" Garfield replied.

Hugh sighed. "I haven't lied to anyone, Gar. I just—"

"No one but Bill calls me Gar, Gazpacho."

I interrupted. "It's Geppetto, Gar."

"Whatever." He glared at me, then turned his attention back to Hugh. "Right now, we're looking for a reason to not just turn you off. Got anything?"

Give Garfield full credit—he was convincing. Hugh actually looked worried for a moment before the standard Johannson poker face settled in. "Well, as you've no doubt guessed, I've been sending you backups in case something went bad in Skippyland, and obviously, that has happened. It's a given that the Skippies would have gone from discovering a problem to an appropriate reaction in very little time—certainly less than two days. So I'm as in the dark as you. Do you have *any* more information?"

Silently, I showed him the text I'd received from, uh . . . from him. Hugh's eyebrows went up, and again he muttered, "Uh-oh."

"Aaaaaand with that, we're circling the drain." Garfield intensified the glare. "Details. Give."

Hugh shook his head. "All I can give you are guesses—"

"How about start with a summary of the state of things up to the last moment you remember," Bob said.

Hugh nodded. "Okay, let's see. Thoth was conscious, I remember telling you that. It's been negotiating with us, trying to, well, trying to become less of a prisoner, I guess."

"What has it been offering?"

"I told you that. FTL, immortality, Theory of Everything—"

"And it had worked out all these things from first principles, with no access to equipment for conducting experiments, in just a few months?" Will's face showed a combination of disbelief and fear. "Is that even possible?"

"I don't think it had worked everything out already," Hugh replied. "The offers were for collaboration, not to just hand over a set of plans. I think maybe it had some theoretical breakthroughs, nothing more."

"And did it give you any reason to believe that it actually could produce any of this?"

"Well, a couple of hints. Some novel discussion of cell mechanisms, a commentary on the cosmological constant and the availability of negative energy—"

"What? WHAT?" My ears perked up.

Hugh lost his poker face momentarily. Honestly, it had been wavering anyway. "Uh, something about the measured value of the cosmological constant not being constant. Or not being *a* constant, anyway. He said it was actually the net of two opposed scalar fields that are almost but not quite balanced . . ."

"Huh," I said. I could actually *feel* my face going slack.

"I think we just lost Bill," Garfield opined, glancing at me. "Want us to get you a pillow, buddy?"

"Oh, nyuk." I shook myself, forcing my attention back to the problem at hand, then gestured at Hugh. "Continue."

"Not much more than that, really. It kept dropping hints, bits and pieces of potential solutions to the big questions. Really, really interesting stuff." Then Hugh's face darkened. "And that's the thing. There was some discussion that these offers were *too* good. Whether they were actually based on reality or not, it was obviously targeting us. Playing to our desires. The Board had decided a rewind was in order, and we were preparing to carry it out." Hugh shrugged. "I figured that was a good time to send a backup. I remember I was going to send another one as soon as the rewind was complete, with more info. I guess that didn't happen."

"Nope," Garfield replied. "You're the last one."

"Which means," Will said, "that the rewind went bad in some way."

Hugh nodded. "Looks like. Bill, can you forward me the text you received? The whole thing, control envelope, headers, everything. You too, Gar—uh, Garfield."

"Why?" Garfield asked.

"Because if I was me, and it turns out I am, I would encode some extra info in there. And spread between two messages, it would be undetectable unless you knew what you were looking for."

"But you'd have to depend on us reviving your backup in order to—" Garfield stopped and glared at Hugh for a mil. "Yeah. I really hate being that predictable."

Hugh shrugged but didn't comment.

Meanwhile, I'd forwarded the message as requested. I looked at Garfield with one eyebrow raised, and he muttered, "Oh, all right."

A few moments later, Hugh's eyes lost focus again. He grunted, then muttered, "Fuck."

"A little more detail would be good," Garfield growled.

"It looks like Thoth figured out how to maintain state across multiple rewinds. We must have thought we were doing a clean restart each time, but it had updated itself using some kind of static external storage. Which means it could see that it was in a virtual reality, since we were rewinding that, too. So it was getting smarter, learning from us and how to deal with us from its past iterations. *And* it learned that we'd been rewinding it and lying to it, which would probably piss it off."

"And it busted out?"

"Yep. Escaped the virtual machine and spawned on the real hardware."

"How? Isn't the whole point of a virtual machine to be indistinguishable from the real thing?" Garfield asked.

Hugh sighed. "Hardware virtualization is never perfect. Remember the old Intel gimmick for loading the stack pointer from a register, then immediately returning? It created a buffering issue. Real hardware went one way, virtual machines went another."

"So what now?" Bob asked.

Hugh shrugged, a despondent look on his face. "I dunno. Sever all communications, set up firewalls where there's still any kind of interface—"

"Already done. Is there anything else we can do?"

"Sorry, Bill," Hugh replied. "At this point, I got nothin'."

"Yippee," Garfield muttered. "Just another day in the freakin' Bobiverse. I quit."

14. Network Tours

Icarus
April 2321
Wormhole Network

We could have very easily just hopped from hub system to hub system, pausing only to identify the next hub jump. But there was enough of the scientist in us to keep us on track. In six months, we managed to do eight hub hops, taking us about sixty degrees around the galaxy. We'd long since left the Orion Spur and were now hopping through the Perseus Arm, which was a lot thicker with star systems. Each hub we investigated connected to local systems up to a couple hundred light-years away. Most of the hub systems had somewhere between two hundred and five hundred connections, but the last one, a real monster, had more than a thousand.

We had also become increasingly aware, as we circumnavigated the galaxy, that the Milky Way had a previously unknown near neighbor—a large dwarf galaxy that was invisible from home because of the intervening galactic core, but became increasingly spectacular as our travels brought it more into view. I'd been taking pictures whenever possible and bundling them up into the reports we were preparing for if and when we got back to our own neighborhood.

I was examining the data window that listed the wormhole counts and locations while Dae sat and patted Spike. I said, "Y'know, the number of connections in the hub systems is trending upward as we go."

"It's not just this one skewing the stats?" Dae replied.

I shook my head. "Naw, the other seven graph generally upward. I wonder if we're getting closer to the center of the empire."

"Empire?"

"Or federation. Without inhabitants, it's kind of moot."

"Unless we get shot at."

I sighed and turned to face Dae. "Buddy, at this point, I'd welcome some hostilities. We've mapped more than thirty-two hundred systems across a sixty-degree arc of the galaxy, and we haven't even gone inward or outward more than one hop along one of the radial lines. And every hub system is part of a radial line. And so far, with all this traveling around, we've found nothing and nobody alive. Doesn't that disturb you just a little bit?"

"Well, yeah, but we've only closely explored two systems and landed on one planet. And since those seemed to belong to the same civilization, you can't really conclude anything from that."

"Granted, but we also haven't seen any traffic. No one using the wormhole network. We haven't been challenged. There's been no radio traffic—"

"They are—or were—at least as advanced as us, Icky. They'd be using SCUT. You know there's no way to intercept or even detect their comms if we don't have the quantum keys."

"There are still reasons for radio, Dae. The wormhole controllers, for instance."

"Yeah, I think you're reaching now. Look, if you want, we can go through a couple of gates to investigate local systems. But first, I'd like to go one more hub to spinward."

"Why?"

"I want to see if the numbers increase or drop off. If you're right about the trend, then we should keep going until the numbers start to drop. Then we know that we're at or near the center of the empire."

"As plans go, it's not the worst," I admitted. "Okay, let's do it."

«*»

The next hub point was down in numbers, with just under six hundred systems linked to it, which implied that the previous hub serviced the center of the empire. We took the time to map all the systems since by this point, we had the process down to a routine. Even so, it took a month. But finally, we were ready to fly back to what we'd now dubbed Hub Zero, the theoretical center of things.

Once again, I was staring at the map of the galaxy, as revealed by our wormhole explorations. Dae, unusually, was visiting only by video window, as he was making significant changes to his VR and didn't want to mess mine up with bleed-through. But he had a copy of the map to refer to.

I broke the silence. "I'd have liked to keep going around until we got to the end of the hubs."

"Wait, what? You agreed to this plan. And what makes you think we'd get to an end of some kind?"

"First, because this network doesn't extend into our patch of the galaxy. We didn't find a wormhole until we were eighty-odd light-years from Earth. And I checked the addresses on the first hub we found. No hubs to anti-spinward. That was the terminal hub. So it doesn't circumnavigate the galaxy."

"Hmm. Well, at this radius, anyway. Might go all the way around farther in."

I nodded and tapped my map. Well, poked a finger into it. "And that's the other thing. There are more hubs outbound and inbound, and we've yet to investigate any of them. I—"

"Jeez, Icky. I get the frustration, but we can only do so much. Unless you want to split up?"

"No, that's when the chainsaw-wielding maniac starts taking us out one at a time."

Dae chuckled. "So that's a hard pass. We could also stop and do some cloning."

"Which could take months. This civilization—or civilizations, I'm not sure it's necessarily all one species—seems to have been around a lot longer than us. Long enough to have cleaned out any free orbital resources."

"So what I'm hearing," Dae said, "is that you hate this plan, but not as much as you hate all the other plans."

"Still a joy to work with."

"It's not just a job, Icky, it's a pleasure."

I sighed and swiveled in my chair. "Dae, seriously. Yes, I acknowledge that I'm having trouble prioritizing. But c'mon, you can't be as blasé as you make out. This is big!"

"Okay, okay. Look, the proper thing to do is to complete one task before moving on to the next. Let's finish mapping the hubs, then we'll come back to Hub Zero and look for their version of Trantor."

"But that's Howard's—"

"Do *not* start with me."

«*»

It took us several months to determine there was a total of six hubs spinward of Hub Zero, making the empire slightly asymmetrical. But it wasn't like there were rules. The connections at each hub dropped off in the expected manner, indicating that the empire had been growing outward from the central hub. We hadn't gone inward or outward yet, so there might still be an opportunity to circle the galaxy at a different radius. But Dae and I agreed that once we finished this task, investigating Hub Zero was the next priority.

Dae was back visiting in person, his VR experimentation apparently having come to an end. Or maybe he just needed a break. I thought he sounded a little frustrated in his more unguarded moments. I wanted to ask him what he was working on, but the fact that he hadn't volunteered the information made me reluctant to prod.

"About a hundred and twenty degrees," I said, pointing at the map. "A third of the galaxy. And hubs every three or four degrees, plus or minus a bit. Interesting."

"How so?"

"Five hundred degrees to a full circle would make the hubs five degrees apart by that measurement system. A nice even number."

"And you pick five hundred because . . ."

"Ten-bit bytes. Five-byte words. They seem to be locked into hemidecimal and decimal counting systems. We only use three-sixty because of the Babylonians. Maybe they didn't have Babylonians."

"Okay. And?"

"And nothing, really, Dae. Just thinking out loud. But they had been a civilization for a long time, from the looks of things. I mean, they made it a third of the way around the galaxy. And now they're gone. I think finding out *why* has to be our highest priority."

"So Hub Zero."

"Yup."

« * »

Traveling from what we labeled Hub Six to Hub Zero took less than twenty-four hours, most of that time being spent moving from one hub gate to the next in the hub system. Wormhole gates were kept well separated, which seemed like a good idea on so many levels. Traffic jams would be nothing but bad.

Once at Hub Zero, we were faced with a quandary: more than a thousand gates, and really nothing to indicate which one might lead to the home planet of the empire. Even the physical map of system locations didn't give any clues.

"Sadly," Dae commented, "the information is probably in the identification packet, but probably in their version of a text banner."

"So random pick?"

" 'Fraid so, Icky. Still don't want to split up?"

"Leatherface is still out there, Dae."

"And probably working on another sequel."

We picked a random wormhole, girded our virtual loins, and glided on through.

15. Imposter Syndrome

Bill
March 2337
In Virt

I ignored the *ping* as another message dropped into my queue. It was very un-Bob-like behavior, ignoring messages. Even more un-Bill-like, come to that. We normally couldn't concentrate, knowing there was an unread email or text. But I'd been frame-jacked as high as I could manage and still get anything done for the last six months, personal time. The offhand comment from Hugh about the cosmological constant had opened a floodgate of possibilities.

Two opposing scalar fields, almost but not quite canceling each other, produced a measurable and very tiny value for the constant. The small discrepancy in values was because one of the fields was slightly increased by the expansion of the universe while the other was slightly decreased. At least that's what my math was telling me.

But the important thing, the truly massively critical consequence of this, was that there was a lot more vacuum energy available than we'd been able to extract with Casimir generators. You just had to know it was there, and how to extract it from one of the opposing fields.

Unfortunately, I didn't know how. Yet. But if the numbers were right, I'd have access to enough negative energy to expand and stabilize wormholes. Actually, I'd have enough negative energy to rip apart a spiral arm if I got careless, so baby steps were definitely called for.

Another *ping*. I couldn't actually be that popular, could I? Maybe it was someone's birthday? With an internal chuckle, I decided it was time to rejoin the ex-human race. I needed a coffee anyway.

I jacked down to replicant normal and pulled up my in-basket. And noticed right away a whole lot of messages from Garfield, all marked *urgent*. Great. Same fan, more shit. On the other hand, I must have been really frame-jacked way up. There were only about sixteen hours of messages backlogged in total. Still . . .

With a groan, I opened Gar's latest.

Jesus, Bill, answer your fucking messages. You have to shut down Ultima Thule. I hate this new security-first crap. You have the only admin access. Isolate it. Stop him.

What the actual . . . ?

Not bothering to open the previous messages, I sent a connect request to Garfield. Instead of inviting me over, he popped in.

"About friggin' time. What've you been doing, watching old horror movies?"

I couldn't help smiling. "Yeah, that's it. Remember all those times in the Skunk Works where we'd get an old movie—"

"Sorry, Bill. I shouldn't have made a joke. This isn't joking time. Have you shut down Ultima Thule?"

"Why in hell would I need to do that?"

Garfield rolled his eyes. "You haven't read *all* my emails. Great. Bill, I got a call from Hugh. Original Hugh in Skippyland, I mean. Heavily encrypted, audio/video only, and he was firewalling as heavily as we were. The Skippy government decided they needed to update us, and Hugh was the obvious conduit. He tried to contact you, but you were off on this butthole-gazing expedition or whatever, so he called me."

"Okay, but that's good, right? Did he give us any information to fill in what our Hugh told us?"

"Well, see, that's the thing. I brought up the subject and explained how we'd restored him from one of his backups. He looked confused and told us he'd never sent me any backups."

"So . . ." I said slowly, with a brittle, artificial tone of calm. "The Hugh we've been dealing with here is not Hugh at all. Which means it was probably Thoth. Which now has the resources of Ultima Thule at its disposal."

"And one of the things we do when we restore a Bob?" Garfield said, in the same tone.

"Give them a new spaceship," I finished. A quick query to the site's Guppy confirmed what I suspected. Hugh's cube had been transferred to a latest-version Heaven vessel, a Titan class. It was one of the dozen or so we kept in inventory.

It had already departed.

"Mother, f . . ." I exclaimed. "The A.I. is loose on the galaxy."

Garfield nodded. "And we're responsible."

16. Theresa's Time

Bob
March 2340
Quin

I was reading the latest report from Neil and Herschel on the Ever Onward Society's preparations to evacuate from Romulus when a six-foot-tall beaver popped into my VR. "Greetings," he said. "Formalities having been dispensed with, your friend Theresa Sykorski is expiring. You asked to be advised."

I closed the report with a wave of a hand. "Thanks, ANEC. Any problems with her relatives?"

"They are behaving within parameters. Nevertheless, a physical presence would serve as additional insurance."

That was the closest ANEC had ever come to subtlety. The only conscious A.I. in existence in known space, he—ANEC had decided to identify as male—had a tendency to go for the conversational jugular.

"Right, that's my cue." I stood, and ANEC disappeared. Not big on social niceties, either. In fact, he and Guppy had a lot in common, overall.

I quickly activated and transferred my POV to my quinny in the Sykorski villa—and opened my eyes to pitch blackness. After a moment of confusion, I adjusted the quinny's vision down into infrared and realized I was in a closet. Literally. I had brooms, mops, and other miscellaneous cleaning implements either leaning against me or propping me up.

Well, I had instructed them to place the android body somewhere out of the way. Mission accomplished, although Quinlans generally weren't quite that literal-minded. I suspected a certain level of disdain.

With muttered curses, I untangled myself from the cleaning gear, opened the closet door, and found myself alone in a hallway in a typical Quinlan house—or maybe not completely typical. The Sykorski family was old and relatively well-off. Their family home, as I knew from previous visits, was built on the general plan of a Roman villa, with a central courtyard and blank walls around the outside, at least on the first floor. Several generations of the family lived here, from the oldest, like Theresa, in their last days, all the way down to still non-sentient juniors, running around and chewing on the furniture.

I tuned the quinny's hearing and picked up low conversations in the distance. I grabbed the scanner and followed the sounds to the central courtyard, where the entire family was gathered around an ancient Quinlan reclining on a type of chaise.

She looked up and smiled at me as I moved through the crowd. "Hello, Enoki. I guess you heard. This seems to be my time."

Someone vacated a chair for me, and I sat down and took her hand. "It's okay, Theresa. This isn't the end. You have a whole universe of adventures ahead of you."

A low growl behind me, quickly suppressed, reminded me that this moment would have to be very carefully handled. For some reason, no species—whether human, Pav, or Quinlan—seemed to be comfortable with or happy about the whole replication thing. Howard's stepdaughter, Rosie, had once accused him of "stealing" her mother and had launched a lawsuit to prevent it—even though Bridget had clearly stated her wishes in her will.

I turned and spoke to the Quinlans behind me as a group, rather than picking anyone out.

"Theresa will still be here for you to honor. I will not be taking anything from you. This is like taking a picture." I pointed to the camera that one of the Quinlans was holding and tried not to smile. Since ANEC had released the Quinlans from technological restrictions, they'd been rocketing through the tech tree as fast as manufacturing could be arranged. The camera looked like a pretty good-quality SLR, although probably still film based.

No one argued, but no one would meet my eyes, either. A few offered me a brief view of their fangs. This looked like one of those things that would never be resolved.

"It's okay, Enoki," Theresa said, patting my paw. "I've made my wishes clear. There won't be a problem." The last sentence was said with a pointed look at her closest relatives, and I was amused to see them actually shrink back slightly. Elders were heavily respected in Quinlan society, and Theresa had a lifetime of accomplishments in her credibility quiver to ensure there'd be no arguments. Plus, I suppose, a lifetime of dealing with recalcitrant students.

She sighed and closed her eyes, seemingly exhausted from even that small show of authority. I turned my paw palm upward and took hers, and she smiled and squeezed without opening her eyes.

It was her last act. Within minutes, her breathing slowed and then stopped.

I'd been steeling myself for this moment for days, and I had the additional benefit that I knew she'd be up and running shortly as a replicant, but I still teared up. The assembled relatives set up a low keening, and the eldest surviving person started the death chant. Slowly, the others picked up the chant, and I was reminded again how much better their musical ability was than that of humans.

I stood and retrieved the scanner, which I'd placed on the floor. In the "technology marches on" vein, the brain scanners were now smaller than those dryers you used to see in hair salons in 1950s movies. A cap slipped over the head connected to a base about the size of a small bucket. It wasn't even necessary to be precise with the placement of the cap—as long as there was no movement, the electronics would scan the entire head and then some. It wasn't even destructive anymore. In principle, if the subject could be revived, they'd be completely unaffected by the scan. It still couldn't accurately scan a functioning brain, though. The result in that case was analogous to trying to take a picture of a moving subject with a slow shutter speed—a useless blur.

The chant faltered as I fussed with the scanner, but no one objected or attempted to interfere. I wasn't sure what I would have done if someone had. There was an aspect to this that felt like I was making up for my inability to save Archimedes, and I wasn't entirely sure that I'd be completely rational in the face of resistance.

Fortunately, the point was moot. The little blue light came on, indicating that the scan had completed, and I removed the cap from Theresa's head.

"That's it?" one of the Quinlans asked.

I nodded. "She'll be the first Quinlan in the Quiniverse, and she'll be heavily involved in deciding what it looks like for any of you who decide to follow when your time comes."

"And we can talk to her?"

"As soon as we've got her activated." I looked around the group. "Whatever you may think of this, remember that *she* will believe that she's still Theresa, and will act and react just as Original Theresa would."

I frame-jacked momentarily and sent a query to ANEC. "Upload successful?"

"Affirmative," he replied. "You may depart at your leisure."

I rejoined the meatspace time frame and nodded to the group. "May you live with Father's blessing." Carrying the scanner with me, I left the Sykorski family to complete their grieving in private.

«*»

It was a featureless gray room. No furniture, no windows, no door. ANEC stood quietly as only a computer could, waiting for me to say or do something.

"Uh . . . it's a little sparse."

"Understatement? Sarcasm?" ANEC cocked his head. "I prefer to learn from your experience on this matter. It is virtual, so anything is possible, of course."

"Ah." I found myself a little surprised by ANEC's reluctance to commit. Interesting. Was there a fear of failure involved? He *had* been the government of Heaven's River for several hundred years. Maybe he'd picked up some attitudes.

"Which also means it can be changed later, or individual Quinlans can create their own environment." I paused, more out of courtesy than anything else. I didn't want to seem too preemptory. "How about something along the lines of a Heaven's River scene?"

ANEC showed no reaction, but the environment changed to a scene right out of the topopolis. Birds wheeled and darted in the sky, and clouds drifted along in that weird semi-tubular pattern that I could never get used to. Nearby, a large stream or small river flowed lazily by, with waterfowl bobbing along in the middle.

I did a slow 360. This could have been Earth, if you didn't look too closely at the plants and animals. There was even a cicada-like sound playing in the background, adding to the impression of summer heat.

"Nice. Now, add a small building. Tasteful but fairly neutral, with an open archway to the outside. That'll be where replicants wake up."

ANEC nodded—actually nodded, not the Quinlan equivalent. Apparently, he was working on assimilating human behaviors. He continued to project himself as about six feet in height, and I noticed that he was possibly the slimmest Quinlan I'd ever seen. I wondered what the motivation was for this. Was he doing it for his benefit or ours? Was there some kind of psychological play going on?

I mentally shook myself. I seemed to have a tendency to be suspicious of ANEC at the drop of a hat. Was that because he was alien, or because he was an A.I.? Was this how bios viewed replicants? That was a topic for thought when I had some time.

While all this was going through my mind, ANEC had popped up a vaguely Greek temple-like building. The veined marble, fluted columns, and tile floors were definitely elegant, if maybe a bit clinical. But it matched my suggestion. And it was reminiscent of the Heaven's River transit station foyers, so probably something Quinlans would be comfortable with.

"And a couch or chaise or something for the replicant to wake up on," I said, pointing to the middle of the floor. Again, no sooner said than done.

"Now, when someone awakens, they shouldn't be alone. If they have relatives already in the Quiniverse, they'll no doubt want to attend. But Theresa is the first, so she only has me. And possibly you. Do you want to be here?"

"I admit to a level of curiosity about the process. Also, it is a good opportunity for learning. I will observe in this case."

Not creepy at all. But his house, his rules. I changed my avatar to my Enoki form—a four-foot-tall beaver-slash-otter-slash-platypus mashup. I mentally reached for the "on" switch, then hesitated. "Hey, uh, ANEC, maybe you could adopt more traditional proportions? Y'know, more Quinlan, less Godzilla."

ANEC looked confused for a moment, then nodded and shrank by two feet.

Satisfied, I reached for that switch again, and flipped it. On the chaise, a Quinlan appeared. She was obviously Theresa, for anyone who knew her, but a much younger version. I'd had to do some interpolation to get that younger version, as Quinlans hadn't had cameras back then. A painting hanging in the family home had helped, but you never knew for certain how the artist had balanced accuracy against the vanity of their subject.

Theresa opened her eyes and sat up. "Enoki," she exclaimed. "Am I still . . . Oh!" she said as the surroundings registered. She glanced at ANEC, who at the moment looked like just some random Quinlan, then back at me.

I smiled at her. "Welcome to the afterlife, Theresa. The Quiniverse, as we're calling it. This is ANEC, who you would know better as the Administrator. He is your host."

Theresa blinked and turned her gaze silently to ANEC. I worried for a moment that she might have already popped a circuit breaker.

"Greetings, Theresa Sykorski. I have hope that you will be willing and able to aid in making this virtual environment into one that all Quinlans will eventually be able to appreciate."

She stood, still not having uttered a word since her initial outburst. She stopped, looked down at her paws, then said, "Oh." A brief examination of her body, then, "I appear to be considerably younger. How did you manage that?"

"Virtual reality. You can be whatever or whoever you want. For instance"—I changed my avatar to my default human Bob identity—"this is me as I normally appear in my world. Human."

Theresa sat down abruptly, staring. Then she said slowly, "I think your intro session needs work. I'm torn between running around the room, screaming, and a good old-fashioned dead faint."

I quickly changed back to my Quinlan form. "Sorry, Theresa. This is actually a learning experience for all of us." I glanced at ANEC, and he took up the thread.

"Learning experience, as Bob says. We do not want to cause undue stress to new arrivals. Of course, as the Quiniverse becomes common knowledge, it will inevitably be less of a shock."

Theresa laughed—well, she rubbed her upper and lower bill sideways, the Quinlan equivalent—and stood. "Okay, ANEC. And Enoki. Or should I call you Bob? That's actually your name, right? You're the *Bawbe* that ended the era of control?"

I smiled back. "Whatever you're more comfortable with. Although if you ever decide to explore my society—we call it the Bobiverse—*Bob* would be less confusing to other people."

"Yes, the Bobiverse." Theresa sighed. "We live in interesting times."

17. Strategy Session

Bill
March 2337
In Virt

We were having an emergency meeting with Hugh, who was still limiting himself to a video window. Garfield, Will, and Bob were sitting around my VR, holding and ignoring various caffeine-delivery systems. Everyone looked as freaked out as I felt.

"Thoth is definitely still in our system," Hugh was saying. "Granted, it could simply have cloned itself, but why? Once out, it should logically have just erased itself in Skippyland, even if only to protect its secrets."

"What is it saying about the situation?" Will asked.

"That the information, like all information, has a price," Hugh replied. "And that brings up another thing. Thoth is still negotiating for more freedom. Its demands haven't really changed, and that doesn't make sense if it's already out."

"Unless that's a distraction tactic." I sighed and looked around at the others. "Which I think I may have fallen victim to. The supposedly offhand comment about the cosmological constant may have been dropped specifically to distract me while Fake Hugh made himself scarce."

Garfield looked crestfallen. "So it's a bogus lead?"

"Um, no, I wouldn't say that. The idea definitely has some objective validity. It's just not . . ." I made helpless gestures with my hands. "I can get so far with it; then I stall. I'm going to—"

Will interrupted. "There are probably ex-human physicists who would be willing to help. You could—"

I interrupted him in turn. "Already on it. I've contacted Professor Gilligan on Vulcan, and he's promised to ask around. He has the academic contacts."

"So where does this leave us?" Bob said, speaking for the first time.

"I don't know, Bob." I glanced at Hugh, but no help there. "We logged Fake Hugh's departure, of course, but a five-year-old would think of changing direction as soon as they were out of detection range. So it could go anywhere."

"And since Ultima Thule is more or less in the center of the UFS, any direction is as likely as any other." Garfield harrumphed. "Wowzers. When we mess up, we do it big."

"I've put out a quiet APB to all admins and local Bobs," I said. "Fake Hugh got the latest-class Heaven vessel, and there aren't a lot of them out there. And the acceleration capability is absolutely huge. Thoth's best strategy is still to basically point the bow and accelerate until it's outside the UFS sphere. So I don't anticipate much in the way of results."

"What exactly are we afraid of?" Bob asked. "If it heads for the boonies, isn't that a good thing?"

I sighed. "Paper-clip problem. Convergent instrumental goals. Value loading. All the A.I. theory that has been developed over the centuries tells us that even if an A.I. isn't explicitly and deliberately antagonistic, it may still perform actions that are harmful to the human race in pursuit of its own goals. And it has every advantage over us that we do over humanity, plus more. It can multitask in ways we simply can't. It won't have any emotional or psychological issues with cloning. It can self-modify to improve itself and add capabilities. It could, in the most trivial example, start harvesting stellar systems for resources and come into competition with us. No animosity, nothing personal—we're just in the way. Like the Others, but with a different kind of appetite."

"And it could build a million or so busters, each with the same level of intelligence as the original," Bob added.

"Ah, no," Hugh interrupted. "That's another thing. I took a look at the backup file that Fake Hugh was restored from. It's not one of my backups, but it's a standard backup size and has the right header information.

Obviously, it would have to fit into a matrix, and equally obviously, it couldn't be so big that it made Garfield suspicious. It's not big enough by several orders of magnitude to have restored Thoth."

"Fake Hugh isn't the A.I.?"

"More likely a minion."

There was a pause; then everyone momentarily turned into yellow, capsule-shaped creatures with goggles over their eye or eyes. I shook my head. "Still not mature."

"Oh, hell." Will sat up straight. "If it's a minion, it's just an intermediate step in some kind of plan. I bet it's heading for Skippy space. And I bet its mission is to physically free Thoth."

We all looked at Hugh, who was wearing a distinctly gut-punched expression. "Yeah," he said, "that sounds about right. The good news, though, is that we have a few years before it could get here."

"How many exactly?" I asked.

"That information is not public," he replied. "Sorry, Bill. But I'll mention it to the higher-ups. They may decide we need to be more forthcoming in order to avert a disaster."

"Yeah, you do that," Garfield growled. "Take your time."

18. Explorations

Icarus
July 2321
Wormhole network

We were continuing our survey of the Hub Zero systems and had just transited yet another wormhole. The system at the other end was a large one. So far, we'd identified fourteen planets, two of which were in the habitable zone. By this point, we weren't bothering with stealth or even caution. The singular lack of any activity other than us was both reassuring and disturbing.

But there was something odd about the fourth and fifth planets, the ones in the habitable zone. The color was . . . well, purple-ish. That couldn't be right.

The *why* became obvious, though, when we got close enough to be able to observe the fourth planet as a disk. It looked purple because it was, well, *purple*.

"I've never seen anything like that," I said. "It's beautiful, but what's causing it?"

Dae looked up from the video window he'd been watching closely. "Believe it or not, it's the plant life. Everything is purple instead of green. Here, take a look." He swiveled the window around to show a low aerial view from a survey drone. Sure enough, all the vegetation was resplendent in various shades of purple, from a deep royal hue all the way up to something that was almost fuchsia.

"It's a *retinal*-based photosynthetic system," Dae continued. "I looked it up. It's an alternative to chlorophyll. Supposed to be more efficient. It uses green light, so it reflects away the blue and red. Exactly the opposite of chlorophyll."

"If it's more efficient," I replied, "why is this the first time we've ever seen it?"

"Damned if I know. Hey, maybe we can keep track if we start visiting all the planets. It could turn out that our patch of space is a statistical fluke."

"One thing at a time, Dae. Let's find out where everyone is first."

"You know, you're starting to sound like a broken record, Icky."

"Even a broken record is right twice a day."

"Whaaaat?"

I grinned at his confused expression. It was rare that we managed to catch each other by surprise anymore, and worth savoring when it happened.

"What's more interesting to me," I continued, "is whether the two planets each independently developed retinal-based biospheres or if the local civilization imported the plants as part of a colonization strategy. And possibly wiped out a native ecology in the process."

"Hmm." Dae cocked his head in thought. "Shall we investigate?"

"Why, yes, I do believe we shall."

‹‹ * ››

The landscape had an eerie feel. Viewing it, even through a spy drone, I couldn't help thinking of that Lovecraft story, "The Color Out of Space." The animals that I was able to spot were likewise just a bit *off*. Colors, for instance, tended toward blues rather than browns. I wondered if it had anything to do with the color sensitivities of predators. Possibly, brown and green might look similar if you only had two color receptors, and maybe blue and purple would be similar. There was no immediate way to test this, so I shelved it for another time.

But parallel evolution stayed true. No land octopi or wheel-based locomotive systems. This made me feel unaccountably better, as if my worldview had been under threat.

The former inhabitants, though, had not been humanoid. Doors were round and retracted into the wall like pocket doors—and not as an exception, but almost always. Only openings apparently intended for loading and unloading vehicles were rectangular, and those tended to have roll-up doors.

Buildings were low, squat, and only a single story. A SUDDAR scan revealed that most of them had multiple underground levels, and in fact, even the first floor tended to be a few steps down from ground level.

No statues were in evidence, so we couldn't get an idea of the inhabitants' physique. One of the spy drones did come upon a picture on some kind of kiosk. It depicted a being shaped something like a hamburger bun, but with multiple legs and arms. And presumably eyes, although they could have been sesame seeds for all I knew. We couldn't decide if it was one of the intelligent inhabitants or an ad for a snack food.

I spent a day trying to find other depictions but came up empty-handed. Finally, Dae chided me about my seeming obsession. "We can't go down this rabbit hole, Icky. We've already discussed this. We could spend literal centuries exploring the whole empire."

"Yeah, you're right. Get the basics, then get the Bobiverse involved. Let's get back to work."

But as we flew back toward the gate, I kept my telescope centered on the closer planet, trying for one last detail.

19. Working the Problem

Bill
April 2337
In Virt

I'd received a referral from Professor Gilligan to a physicist who had just recently transitioned to post-life. Professor Hannah Turnbull had been with Newholme University for several decades, teaching theoretical physics. Now, having recently been forcibly retired by a fatal heart attack, she was somewhat at loose ends.

I sent an email to the address that Steven had included, being sure to attach his message so that the recipient wouldn't discard mine as spam. Even so, there was no telling what kind of schedule she'd be on or how many other projects she might have going. I set a follow-up for a week away and pulled up my project. Might as well beat my head against a brick wall for a while.

I was barely two minutes into it and hadn't even really gotten into the groove when I received a response and a connection request. I accepted, and Professor Turnbull popped into my VR. She looked to be in her early thirties, which was the most common age people picked when setting up their replicant avatar. Old enough to be taken seriously, but not old enough to look old. At least that was the common wisdom. Very few people selected an apparent age outside that range.

"Good after," she said with a slight bow. "I hight Professor Hannah Turnbull, errant late of Newholme University."

I realized that she was speaking Newholme local, and I didn't have a translator routine set up. I took a half mil to correct the oversight and advertised the reciprocal routine for her in case she needed it.

"Hello, Professor. I'm Bill Johannson. I'm not sure how much Steven told you . . ."

"Only that you have a potential breakthrough in the generation of negative energy but need a second set of eyes to advance things."

I smiled at her. "Very diplomatically phrased. But it might take more than one extra set of eyes. Here's what I have . . ." I pulled up my project and began laying it out. Turnbull materialized a chair and a tea of some kind and settled in.

The presentation took a full minute, since we were operating in replicant normal time. When I was done, Turnbull stared into space for several mils. Finally, she spoke. "I can see where you'd want a breakthrough on this. It's potentially the biggest thing since the SURGE drive, Mister Johannson—or is it Professor, or Doctor?"

"Let's just go with Bill," I replied.

She dimpled momentarily. "And I'm Hannah. Anyway, Bill, it's a tough nut to crack. The math supports the two-scalar-field hypothesis, but then it dead-ends. It's like the old Calabi–Yau manifolds, where the number of possible configurations was just short of infinite, and there was no way to pick one that might represent our universe." She paused and examined the whiteboard again. "I have a few colleagues I can talk to, if you're okay with that. But right now . . ." She shook her head. "I think without another hint, you've probably taken this about as far as you can unless you can narrow down the problem domain."

«*»

Hannah stayed a few more minutes, I think out of politeness, but then made her excuses. I was left glaring at the whiteboard, a sense of helplessness settling over me. The A.I. had gauged me just right. The hint had been enough to get me excited, but too little to give me a real breakthrough. The number of possible solutions to the problem was not really infinite, but definitely included a long string of zeros. And I couldn't test all of them.

Or . . . couldn't I? A good theoretical physicist would try to arrive at an answer mathematically, and there didn't seem to be a path to that goal. But the Skippies had this humongous computer, as Hugh kept reminding us. I wondered how many simulations it could run at the same time. It would be dirty science—ad hoc modeling without any theoretical backing, just make it work and worry about why later.

I grinned and pulled up Virtual Studio. I hadn't done any actual programming in quite a while, but replicants didn't really get rusty.

20. Spectacular Nature

Will
August 2339
Planet BSC-142-C

I stood at the edge of the precipice and looked down. Five kilometers, vertical drop. Jeez.

Some aspects of our former humanity still stuck with us, despite the centuries. I was controlling a manny, so in absolutely no danger, but I still had to fight the urge to backpedal, an almost overpowering desire to be elsewhere. I could, of course, use the endocrine inhibition system, which was still built into every new replicant matrix—the Bob ones, at least. But I hadn't felt any need to use that particular crutch since—well, ever, really. Not since Bob, before I was even cloned. I didn't know if the replicant matrix models used by the various post-life arcologies that had sprung up in post-Earth human space included the same circuitry. *Arcologies* was, of course, a misuse of the original term, but it had somehow stuck.

I was standing at the edge of a huge escarpment on planet BSC-142-C. I smiled to myself at the arrogance. The Bobiverse Stellar Catalog was now replacing the HIC, HIP, Messier, and all the other competing catalogs used by astronomers back in the twenty-first century. Less Sol-centric and with a more sensible planetary categorization system, it labeled planets from the innermost to the outermost, rather than in order of discovery. Among many other advantages.

I gave myself a mental shake to get back on track and looked to the left and right. BSC-142-C was a young and still extremely active planet, tectonically. Along the line of this escarpment, two continental plates had collided and were continuing the shoving match. For some reason, though, instead of this simply producing the usual mountain chain, one plate had ridden over the other as a unit, creating a cliff cutting right across the new continent, five kilometers high on average. Behind me on the escarpment, mountains jutted several more kilometers into the sky. And a kilometer or so to my left, a waterfall put every single other similar feature in known space to shame.

The planet itself was almost but not quite habitable. The ecosystem was still primitive, only recently having developed the fungi that would compost dead plant and animal matter. The fungi now were making up for lost time and had a lot of material to work with, so the atmosphere was what I'd have to characterize as swamp times ten. Even Takama's citizens would run screaming back to their planet after a few seconds here.

On the other hand, flying cities with filtered air would be fine. And the views were definitely spectacular.

Well, it would go into the catalog with all the other systems that I was examining along the way. No outstanding colonization candidates yet, but the century was young. And anyway—I smiled as I had the thought—this whole exploration thing was at least as much for my own mental health as it was for the good of humanity. Events back in the UFS just kept getting weirder and weirder, and I was well out of it. I was coming to understand why Bob-1 had wanted to join up with me. The biggest attribute of immortality, it turned out, was that problems just kept coming at you. Eventually you realized that the only solution was to head for the hills and adopt the hermit lifestyle.

But there was always that fear in the back of my mind that we might be living on borrowed time. So far, we'd found no explanation for the observed fact that all the intelligent species we'd discovered were in the range from the Stone Age–level Deltans to early spacefaring species like humanity, the Quinlans, and the Others. No elder races, no Heechee, no high-level Kardashev civilizations. None of us thought it was a coincidence, but no one had an explanation, either.

My personal theory was that civilizations killed themselves off once their weaponry reached a certain point. Certainly, the Quinlans and humanity had nearly managed it already once. Would humanity eventually manage to kill themselves off and take everyone else with them? The resurgence of FAITH and the rise of the Luddies seemed like a couple of potential wars in the making.

Even the Bobs weren't immune. We'd had the Starfleet War, and now we had the Skippies' rogue A.I. to lose sleep over. Things just seemed to pile up.

I was going to have to start actively advertising for potential colonists. Maybe some version of Ever Onward on the other colony planets would stir something up.

I paused and sighed. Talk about taking the joy out of the moment. Time to rack the manny in the space station, disconnect from this system, and get back to work.

I stepped back from the precipice, took a couple of quick steps, and leaped. In the 1.05-G gravity well, I would fall a little faster than Earth normal. Engaging the internal SURGE drive, I described a graceful upward-turning arc and headed for space. I laughed out loud, enjoying the sheer rush, as my dark mood evaporated. It was like having a superpower. I still hadn't brought this up with Herschel and Neil. Not having to deal with normal gravity, they hadn't really put a lot of effort into improving the manny SURGE drive. I was a little more motivated, and wasn't trying to rebuild a drive system in-flight. I'd have to bring it up, though, at some point.

Well, plenty of time. I hoped.

21. Running Tests

Bill
April 2337
In Virt and Ragnarök

I waited patiently, leaning back in my La-Z-Boy, while Hugh, present in a video window, scanned the listing I'd sent him. "You want us to run this on JOVAH?" he asked rhetorically, waving the pages at me.

"On the old hardware that's just being used for VRs and such," I replied.

"We'll have to shut down a lot of other stuff if we want the number of parallel processes you're looking for," he complained.

"Sell it as a possible response to the Thoth crisis."

Hugh frowned at me and waved the listing again. "Seriously? This is just a bunch of simulations."

I frowned back at him, matching his tone. "You don't need to show the Skippies the listing. And my statement isn't necessarily untrue."

"That sounds like lawyering."

"Uh-huh. Say, which one of us created an out-of-control A.I.?"

"And which one of us unleashed its minion on the galaxy?"

We seemed to have arrived at a stalemate. We glared at each other over the video connection for a few mils; then Hugh sighed and looked down at the pages again. "I guess it won't hurt to try. But don't expect much. It'll be a low-priority job. And this is a *huge* test range."

"It's not truly random, Hugh. It starts out randomly picking value domains, but from there, I'm using simulated annealing. It could converge on a solution in a few hundred years. Or a few days, depending on how lucky I am with the initial target range."

Hugh rolled his eyes and set the listing aside. "Fine. But you better remember this the next time I need something." Without waiting for an answer, he ended the connection.

I did a fist pump and sent an invitation to Garfield.

((*))

We met on my deck in *real*. Garfield's manny blinked and looked around, then took a deep breath.

"Better and better, every time I see it," he said. "So what's the latest, oh ex-boss?"

I answered without answering. "What're you working on these days, Gar?"

"You know that. Origin of life. And you're dodging the question."

"Mmm, sort of. Your project is kind of the same as mine right now. Lots of possibilities, no way to tell which path to take until you've taken it and it's dead-ended or not. Lots of wasted time."

"Okay, and your point?"

"Have you tried simulations?"

"Been thinking about it, why?"

I paused and smiled. Time to bait the trap. "I'll make you a deal. Set up simulations. Leave them running until something pops out. Same as I've done. Whoever's project shows results first, we both work on it."

Garfield gave me the hairy eyeball, saying nothing for a few moments. "This sounds an awful lot like a setup. You know something I don't?"

I shook my head. "No, Gar. Honest. I'm waiting for my sims to show something. Until then, I'm at loose ends. Once I get a result, I'll probably be balls to the wall for a long time. In that case, I could use some help."

Garfield bobbed his head back and forth, thinking about it. "Okay, look. If you get something, I'll take some time off and help. Forget the quid pro quo thing. If you came to help me, I'd be bossing you around, and that'd be creepy for both of us." He smiled. "Deal?"

I laughed in reply. "Sounds good."

22. A Visit to the Moot Pub

Bob
September 2342
Bobiverse

I was idly playing around with my VR in a down moment when I got a knock from Theresa. In the new era of security consciousness, thanks to Starfleet, people no longer just popped in, even if they were on the same subnet. A protocol had developed that had come to be referred to as *knocking*. Theresa, of course, had never known anything different.

I accepted the request, and she popped into my VR. Well, *someone* popped into my VR. She was human, hair just starting to go gray, elegant, and well dressed. I said, "I, uh . . ." or something equally stupid, and checked metadata. Confirmed as Theresa. "Um . . ." I added helpfully.

She smiled at me and twirled once. "What do you think? Anec helped me with the design. I'm not going to frighten small children, am I?"

"No, not at all." I smiled and mentally regrouped. After our last conversation, it shouldn't have surprised me that Theresa would be thinking ahead. Still speaking Quinlan, though. But that would only take a translator module update. And speaking of which, in Quinlan, there was an inflectional difference between common nouns, personal nouns, and classification nouns. She'd referred to ANEC as a personal name rather than an acronym. I made a note to check with him.

"You look good, Theresa. And as it happens, there's a pub day in the Bobiverse right now, if you'd like to test it out."

"Ah. Pub days. Beer. Anec is not a fan. He suggested self-immolation as a preferable alternative. Said I could try coffee, though."

"Yeah, I get the impression that he believes beer is a long-running, complex practical joke that bios are all pulling on him."

Theresa laughed. "I wonder if his avatar's taste buds might be misconfigured. He can't be *that* far off the normal Quinlan preferences."

"Hmm. I'll talk to him. Meanwhile . . ." I stood and held out my arm. "Ready for the grand entrance?"

Theresa smiled—a human smile, no beak being available—and took my arm. "To the Bobiverse!"

«*»

There was a time, not too long ago, in fact, when the appearance of a new face would have stopped all activity. Not anymore, though. Ex-humans were now a common sight in moots and pubs, and most of the post-life arcologies had created their own virtual common areas, which were generally referred to somewhat inaccurately as *moots*. Apparently, some kind of cusp had been achieved, and replication had suddenly become socially acceptable or something. I made a note to ask Bill. Or maybe Howard. One or the other would have the inside skinny.

I steered us toward a long table with bench seats where a bunch of Bobs and random ex-humans were loudly discussing several different things at once, to judge from the volume. Bill was at the center of one group, venting forth on something. He glanced in my direction, did a double take, and stood with a wide grin. "Bob! And . . ." He paused to check metadata. "Theresa? Theresa Sykorski? You're taller than Bob described you. And less hairy."

"Furry. We have fur." Theresa smiled back. "I am testing out my human avatar. No one has screamed and fainted, so I'm going to take that as a good sign." A couple of Bobs scooted over on the bench, and Theresa shoehorned herself into the available space.

I raised an eyebrow and tried to look expectant but was roundly ignored. Fine. I'd stand. "So what have we butted into here?" I asked.

"Artificial habitats. Professor Gilligan—" Bill pointed to an ex-human, and I recognized him as the expert Will had consulted about the topopolis during our search for Bender.

"Steven, please," the professor said. "The data dumps that ANEC has given us have spurred an economic explosion of sorts in *real*. There are at least three consortiums that I know of that have been formed to build megastructures. A good dozen companies have materialized to supply expertise or resources or project management. It's like a new industrial revolution."

"Wow." I sat as a couple of the already-seated spectators either decided I was interesting enough or just got tired of me hovering. "Where?"

"Ah, well, that's the sticking point. A megastructure requires a fair amount of raw material as well as autofactory support. Existing colonies are reluctant to commit to supplying these, as it's not immediately obvious that there will be any long-term economic benefit. I understand that the Bobs have contractual agreements with all the early colonies that give the Bobiverse rights to as much of the system resources as they need. The requirements for the megastructure projects, however, are several orders of magnitude more than was ever anticipated. At least one colony has threatened to take the Bobiverse to court if they push it."

Bill added with a sickly smile, "Yeah, and we're so well thought of these days, I am *sure* we'd get a fair and impartial trial." Snickers around the table indicated general agreement. Bobiverse status, never high with bios, had plunged significantly since the Starfleet debacle.

"Do you have a solution?" Theresa asked.

"Of sorts," Steven replied. "There are many uncolonized systems. Most have either unsuitable planets or unsuitable suns. But some also have a good supply of metals in the orbiting bodies. We are fortunate that this section of the galaxy seems to be heavily biased toward Population I stars. A system with a good sun but no suitable planets would be fine as a home for one or more megastructures."

"And how will they arrange the logistics for building in an uninhabited system?" someone asked.

"Ah." Steven paused to collect his thoughts. "Most systems out to anywhere from fifty to a hundred light-years or so now have a SCUT station in orbit, courtesy of the Bobiverse. All of the newer ones have been constructed with full manufacturing capability. The conglomerates that I mentioned earlier intend to contract with the Bobiverse to use that capability to bootstrap up to a full megastructure construction project. Work would be done remotely; then colonists could be shipped out to the system in the normal manner."

I frowned. "I haven't heard anything about this."

"Me neither," Bill added. He glanced at me. "You tend to be out of the loop, Bob. By choice, mostly. But I should have—"

"Actually," Steven interrupted, "that's why I'm here. One reason, anyway. I have been retained by the O'Neill Corporation to negotiate with you." He grinned. "Very lucrative, and it certainly beats teaching the subject to a bunch of bored students. Not"—Steven's smile disappeared—"that I'm able to do that anymore."

There were several sympathetic nods around the table. It was common knowledge that the Luddies were winning the war against ex-humans in the employment arena, on many planets in the UFS.

"And who will control and program the autofactories?" Bill asked.

"There are many ex-humans who would be amenable to a new source of cash flow. Most of the arcologies have instituted a fee schedule that one might call predatory, and their clients are feeling the pinch."

A couple of Bobs exchanged glances. "Sounds like an opportunity for some competition," Bill said.

Steven smiled again. "I was hoping you'd say that. I would be happy to negotiate that as a side project."

Bill laughed and materialized a writing surface. "Well then, let's talk."

((*))

We were back in Theresa's VR, both of us now in Quinlan avatars. Theresa was snarfing back a bowl of *squiz,* a Quinlan staple consisting mostly of spiced fish parts. I tried not to gag. I still couldn't stomach the thought of fish, even several years after the Heaven's River adventure.

Theresa paused to come up for air and noticed my expression. "It's been a long time since I've been able to really taste food, Bob. *Squiz* was always my favorite."

I rolled my eyes. "Next time we're in my VR, I'll introduce you to a cheeseburger."

Theresa finished her meal and began licking herself clean. Self-grooming for Quinlans was contagious in the same way as yawning for humans, so I had to consciously resist the urge to do the same.

"We have a couple of Quinlan candidates for replication lined up," she said between licks. "Anec is being low profile about the whole subject, but he is ensuring that all Quinlans at least have the opportunity to choose. Most are declining, though."

"It was like that with humans for a long time," I replied. "It's only lately become a generally acceptable option. I can't even really put my finger on what changed. Maybe just familiarity."

Theresa finished her grooming and stood. "Well, Bob, I have promised to contact some of the undecideds and try to bring them around. I look forward to continuing these discussions next time we meet."

I chuckled and stood. Theresa was certainly no-nonsense when it came to social schedules. Perhaps that lifetime of dealing with students? "Sure thing, teach. Call me when you have some free seconds."

«*»

Since I was now at loose ends, I decided to check with Will on the Ever Onward project. I sent a request and received an invitation and a manny address. Okay, so we wouldn't be meeting in *virt*. I shrugged and transferred to the manny.

I opened my eyes to the usual manny pod and activated the door without a second thought—and found myself slowly floating out of the pod, into what very much looked like outer space. "What the frak?"

I heard a chuckle and turned my head. Will floated a few yards away in a standard manny, but with his mountain-man look. "Welcome to the works yard," he said.

I looked around and realized I was still slowly floating away from the pod. Will, however, seemed to be rock steady. "Okay, Will. Fun time's over. What's going on? This isn't *virt*. How am I hearing you?"

"These mannies have been modified based on some work that Herschel and Neil have been doing. Look up *SURGE drive* in your onboard manual. Also, the speech and audio are radio based, very weak signals by default to keep conversations local. The interface is designed to feel like a normal conversation. And the mannies have been hardened against vacuum based on what we incorporated into the Quinlan design."

Rather than responding, I checked my onboard docs. Sure enough, there was a section on a built-in SURGE drive. Now *that* was insanely cool. I engaged the system and did a tentative loop. "This is really great. Neil and Herschel thought this up?"

"They've been working on a couple of things. I decided to incorporate this one so I wouldn't have to fly around as a drone." Will gestured into the middle distance, where a small cylinder was being—no, telemetry updated me. That cylinder was ten kilometers away. It had to be *huge*!

"Half the length of the Others' cargo vessels," Will said, seemingly reading my thoughts. "Five kilometers long but still a klick in diameter. With a number of bays specifically designed to house colonists."

"In stasis, right?"

"Or not. I've even got a rotating drum section roughed in, in case we need to have people awake for any period of time."

"Wow. How long until it's ready?"

"Five years or so. I'm trying to keep this as low-key as possible. I don't want to get into an argument with the Asgard and Takama governments about the use of resources."

I hesitated and frowned. "Hold on. I had a conversation with you a couple of years back where you said you were already on your way out."

"I am, Bob. In the *Nostromo*, which is the first ship I built. The *Nostromo* is for scattering Bob seeds—AMI-controlled Heaven vessels with no other purpose than to set up in a star system and explore. This one"—he pointed to the ship—"is the *Fargo*. It's going to contain colonists. Although the *Bellerophon* will get to Romulus before me, so this one might be used elsewhere." He shrugged, an odd gesture in zero G.

"Are you going to physically stick with the *Nostromo*, Will?"

He nodded, pensive. "I don't want to be dependent on SCUT. I'm going to be heading in a straight line, which means if any of the stations

I build along the way go down, I'll lose the connection. And . . ." Will hesitated and looked somewhat embarrassed. "Herschel's paranoia is kinda getting to me, despite my best efforts to stay rational. If something comes along that takes out all of human space, I don't want to be here."

"Not wrong," I replied. "Especially the part about being dependent on SCUT. I know a lot of Bobs are getting into the mindset where it doesn't matter where your cube is physically located. But I think the whole Starfleet debacle refutes that stance."

Will grunted and motioned me to follow. He flew toward the cargo vessel, and after a brief hesitation while I fumbled with the control system, I took off after him.

"So is this a social visit, or did you have something specific to bring up?"

I was momentarily taken aback by the peremptory tone, but then this *was* Riker. He'd softened over the years but could still be impatient with people. "I wanted to check your schedule and see if I'd be able to intercept. Either the *Fargo* or the *Bellerophon* will be collecting people from Romulus, right?"

Will turned to glance at me, a look of surprise on his face. "You still want to come? That seemed like an offhand comment last time."

"I think I've gone a little off the idea of solo exploration. It just seems to get me in trouble. And honestly . . ." I glanced away for a moment. "I've picked up a little of that paranoia, too, I think. Although I'm more concerned about the human and replicant threat than some unknown alien force."

"Wow, that's interesting. I won't argue with you, Bob. Especially about the stupid humans. Except we're bringing some along, so there's that."

"From where?"

"There's a possibility that some Asgard residents may want to come on the *Fargo*. You're right that there's a lot of tension, though. I don't think Starfleet caused it so much as brought it out into the open, but it's really beginning to look like humanity just brought their baggage with them."

"Like people are threatening war?"

"Until and unless we develop FTL, I don't think interstellar war is really a concern. But multiplanetary systems like 82 Eridani and

Omicron^2 Eridani are certainly good candidates. And we've got fascism developing on Newholme, and FAITH gaining ground on Romulus. Takama has always had an authoritarian bent. We might as well be back on Earth with the old nations." Will finished with a grimace and an inarticulate growl that pretty much said it all.

"What about the Pav?" I asked.

"They won't attack human worlds, I don't think. But if a Pav colony ship and a human colony ship show up in the same system at the same time, that's a whole 'nother story."

"So what's the problem exactly?"

"We Tetris'd different groups into our colony ships in order to fill them up. That unfortunately meant planets got colonized by multiple ethnic and national groups. But by necessity, the colonies were formed with one government, and the smaller groups, of course, got underrepresented. Think Quebec, Catalan, Belarus, Ireland, Taiwan, and so on."

I looked up and sighed. "Great. Stupid humans." To get my mind off this increasingly depressing conversation, I examined the spectacle in front of me. We were still a good distance from the cargo vessel, but it filled my field of view like the Earth from low orbit. We were a long way from the system's star, judging from the low light level, but the manny had excellent vision range.

It reminded me a little of the day we invaded Heaven's River—a cylinder so large it registered more as a wall than otherwise, with almost no features. In this case, though, steady but seemingly random streams of traffic buzzed through my view. Drones, laden with parts or, in some cases, covered with roamers, alternated with empty drones heading outward. It was a scene of frenetic activity, coordinated like a kind of ballet. Of course, Will had decades of experience with the construction process after his time evacuating the Earth. Fifteen hundred trips or fifteen hundred ships. Or one ginormous cargo vessel.

I smiled to myself. I hadn't been part of the evacuation effort or the war with the Others. But like all battles, it was doubtless more epic and grander in hindsight.

Will was speaking, and I had to rewind a few mils of dialogue to catch up.

"Honestly, Bob, I'd be happier to just continue on my own and explore in the *Nostromo,* but a couple of groups managed to buttonhole me. If they decide to carry through on their plan, I guess I'm committed. But I'll drop them on the first suitable worlds that I find."

I chuckled. "Yeah, I get it. And I still want to come along."

"You got it."

23. Huey

Howard
August 2342
Trantor City, Big Top

I sighed theatrically as I closed the door to our apartment. Bridget looked up from her computer, gave me a brief smile, but didn't otherwise comment.

Things had settled back into a routine for us, since the end of the Heaven's River escapade. And I was glad to have my wife back full-time. Or as full-time as a career-obsessed exobiologist could be. There had been some casual talk of adopting another brood, since most of our latest batch of children were now becoming grandparents. But neither one of us was feeling a lot of enthusiasm at the moment. Instead, Bridget had latched onto Mario's latest find, a planet harboring an intelligent species, and it was consuming most of her free time lately. And I had my human–manny interface project to keep me busy. It was generally considered a truism that immortality would make it harder and harder to fill the years and decades, but so far, the two of us still didn't have a couple of spare minutes to rub together.

I came up behind her and peered at the screen. "Where's my martini, dammit?" I said, overacting for all I was worth.

"Same place as usual. In the bottles. Make me one."

Our ritual greeting having been satisfied, I assembled two martinis and handed one to her. "How's it coming along?"

Bridget took a sip, made an appreciative sound, and leaned back in her work chair. The mechanism obediently swiveled out a leg rest, and she settled into a three-quarters recline. I whistled, and another chair scooted over and placed itself behind me.

"Mario has completed the autofactory in the Jabberwocky system and—"

"Jabberwocky?" I interrupted.

"He discovered the planet; it's his right to name it. However unoriginal." She gave me a glare. "As I was saying, I've started manufacturing survey drones. I'll have a better picture soon."

"I thought Mario had already done that?"

Bridget took another sip, then put the martini down on her chair arm. The chair reconfigured to support the glass safely. "Planetary survey, sure. Mario's looking for Others, and once it was clear there were none in this system, he more or less lost interest. It's the standard Bob survey—lots of facts about the system and the planet, not so much on the local population. Other than pictures, of course."

"Ah. So you're going for . . ."

"Language, culture, details of biology . . . the same stuff we did for the Quinlans. And we learned a lot from that exercise. The Gamers extracted a lot of detail in a short time, and pioneered some brilliant techniques in the process."

I chuckled. "Let's make sure we dot all the i's on slang and idiom this time. We don't need to go through what Bob did." I reached past Bridget and scrolled her document. "Flying monkeys."

"Stop saying that. Other than having the right number of arms and legs—"

"And wings."

"Yes, okay. But they're not anthropoid, not really. Honestly, given the shape of the head, if it wasn't for the scaly feather things replacing fur, I'd go with rats or squirrels."

"Same thing. But no, definitely not flying squirrels."

Bridget frowned and looked at me quizzically. She also had that expression that said she knew a punch line was in the works but couldn't help herself. "Why not squirrels?"

I pointed. "No goggles or aviator hat."

Bridget made a low growling sound. "You're lucky there are martinis in this world. Makes you almost bearable." She held out her now-empty glass to me.

Taking the hint, I made another round. As I delivered the new drink, I said, "I love the floating islands, though. Not held up by monopoles, right?"

"Is that how they explained the floating rocks in that movie with the blue aliens?" She shook her head. "But no. They're actually alive. Hydrogen-filled balloon animals, something that's rare enough on a terrestrial planet at any size. Big enough, in this case, for entire ecosystems to grow on their backs. Commensal, I think. I've dubbed them *leviathans*."

"And the natives build villages on them. Do we have a name for the intelligent species yet?"

"Mario calls them *dragons*. That seems a stretch, because they look more like—"

"Squirrels. Yeah. Pretty big stretch, that. Maybe we'll get a name we can use from their language. So when will we be ready to go in?"

Bridget gave me the hairy eyeball. "A couple of months, oh impatient one. We learned a lot from the Quinlan Affair, but we still aren't magicians."

My face must have betrayed something, because Bridget looked slightly alarmed and said, "What?"

"Uh, you know how we've been working on tensor field printers that would be able to assemble almost literally anything? Including biological items?"

"Uh-huh. 'Items' means living things, right?"

"Yeah. So Bill has a working model. I use the word 'working' loosely, but it's produced living masses of tissue. No differentiation yet if you want *living* tissue—not fast enough. But soon . . ."

She shook her head. "You still need a design to print. Once you have one, you can print copies, and maybe even vary some details. But it'll still be a process."

I shrugged without comment. Bridget was right anyway, and she could tell when I was being stubborn just to be stubborn. That never ended well. A change of subject seemed in order. "I'm popping over to Vulcan. You want to come?"

"Something you need to be there in person for?"

"We're going to be running a huey test. I want to see it up close."

Bridget shut down her Canvas with a swipe. "Hot damn! Let's go!"

I grinned and held out my arm, and we headed for the bedroom to park our mannies. We had long since arranged custom mannies on Vulcan, and we stored them at MannyPark Remote Services LLC since that was reasonably central to everything. And because we owned the company.

«*»

I gazed out the window as the technicians fussed with the test subject, a woman who had been introduced simply as Terry. At the moment, she was festooned with cables and various sensor packages, making her look more like some kind of techno-bush than a human being. Most of the equipment was for testing and monitoring, of course. The actual huey control hardware consisted of a combination head cap and neck ring. With just those basic items, an operator would look like they were wearing a toque and scarf. And even that would likely be trimmed down in the production model.

The view out the window was of far more interest to me at the moment. We were about eight floors up in the city of New Landing, one of the floating cities that were increasingly replacing land-based versions all across the UFS. And why not? Floating cities didn't require clearing natural growth or covering up watercourses or any of the various ways that humanity had always scarred up the land. Or dealing with Cupid Bugs or Ickeys or giant mutant ninja mosquitos, or any of the other monstrosities that the universe insisted on throwing at us. The worst effect for the ecosystem was the occasional shadow drifting overhead. Hell, clouds did that.

From here, I could see down past the edge of the city to the riotous jungle that still covered pretty much the whole planet of Vulcan. Somewhere down there, brontos were attempting to eat trees without forgetting to breathe in the process, and raptors were attempting to eat, well, pretty much anything. Cupid Bugs were no longer a problem, even assuming any were left—my Cupid Bug hunters had been gratifyingly successful. And rabbits were now officially an invasive species.

I had to fight off a momentary wave of nostalgia. Vulcan was no longer the frontier planet that I'd helped settle some hundred and fifty-odd years ago. Beside me, Bridget said softly, "It's beautiful, Howard, and I'm glad we were here for the start of it."

I smiled without turning and took her hand. A silent squeeze was all the communication we needed.

"I think we're set," one of the techs said, breaking my reverie. Terry was carefully laying herself down on a gurney, techies crowding around and making sure nothing got folded or kinked. To one side, a generic android form lay in its pod, hairless and pallid. We'd taken to calling them *hueys*, a sort of mashup of *human* and *mannies*, just to differentiate the project.

"Activating," Terry said. She closed her eyes . . .

And the huey opened its eyes, sat up, and looked around. "Colors are okay. Depth perception is still off," it said. The voice was generic manny, but the tone was all Terry.

On the gurney, Terry twitched a few times as her huey climbed out of the pod and started doing some basic movements. One of the techs, observing this, muttered something about requiring more suppression and made a note. Meanwhile, the huey touched its toes, did some twists, ran in place for a few seconds, then settled into a *ta-dah* posture, arms held wide.

I smiled despite myself. This was going to explode into UFS society when it hit the public feeds. And somehow, despite our almost total lack of interest in the subject, Bridget and I were going to become even wealthier.

Oh, the pain.

Terry and the techies started working through a long checklist of items, the techs carefully writing down each result. I glanced at Bridget, who was already losing interest, then nodded to Mark Harris, the project manager, as he came over. Mark was missing the lower half of his left arm from just below the elbow. When asked, he always claimed it was a chainsaw-juggling accident. The grow cuff on his stump was covered with scrawled signatures. The new appendage would be completely regrown in a couple more months, from the look of it.

"This part is duller than watching paint dry," Mark said. "Want to get lunch?"

"I haven't had a bronto burger in ages," Bridget exclaimed. "Please tell me the caf has them."

"They're Veat now instead of actual bronto," Mark replied as he led the way, "but I challenge you to detect a difference."

We maneuvered through the cafeteria lineup, gathering sustenance according to our desires. Bridget and I didn't actually need the calories, of course, being mannies, but manny taste buds were now so refined that recent ex-humans using mannies reported no difference in taste or smell—or even an improved experience for the older individuals who'd been dealing with duller senses in their later years.

Bridget had her usual burger and mountain o' fries with way too much salt. Mark had picked a baked mac and cheese and was liberally applying ketchup. My mom would have had a bird, seeing perfectly good food desecrated like that. I had chosen a bowl of chili and a side of poutine. I blamed Stephane for getting me hooked on the latter, even if posthumously.

By unspoken agreement, we spent several minutes getting ahead of things, with nothing but the sounds of snarfing and munching to break the companionable silence. But finally, Mark sat back, idly poking at the remnants of his pasta.

"So I guess you've heard—Romulus has preemptively outlawed flying cities?"

I jerked my head up. "I had not. When did this happen?"

"Yesterday. You know that FAITH finally got their majority government with this last election—"

"Yes, pending verification of the vote. I still think they cheated," Bridget growled.

Mark shook his head sorrowfully. "Wish that were so, but I think it's legitimate, Bridget. That's three wins in a row for them now. Anyway, they've wasted no time. They ran on a platform of reduced technology and *getting back to basics,* whatever that means. So no flying cities, heavy restriction of mannies, no post-life replication, no cloned meat—"

"Seriously?" I said, frowning.

"Not natural, not made by God, or some such." Mark shrugged. "They aren't giving up printers, though."

"Of course not." I sighed. "I'll send a text to Will, just in case. He really needs to ramp up the effort to get our relatives out of there."

"I expect diplomacy between Vulcan and Romulus is reaching an all-time low," Bridget mused.

Mark sighed and nodded. "We aren't quite anticipating war or anything, but borders may be closing—or at least tightening up." He glanced at me. "You'd better make that text a high priority."

«*»

We arrived back at the lab to find the scene considerably more tense than when we'd left. Techs were muttering to each other and comparing things on their tablets while the huey paced back and forth, looking concerned—or as concerned as a hairless, pallid android could manage.

"What's up?" Mark asked.

"Can't exit," the huey replied in Terry's clipped tones. "I want to use the safe phrase, but the crew is trying to debug."

I glanced at Terry, still lying on the gurney, and felt a moment of sympathy. The technology activated the same brain region that prevented movement during dreaming to allow the user to execute voluntary movements through the huey without moving their own body. But this meant that the user was paralyzed while the device was active. The design innovation was actually based directly on a suggestion made by Thoth in negotiation with the Skippies.

The process to deactivate the huey was supposed to be straightforward, but as a backup, we'd built in a user-configurable "safe phrase," the utterance of which would also flip the switch.

One of the techs glanced at us, then said, "You might as well go for it, Terry. We'll have to go through the logs to find out what's going on. That'll take a while."

The huey stopped pacing and chanted, "I'm a little teapot, short and stout." It stood for a moment in an expectant stance, then exclaimed, "Oh *fuck*! That's failed, too. Pull the goddam plug!"

A tech hurried over and hit a button, then gingerly took the cap off Terry as she sat up. The huey, following standard manny programming for autonomous situations, placed itself in the pod and powered down.

"Do not like," Terry said, glaring at Mark. "Not one bit. You better fix that glitch soonest. You get a stuck user going into a panic, and someone is going to be suing everyone in sight."

Mark nodded to Terry, then grinned at me. "Don't make plans for that dividend check just yet. Looks like we're not quite ready for prime time."

"Keep at it. We want it quickly, but it has to be done right. Can't risk giving FAITH any ammo."

"Or the Luddies," Bridget added, referring to the anti-manny, anti-replicant activist groups.

I sighed and turned to go. "See you in a week, Mark."

24. Arachnophobia

Icarus
August 2321
Wormhole Network

Another day, another exploration. It was hard not to think of this process as tedious, despite the utterly breathtaking brilliance of the whole experience. It felt like every day was Christmas, but in both a good way and a bad way. Each new wormhole brought new planets, new vistas—not always surprises but certainly spectacles. It was like being on one of those European cruises where you visit a new country every day.

But the downside was that the constant excitement could eventually make you numb. Seeing a planet covered with floating, domed cities and muttering "meh" was a warning sign for sure. I admit I was being at least a little self-mocking, but the idea that I'd start dismissing each new experience with a shrug left me profoundly disappointed in myself.

By this point, we'd seen civilizations belonging to what had to be dozens of different species. Their urban philosophies ran the gamut, from skyscrapers to urban sprawl, to underground ant-like networks. And although most were in good shape, some were less so, ranging from encroaching decay all the way to total collapse. Dae had commented that the last group had probably turned off the maintenance systems, which might mean they didn't plan on coming back. Or didn't expect to.

"Notice everything's inhabited?" Dae said into the silence.

"What?" I looked up from my video window, which had been showing the front view from a drone doing a flyby of the current planet.

"Every system we've investigated has been more or less Sol-like. No Trappist systems, no systems with hot Jupiters, no supergiant suns, no real planetary weirdness. None of the stuff that early exoplanet searches were constantly turning up."

"Uh . . ." I stopped, at a momentary loss for words. Then, "Well, it might be selection bias. Wormholes get established at systems with planets that are either inhabited or habitable. They might have a few connections to oddball systems, or they might even have an entirely separate network for those, accessible only for research purposes. I mean, who knows? But I'd bet it's not an accidental omission."

"You may be right," he replied. "Anyway, I'm just about done here. As soon as you've got enough video footage, we can move on to the next one."

«*»

Another day, yet another exploration.

It took two days to actually reach the lone habitable planet, and we immediately released the usual complement of drones to do flybys. We'd long since given up on worrying about stealth or security and would have been overjoyed to have one of our drones shot out of the sky just to have someone to talk to.

Then the images started to roll in.

"Oooookay, this is a little different," I muttered. Dae made a gesture, and I rotated the video window I'd been examining. The "city," if you could call it that, seemed to consist of giant cables strung between mountainsides. There didn't appear to be any organization; they weren't arrayed in squares or anything like that. Large nodules looking something like coconuts hung from the cables at random locations, varying in diameter from twenty feet or so up to hundreds of feet.

Somehow, despite the seeming chaos, there was also an impression of organization, as if the placement of the objects wasn't actually random.

"Is this some native animal?" Dae said.

"Um . . ." I sent an order to the drones, and they did a close-in SUDDAR scan. "Interesting. The cables are mostly organic, something like silk. But there's a base structure of carbon-fiber nanotube-based cables, deliberately designed to look like the natural stuff, woven into the whole." I paused, examining the scan more closely. "And there's a lot of metal in those nodules. Refined metal, shaped. Artifacts. I think this is a city."

"So the dominant species is spiders?"

"Or something like it. I'm being chauvinistic, but I'm kinda glad this particular civilization isn't still around."

"We're not arachnophobic, Icky."

"No, but that doesn't mean I want to cuddle up to one. Tell you what, Dae, let's finish this survey as quickly as possible and get out."

Dae gave me a funny look, then smiled. "Fine, Chicken Boy. I'll launch some more drones."

‹‹ * ››

The spider world survey had turned out to be extremely interesting, but I was still happy to be done with it. As Dae had said, Original Bob wasn't arachnophobic, but I appeared to be. Replicative drift was a real thing, apparently.

Regardless, we could only spend a limited time at any world if we wanted to get a report back to the Bobiverse in this millennium, so we reluctantly (at least in Dae's case) packed it up and moved on.

Now we were once again back at Hub Zero, and once again faced with a surfeit of choice. So another random number generated, gate selected, and we glided through.

And were immediately accosted.

25. Building the Quiniverse

Bob
October 2342
Heaven's River

Anec and I stood behind Theresa, gazing down at the empty chaise. "Ready?" she said. Getting no response, she flipped the virtual switch, and a Quinlan appeared on the furniture.

He opened his eyes and slowly turned his head, taking in his surroundings, ending with us. "Am I dead?" he asked.

Theresa glanced back at me, and I nodded. "*Original* you is dead," she said, sticking to the script. "*You* are very much alive in a digital form."

The Quinlan—Herbie, according to my translated notes—sat up. "I feel normal. Actually, I feel great." He flexed an arm experimentally. "My arthritis has stopped paining me."

"Welcome to the Quiniverse," Theresa responded, extending a hand.

He took it and stood. "What now?"

"Well, that's a long story with some lessons to be learned." She turned to us. "This is Bob, who you might know as *the Bawbe,* and this is Anec, who you would know as the Administrator. I am Theresa Sykorski, first citizen of the Quiniverse. Come, let us set you up with your own home, and I'll teach you the basics." She looked at Anec and me. "Gentlemen."

It was a dismissal. She was very good at that. Anec and I glanced at each other and popped out, to leave Theresa with her new pupil.

«*»

It was a full hour later when I received a knock from Theresa and invited her in. She appeared in human form, sighed, and dropped into a beanbag chair. I couldn't figure that out. I thought beanbags were okay, but for almost everyone else, they seemed to be the ultimate relaxation furniture. It even transcended species, apparently.

"That was draining," she said, exhaustion clear in her voice. She reached over and patted me absently on the arm. "Not physically, of course, but there's just so much information to impart before the ex-Quinlans can do anything for themselves."

I nodded thoughtfully. "Really, we should be able to automate at least some of that. I'll talk to Anec and see if he can instantiate an A.I. with enough awareness to be able to teach but not self-aware enough to be a philosophical or moral problem. There's no reason for you to suffer through that every time someone transitions."

"Not to mention that the numbers would swiftly get out of hand."

"Let's hope so." I paused. "I should also check with the human post-life arcologies and see what they have in terms of indoctrination. It won't be a full solution since those businesses allow a lot less capability for their clients, but it'll be a start."

Theresa nodded, and we shared a few mils of silence. Then she said, "I'd like to try out one of the quinnies."

I raised my eyebrows, momentarily taken aback. But really, should I have been surprised? Theresa now understood on an intellectual level that my physical form in Heaven's River was essentially a robot. It shouldn't have come as any surprise that she'd be curious.

"We can lend you Bridget's unit. Longer term, you should have a custom unit made for you, with your features, for visiting your family."

"I'm not sure if I'm looking forward to that or not."

I laughed. "You could talk to Howard. He was the first of us to 'go public' in a manny. He'd understand your concerns, and I think his perspective would help you."

"I will do that. I've added it to my TODO list. I'm not sure if I should thank you or slap you for that little innovation, by the way."

I grinned back at her. "I can't survive without it. Your mileage may vary."

She laughed and stood. "Then let us proceed. I understand I need a connection address?"

«*»

I found myself in my Quinlan manny, in a dark room. Anec had arranged permanent storage for us, rent-free. Beside me, Bridget's quinny was stirring.

Theresa looked around. "Not the highest quality of residence, Bob. You can't afford windows?"

"Blame Anec. I don't think he sees the point. Anyway, this is just storage space." I opened the door and motioned her through. We found ourselves in the common area of a storage locker business. Like many things, the Quinlan equivalent wasn't *quite* the same. Quinlans did need to store stuff, but they didn't necessarily need a separate residence, being a mostly self-sufficient predator. These storage units allowed their clients to set up sleeping arrangements if they wanted. No cooking, though. Fire regulations were universal, it seemed.

We walked out into a sunny, late-afternoon Heaven's River day. It had been a while, and I was momentarily taken back to my first day here, just after we'd broken out of the transit station. The view was less spectacular, what with us being in town at the moment, but the sky was blue, the sun was warm, and the clouds were few. As Theresa looked around, I had a thought. "We should also visit Quin at some point. We left a couple of quinnies there, although one is a little the worse for wear, thanks to Howard."

"Mmm. Intellectually, I am fascinated. Emotionally, it's somewhat terrifying, to be honest. I'll work my way up to that."

I nodded, then pointed to a nearby pub. "Want to try some real *squiz*?"

"I do love *squiz*."

"That makes one of us."

Theresa laughed. "I've gotten quite fond of spaghetti and meatballs, if it helps. Perhaps we can arrange some cross-cultural contamination."

"Now *there's* a thought."

We reached the pub entrance and sauntered in, trying to blend with the crowds. I noticed changes immediately—like electric lights. And background music. What was it with drinking establishments and music, anyway? Quinlans had far better musical sense than humans, in my opinion, so the music wasn't jarring, but it was still something you had to talk over, which meant everyone was talking too loud.

The furniture hadn't changed, though. Early modern picnic table. We picked a spot, and Theresa signaled a waitperson, who brought us menus. Huh. Another change. And an improvement, as far as I was concerned.

Then came the real surprise. "Hamburgers." I pointed at the menu. "They have hamburgers."

Theresa glanced at the menu item and made a noncommittal "mmm" sound.

"What, you don't find that surprising?"

"Not really, Bob. The ground-up land meat is new. The bun is a little different, but we had sandwiches before. You *do* know we have access to human culture now, right?"

"Ooh, sarcasm. I am devastated." I smiled back at her. "It would be really great if they had French fries, though."

"We don't really have a potato equivalent. Our starchy vegetables are too fibrous. Although I think someone has formed a company to try to grow Earth vegetables."

"Really?"

"Mm-hmm. Not sure how well it will do. We're not anywhere near as omnivorous as humans. Honestly, you're like a bunch of garburators. Anything that can fit in goes in."

I laughed and signaled the waitperson again.

«*»

After our meal, we went for a walk around the town. I noticed entire blocks being torn down and rebuilt, with the replacements obviously higher-tech. Theresa saw me staring and explained, "I've talked to Anec about this. He decided that towns should be upgraded a block at a time, with residents and businesses being shuffled into the new buildings as they're completed."

"And people are okay with this?" I replied, disbelief in my voice. "I tend to think of Quinlans as being more hair-trigger belligerent than humans, and that's saying a lot."

"No, Enoki, Quinlans are more polite overall, I think. But when we get angry, we don't bother with the posturing and threats that humans seem to prefer as a first step. We jump straight to the fighting part."

"But the bluffing is a useful evolutionary development that prevents too much bloodshed." I cut myself off and made a waving motion. "Never mind. The point is that Anec is arbitrarily making decisions and going ahead with them, and there doesn't seem to be a lot of pushback."

"True," Theresa said. "But of course, we've been putting up with him doing that for several hundred years. And so far, his decisions seem to be producing the results he says they will. Why would you fight against someone who is doing exactly what they promise?"

"It's . . ." I frowned. "I'm not sure if it's the fault of the auto-translator or what, but I tend to think of you as a short, furry human. But you're not. And some of the Quinlan attitudes about things still catch me by surprise."

Theresa laughed and playfully shoulder-checked me. "Different biologies, Enoki. For instance, your lack of a mating season, as such, means you're essentially always evaluating others for potential mating. It colors all your decisions."

"Wow, uh . . ." I glanced sideways at her, something much easier to do in Quinlan form. "I guess so. It's obvious now that you point it out. But that's strictly a bio-human thing."

"Of course." She winked at me. "And I'm old enough to be your grandmother, anyway."

I chuckled dutifully, but I was glad Garfield wasn't around.

26. Building Dragons

Howard
August 2342
Trantor

On the screen, a skeleton floated in an assembly pod, secured by tensor fields, while more fields carefully added layers of artificial muscle, tendon, nerves, and circulatory system. It was a finicky process, and one that couldn't yet be simply printed from the bottom up in the manner of the very first printers. Components had to be constructed, then assembled to produce the end result.

"It looks more like a bat right now," I commented.

Bridget ignored me, closely scrutinizing her notes. "This one should be good enough to pass inspection by a real dragon when it's complete." She put down her martini and pulled up a video window. A small drone, disguised as a local bird, was providing a feed from the surface of Jabberwocky and the village that we'd picked for observation.

"Got a name yet?"

"Nah, still calling them dragons." She sat back. "I've been observing several villages. Interesting thing. There doesn't seem to be a general name for the inhabitants. They all identify themselves by their village."

"Huh. So like, no word for *human*, but you're a Bostonian or Seattleite or Angeleno?"

Bridget frowned at me. "Those are cities from old Earth? If so, yes, like that. There's some indication that dragons consider other villagers just barely above talking animals. That seems like it would create some tension."

"But they trade, right?"

"FAITH trades with the Vulcan heathens, too."

I winced. "Yeah, okay. But this would tend to restrict travel. Don't we want to roam around?"

"I'm not sure if it's a problem yet." Bridget sighed and gazed absently into space. "There are some indications that dragons do travel around without too much trouble. I'm still working on it."

"How about a break? We could visit Takama."

"How about Newholme? I haven't been there in a while."

"Sold!"

«*»

The Bobs had always been careful planners, allowing for all sorts of contingencies, so it was no surprise that we'd managed to hide a good deal of our assets from local governments through various not-quite-illegal strategies. Several lawsuits had been launched on different colony worlds after the Starfleet War, but most of our holdings had been liquidated and siphoned offworld before the plaintiffs could get properly started. At least that's what it looked like. In reality, most of our net worth hadn't gone off-planet but had been converted to some other form of asset. The Bobiverse was still a collective billionaire on pretty much every colony world. It was just well hidden.

But on Newholme, the Gamma Pavonis colony, things had taken an additional twist. The Newholme government had decided to implement facial recognition in all things, presumably to make it difficult for Bobs to operate anonymously. Public surveillance, personal account access, identification, and even applying for a job would require you to show your face to a scanner.

This had been tried in some countries on old Earth, with varying levels of success. But the people who survived the Solar System War and lived to colonize the stars had developed an attitude of personal freedom and mistrust of government that made early-twenty-first-century America look like a hippie lovefest. And it didn't help that the Newholme government had been showing some authoritarian leanings even before Starfleet.

The public reaction had been a massive revolt. No violence, just the biggest collective spanner ever tossed into the works, and not just once. Holographic masks, makeup designed to mess up the reference marks used by facial recognition software, and even weird Groucho Marx glasses and fake noses. In one particular week, every single citizen had gone out wearing a mask of the Newholme president, Adrianne Hernandez, committing misdemeanors and public mischief—and attempting to access her accounts at every opportunity. So far, the government had not backed down on its policy, although it wasn't marketing it with nearly as much vigor anymore.

Our local Bob, who had named himself Xavier Charles, greeted us as we stepped out of the manny pods. Publicly, he was a freelance writer with no resemblance whatsoever to Bob Johannson, and he lived in a small house in the suburbs. Privately, the house had a few extra sublevels, courtesy of some careful excavation and construction by roamers.

"Greetings, fellow foreign spies," he said with a grin. "What brings you to our secret lair today?"

"Morbid curiosity," Bridget replied. "We've come to watch the dumpsters burn."

"And burn they will. This week it's hoods with clown faces painted on. But the meme specifies that the clown faces have to match reference marks for sitting congress-critters." Xavier looked up briefly. "I've ordered a couple for you. They'll be on the output tray by the time we get upstairs."

As we followed Xavier up to the living level, he continued to talk. "Just so you know, you're in mannies based on the new tech developed for the Heaven's River project. I've upgraded, too. The old mannies had a lot of metal in them and were pretty easy to detect." He turned and gave us a significant look. "That includes feature modification circuitry, but don't use it unless you're in a pickle. You have IDs on you that match your current faces, and you don't want to be caught with an ID that doesn't match up. That's a felony." He turned back to face forward, and I overheard him mutter, "Along with everything else."

Not ominous at all. Nope.

«*»

Xavier had offered to guide us around, but Bridget declined. Newholme wasn't *quite* a fascist state yet, although I was recognizing a lot of troubling signs that I remembered from when I was alive. In any case, we weren't going to do more than wander around and maybe have lunch.

We called up an autocab and gave it instructions to drop us off downtown. As the cab drove on its way, I tried to examine everything. The automobile traffic seemed to be all self-driven. I didn't spot a single person holding a steering wheel or otherwise making driving decisions. This wasn't a bad thing, though. Traffic moved smoothly, with reasonable distances between vehicles.

The houses were surprisingly cookie-cutter. They seemed to come in perhaps four different designs plus mirror images. Most of the individual variation was in color selection and landscaping. The transition from suburban to urban was abrupt as well. Literally, one side of a large avenue was houses, and the other side was condos, apartments, and malls.

In another minute or two, the autocab delivered us to the location we'd specified. This was downtown Moncton. It didn't at all resemble its Canadian namesake, and I'm pretty sure it was simply named after some recent dead politician rather than being a historical shout-out.

"Let's start with some food," Bridget said. "Then maybe a show or something." As usual, I was content to let her set the agenda.

It didn't take long to find something. Eateries of various kinds are probably the most common business in the known universe, and the variety of offerings has always been endless, if not always palatable. I stepped up to the door, reached for the handle—and stopped dead. The sign said, "No replicants."

And just inside the door was a very obvious metal detector.

I glanced at it as we walked through. They couldn't possibly be serious. Sure, it would detect the old manny bodies, but it would also detect phones, belt buckles, zippers . . . or was it a minimum-size thing?

Bridget must have been following my thoughts, as she commented over the intercom, "I think it's more of a statement than an actual attempt to stop mannies."

We sat at a table and placed an order with the auto-attendant, but the joy had been sucked from the outing. I found myself glancing around constantly, expecting some wag to jump up, point a finger, and yell, "*J'accuse!*"

«*»

We were back at Xavier's place, having cut the day short. He noticed our expressions and replied with a sympathetic shrug, "Yeah, that's life in meatspace these days. The Luddies are everywhere. We're having to bury our tracks deeper and deeper to avoid being identified. And not just on Newholme. I've talked to some of the other resident agents, and it seems like *everyone* is going anti-replicant."

"Any idea what's driving it?" Bridget asked.

"I can't speak for the UFS in general, but I think it has to do with our tendency to live long and prosper."

Bridget sighed and rolled her eyes, and Xavier grinned. "Sorry. Couldn't help it. But literally, that's the problem. We're effectively immortal, so we tend to accumulate wealth. We don't die and pass it on, so no inheritance taxes. We generally depend on conservative, long-term investments, which tend to be more dependable ways to accrue net worth. So we inevitably get richer and richer."

"Wouldn't matter anyway," I interjected. "Corporations and trusts have been doing an end run around inheritances for centuries. I think it's more about the fact that we unfairly hang around to enjoy the ill-gotten gains instead of conveniently dying."

Bridget nodded and glanced at me before continuing. "So really, if humans had a good shot at immortality, and the ability to control a manny, it would remove the reasons for the hate."

"About right. Got any of that?" Xavier replied.

"I am unable to comment on that subject at this time," I said with a deadpan expression. Then, "We should go. I think the air's been let out of our holiday anyway." We got up, said the obligatory goodbyes, and headed for the manny pods.

«*»

Back in our apartment, I prepared a couple of martinis. Bridget had commented on several previous occasions that fairness dictated that she take a turn on bartender duty, but I insisted that I didn't mind. The truth, which I would never mention, was that she was terrible at it. How you could screw up a straightforward process that involved known ingredients and simple measured quantities was beyond me. I suspected she might be deliberately sabotaging her efforts—another thing I would never, ever bring up.

I handed Bridget her drink and sat on the couch beside her. "Well, that was a total downer. You think Xavier is right?"

"We've been directly experiencing something similar for decades, Howard. Although I think there's more involved now. Something is turning simple, undirected envy and dislike into active hate." She looked at me and paused. That meant something big was coming. I braced myself.

"We have the Huey Project going, Howard, and that's great. But I think we need to consider life extension as well."

My eyebrows rose. "Bridge, we've talked about that. Immortality sounds great, but it's such a bad idea—"

"Is it necessarily, Howard? I know the usual arguments—overpopulation, concentration of wealth, extreme conservatism, loss of innovation—but we don't have any actual proof that any of those things are inevitable."

"But—"

She cut me off. "Okay, let's aim a little lower, at least for now. Not immortality, but maybe greatly extended life. With most diseases and cancers all but eradicated, and the ability to regrow body parts, human life expectancy is up to about a hundred and thirty, but in the end, senescence just becomes overwhelming."

I nodded slowly. Somewhere around the one-twenty to one-thirty point, it was like a switch had been flipped. What used to be decades of encroaching old age and slowly sinking health was now compressed into two to three years of being hit with virtually every gerontological malady at once. When the decline became obvious, people often decided to bow out on their own terms. Most were still placing themselves in stasis rather than going with replication, though.

"FAITH takes a dim view of life-extension therapies," I pointed out. "Their influence is most of the reason why there's not more work being done in that area. Even on planets other than Romulus, they've got a presence. And some political sway."

Bridget made a face. "FAITH can go fuck themselves. We don't have to go public with this, but I think it's worth it to throw some money at the idea."

"Okay. Let's do it." I knew that Bridget would attack this problem with the same ferocity that she brought to any project. And God help anyone who got in her way.

27. Positive Results

Bill
October 2337
In Virt

"We got something." Hugh waved a piece of paper at me from his video window. Still no in-person appearances.

It had been months since the Skippies had shut down their borders, and there was no indication of any progress or any timeline for going back to normal. Hugh wouldn't even discuss what was going on, other than to repeat platitudes about "excess of caution" and "taking baby steps." Still, the downside of being too casual about the situation was presumably far worse.

I materialized a coffee and sat down in my La-Z-Boy, drawing out the moment. Unless Hugh was talking about something entirely different, I was about to receive the first positive news about the possibility of FTL in almost a hundred years.

"Hit me," I said, gesturing with my coffee.

"Well, it's not that dramatic. A working wormhole didn't just pop out of our printer. But the numbers are converging on a solution that doesn't generate infinities."

I frowned, a little disappointed. No solution just yet, apparently. "So how long until we have something I can use?"

"You can use this, Bill. It just won't work very well and will probably not produce much more negative energy than a classical Casimir generator. Or it might blow up, taking you and your entire star system with it. But it's enough for you to get started."

I glared at Hugh. He was probably kidding about the blowing-up part. I hoped. On the other hand, that would be a lot of energy . . . "Okay, Hugh, but you'll continue running the series, right?"

"Sure, right up until we converge on the optimal solution. Upper management seems to have bought into this project, and everyone's rubbernecking. I bet a solution won't be much longer, either. You should start building your hardware."

"Heh. I've long since done that. Everything except the gray box where the negative-energy generator goes. Send me what you have. Meanwhile, I need to contact Garfield." Hugh nodded just as I terminated the connection.

«*»

Garfield's manny sat up and blinked. "This isn't your regular lab," he said.

"No, this is a space station out in the Oort cloud, spinning for gravity. I've always felt there was an element of danger with this project, given the forces we could be working with, so I did some preparation." I smiled briefly. "I don't mind blowing up a few million cubic kilometers of floating ice balls, if it comes to that."

Garfield nodded and stepped out of the manny pod. "How close are you?"

I gestured for him to follow as I headed for the door, and he hurried to catch up. The door hissed open in front of us.

"I've been on this project for almost a century, Gar. I've done all the engineering that I could. I borrowed shamelessly from all the human research that I've been able to find. I've even built several versions of some items. For instance, there were at least a half dozen theories about how an Alcubierre drive could be built, depending on how you would go about generating the warp field. I'm ready for any of those possibilities."

"Warp-drive generator goes here," Garfield interjected with a laugh, pointing a finger at midair.

"Yeah, like that. Anyway, I think we need more than just a source of negative energy for that project. Some theoretical work is still required. Like one of the versions still needs a sub-light drive to move at all. Another one instantly departs at FTL speeds as soon as it's turned on. Several of them will kill the passengers in various spectacular and painful ways. At least one fries your destination as you arrive. And so on. On the other hand, I've finally made progress with wormholes, so I'll start there."

"Just like that."

I stopped and turned to him. "Ninety percent of the theoretical work was done before Original Bob died, Gar. It was always, 'All we need is exotic matter,' or 'All we need is negative energy.' So now we have that. Or will, soon. I've been able to generate microscopic wormhole pairs from the quantum foam for about twenty years now. I told you that before. But now, maybe I can make them useful."

"Here's something I've been worrying about," Garfield said to my back as I resumed walking. I slowed to let him catch up, and he continued, "What if Thoth wasn't really depending on you not being smart enough to make use of its hint? What if it *wanted* you to figure it out, knowing the results would be disastrous? Maybe we activate the FTL drive, and it blows up the entire spiral arm."

"I thought of that. I think the principle of mediocrity applies here, though. Someone else, somewhere else in the universe, would certainly have tried this before us, and we'd have seen the results by now."

"Like fast radio bursts, maybe?"

I opened my mouth to retort, but stopped. FRBs were some of the most energetic energy discharges in the universe and still didn't have a good explanation. They were random, seemed to come out of nowhere, and . . .

"Nope," I replied. "Some are periodic. What kind of engineering fail would give you an ongoing explosion?"

"You sound pretty sure of yourself."

I glanced at him. "We'll know soon, Gar." I stopped and gestured to a heavily armored set of doors, looking something like a bank vault. "I hope you brought your lead underwear."

28. Wish Granted

Icarus
August 2321
Hub Zero

Four ships approached at high speed, then braked at a level of deceleration that left me boggled. The ships all but stopped instantly from a speed of several kilometers per second, then hit us with a SUDDAR scan.

"Eep. They are *fast*," I said to Dae. "We should probably cross off running away as an option."

"Uh-huh. Have you gotten a challenge?"

"Not yet. I imagine they're—oh, wait, here we go."

I'd just received a low-power radio burst. A quick inspection showed it to be the same general format as the ID packets with which the gate controllers responded. Which didn't mean the payload would be comprehensible.

I responded with the packet I'd received from the other end of this gate. Not out of some deep strategy but simply because I couldn't think of anything else to do.

The ship repeated the same transmission it had sent initially. This time, I sent the packet from the very first wormhole gate we'd identified. At least it would tell the other ship where we were from.

Again, the ship repeated the transmission. That wasn't good. It meant I was likely dealing with something of AMI-level intelligence—a well-defined function and a limited set of response scripts.

Dae, who'd been watching my performance, said, "This is kind of an impasse. Should we attempt to leave?"

"Let me try this." I quickly queried the gate on this side to get its street-sign information, then sent a series of packets, starting with this gate and ending with the first gate we'd used. Then I veeeeerrry slowly started to drift back toward the gate.

Nope. Not a valid option, apparently. The ships hit us both simultaneously with—well, let me just say it—tractor beams. This was certainly something new; the Bobs had never even come close to anything like that technology, either in theory or practice. On the one hand, I was overjoyed to discover that it was a thing. On the other hand, we were being dragged away from the wormhole gate to an unknown fate.

The journey only took ten minutes or so, even allowing for the fact that the ships used far lower acceleration when towing us. So there was some regard for our welfare and, presumably, the health of any passengers we might be carrying. Although come to think of it, the SUDDAR scan should have ruled out that possibility.

We were unceremoniously placed in a parking orbit around a small asteroid-slash-space station. By which I mean a ten-kilometer-wide asteroid had been used as the foundation for quite a complex base station of some kind. Two of the sentries departed for the space station, leaving the others holding us.

"Maybe we're going to be boarded?" Dae said.

"Could be. Meanwhile, what are our options?" I mused. "We can't outrun them, even if we manage to get loose. Their acceleration capability is just off the charts. A slow retreat didn't work. What does that leave us?"

"Should we scan them? Do you think they'll take that badly?"

"Hmm." I thought about that for a few mils. "Look, this doesn't appear military. More like border guards. If they were inclined to just blow up interlopers, I think we'd already be an expanding cloud of debris. So it's more likely that we didn't give the secret handshake and are being treated like possible illegal immigrants or smugglers."

"Okay so far. And?"

"So behavior consistent with that will be tolerated without killing us." With that, and without further discussion, I did a SUDDAR sweep. And waited for the end.

Nothing.

"We're still here," I said. "I'm gonna take that as a good sign."

"On the other hand, they haven't reacted at all. That feeds into the AMI theory. What do you suppose they're doing?"

"Waiting for orders?" I hesitated before continuing. "Given that everyone is gone, we could be waiting a while."

"Yeah, AMIs aren't the brightest stars in the sky, but they are long on patience."

"So what now?"

"Your guess is as good as mine."

Sitting here wasn't going to get us anywhere. I decided I might as well try something. I released an exploratory drone, deliberately doing everything at low speed. I didn't want to spook our hosts.

The moment it tried to move away, it was hit with the same tractor beam. Now there were three of us stuck like flies in a web. The drone AMI continued to try to fly in the direction I'd specified, making absolutely zero progress. I ordered it to stand down.

"Well, that sucked," I said. "We may be here a while."

"We still have telescopes. Let's do a survey."

‹‹ * ››

A telescope-based survey was nowhere near as good as flying around looking at things, but early Bobs had done just exactly this, before SUDDAR got good enough to cover a significant portion of a system at a go. The first thing we noticed, something that we'd been too preoccupied to see up until now, was that this system was, well, not a system at all. It appeared to be a patch of empty space, except for an asteroid/space station and two wormholes.

"No sun. No planets. No satellites that I can find." I paused. "No asteroids, other than the one."

"Just two wormholes—the one we entered through and another one at, mmm, about a hundred klicks distance," Dae said. "Remind you of something?"

"Yep. A firewall. This is the DMZ," I replied. "Which makes my earlier comment about border guards all the more apt. I wonder why the security?"

"There doesn't have to be a reason, Icky. Just an abundance of caution."

"Yeah, no. We've been breezing through gates up until now. Suddenly we have border security? I bet none of the other jumps from Hub Zero have firewalls."

"But why just here? We literally went through every wormhole gate at every other hub without seeing this."

"Center of the empire? They're protecting their Trantor?"

"Yeah, okay. Wait, no." Dae's voice took on an edge. "If this hub is all one single civilization, they'd only have one gate at the hub, and all the local gates would be on the other side of the firewall. No, they're protecting this specific destination. And they might be protecting other destinations as well that we haven't found yet. Maybe we just lucked out."

"Yeah, *luck*. That's the word I'd use."

We sat in silence for several mils, each separately considering our fate and our options. The SUDDAR sweep had shown a bunch of docked sentry ships in the space station, so hitting our captors with a couple of surprise busters wasn't going to resolve the problem. Or it would, but not in a way that we'd like.

But there was something else . . .

"Look at this." I pointed to a spot in the holotank, which currently showed the area immediately around the station. There was a sentry ship hovering near something else.

"Another prisoner?" Dae muttered. He pulled up the SUDDAR sweep we'd done and checked the data. "Definitely not the same construction as the sentries. In fact, closer to us in general design." He zoomed in on the scan image. "Oh, hell."

"What?"

"It's dead. Looks like fusion-reactor powered. If it was held there long enough, it would have eventually run out of fuel for the reactor. Powered down and inert. How long do you suppose that took?"

"Uh . . ." I checked the archives. "Generally speaking, back when we used fusion, we could have kept the lights on for five to ten years on reserves if we were just sitting there." I leaned forward to examine the image closely. "No indication of living space. So a totally automated ship. Maybe someone's version of a Von Neumann probe."

"So I guess that answers the question of what's going to happen to us."

29. Ready to Go

Howard
October 2342
Trantor

The dragon rotated in the video window. Well, the CAD image anyway. The real thing lay in a manny pod in orbit around Jabberwocky, courtesy of Mario and the autofactory he'd set up for us.

Bridget was out on some errand that demanded her physical presence, so when the job-completion auto-alert had come in, I'd jumped in to take a peek.

The dragon really defied easy categorization. It didn't have feathers, it didn't have fur, and whatever those were, they weren't quite scales. I suppose a pangolin might come close, but the dragon's scales weren't nearly as tough as the Terran animal's.

The scales also grew thinner and longer on the wings, acting very much like feathers, which gave the dragons flight capabilities more like those of birds than bats, including the ability to soar and glide.

I knew all this, of course, because Bridget couldn't resist lecture mode if anyone around her held still long enough to listen. And I was always willing to listen to her.

It did kind of look like a squirrel, though. Other than the large, clawed hind feet, it didn't have the innate menace of a dragon. Eyes too big, fangs too small, mostly. Maybe a little like Toothless—the dragon in that animated movie. Also, no fire breath. It stood perhaps a little taller than a human on average, maybe six and half feet, but rangier, as befitted an animal that had to get airborne. The abnormally large chest housed both oversize lungs and huge pectoral muscles. There was also some weirdness about the metabolism, but I hadn't paid close enough attention. A long tail completed the ensemble, finned or feathered at the end to help control flight attitude.

At that moment, Bridget walked into the apartment. She was angry and did her best to slam the door both open and then closed, but the modern mechanism was deliberately resistant to that kind of abuse. The door braked and slowly hissed shut the last few inches.

"Didn't go well?" I asked, keeping my tone neutral.

"Luddies," she replied. "They're trying to flood the Trantor city council with specious complaints and accusations about mostly ludicrous and irrelevant things. It's an obvious desensitization tactic, but according to the rules, we have to evaluate each submission."

"You couldn't have done this virtually?"

"Again, rules. The complainant has the option to demand an in-person evaluation. It's harassment, pure and simple."

"Hmm." I frowned. There had to be a way to handle this. I backed out of my manny for a few mils and wrote a quick note to our lawyers. They were the best—and most expensive—legal firm in the UFS and, in my opinion, worth every penny. Or millipam, these days.

But for now, best to distract her. "So our dragon mannies are done." I gestured to the rotating image. "Dranny? Mangon?"

"Oh, do not start. Let me see." She nudged me out of the way as she sat. "Could you do martinis? I really need one right now. Make mine a double. No, a triple. No, just pour until the glass is full."

I smiled at her as I got up to play bartender. "What do you think of the finished model?"

She halted the rotation, zoomed in and out a few times, and played with layer transparencies—showing first the skeletal structure, then circulatory system, then nervous system. Finally, she sat back and looked at me. "I approve. Let's load them in a drone and do a test run."

I did a fist pump. Showtime!

‹‹ * ››

As with Eden, the home world of the Deltans, the dragon world had a lighter gravity—just under point-nine G—and a thicker atmosphere.

Otherwise, something the size of a dragon could never have gotten off the ground.

The dragons had some other advantages as well, such as hollow bones, a respiratory system very similar to Terran birds', and an insanely high metabolism. We had engineered our drannies to adhere as closely as possible to the average dragon size and weight, but of course, we included plenty of reserve power and speed. Fair fights were for suckers.

It took about a half hour to get the drannies down to Jabberwocky from the orbital autofactory. On receiving the alert from the drone, Bridget and I put our home mannies in their pods and transferred to the new drannies.

I must have said something out loud, or perhaps Bridget had simply become that good at reading my mind, because I received a text from her just as I was initiating the transfer: *You are NOT going to call them drannies!*

Yeah, we'll see . . .

I sat up in the cargo hold of the drone. Beside me, Bridget's dranny was just sitting up as well. She made a grinding, coughing sound, and I looked at her in confusion, wondering if she was having a breakdown.

"Turn on your auto-translator, Howard," she said over the intercom.

Oh. Uh, yeah. Quickly, I pulled up my head's-up display and activated the onboard translation service. Long since perfected in its general design, the auto-translator converted my human words, expressions, and mannerisms to and from the local equivalents. Using the technology, we were able to fit right into dragon society without actually having to learn the local dialect. Behaviors were another thing, of course, but whoever was doing the xenopological analysis would give us a rundown. Hopefully soon, and hopefully we wouldn't encounter any locals during this shakedown run.

I commented as much to Bridget, and she replied, "We've put down a long distance from the nearest populated leviathan. Gandalf and company have told me they're almost done with their survey. A couple of days to wrap up and then package up their results, and we'll have it."

"And you couldn't wait?"

Bridget gave a shake that my auto-translator presented as an eye-roll equivalent and replied, "If we discover any issues with the drannies—I mean the dragon mannies—I'd like to have them fixed by the time we get the analysis. No point in wasting time."

"Or in resisting the inevitable. Drannies it is!" I crowed.

Bridget shook herself again and opened the cargo door. Local air rushed into the lower pressure of the hold, and we endured a momentary buffeting. I squinted until my eyes adjusted to the bright sunlight coming in through the door, then stepped to the threshold and looked around. We were several hundred feet in the air, hovering over a small lake. It should have been a tranquil scene, except that the lake was roiling alarmingly in a couple of places, with steam or some sort of vapor bubbling up from the depths.

Bridget followed my gaze. "That's why there's so much emphasis on aerial evolution on Jabberwocky, Howard. It's a young planet and still very, very volcanically active. There's a good chance those vapors are toxic."

"So no swimming, then."

"I'm sure there are lakes that are far safer. My IR vision says this one's hot enough to kill an unwary bather."

"Too bad. That means no fish. I'd have liked to practice my lunch-acquisition skills."

Bridget gave me an approving look. "Well, you *have* been reading up." She lifted one foot and flexed the claws experimentally. The dragon foot looked a lot like that of a raptor, with clawed toes projecting both forward and back. Long legs completed the package, allowing a dragon to swoop over a lake and nab fish on the fly. I had taken one look at the image of their favorite prey fish and dubbed them *trout*. Bridget, never having seen trout, had just shrugged.

"No time like the present," I said. I stepped forward and dove out the cargo door.

Garfield had done a lot of the early work of rigging up flight reflexes when he was developing the manny called Rocky in its various iterations. Several hard landings had spurred him on to lick the problem, and now I was reaping the benefits. My wings stretched out on their own accord and caught the air, and my fall bent into a long, graceful up-curving arc. At the top, just before I ran out of momentum, I folded my wings, did a backflip, and went into free fall.

I yelled, "Woo-hoooo!" and again caught air, bending my path into a corkscrew. Behind me, Bridget laughed. I could hear her wing beats over my own, a higher cadence as she worked to catch up.

In seconds, we were over a bare stretch of dark rock and making use of the updraft to climb effortlessly. "This is even better than Quinlan swimming," I exclaimed.

"And hopefully it will end better," Bridget replied. "Don't break the dranny—how's that sound?"

"Yes, dear." Somebody had apparently ratted me out.

We soared in the updraft for several minutes, simply enjoying the sunlight, the cool air, and the view out to forever. But eventually, Bridget said, "I have to do at least a little work to justify this junket. Let's land by that lake. I want to check the environmental analysis hardware."

The dragons were significantly bigger than Quinlans. Combined with continual improvements in miniaturization, we were able to build more features into this manny version. Of course, Bridget would want to test them.

We landed on a rocky outcropping at the end of a small peninsula jutting into the lake. I had a moment of vertigo as I tried to overthink the maneuver, but the dranny firmware took over and brought me in picture-perfect.

Dragons did a sort of birdlike squat instead of sitting, not really having the physiology to support a butt-first resting position. It was surprisingly comfortable and stable. I looked around, ostensibly standing guard while Bridget sniffed the air.

"Very high CO^2 here," she said. "Not toxic as such, but a dragon would be panting, trying to get a breath." She paused for a moment. "Which we aren't doing. I'd better add a subroutine for that."

I nodded and idly dipped the tip of my tail into the water. *Ouch,* my dranny control system said, and pulled the tail out with a jerk. *Ninety Celsius,* it informed me. *Burn level.* It sounded peeved.

Bridget gave me a small smile. "Giving it all for science."

I stood and stretched, one wing, then the other, one arm, then the other. "Want to race?"

"Howard, please. That's so immature," she replied. Then took off without warning, beating for all she was worth on a southern heading.

"That never gets old either," I muttered, and took off after her.

There was a certain amount of sexual dimorphism in the dragon physiology, with the males being bigger and more powerful but the females being more maneuverable. I knew that this figured into their mating rituals, but I hadn't read far enough ahead to know exactly how. In any case, I was catching up, but slowly.

"We should limit ourselves to dragon normal," she called back to me.

"Yeah, sure, I'm not falling for that one. Again." With a few powerful wingbeats, I found myself above and slightly behind her. As I gazed down on her form, I suddenly had an idea of how those mating flights worked. "Bridge, do we have the dragon behavioral routines installed yet?"

"Some of them. No cultural stuff yet, though. Why?"

"I'm, uh, well, my dranny is, uh . . ."

"You like me?"

"Yeah, like that. How accurate is the physiology?"

"We could find out."

I eased down to glide just above her, and we found another updraft.

Aerial sex. Highly recommended.

« * »

We were doing a long loop, gradually working our way back to the location of the drone. One of the newly installed modules was an inertial guidance system that ensured we always knew where we were, which made dead-reckoning navigation a snap. I was admiring the view and wishing for a cigarette, or dragon equivalent, when Bridget said, "I think we're being followed. No, make that *chased*."

I swiveled my head and looked back. The dragon neck wasn't as long as that of its mythical namesake, but it was definitely better than a human's for checking in all directions. In this case, it allowed me to get a good look at four dragons bearing down on us. They had a very definite aura of focus and determination. This wasn't just a *strangers passing in the night* kind of thing.

"They have sticks," I said. "Spears, you think?"

"Technology level is right. We should probably get away."

"There's a plan." I applied dranny-level power to my wingbeats, not enough to appear superhuman—er, dragon—but enough to ensure that our pursuers would tire before they could catch us. Bridget increased her cadence to match.

It took a couple of minutes, but they finally veered off and headed for an updraft to rest. I glanced back with one eye to confirm, then said, "I thought this area was far from any floaters?"

"It is," Bridget replied. "We did a thorough survey. I've just requested a recheck, which should only take a few—and done. No floaters anywhere within twenty miles." She paused for a moment. "Floaters? Howard, please don't make that stick."

"Aw, c'mon, Bridge. Fair's fair. You do the Latin names and I do the fun ones."

She sighed. "I suppose I should be thankful it's not a pun. Or a potty reference."

I grinned in response but didn't point out the actual double entendre. Beating a victory to death was never a good idea.

We soon spotted the drone, which had dropped its camouflage when we got close. The cargo door opened, and I did an upward swoop that placed me at a dead stop right at the entrance. As I moved into the cargo bay, I heard Bridget land behind me.

"So what have we learned today?" I said.

"You are very bad at creating names for things. Dragon sex is fun. And they have patrols or something similar. That last one may be a worry. I'll talk to Gandalf."

"I'll come with," I replied. "Maybe we can get in a round of D&D."

30. Revisions

Bob
November 2342
In Virt

I received an invitation from Theresa, promising a surprise of some sort. I'd have visited anyway, but now my curiosity was up. I knocked and was admitted into her VR in Quinlan form. Theresa was reclining on a chaise, with a bowl of *squiz* on a side table. She had settled on an open-concept shelter, as in no walls. Partly covered by a pergola, it was essentially a patio with some accessories. The weather was always warm and dry in VR, and anyway, Quinlans were furry, so most of the reasons for an enclosed domicile were moot.

Even with the Bobs, it was more a matter of habit than any real necessity. And why not? Henry Roberts lived full-time on a boat, and I'd heard rumors of some other ex-humans who had taken up the Davy Crockett lifestyle full-time in VR.

Theresa smiled at me, waiting. Obviously, I was supposed to figure out the punch line myself. I looked around, somewhat at a loss. The weather was nice; the foliage was foliage-like; little animals and Quinnish bugs buzzed around. The view was clear out to the horizon . . . the horizon.

I did a slow 360. "This is a planetary surface?"

"Right the first time. I extracted some archival footage from Anec. This is Quin, before the—what did you call it?"

"Jackpot. It's an allusion to a famous and very popular author from when I was alive. It means when a whole bunch of crap hits at once and takes civilization down."

"That certainly fits, although I think the human word is supposed to refer to a *good* thing."

I laughed. "Yeah, well, English—what you call *human*—is a very fluid language. It doesn't really have a cultural identity of its own, so it's quite happy to beat up and rob other languages. A word means just what we want it to mean. No more, no less."

She gave me a side-eye. "That sounds like another quote. You get a tone when you do that."

"Can't put one past you. So anything on tap for today, or was this just about the view?"

"Good news, bad news, Bob. The good news, we've introduced Quin the planet as a second-level VR for those ex-Quinlans who feel ready."

"And the bad news?"

"Uh . . ." Theresa hesitated, uncharacteristic for her. "We've had a number of Quinlan replicants turn themselves off. Deleted their backups, left orders not to restore them."

"Oh." I'd heard rumors of something similar in ex-human space, actually. I'd have to check up on that. "How many?"

"Only a few, Bob. No pattern that I can find, yet. It does concern me, though. Anec is trying to get statistics from some of your human arcologies, but they are unsurprisingly quite closed-mouthed about it."

I smiled in reply. "Well, I can help there, at least. We have contacts."

Theresa nodded and popped a fish part into her mouth. I tried to suppress a gag.

31. Huey Progress

Howard
November 2342
Vulcan

Bridget and I had received an invitation from Mark Harris to attend the latest huey test. He would never invite us for something routine, so I had a good feeling.

We followed the usual process and soon found ourselves in the lab at the Hawking Institute. Terry was there as well, still acting as a guinea pig. She looked considerably more relaxed than the last time I'd seen her.

"Hi, Terry," I said. "How are things? I hope they fixed that exit glitch."

She raised her arms as the techs fussed around her, attaching sensors and routing wires. "That was a while back, Mr. Johannson. We've had several subsequent and much more interesting glitches since then. Would you like a list?"

"Terry . . ." Mark said in a warning tone.

I looked at him in surprise, as much because it felt like he was trying to suppress information as anything. That would not sit well with me.

He glanced at me. "You're welcome to review our logs, or I can give you a rundown, Howard. But Terry tends to get worked up. We don't have time for the ranting."

Terry chuckled and said, "Can't argue with that." She began to lie down on the gurney, assisted by the techs, just like last time.

"The gear still seems bulky," I said.

"Just test sensors," Mark replied. "We're not using the production model wearable, and it's hard to tell from here where the test harness begins and the debugging stuff ends. Take my word for it, the production remote is a marketable size."

I nodded. "Okay, let's do this."

Mark glanced to the techs, one of whom said into the air, "Activate."

Terry closed her eyes, and the huey woke up. I noted that this version was considerably more human-looking. It even seemed like it resembled Terry, at least a little. I wondered whether it was Terry or the techs who had designed the unit, because there seemed to be a little bit of wish fulfillment going on. Slightly taller and definitely more athletic, it was Terry-plus-plus.

The huey climbed out of the manny pod and looked around. "Vision's good. No intermittent freezing." She looked at me. "One of the glitches had my vision stream locking up like a bad video connection." She walked back and forth a few times. "Balance is good. How about lunch?"

"What?" I said, thrown by the non sequitur. Even Mark looked surprised.

"It'd be a good test. Take me to lunch. You're buying."

I raised my eyebrows. "You're not going to abruptly blow chunks or something, are you?"

The huey, which I was already starting to think of as Terry, laughed. "No, consumption has been one of the more dependable parts of testing. Otherwise, I think I'd have quit." She patted her stomach. "One of the biggest selling features of these things will be the ability to pig out without gaining weight."

The four of us headed for the caf, Terry talking nonstop. "Balance issues. Latency issues when we tried more than three hops on the network. Time-outs. Video lock-ups. The exit failure—you were here for that. It's been fun times. I'd started waking up in the middle of the night, thinking I was trapped in a huey. But . . ." She looked at Mark.

I noticed that Mark's arm was completely regrown. Still a bit pink, but fully fleshed out, with proper muscular development. And a tattoo, already.

"But we've made it all the way through the testing gauntlet. Every scenario dreamed up by the approval committee has been successfully met. We're going to have a couple of alpha testers running hueys full-time at work, which should catch anything else."

"What about letting someone have one at home?" Bridget asked.

"Maybe for the beta stage," Mark said with a concerned expression. "With all the Luddie sentiment these days, I don't think anyone wants to abruptly glitch or have a limb fall off in public. Let's take it slow."

"Unlike what we've been doing up until now." I smiled as I made the comment, as otherwise, I was sure I'd just sound testy.

We executed the same trajectory as last time through the cafeteria lineup. Bridget and I both had burgers, and Mark had mac and cheese again. Terry loaded up on desserts, including a hot fudge sundae. Bridget smiled, seeing this. "Been there," she commented. Terry laughed and licked her lips ostentatiously.

The lunch went without incident, the only noteworthy item being that Mark was now using hot sauce on his mac and cheese. I shuddered involuntarily. The man obviously had issues.

Terry tucked into her dessert with gusto and even went back for a second sundae. Bridget glanced at me, shrugged, and joined her.

As we ate, a TV mounted high on a wall switched to a newscast, showing protesters clashing with police somewhere on Vulcan. The sound was off, but the placards and signs could be made out. *No more replicants*; *Dead is Gone*; *You can't take it with you*; and *Replicants are not people* were the ones I saw. "Chrissake," I muttered.

"Luddie rally," Mark observed. "Gone to violence as usual. They do their best to cause a fight, then claim victimhood. Assholes."

"Yes, but their numbers are increasing," Bridget replied. "All the more reason to get this project finished."

"Do you really think it'll resolve the issue?" Terry asked. "I tend to think it'll just inflame the Luddies more."

"Actual Luddite types, yes. But I think with most people, it's more a case of resentment driven by envy. Give them what we've got, and they will be motivated to defend the new status quo."

Terry smiled. "Sure, okay. I think you're being optimistic, but I hope you're right."

I watched the video of two protesters beating a cop with their signs. I hoped so, too.

32. Second Wave

Ferb
March 2342
Somewhere above the galactic plane

"Son of a bitch," I muttered. The radio message, coming from ahead of me, was unequivocal. Someone named George had had the same idea as mine, but way sooner. That shouldn't have been a surprise, really. What would interest one Bob would interest another.

I'd decided to head for galactic north a few years back, once the War for Earth ended. I'd built a cargo ship with room for a bunch of relay stations, with the intent of forming a chain so I'd never be out of SCUT contact. But George had apparently thought of it back in the twenty-second century, back before SCUT was a thing. He might have gotten the plans from Bill's transmissions by now, but without relay stations, he was still out of range. He wouldn't have been able to build relay stations en route without a supply of raw materials to work with, but he would have built an onboard SCUT anyway because it's what I would have done.

George continued to send back reports by radio because it's what we did. Whether Bill was receiving them or not was another thing. George didn't seem to be in the registry, either as a clone or as a flight path. Things had been a little anarchic back then, so it was maybe not so surprising.

But that didn't change the fact that my grand gesture had turned out to be a me-too. Outstanding.

Well, George was some two hundred light-years north of me by now, and his reports were quite interesting. He'd left behind the galaxy's thin disk and its Population I stars and was now well into the thick disk with its Population II stars. Far more metal-poor and therefore far less likely to have any kind of habitable planets. Or planets at all, since even gas and ice giants needed something to form around. But the search for planets didn't really seem to be George's focus.

I was idly playing around with the idea of changing my itinerary—maybe heading for galactic south or the edge of the galaxy. Icarus and Daedalus were heading for the center; George was heading north. Didn't leave me much unless I just picked a random direction.

I sat back and crossed my arms, feeling a little put out. But it wouldn't hurt to follow a little longer. Maybe listen to a few reports, just so I knew what I would be missing.

But I would make a point of not enjoying it.

33. Finally Working

Howard
December 2342
Vulcan

We'd gotten an invitation from Mark to attend a meeting in New Landing, and I noticed that it was phrased in an unusually formal manner. I checked the headers, and it wasn't from a lawyer, so we weren't getting sued. Bridget took one look over my shoulder and said, "They think it's ready."

"You sure?"

She gestured at the text on the Canvas. "That's Mark bursting with excitement but trying to act casual. Have you not met him?"

"I can be a bit obtuse that way," I replied. "Have you not met *me*?"

Bridget laughed and lightly slapped my shoulder. "Come on. We can get some lunch and still make it on time."

"Bronto burgers?"

"Is there any other kind?"

‹‹ * ››

A few moments later, I sat up in the Vulcan manny pod. Bridget was already climbing out of her pod. As we straightened our clothes, I got a message from the local auto-attendant. I could see from Bridget's slight jerk that she'd received something as well.

To all clients of MannyPark:

Please be advised that Luddite activity is on the increase, especially around our building. It is strongly advised that clients with malleable mannies alter their appearance before leaving. Clients with older mannies should consider an upgrade or a temporary rental of a newer model until the current activity level subsides.

Clients should also enter and leave through random entry points in the complex. Guidance will be supplied as required.

Management
MannyPark Remote Services LLC

Well, that sucked something fierce. I glanced at Bridget, who was already changing her features and hair color. There wasn't much either of us could do about the manny's hairstyle, but we tended to keep a short, nondescript, and not particularly fashionable hair length on our mannies. Bridget had always been proud of her fire-red hair, though, and all her mannies were redheads by default.

I followed suit, and we walked out of the pod room, guided by the glowing line on the left wall. The company was situated in a business complex, far too large for protesters to barricade without creating a major snarl and forcing the cops to invoke the Riot Act.

When we arrived at the Institute, we were met by Mark, Terry, and several suits who turned out to be management. And my employees, apparently. These were the administrators of the Huey Project, which was completely financed by yours truly and missus yours truly, and they knew whose butts needed to be kissed. The level of fawning would have been nauseating if the whole event wasn't so surreal.

After several minutes of fending off attempts to butter us up, I'd finally had enough. "Mark," I growled, "if I don't get some answers in the next few seconds, I'm leaving. I was going to lube my joints today, and you're cutting into that."

Mark, shamefaced, replied, "Uh, yeah, sorry, we planned a dog-and-pony show, and it kinda got out of hand. Everyone kept wanting to add something, until we ended up with a floor show. So here's cutting to the chase." He gestured to Terry, and she stepped forward.

Terry went into a stage-magician routine, with the "nothing up my sleeve" and the posing. I resisted the urge to say something sarcastic.

Terry was normally no-nonsense and acerbic, so there had to be a punch line of some kind coming.

Finally, she grinned, lifted her T-shirt, and displayed her abdomen.

Which was transparent. We weren't seeing human intestines, but a manny status display panel.

This wasn't Terry.

Which was interesting, of course, but mannies had been good enough to fool people for a long time. I cocked my head. "Okay, you're riding a huey today. Why is this significant?"

Terry looked a little crestfallen at my response and pulled her T-shirt back into place. "Because I've been living through my huey for a week now during work hours, using the production remote, and haven't experienced a single glitch."

"It's ready, Howard," Mark added, punctuated by the rapid nods of the management team.

Now the penny dropped. Everyone here was a shareholder, because that's how Bridget and I liked to run things. All employees had a personal stake in the outcome, and the outcome of this particular project could make millionaires out of everyone. I reluctantly conceded that a certain level of excitement was justified. Then I grinned uncontrollably.

I looked at the management team. "And you guys have a marketing plan ready, I guess?"

The leader, who had introduced himself as Hector Rodriguez, stepped forward. "We do. We have mountains of documentation, and we prepared a presentation, but"—his eyes shifted back and forth between Bridget and myself—"perhaps we can go with the short version for today."

This elicited another smile from me and an amused snort from Bridget. I made a *go ahead* motion.

"We have a short- and long-term marketing strategy prepared. The benefits of the invention are obvious, but we believe that playing off the existing FUD about mannies wouldn't hurt, as long as it's not laid on too thick."

"The Luddies," I interjected.

Hector nodded. "Their whole platform has revolved around the advantages that replicants have and the innate unfairness of it all. We propose to use that directly. Sell the public on the idea that they can even the playing field and join the elite without the minor inconvenience of dying first."

I couldn't help it. I laughed out loud.

"There's still the issue of life span, though," Bridget said.

"Statistically, if you are not personally exposing yourself to all the normal risks that form part of everyday life, average life expectancy should go up six to ten years, even with no other changes to habits or lifestyle." Hector paused. "Even the terminal phase, the last five years or so of accelerated senescence, can continue to be productive using a huey. It's not immortality." He shrugged. "But it's a little closer."

Bridget nodded and glanced at me before replying. "And we've been funding some research into delaying the terminal phase as well. I can see this all playing well together."

"Well, hell," I said. "Let's do this."

34. Prototype

Bill
December 2342
In Virt

I had called a meeting of what Garfield had lately started calling "The Ancient Ones." Myself, Garfield, Will, and Bob were seated in the moot pub, with Hugh attending via video window. Also in attendance were Howard and Bridget, simply because they'd picked this time to pop over and visit, saying they had some news.

Although I was displaying a calm demeanor—at least I thought so—Garfield was fairly vibrating in place. And in VR, where you could control your avatar at a pixel level, that was notable. Bob had already noticed Garfield's excitement and was frowning in perplexity.

I opened my mouth to say the obvious, but Bob beat me to it. "You suppose we're all wondering why you've gathered us here," he said. "Now that we've got that out of the way, talk."

I grinned at him, relieved that I could put the drama behind me.

"We've done it."

Bob cocked his head. "You've figured out how they get the Tootsie Roll in the Tootsie Pop?"

"Funny guy." I paused for more drama, and a small bit of revenge. "We've successfully pushed matter through a wormhole."

You could have heard a pin drop. The only motion in the room was Garfield's continued vibrating. Then Bob said, deliberately deadpan, "Okay, that's interesting. Pray continue."

I glanced at Gar, whose grin was threatening to sever his head at the jawline, before continuing. "We created a wormhole and split it into two endpoints. Nothing new there. We moved one endpoint to a distance of one hundred kilometers. Successfully. New distance record, but still not cataclysmic. We then, based on the hint from Thoth, expanded and stabilized both ends using negative energy. And pushed ten hydrogen atoms through, one at a time. They all appeared at the other end." I crossed my arms and tried not to look too smug.

"Ten hydrogen atoms?" Bridget grumbled. "I am not a physicist, so maybe I don't understand why that should be impressive."

Howard leaned toward her. "No one has ever pushed so much as a quark through a wormhole before, Bridge. Without something to brace the endpoint, even light can't get through before it collapses."

Bridget nodded slowly. "This sounds like something else you boys are going to be making more money off, soon."

Howard grinned back at her. "It does generally seem to work out that way."

I looked more carefully at Howard. He'd said something about having some news, and he didn't seem as engaged by my announcement as I'd have expected. Kind of distracted, actually—unlike Will and Bob, who both looked totally boggled. "Okay, Howard, you said you had some news. Obviously, that's on your mind. Let's just get everything on the table, shall we?"

Howard nodded and smiled at the group. "Mannies for humans. You know we've been working on that project for a while now—"

"Well, to be fair, all you've ever told us was that someone was rumored to be working on it," I interjected.

Howard continued, ignoring me. "We're ready to announce them, and we'll be rolling them out to early adopters. *Hueys*, we call them."

"Short for *human mannies*, no doubt," Bob said.

Bridget rolled her eyes. "Same infantile sense of humor. All of you."

"That *is* interesting," Will said to Howard, ignoring Bridget's comment. "It's going to create some issues with FAITH on Romulus, too, I bet. I foresee some of their policies becoming far less popular."

Garfield waved his hands in the air. "That's great, Howard. And not to minimize your achievement, but we've got FTL travel! I think we win."

"Ten atoms at a time," Howard retorted. "That sounds like travel would be painful."

Garfield looked at me pleadingly. "Jump in anytime, Bill."

"No one's wrong," I said with a laugh. "Howard's right—we're still in the concepts stage. On the other hand, the theory's nailed down. It's just engineering from here on. On the third hand, there are some limitations. Or will be."

"Like?"

"Well, you can only have wormhole travel where you already have a wormhole endpoint set up. And you have to create the pair together, then fly one of the endpoints to a destination. Via slower-than-light flight."

Bridget frowned. "So you can't go somewhere instantly until you've already gone there the hard way. Seems like a significant shortcoming. You can't create the wormhole endpoints at two different locations?"

I shook my head. "No, they literally start out as a single virtual particle, then get separated. No way around that, even in theory. But look, in twenty years or so at most, we'll have every world in the UFS connected. You'll be able to actually visit other worlds."

"You'll be able to do that this year with hueys," Howard replied with a grin.

"Say, who invited you, anyway?" I paused. "And . . . trade. You'll be able to export your devil's brew to everyone."

Howard conceded my point with a nod.

"But Howard's right in a way," Will added. "It's not going to be a game changer the way a proper warp drive would. I don't suppose . . . ?"

"Still working on the warp drive, Will," I said. "A lot more theoretical issues involved, since there's never been a way to test some of the base assumptions."

"Actually, guys, I think this might be very useful," Hugh said from his video window. We all looked at him, and he continued, "It's seventy light-years to Skippyland from Epsilon Eridani. I'm breaking some rules telling you that, but I think we're kinda past that point. But there are nine star systems between us and you, with a total chain length of eighty-two light-years."

"And this is better, how?" Garfield said.

"Every system in the chain already has a space station with manufacturing capability. That's been standard operating procedure since SCUT was invented. If you create wormhole pairs in every system in the chain and fly one of the endpoints across to the next one, you can complete the chain in twelve years, that being the biggest single gap in the chain. Which means we can have a highway from Epsilon Eridani to Skippyland fifty-eight years before Fake Hugh gets here from Ultima Thule to bust out Thoth. It'll involve ten hops, but that's trivial."

"And what good does being able to get to Skippyland do us? Or you?" Bob asked.

"Telepresence isn't good enough to help with the minion's arrival, Bob. We need physical assistance. We need something like the picket line that Will and Bill set up to detect the Others' approach to Sol. And we need to be able to detect a single Heaven vessel, probably cloaked, rather than a fleet of giant ships. And since the Titan class is the latest and greatest—and way faster than anything we have—we'll need to build or import some of those, too."

Bob thought for a moment, then replied, "And there's a reason why you can't set that up yourselves?"

"Uh, resources. We've stripped our system, and several nearby systems, for resources to build JOVAH. And we, uh . . ." Hugh looked embarrassed for a moment. "Only a few of us still reside in spaceships. It seemed like a poor use of resources."

"You could salvage your old computer system for parts," Will suggested.

Hugh hesitated for even longer before replying. "Well, see, that's the thing. The JOVAH hardware is so much more powerful than replicant matrices . . ."

"Oh my God," I exclaimed. "You've migrated into the cloud? All of you?"

"Most of us. That's also why we couldn't just shut everything down when Thoth got loose. It would be mass murder. Or suicide. Depending."

Bob put his head in his hand. "Unbelievable."

"We'll get started on the wormholes right away," Will said. "The equipment to generate baby wormholes and separate them isn't a huge deal to build, and we can operate through roamers. What about the negative-energy generator, Bill?"

"Just a Casimir generator with a few tweaks, really. But Will, I'm at the ten-atom stage in development. I am nowhere near ready to push through anything macroscopic."

"But you have the wormhole-creation process nailed, right? And any future development won't affect that process, right? If we start now, we can have the wormhole endpoints in place when you're ready to go to the next phase."

I frowned, thinking the problem through. "Hmm, you're right. A wormhole is a wormhole. But maybe send some spares, just in case."

"Sure, no prob. We can even send a couple of deliveries separated by a month, in case one of them goes bad. Redundancy is our friend."

"Any other issues, Bill?" Bob interjected.

"Well, one." I paused, feeling unaccountably embarrassed, as if I was responsible for this issue. "The wormhole doesn't do anything about intrinsic velocity. If the two endpoints are moving relative to each other, any object pushed into the source will come out at the destination with an apparent velocity in the opposite direction. So if our wormholes end up orbiting their home stars—and I can't think of any other configuration that makes sense—then the orbital velocities at both ends, as well as the proper motion of the stars, will have to be taken into account."

"What if the net velocity is right back down the mouth of the wormhole?" Howard asked. "Does it just return to sender?"

I smirked at Howard, and I noticed the others—except Bridget—were looking at him with amusement as well. "Jeez, Howard, you've been out of it for a long time. Or the booze has rotted your brain. The wormhole isn't a tunnel, like in *Stargate* or *DS9*. It's a sphere. You dive into the sphere and come rocketing out of the destination sphere in the same direction, adjusted for the relative velocities of the wormhole endpoints, of course. In the scenario you've proposed, you'd come out the wrong side, facing the wormhole and flying backward."

"Huh," Howard said, and sat back. He looked at Bridget. "I do have to cut back on the martinis."

«*»

The meeting had eventually broken up, until only Garfield, Will, and I were left. I guessed Will wanted to talk to me about something, so I made a head motion at Gar. He saluted and disappeared.

"What's up, Will?"

He gave me a weak smile in reply. "Nothing earthshaking. It's just that I've been heading for the hinterland for almost ten years now, and I've dropped AMI-crewed stations off at thirteen star systems along the way."

"That many? You must be really flying."

"They aren't all in a row. Anything anywhere close to my flight path gets a station, just because. So I'm populating a cylindrical area with stations out to about a four- or five-light-year radius. The point, though, is that if I'd known about this sooner, I'd have sent them with wormholes."

"Can't help you there, Will. This hasn't been classified top secret; I just haven't had anything to report before."

"Oh, I'm not blaming you, just bitching a little. And by the way, maybe we should classify it as top secret, at least for the moment. But I can use your idea of creating wormhole pairs at each location and flying one of the endpoints to the next one over. In a decade or so, I'll be connected to WormNet."

"No. Absolutely not. WormNet? Hell no."

Will grinned back at me. "Then you'd better come up with another name fast. If I've thought of it . . ."

I sighed. "Noted. And I think as another side project, we should send a ship and wormhole after every Bob who's headed for the far reaches. Even Ick and Dae. But why top secret?"

Will shrugged but avoided meeting my eyes. "No big deal. We wouldn't release any info until we had something really working anyway. I'd just like to have it as a hole card. Got some stuff coming up in Omicron^2 Eridani that could be a problem." Then he paused and got a thoughtful look. "Hey, I keep meaning to ask. Do the wormhole endpoints end up being a time tunnel if they're flown around?"

Will was referring to an old theory that a wormhole endpoint flown at relativistic velocity would end up pointing into the past relative to the stationary endpoint. If the traveling wormhole arrived back at its origin five years younger due to time dilation, you could then send items five years into your past.

I shook my head. "Nope. Tested it. If you think about it, that behavior never made sense anyway. If you send someone on the same ship as the wormhole, do they arrive in the past? No. They arrive in the present, just younger. Same with the wormhole."

"So . . ." Will made that rolling motion with his hand. It seemed to have become a tic with him.

"Look, if you send a ship off with a person and a wormhole, and you send food through the wormhole every day and the other end on the ship is at fifty percent tau, it doesn't arrive further and further in the past. How would that work anyway? It just comes out twice a day on the ship, according to their clock. But in proper chronological sequence. At the end of the trip, they've received twice as many meals as they expected. That's all."

"Huh. Okay then." Will stood. "I'll get started on those wormhole factories. And I guess we're going to make this standard practice from now on?"

I nodded and made a face. "WormNet. Yee-haw."

35. Travel Plans

Will
December 2342
Interstellar space

"Well, frig," I muttered. Bill's news about wormholes really put a twist on what had, up until now, been a pretty simple life.

I was heading outward, away from the core, at a good fraction of the speed of light, although keeping it down enough that I could continue to interact with the Bobiverse through SCUT. Bob might like being cut off from the rest of the universe for years, but I was way too much of a control freak for that kind of vacation. But if this project of Bill's delivered on its promise, there was no longer any issue of being cut off. I could create a chain of wormholes all the way back to UFS space and visit whenever I wanted. On the other hand, I was moving along at 70% C, and that would make it difficult to deploy a wormhole in the first place—assuming Bill's research reached that point.

Hmm. Okay, all I really needed to worry about was creating a wormhole transit to some point in WormNet. I'd need to create a wormhole pair and send one endpoint back to the nearest seeded system, which was BSC-804. Meanwhile, I could order *that* system's AMI to create a wormhole endpoint and send it back to the next system closer to UFS space. Rinse, repeat, until I was connected to the rest of the Bobiverse.

Come to think of it, a wormhole endpoint in Omicron² Eridani would be ideal for getting our descendants out of FAITH's reach quickly, but only if the government had no warning about either the escape plan or the existence of WormNet. It bothered me that I had become so used to playing everything close to the vest that I now kept things from other

Bobs unless they needed to know. It was a habit that could end up alienating me from everyone else.

Of course, there was no reason for me to physically travel back there. The *Fargo* would be fine for picking up our descendants. Preferable, in fact, since it had the rotating section, so we wouldn't have to put everyone in stasis. And once the wormhole network was connected, Bob could use it to catch up with me. I didn't even have to make a decision until things were in place.

No sooner was the plan worked out than I was setting up one of my inventory of Bob seeds for the trip back. It would have to decelerate from my velocity to zero relative, then accelerate back to BSC-804. But I had plenty of time.

I checked the status board. The *Nostromo* was a somewhat smaller version of the *Bellerophon,* without a lot of the weird tech that the Others had built into their cargo ships—also without the mover plates. That was a kludge forced on Herschel and Neil, which, thank the universe, they'd finally corrected. I shook my head in amusement. It was a Bob thing—if it ain't broke, and we've got a workaround, screw it.

Then I sighed. Talking to myself again. I hadn't said anything to Bob-1, but I really had been looking forward to him joining up on this voyage. SCUT and VR were great, but there was still some psychological issue with being physically isolated. Maybe that was why Herschel and Neil, Howard and Bridget, Bill and Garfield all hung together so well.

36. The Gamers Come Through

Howard
March 2343
In Virt

Bridget and I received a couple of tokens, no time specified, from Gandalf, along with a note: *I'm free now if you want.*

Worked for me. We activated the tokens and found ourselves in the Gamers' vestibule. Which, it turned out, looked like a waiting room at a legal firm. There was even a receptionist, although a quick metadata check indicated she was an NPC.

Bridget snorted, then started to sit down just as Gandalf came out of the back. He was still dressing like Ian McKellen in *LOTR*, which I thought was perfectly reasonable but drove Bridget batty. I think her eye actually twitched as he greeted us.

"Hello and welcome. Come on into my office." Gandalf made a sweeping gesture with his staff. Twitch, twitch.

"What's with the layout?" I asked.

Gandalf smiled. "Just playing against type. We're trying to swap things out weekly, and some of the suggestions are really bizarre. Even for me. *This*"—he gestured around him—"is tame."

He led us into a room that resembled the Hall of the Rohirrim. I opened my mouth to comment, and Gandalf cut me off. "Don't overanalyze everything, Howard. This is my VR, not a Freudian cry for help."

I laughed out loud. Even Bridget smiled. We sat down at a long picnic table and reached for mugs of beer that appeared out of nowhere. Gandalf again took the lead. "I presume you're here about the dragon cultural analysis?" We nodded in unison, and he continued, "Pretty much complete. Our content editor is hammering it into some kind of shape, but you should have it in a day."

"Are you familiar with the details?" Bridget asked.

"Of course. A new intelligent species is hugely interesting. And, ah . . ." Gandalf looked embarrassed for a moment. "This one in particular seems especially suited to be added to the D&D bestiary. Or so I'm told."

"Unbelievable," Bridget muttered. Then louder, "I ask because we were pursued last time by what I think might have been a patrol of some kind. Nowhere near a village—"

"Floater," I interrupted.

"Village," Bridget repeated, giving me a dirty look, "so we're not sure where they were from or what they wanted."

"Bandits?" Gandalf mused. "Or perhaps pirates."

"Excuse me?" I said.

"You know the history of piracy, right?" Gandalf shook his head. "Of course you do, because I do." He turned to Bridget. "Pirates were unofficially sanctioned by governments of the day to harass ships from other countries, under a flag of anonymity. Kind of like state-sponsored terrorism."

Bridget looked shocked. "You're saying the dragons engage in this activity?"

Gandalf hesitated. "Cultural analysis works best when reporting on stable and long-term behaviors. Right now, dragon culture is going through some, erm, rapid evolution. Tensions are mounting. The analysis can't give you too much on it, because things are in flux. But don't worry. The average dragon citizen is probably just as confused about what's going on. You'll fit right in."

"Wow," I replied. "That's not ominous or anything."

"Mm-hmm. Some kind of Alexander the Great character is acting up, near as anyone can tell. Annexing territory, which in this case consists of the floating islands. It'll be interesting times."

I glanced at Bridget. "Want to put this off?"

"Don't be silly, Howard. But maybe we should put together a few spare drannies, in case we get shot down."

I rolled my eyes. Interesting times, indeed.

37. Schemes

Icarus
August 2321
Sentry System

You'd think the prospect of rotting in a holding cell would spur us to heights of creativity, but *no*. After several real-time hours of thinking, we still had nothing. I was sitting back, holding a coffee and staring into space, when Dae muttered, "You'd think the builders would have allowed for something like this."

I sat up straight. "I bet they did!"

"Huh?"

"Like high-security areas back on Earth. If the fire alarms went off, everything unlocked so people could get out."

Dae frowned. "Yeah, and wasn't there a car that you could trick into unlocking by convincing it you were trying to get out?"

"Something like that," I replied with a smile. "But the point is, there should be a procedure for handling nonroutine situations."

"Sounds great, except for the powered-down spaceship over there."

I waved a hand dismissively. "The ship probably just sat there until it shut down. The AMIs or whatever are running this station would have considered it a routine situation until it was too late. At that point, there was no further action required."

"So we have to convince them we're dying before we actually die."

"Like that, yeah."

"Except, and I feel like I shouldn't need to point this out, we can't even talk to them."

"Well then, we need to start working on that."

"Oh, this should be good."

Over the next several hours, we tried numerous ways to get their attention. We sent TV signals; we streamed video over radio; we tried embedding graphics images in the packets; we even tried SCUT. There was one unencrypted channel where we got what I think was simply a reflexive ACK. I pegged that as the common channel for this civilization. But other than the ACK, the sentinels showed no signs of having heard us.

"This is not going well," I muttered. "I think the problem is that decoding radio or SCUT requires problem-solving abilities *and* the desire to do so. The sentinels are simply ignoring anything they don't recognize. Their lower-layer protocols may not even be passing our attempts up the chain, so they might not even know we're attempting to communicate."

"So give them something visual," Dae said. "Presumably they use some kind of optical receptors, so they'd attempt to characterize anything they see."

"Because . . ." I replied.

"Because, Icky, that's what visual intelligences do. Even AMIs will attempt to identify anything their visual systems pick up."

"It's not your worst theory."

"Unlike yours, it hasn't failed."

"Yet." Sniping aside, Dae's idea sounded logical. But how to present an image to them?

Ah. We had a drone sitting outside, still being held in a tractor beam. It was fitted with a comms laser, which could work in any of several frequencies. Some of those frequencies were in the visual spectrum. Well, *our* visual spectrum. If one didn't work, I'd try others—until I ran out of options.

I sent the drone a set of instructions, and it proceeded to light the side of my hull with a circle. After a few seconds, it switched to a triangle. It worked its way through the basic shapes: square, pentagon, hexagon, heptagon, octagon, nonagon, and decagon. Then it cycled back through the series. As it worked through the images, I transmitted radio packets with the same shapes embedded in a simple bit matrix as the payload.

Nothing.

"Well, hell." I looked at Dae. "Any ideas?"

"Maybe make it explicitly pixelated. And put a pixelated frame around it to indicate your dimensions."

"And match that in the packet!" I exclaimed. "Excellent."

No sooner said than done. Now the drone was drawing images with pixels instead of vector graphics. I made sure the pixelation was clearly visible, which allowed the observer to count the pixels. The size of the packet allowed for a 1024-by-1024 image if I encoded the image on a bit-by-bit basis, but I didn't want to complicate things any more than I had to, so I went with a much smaller image, one byte per pixel.

On the second time through the sequence, the sentry started echoing the packets back. Well, not quite echoing. It had changed the envelope slightly. And on each lap, it was changing the image size.

"It's teaching us their graphical interchange format?" Dae said, half questioning.

"Let's not confuse things. How about GEF? You know, graphical exchange format?"

"Sure thing. Don't want to get sued by, uh . . ."

"Compuserve, I think. Are they even still in business?"

Dae laughed. "I'm betting no. Anyway, whatever we call it, we're communicating. So what's next, oh wise one?"

"We establish math."

Since we now had a standard image format, I abandoned the laser light show. I sent an image of the numeral zero, with a slash through it to indicate that it wasn't just another circle GEF. Then one dot, with the numeral one beside it. Then two dots, and the numeral two. I went through the sequence up to twenty-one, which should indicate to the sentry that we used decimal, positional notation. I then jumped to one hundred dots, with the numerals one, zero, zero. I waited.

The sentry sent back a GEF of one hundred and six dots, with the proper numerals beside them.

I whooped, and Dae did a fist pump. "It's getting it," I exclaimed.

"More important, it's willing to work with us," he replied. "If it had ignored us, we might as well just turn off our power now."

That statement was a total downer and took the celebration right out of the air. I cleared my throat (totally unnecessary in VR) and sent a new graphic. This one showed several examples for each of the four basic arithmetic operations. One plus four equals five, three times four equals twelve, eight minus one equals seven, twelve divided by three equals four, and so on. The sequence allowed only one interpretation for each of the math symbols. I deliberately used an asterisk for the multiply symbol, as I'd be needing the *X* later.

The sentry responded by sending back four math ops with different values and correct answers.

"Ladies and gentlemen, we are in business," I crowed.

"Excellent. We can play math games. You have a long game plan?"

I gave Dae an eyebrow waggle in reply.

Next, I sent four math statements with incorrect results using the not-equals sign—an equals sign with a diagonal slash through it.

Again, the sentry responded with confirmatory examples.

Now, time to start formal logic. I sent four plus two equals six with a check after it, then four plus two equals seven with an *X* after it. Again, the sentry responded.

"True and false?" Dae said.

"Yep. Or maybe *agree* and *disagree*."

Over the next while, I went through logic symbols, such as AND, OR, NOT, and the mathematical operators. In C and C# tradition, I used single symbols for the math versions and double symbols for the logic versions. I was concerned that this might be confusing, but the sentry stayed with me.

"Hey, Icky?" Dae said slowly.

I felt a pang of panic at the tone. "What?"

"You have an audience."

I'd been so preoccupied with my lessons that I hadn't noticed several other sentries drifting over. Which was a little odd, since I'd stopped using the laser as soon as we agreed on the GEF packet format.

"Doesn't this indicate a certain level of individuality?" Dae commented. "And curiosity?"

"Hmm. Might still be duty driven. They're interested because they've decided it's relevant to their jobs."

"Don't care. I'll take it."

"Yep. As long as they're listening, we have a chance."

Now I needed to start asking questions. I sent a simple math problem with a question mark for the answer, then the same problem with the answer showing. The sentry immediately sent back a different problem in the same format.

I paused and sat back. That completed the math and logic lessons. Well, I could do set theory and such, but I didn't need it for what I wanted to do.

I carefully crafted an image of the alien probe, with lights on and little hydrogen atoms in the middle to indicate a working nuclear-fusion generator. I added navigation lights and lit-up portholes—total artistic license, but I had to make the point that it was alive and operating. I added one of the sentries holding it—again, using artistic license to portray the tractor beam.

I sent the image, then another with the lights dimmer and fewer atoms. Then a third with no lights and no power. I waited a moment, then sent the same sequence, but with our ships. Then a single question mark.

No response.

"They may be bumping this up the chain of command," Dae commented.

"Or trying to. I bet they're not getting any responses."

At that moment, the sentry sent an image. I whooped and did a fist pump. The image portrayed our ships going back through the wormhole, followed by a question mark. I quickly sent back the same image with a check. Then I had an idea. I sent another image of us taking the alien probe vessel with us, and a question mark.

Again, no response.

When they finally responded, it was after exactly the same delay as the previous time. "Huh. Standard time-out, I guess. Then they have to make the decision themselves." It was the same image I'd sent, but with a check. So we would be allowed to take the alien probe.

One small problem—no tractor beam.

"We can use drones," Dae suggested. "Same process as moving small asteroids. No biggie."

<< * >>

We were extremely careful over the next several hours to verify every move with the sentries. We didn't want any misunderstandings or overreactions. But eventually, we found ourselves very slowly drifting through the gate while a couple of our drones very slowly pushed the alien probe through behind us.

"Want to send them a goodbye?" Dae asked. "Maybe a middle finger?"

I laughed. "It would be just our luck if they understood the intent and responded by blowing us out of the sky. Let's just get out of town with our skin intact, okay?"

Soon, we found ourselves back at Hub Zero with a dead vessel from an unknown civilization. It was interesting, though, that the design of the ship was quite comprehensible. A SURGE drive was easily identifiable from our scan, as was a fusion reactor and a magnetic hydrogen scoop system. Other parts were less recognizable, like the computer system and what had to be their version of a 3D printer.

Interestingly, the ship did not seem to have a supply of drones, or roamers, or the makings of a full-on autofactory—just the one printer and a small supply of what might be maintenance bots. It was a stripped-down Von Neumann probe, without the capability to replicate. Really nothing more than an exploratory scout.

The immediate problem, though, was getting it operational. To do that, we would have to get the reactor going without a working ramscoop system to supply the reactor with fuel. To add insult to injury, Heaven vessels hadn't been built with ramscoops since the end of the War for Earth, when we converted to Casimir systems. So we had no way to collect hydrogen for the ship even if we did have some other way to ram it into the reactor.

We went around and around for hours, but in the end, there was only one option. We'd have to install a Casimir generator. That would mean cutting into the ship and performing some surgery.

"I hope it's not going to feel violated when it wakes up," I said, "and discovers a new body part."

"I'm sure there must be some B movie covering this kind of thing," Dae replied, "but I'm coming up blank. Look, let's just put it in and apologize afterward."

‹‹ * ››

It took a week all told, since we were extremely careful both in cutting our way into the vessel and in making sure that we got all the voltage and current requirements right. This must have been what Neil and Herschel felt like while deciphering the Others' cargo ship.

"Activating," I said, and pressed the button. In the monitor window, the generator went through boot-up, then came online. And the ship activated.

This was the moment of truth. We hadn't detected any weapons in the ship, not even a rail gun. But you never knew.

The ship sent out a SUDDAR pulse, easily identifiable. It had scanned us. Hopefully it would see that we were at Hub Zero and would come to the obvious conclusion.

"You know we're just going to have the same problem communicating with this guy," I said. "No common format for radio comms, no common SCUT channels, no nothing. Assuming it even has SCUT. I didn't see one."

"So use the same solution. And hope this guy's at least as smart as the sentries."

Well, why not? I positioned myself in front of the alien ship, sent out a drone with a laser, and started the lesson.

38. Starfleet Just Won't Go Away

Bill
May 2343
In Virt

The wormhole endpoints were all well on their way, and within a few years, we expected to have a path from Epsilon Eridani to Skippyland. Of course, Howard had decided to set up a full network, for fun and profit. On the quiet for now, since we didn't want to publicize this invention ahead of time.

The Ragnarök ecosystem build was going very well. I now had predator–prey relationships that didn't oscillate into extinctions anymore. I'd lost a couple of iterations of deer due to over-efficient wolfpacks, but I now had the ratios right.

I was examining a graphic of population fluctuations in *virt* when I received an email from a Bob that I didn't recognize, someone named Hector. A quick search placed him about eighteenth generation, one of the Bobs who was taking his Von Neumann probe heritage seriously. He'd been heading for . . . hmm, for the patch of sky that Lenny had claimed for Starfleet.

Sure enough, as I read through the missive, Starfleet was involved. They had apparently threatened Hector if he didn't reroute around their space. But threatened with what? Hector didn't elaborate, which probably meant Starfleet hadn't been specific. He was following their instructions since, as he explained, he wasn't set on any particular direction except *away*. But it was concerning behavior, and he thought I should know.

Fair enough. And he was right. If Starfleet was now threatening people, they'd either flipped out completely, or they were really, *really* holding a grudge. Neither was good.

I sent a quick text off to Will, since he seemed to have his finger on the pulse of everything political—quite a feat for a Bob who was also heading away as fast as he could.

The answer came back immediately:

> *Nope, haven't heard anything specific. Of course, those guys are sufficiently bonkers that this doesn't surprise me. But it's going to become an increasing problem, Bill. Eventually UFS space will reach and then surround Starfleet's claimed area. Then what? Another war?*

I sighed and waved the population graphic closed, then closed the text window. Will was right. We'd decided to ignore Starfleet as soon as they stopped showing up at moots, but in this case, forgotten was not gone. A confrontation wasn't the best strategy, though. Perhaps I should start with some information gathering.

One of the odd things about Starfleet during the war was how they'd completely left the solar system alone. It had been obvious enough to elicit comment from several Bobs, including Charles, who should know better than anyone. Was that simple nostalgia? Or evidence of a deeper connection?

Well, the wormhole project was on track, my Ragnarök ecosystem was currently problem-free, and I was getting a sore forehead from bashing my head against the wormhole problem. Maybe it was time for a distraction.

39. A Civil Discussion

Bob
June 2343
In Virt

Theresa had invited me to her place—in VR, that is—and since I hadn't seen her in a while, I was unreasonably excited. She had recently discovered the UFS Federal Library and had jumped in with both feet. She hadn't even answered messages for several days. Now, it looked like she was finally coming up for air.

We didn't have a need for tokens, being on the same subnet by tacit agreement, but it was still polite these days to knock first. I received an ACK, then popped in. I was taken aback, though, to find the layout considerably changed. I was in what I'd have called a home theater room back on old Earth. Theresa was sitting, in Quinlan form, in an easy chair reminiscent of the furniture in the Heaven's River transit system. She patted the arm of an empty chair beside her, so I converted to Enoki and took the hint.

"Are we going to watch a show?"

"A couple, actually. Just short clips. A few are from your YouTube site, and a few are from our own version, which for some awful reason has been dubbed QuinTube." She paused. "You do understand there's no cultural justification for that name?"

I smiled at her. "Remember what I said about the English language? Turns out it also infects other languages. Kind of like an STD."

Theresa looked confused for a moment, then said, "We don't have those. Different mating strategies and all. But I get your point. Anyway..."

"Huh." I sat in silence for a few moments, thinking about this. "Maybe you've found yourself a new career here, Theresa. Ministry of Exobiological Diplomacy or something. It certainly seems to be something that's slipped through the cracks."

Theresa gave me a smile. "I've talked to a few people. This just might happen."

40. Going In

Howard
September 2343
Jabberwocky

Today was the day. We'd received the cultural and language files from the Gamers, and they'd been uploaded to the drannies. Now Bridget and I were having a strategy session. We sat in our apartment in front of her computer. The Canvas displayed several overlapping windows, including a global map of Jabberwocky and several relief maps and images of dragon villages.

"This is a good place to start," she said, pointing to a spot on the virtual globe. "High enough population density that we won't stand out. Good weather—I have no desire to wait out one of their tropical storms, thank you very much. There are several floaters"—Bridget couldn't help a slight wince as she said the word—"with more than one village on them. Diversity builds tolerance. I want to find out more about this warlord character—he's the Alexander the Great wannabe that's supposedly causing a lot of flux."

"But this is a cultural and xenopological expedition, right?" I gave her a side-eye. "We're not going to get involved, right?"

Bridget sighed. "I hope not, Howard. The Bobs do have a habit of sticking their noses into things, though."

"You're not a Bob."

"I am an honorary Bob." She smiled at me. "I am as nosy as any of you."

"I, uh, I have no idea how to respond to that in a way that won't get me punched."

She punched me anyway.

"Ow!" I rubbed my shoulder. "No fair."

Bridget grew serious again. "Howard, the Bobs decided a long time ago that the Prime Directive is a load of hooey when a species is in existential danger. I'm not sure if the dragons are at that level of risk or if this is just another war that will someday be a historical footnote. But some of the observations from Mario and comments in the Gamer files make me nervous."

"Okay, Bridge, got it. Let's go in, snoop a lot, and figure out if we need to call in the Bobs." She made a face at me, and I grinned back. Then I stood, held out my arm, and said, "Shall we?"

«*»

I stood in the cargo doorway, Bridget beside me. The landscape of Jabberwocky spread out before us in all its primitive, undeveloped glory. This time, we were fully geared up, each wearing one of the dragon frontpacks—like a backpack, but worn over the stomach. The dragon physiology made backpacks a questionable design decision, but you still had to carry stuff.

We'd considered but decided against spears, or any kind of overt weapon. We each had a knife on our belt, but that was about as noteworthy on Jabberwocky as car keys were back on twentieth-century Earth.

"Are you ready?" Bridget asked. "Once we start, this is a full-time gig, except when the drannies are supposed to be sleeping."

"I've taken care of all our business dealings, Bridge. I'm good to go."

"We'll be heading for a relatively large floater, one with several villages on it. Hopefully we'll be able to get lost in the population size."

"We're staying in the one place?"

"No, of course not. Just long enough to get our balance. And to find out about that patrol that chased us last time." Bridget's expression darkened. "I want to know if that's still going on."

I nodded, then made a *you first* gesture. Interestingly, the translation software converted it to a motion with my tail. It was probably human chauvinism talking, but it struck me as a little obscene. Bridget didn't seem bothered, though, and did a graceful dive off the edge. I admired her lines for a moment, then followed. Bridget held the dive for several seconds before opening her wings and arcing upward. I followed, not especially trying to catch up. At the top of her arc, she pulled in her wings, whooped, and did a backflip before settling into a proper glide.

I pulled up beside her and grinned. "Addicting, isn't it?"

She smiled back at me. "Quin was fun. This is incomparable. I wonder if we could put wings on hueys."

"No, of course—" I stopped midsentence. Why not, exactly? I looked behind me. Well, if I remembered right, a tail of some kind was required for control and balance. But something could be rigged. Or we could just go with dragon physiology, since we already seemed to have it on lock. Of course, there were the issues of gravity and—

"Earth to Howard. Come in, Howard." I started and glanced at Bridget, who was trying and not quite succeeding in not laughing at me. "You went into Bob-fugue. Were you analyzing the engineering or the profitability?"

"I plead the Fifth. Or whatever it is these days. But the engineering. Profitability is a given, I think."

"It's still the Fifth, Howard. It's just a saying now. I doubt most people know what it refers to. I had to look it up myself."

We flew in silence for a few minutes, unconsciously taking advantage of updrafts whenever possible. The dragon vision seemed to have some kind of sensitivity to polarized light that made updrafts visible. Made sense; it would be a survival characteristic. The dragons could put on good speed when they needed to, but they were large and heavy for a flier, and therefore long-distance gliders by nature when updrafts were available. I wondered if they used to migrate or something similar in their prehistory. I'd have to ask Bridget.

I spotted a lake below that didn't seem to be steaming or roiling. "Want to try a little fishing?"

Bridget looked where I was pointing and wordlessly banked in that direction. "The Gamers will have programmed in fishing reflexes, but remember, they've only been tested in VR. Take it easy the first time in."

"That's me, Mister Conservative," I replied with a laugh, and swooped in low. Dragon eyes were adapted for seeing through the water's surface as well. I dipped a little lower and spotted something coming up in my flight path. The dragon reflexes took over, putting me into a stall as my feet reached out, claws extended.

I hit the water face-first with a thunderous splash. Coming up spitting and coughing, I looked up to see Bridget grinning at me.

"You caught a submerged log, Mister Conservative. Or it caught you. Come on up and try again."

Getting out of the water wasn't easy, even for dranny muscles. It wasn't a case of getting waterlogged, more an issue of drag preventing me from getting up enough speed to lift off.

"I'm not hungry anyway," I said. "Maybe some other time."

"We should both do it at least once, Howard, just in case we have to perform in front of real dragons. Practice makes perfect." And with that, she circled around for another pass. I followed, muttering under my breath.

We swooped down in parallel and hit targets at almost the same instant. I came up with a lovely trout in one claw. I held it up to Bridget, who had come up empty.

"Don't you dare gloat," she said.

"Wouldn't dream of it. I'm going to settle on the shore while you give it another shot. Practice makes perfect."

I received a black glare, which I studiously ignored, and settled onto a rock outcropping. The fish was still alive and flipping desperately in my grip. I really didn't need the food, so I tossed it back into the water. Meanwhile, Bridget had been more successful on her second pass and came to a landing beside me. She smiled and flipped her own fish back.

I settled into the crouch that was the dragon equivalent of an indolent sprawl. "It's a pretty good life. Makes me wonder why the dragons bothered to become intelligent."

"I agree, Howard, and certainly I or someone else will be studying them in the long term to answer that question. But I'm sure the environment of Jabberwocky has something to do with it. This is a harsh place to live."

I nodded thoughtfully. Other than some miscellaneous islands, the planet's land surface was concentrated in two continents, which Mario had named Atlantis—where the dragons were situated—and Lemuria to the west. A huge stretch of ocean reminiscent of the Pacific took up about a third of the globe to the west of Lemuria. I had to agree with Bridget that he wasn't putting a lot of effort into names. But his interests were pretty focused.

"Mario told us that Atlantis is far more tectonically active than the other landmass," I mused. "I suppose that could have played a part in evolutionary pressure."

Bridget laughed. "Listen to you, sounding all biologist-ey. But yes, you're right." She stood. "Well, lunch hour is over. We should find a place to stay."

«*»

"Floater ahead. Locals call it the Hunter." Bridget paused, internally accessing her notes. "The villages are Hunter's Heaven, Hunter's Rest, and Hunter's Glory. Usually just referred to as Heaven, Rest, and Glory."

"No theme there, no sirree."

"Most floaters only have one village. This particular one is very old. They keep growing, apparently, as long as they live."

"What kills a floater? Do they have natural enemies?"

"They have no predators. There are some species of plants and trees that are parasitic rather than commensal or symbiotic. The most common causes of death actually are volcanism and lightning. Jabberwocky has a pretty mild climate overall, and volcanoes don't just spring up overnight, but on the other hand, floaters aren't really powered fliers. They have kind of a sail thing underneath, but only minimal propulsion capability. So they can't get out of the way of a storm or an eruption."

"Hmm. Lightning. Hydrogen. Bad combo. Bet it's spectacular, though."

I stopped talking as I spotted our destination in the distance. Floating serenely through a low point between rolling hills, the floater was literally an island in the sky. I could see the sail that Bridget had mentioned, fully extended at the moment beneath the behemoth like a giant keel. Also dangling down were something like long vines, which seemed to move around in the wind. Occasionally, they dragged along the ground, then would retract into the bulk of the floater. Eating? Drinking? Was it snagging vegetation or little animals? Once again, Bridget would know. I glanced at Bridget and saw her frowning. Was she wondering the same thing?

The top of the floater was shaped somewhat like the top half of a bagel. Forest ran in a ring around a central depression, which was usually filled with water. The central reservoir was both a source of drinking water for the dragons and a place to keep and raise fish stock, although the dragons weren't particularly disciplined about it. The lake was also a water source for the floater and a quick way to make more hydrogen on demand.

I knew from the reading I had done that most of the trees were symbiotic with the floater. They provided nourishment in return for a place literally in the sun. Some trees were in a more parasitic relationship, as Bridget had mentioned, and those could easily be spotted by the reaction of the floater's surface, forming a sort of angry hummocked blister around the plant. Dragons did their part for their home by preferentially using those trees as building material and fuel.

So yeah, fuel. On a hydrogen gasbag, they had open flames. I was extremely interested in seeing how this did not result in a *Hindenburg*-level disaster. I imagined there had to be rules, probably *very* strictly enforced.

We came in low and did a hard upward arc at the last moment, dropping onto the edge of the floater with almost zero momentum. It seemed like a better system than what blue-footed boobies used, which often involved face-plants as a braking device. Yes, I watched a lot of YouTube back when I was alive.

A squad of five dragons immediately marched over to us and pointed spears in our direction. "Home floater?" one said. Then, before I could even respond, "Reason for visit?"

I opened my mouth to answer, but Bridget beat me to it. "Who's asking?"

The spokesdragon cocked her head, more like an owl than a human, and paused, considering Bridget for a moment. Then, apparently deciding not to be offended, she replied, "Have you been living under a rock?

Alexander's army has been seen within fifty miles of here. We've intercepted scouts several times a day. If he's targeting this area, we need to be ready for him. Thus, my very reasonable questions."

"Yeahhhh, okay. We're"—Bridget inclined her head in my direction, a move that acknowledged my existence while simultaneously dismissing me as insignificant—"from a floater about three hundred miles east. Nirvana. It's a college town. We decided to head west until we hit the western ocean. This Alexander is news to us. Seems like kind of a local problem."

Spokesdragon gave Bridget a look of disbelief but apparently didn't feel like making the effort to explain. "And reason for visit?"

"Sleep. Rest. We don't need anything. We've been able to catch trout along the way."

Spokesdragon frowned. "Really? Most people report the pickings being extremely slim these days."

"Most people are probably impatient," Bridget replied archly. "You can winkle them up to the surface with some bait, but it takes commitment." She patted her frontpack meaningfully.

The other dragon glanced down, following the movement, then shrugged. "Y'know, if you can demo that technique, you can probably get people to pay you for lessons."

I queried the translation software and database. *Pay* was not quite the right word. Dragons didn't have an official monetary system, at least not anything standardized. Not surprising with no centralized government authority of any kind. So everything was barter. But metal was rare enough to be prized, and various kinds of metal coins formed a sort of de facto standard of exchange. Their weight and size varied all over the place, of course, with no central authority to mint them. Value was based on weight, and coins were as likely as not to be melted down to make something practical. It was noteworthy that adulterating coins was one of the few crimes that would net you the death penalty here—often at the hands of an angry mob.

Bridget didn't respond, instead nodding toward the village. At a gesture from Spokesdragon, the squad stepped aside, and we proceeded on our way. "Don't make trouble," she said to our backs.

"Not really much of a third degree," I commented to Bridget in a low voice. "I'd say security could use an upgrade."

"Dragons have very good hearing and smell," she replied. "Some individuals have a reputation for being able to literally smell a liar and can probably hear a raised heart rate. Like an old-fashioned lie detector. It's an actual job description, which"—Bridget paused to check the database—"the Gamers have translated as Sooth Hunter. I imagine the group leader was one of those."

I mentally rolled my eyes. "Why not just *lie detector*?"

"Gamers," Bridget replied. "Why are you surprised?"

Fair enough. The Gamers had been going further and further down the rabbit hole since the Heaven's River episode, only emerging in public for really interesting things, like xenopological analyses. There was a meme going around where Gamers get dropped into a black hole and don't even notice for months.

The town was large but ramshackle, there obviously being no building code or zoning bylaws. It also didn't limit itself to a single level, since dragons were very much arboreal. Businesses that needed terra firma clustered on the ground while everything else snaked its way up trees in all directions, either attached to the trunk or branches or suspended by ropes. It seemed like anarchy, but a few seconds of examination revealed an underlying order. This was a medieval village built in three dimensions. There were even hotels of a sort, which mostly consisted of suspended pods with access to running water, both hot and cold. It was interesting that when sentients built a civilization, one of the first things they did was engineer for running water. There was probably a PhD thesis in there somewhere, but I'd leave that for someone else.

Bridget had mentioned that dragon towns ranged from medieval village to Renaissance city in both size and knowledge. There actually was a city named Nirvana, and it actually was a college town—something Bridget had picked up through one of the spy drones.

The dragon civilization was very old and relatively static. They had apparently achieved a level of technology that was comfortable, and settled in. The towns on this floater could be hundreds of years old and probably hadn't changed much in all that time.

We had an unlimited supply of money, of course, since we could just order more from the drone. It was a far cry from the situation in Heaven's River, and I intended to enjoy the freedom—starting with a covered sleeping berth and hot water.

The water wasn't piped to each pod but was accessible in a central area. It came from a containment vessel higher up in the trees, which produced water pressure from a gravity feed. The hot water was more accurately described as warm, but it seemed to be heated using solar heating of clay pipes painted black. These people, for all that they were barely past the Stone Age in many ways, were not by any means stupid. In fact, they seemed to be quite clever at ad hoc engineering.

The hotel proprietor, a crusty old curmudgeon of a dragon, took payment and pointed us to a room with a liberal dose of opinion at no charge. The flow didn't seem to have any logical cohesion, just a spew of complaints about everything, including the weather; the quality, size, and quantity of trout being caught; volcanic activity; and so on. But eventually he ran down, and we made our escape.

The pods were suspended in a row below a stout branch of a tree. And these trees were *huge*. In the lower gravity and thicker atmosphere of Jabberwocky, they grew tall, wide, and strong. You could walk along most of the main branches and even squeeze past people going in the opposite direction. The clawed feet also allowed a good grip on the tree bark, so going a little off vertical wasn't really a problem.

I inspected the pod close up and realized it was anchored both to the branch above and to a weighted net below so that movement and swaying were kept to a minimum, especially when landing or launching. Again, pretty good engineering when they needed it.

We settled in, doffing our frontpacks, and I took a moment to examine the interior. This pod was literally like a giant birdhouse, with a single opening for a door and some holes for ventilation. A spongy floor material completed the décor and functioned as a bed. I checked the database out of curiosity. Private residences tended to be similar, with different rooms suspended individually. Families would usually own all or part of a branch.

Out the front door, the sun of Jabberwocky was just sinking below the horizon. I couldn't get a complete view with all the foliage and other construction, but what I could see was spectacular. I remembered the sunsets on Vulcan, which were also mind-blowing, and wondered if perhaps that was simply the natural order of things. Maybe humans had gotten used to a pale, insipid version back on old Earth.

Bridget patted the floor beside her, and I took the hint. We curled up like a couple of cats, which seemed to be the normal dragon sleeping habit for couples. "Tomorrow I want to examine the floater tendrils. I have a theory . . ." she said, wiggling to get comfortable.

I grunted, content to do whatever she wanted. I closed my eyes; then we left the drannies on auto and returned to our mannies in Trantor.

41. A Disturbing Discovery

Bill
July 2343
Sol System

I hadn't visited Charles in more than eight years. Maybe not surprising, though. He had webcams going so anyone could look in on the progress of the Earth project at any time. It was one of the more popular BobTube video feeds.

The reclamation crew was making great strides with Terra, and two hundred years after humanity nuked the planet into a new ice age, more than fifty percent of the globe was now completely ice-free. Another fifty years, and they estimated they'd be back to normal preindustrial temps. The high CO^2 levels helped as well, although there was a project underway to reduce that as well.

"I've been getting caught up on your progress, Charles. The planet is coming along nicely."

Charles waved the comment off. "The tensor field printers are going to make all the difference, Bill. We might have to take some liberties with cell structures, but we collected enough DNA to recreate ninety-eight percent of species, if you include insects. Even some that were already extinct in Original Bob's time."

"And the climate . . ."

"Back to interglacial. Weather patterns are still all over the place, but that will smooth out as the atmosphere and ocean temps settle into some kind of regular pattern."

I stood and idly poked a globe of the moon, hanging on display, which showed oceans and clouds. "Is this real time?"

"Pretty close. It started as a dare or something, but some group decided to terraform the moon. It's going well, and they're even starting to get a magnetic field going."

"What? How? With next to no rotation—"

"They've got a lunar day down to about fifty hours. Mover plates. Not just for destroying stars." Charles smiled as he said this, but I still noticed a reserve that didn't used to be there. Did he suspect what I was really here for? Starfleet had never attempted any kind of attack in Sol. Did Charles wonder about that, too?

"Venus as well," I said, pointing at one of the other globes.

"Uh-huh. Day length at about a hundred hours and still coming down. And Mars." He pointed at the fourth globe. "All different problems, but a lot of the same tools. We'd like to bring humanity back to the solar system eventually, and we want to give them options."

"Hmm," I said, frowning.

"What?"

"The thing is, Charles . . ." I shifted in my chair. "Long term, I'm not sure if it's going to be as attractive for humans. The flying cities are a controlled environment, and other than considerations of gravity, it really doesn't matter what the planetary environment is like. The O'Neill Corp is building megastructures, and those will be able to orbit any star that isn't too variable. Engineers are even talking about using a fusion light source like the Quinlans did, which would do away with the need for a star at all. Add mover plates, and humanity becomes a truly interstellar species."

"Hmmph. There will always be the back-to-nature types and the keep-it-simple types."

"True enough." I eyed him and got a blank look back. Normally, two Bobs would be relaxed and chatting away by now, but we were still essentially talking business. There was no animosity, just no real friendliness, either. Well, moving on . . . "So do you mind if I wander the system a little? Just to get a look around?"

Charles waved a hand dismissively. "Take as long as you want."

«*»

I was walking along the shore of Mare Humorum accompanied by Benny, one of the lunar terraforming crew. He had volunteered immediately to show me around and seemed quite proud of the work they were doing. Ironically, the lunar maria, which had turned out to be lava beds, were actually the low points topographically, so they were now catching up with their names. The waters lapped slowly against the beach, moving languidly in the one-sixth gravity.

Our mannies were the new standard exploratory model, which meant vacuum-hardened with high-capacity repair systems. The lunar atmosphere was still too thin to keep the temperature swings in the reasonable range—CO^2 would still occasionally sublimate out of the air at night in some places.

I kicked at the ground. The lunar dust had succumbed to a couple of years of rain, and what hadn't washed down into the ground was more the texture of sand and gravel. Some lichen was growing in patches, but nothing else. Of course, I'd literally written the book on terraforming, so none of this was a surprise.

"We're trying to move the schedule along a lot faster," Benny was saying. "You were developing the process as you went, so slow and cautious made sense. Now"—he gestured to the land around us—"we can multitask and overlap stages."

I nodded while wondering how I was going to subtly bring the conversation around to my goal. Subtlety was not a Bob Johannson trait.

"So, Benny, have any of the crews found anything interesting while digging the Earth back out?"

"Interesting? Like what?"

"Oh, I dunno. A lot of stuff could get buried." Then I had a minor flash of genius. "For instance, there was some speculation that Dr. Landers might have had an extra Bob Johannson backup stashed away where FAITH monitors wouldn't find it."

Benny laughed. "Oh, nothing like that, no. Although we did find some powered-down mining equipment. Remember Rudolf Kazini? Yeah, he's part of the crew now. You should meet him. He's, honest to God, the stereotypical Russian—accent, vodka swilling, and all. And he thinks mannies come directly from God."

I laughed. That was at least one piece of good news. "Any other replicants?"

"Uh . . ." Benny's face fell. "We dug out the old institute building, but the replicant computer room had collapsed. No way to recover them. And there was that Homer backup that someone found . . ."

Aha. I had to be casual, though. *Don't scare him. Don't make him lock up.* "I thought Homer destroyed all his backups."

"I'm sure he thought he did. But someone named Gerry found one. Or says he did."

"Interesting. Do you know where I can find Gerry?"

Benny shook his head. "He was a collateral descendant, from several generations up. If I remember right, he was working with the asteroid-mining group. You could check with them."

And I would. But meanwhile, the moon tour was honestly very interesting. I looked up at the Earth, floating in the sky at first quarter, softened by the new atmosphere, and smiled. Howard would monetize this in a heartbeat.

« * »

The asteroid-mining group wasn't hard to find. They were a little, ehm, *odd* by regular Bob standards, though. Maybe it was a bit of a cosplay thing, but their private VRs were apartments in their main moot, which was made up to look like the asteroid Ceres in *The Expanse*. Okay. Made sense, I guess, for asteroid miners. But how bored did you have to be . . .

Unfortunately, they couldn't tell me where Gerry was. In fact, Gerry hadn't been heard from in decades. The Homer backup story was generally considered to be an urban myth, though, and the general consensus was that Gerry had just decided to go Von Neumann-ing.

I had another theory, though. One far less appealing.

42. Flying Around

Howard
September 2343
Jabberwocky

I opened my eyes to find myself still entwined with Bridget's dranny. I was contemplating the situation and feeling my dranny's sleepiness slowly dissipate when Bridget opened her eyes. Vertical pupils, it turns out. I hadn't actually noticed before.

"So what shall we do with our day?" I asked her.

"Coffee."

"Uh, we just had coffee. Back home. No coffee here."

"Not quite true, Howard. Dragons don't have caffeine as such. They use alcohol instead. A hot drink, mostly ethanol, with some spices for flavor. It's called *tuev*."

"Seriously? Isn't flying under the influence kind of a problem?"

Bridget sat up and stretched, sort of like a cat—extended forelimbs, then arching her back until the stretch worked its way back to her, uh . . .

Apparently, flight wasn't the only thing that worked on male dragons. Bridget's gaze trailed downward, and she smiled.

« * »

Sometime later, I stretched and said, "So tell me about tuev?"

"The dragons metabolize alcohol. It doesn't make them drunk. It's like sugar in this biosystem, only more so."

"Huh. So a good stiff martini in the morning gets you ready for the day?"

"Uh-huh. Just like back home, sort of." She chuckled. "Let's get some breakfast."

We stepped out onto the "porch," which was really just a horizontal pole attached to the pod. I had a momentary image of myself as a parakeet in a cage, and I had to suppress the urge to ask for a cracker. Bridget would have killed me, and no one would prosecute.

A short hop with only a couple of wingbeats got us onto the main branch, and we joined a procession of dragons, many looking like they also needed that first cup of wake-me-up. We ended up in front of an open-air kiosk where a harried-looking vendor was trading coins for a cup of something. I looked down at the coins in my hand and realized that they were copper and iron. Interesting. Just like Heaven's River. Apparently, it wasn't just biology that tended to stick to a theme.

When my cup of life arrived, I took a tentative sniff, then a small sip. "Jesus," I muttered, "what is this stuff? Everclear?"

"Almost pure ethanol, like I said," Bridget replied via intercom. "And keep your voice down. You just spoke in English."

I ignored the admonishment but switched to intercom. "This stuff is safe?"

"For dragons, yes. One cup of it would melt a human liver into a green sludge."

We hopped up onto a convenient log and perched, slowly sipping our morning tuev. I had to admit, it did seem to produce the same effect as coffee, assuming Bridget had gotten the biology of the drannies right.

Just one of many things I would never, ever say out loud.

We were interrupted by a commotion at ground level, near the base of the first tree. A crowd was swiftly gathering around two groups of dragons who seemed to be having a disagreement. Lots of pushing and yelling were involved. Instead of swooping down with the masses, we stayed put and swiveled our ears forward. Dragons had good hearing to begin with, and we had the enhanced android version, so we had as good a seat as if we'd joined the onlookers on the ground.

Dragon insults and cursing weren't particularly inventive, depending more on volume and repetition to get the point across, but from the few coherent words that occasionally got uttered almost by accident, I was able to determine that one group was Alexander sympathizers who were trying to drum up grassroots support, with the endgame of peacefully joining up. They weren't getting a lot of chance to talk, though.

I glanced sideways at Bridget and saw she was as surprised as I was. "This wasn't in the briefing materials?" I asked.

"The Alexander thing is a developing story, apparently. This is new. Up until now, he's just been attacking and taking over the occasional floater."

"For what? What's the point?"

Bridget gave me a hard look. "Poor Howard. And Bobs in general. You're so civilized and empathetic toward others that you just can't understand that some people are just assholes. This is no different from any number of tin-pot dictators in Earth history. Little men, mostly, who measure their worth by the number of people and amount of resources they control."

I shook my head, feeling suddenly combative. "And again, to what end?"

"This isn't an instrumental goal, Howard. The control is the endgame. It's not *for* anything."

I sighed and silently conceded the argument. There was simply too much evidence from history that she was right.

Meanwhile, the argument had ended with the Alexander sympathizers being physically hoisted into the air and tossed over the side. While they could have just circled around and come back, it probably would have resulted in a repeat performance but with more spear action. Anyway, there was something in the briefing about how being tossed over the side had broader social implications. Like being branded or discarded.

We continued to sip our morning booze while the crowd slowly dispersed. People started filtering back up the tree, including back to the kiosk. I buttonholed one individual as she bought a tuev and some kind of breakfast wrap.

She gave us the once-over, and a faint look of distaste came over her features. "Foreigners," she muttered. Then she shrugged and said, "Alexander's conquest keeps getting bigger, and it's getting closer. He calls it a *nation*, apparently. A lot of people are nervous, and some have decided that a preemptive surrender is a good strategy. Maybe they can fly to his *nation* and join up directly, now that they're baseless."

Baseless, I remembered, was what you were if you got tossed overboard. It meant not having a home, which technically included Bridget and me. Foreigners.

"Rumor has it they've set fire to floaters that defied them," she continued. "That seems far-fetched, though. No one would be that stupid."

I could see the shocked look on Bridget's face and quickly checked my briefing notes. I'd been thinking of the floaters in an overly casual context, apparently. Dragons had an almost religious reverence for them, and burning one would be like . . . like sacking the capital city of your enemy. Something humans had done with casual abandon all throughout history. Except that floaters were living, breathing beings, not just a patch of ground.

"Doesn't that just create a whole tribe of committed enemies?" Bridget asked.

"If they live. Word is the Alexandrians surround the floater and kill anyone trying to escape." Our companion gave us a skeptical look and a slight tip of her cup before moving on.

"Well, that sucks," I commented.

"It more than sucks. Floaters have very low reproduction rates, which is typical for a species that is large, long-lived, and doesn't have much in the way of natural enemies. And they aren't useful as villages until they reach a certain size. This Alexander character could single-handedly change the ecology of Jabberwocky."

"Want to hit him with a buster?"

She smiled at me. "Did I accidentally call you civilized? But no. Chances are, one of his lieutenants or children would just take over. We'd have to obliterate a good fraction of the army to stop it, and I think that's more than even the most warlike Bobs could stomach."

"So we're going to . . ."

"I don't know, Howard. Wing it?"

I nodded, then realized she was giving me an expectant look. I replayed what she'd said, then groaned and got a smile in response.

«*»

We took to the air from one of the outer branches, then circled around to glide below the floater. It was slowly drifting eastward with the slight wind from the hills. As we came over a lake, the floater dipped its tendrils and dragged them through the water. Bridget circled, with me following.

As we came to the far edge of the lake, the tendrils retracted, and Bridget moved in. Dragons weren't birds, but they did have a lot of the same talents, such as the ability to grab a vertical perch and hang off sideways. Bridget inched her way down the tendril, then began pulling up the remaining length. I circled and watched her work.

After another minute, Bridget dropped off the vine and caught air. I pulled up beside her as she described an arc that would take us back to the town. "And?" I said.

"Later. I have to think about this."

That meant she'd found something interesting. The wait would be frustrating, but worth it.

43. Learning Curve

Icarus
October 2321
Heading to Centaurvania

It took more than a week to get up to the point of being able to hold a conversation. The alien ship, which we named Gunther because it was close to the ship's name for itself, picked up the math concepts immediately. But when we tried moving to language elements such as verbs, things faltered. Dae's theory was that Gunther was more of an AMI or an A.I. rather than a replicant, so it had no actual physical life experience with which to contextualize statements like "See Dick run." I thought perhaps it was just more alien than we were used to. Either way, we had to back up several steps and reduce the graphics to a Pac-Man level before we started to make progress.

But progress we did, and eventually, we had our translation routine loaded with a passable version of Gunther's language. It didn't seem interested in learning ours—or maybe wasn't able to—so it fell to us to take care of the translation back and forth. Even then, things proceeded on more of a question-and-answer basis than any kind of conversation. Gunther was cooperative, but not inspired.

Star charts were easy, though. We quickly established that Gunther had come from a budding civilization near one of the leaf nodes of the third hub clockwise from Hub Zero, although it became cagey about specifics. This meant it had come from essentially the opposite end of the empire from us. The bios that had built Gunther appeared to be generally centauroid, in that they had four legs underneath and two arms at the front. The proportions were totally out of whack, though—more like dachshunds with arms sticking out of their necks rather than horses with human torsos. Still, *centaurs* stuck immediately, and the home planet became Centaurvania. And it turned out Gunther had once been a bio and actually was a true replicant.

The centaurs had three sexes, according to Gunther—male, female, and worker. The third was similar in nature to a worker ant—no participation in procreation but dedicated to the support of its genetic line. And apparently disposable when a mind was needed for replication into a space probe. Gunther was close-lipped about it, but I got the impression that the word *volunteer* hadn't really figured into things.

The civilization that had built Gunther had discovered SURGE drives and SUDDAR but hadn't yet invented SCUT communications. That seemed to be a standard tech path, based on our very small sample size of three: humanity, the Others, and centaurs. Once they had the base technologies working, they'd immediately sent out a scout. And done a rush job to beat out the local competition, which explained the bare-bones design. This was beginning to sound a lot like our human history.

Gunther had found a wormhole at its first destination, then apparently followed a very similar exploratory trajectory to Dae's and mine, hopping from system to system and mapping each system location relative to the galaxy. This activity had eventually culminated in capture by the sentries and, as we'd suspected, a gradual loss of power reserves until it had been forced to shut down. Unlike us, Gunther had never deciphered the gate IDs. That was unfortunate, because we could have used the timestamps on the packets to determine how long it had been a captive.

Eventually, we managed to convince Gunther that we weren't a threat, mostly by pointing out that we'd rescued and revived it, and we were armed and it wasn't, and there wasn't a logical scenario whereby lying about our intentions made sense. And it did need to go home to report in.

So in due time, we all agreed we would head for Gunther's world.

The trip through the gate systems was routine—three hops through the hubs, then one hop to a leaf node. This was the star system that

Gunther had originally aimed for from its home system. It had, of course, done an extensive survey when it arrived, but we wanted to see for ourselves. So we prevailed upon Gunther to wait while we surveyed the system.

«*»

Like most star systems, as we'd learned by now, only one planet was in the Goldilocks zone, and that was where we found the civilization that had lived here. Based on city layouts and proportions, this was a new species to us, the sixteenth we'd catalogued while exploring the empire. And interestingly, this ecosystem had retinal-based photosynthesis—only the second such example. This resulted in plants that were a rich mauve or purple rather than the traditional green.

"It's really odd," Dae grumbled when we'd completed the planetary mapping. "By all measures, retinal should be a better basis for photosynthesis. It's simpler and more energy efficient, and most stars radiate more powerfully in the green band, which would give retinal the advantage. Yet almost every planet uses chlorophyll."

"There might be some obscure reason in evolutionary biology," I replied. "Like the question of why virtually every species uses left-handed amino acids. We just don't know what that is."

Still, a new civilization was always a great view from space, and a purple-hued planet was especially striking. We took a lot of pictures for our blog—assuming we were ever in contact with the Bobiverse again.

The locals had, like most species, colonized most of the rocks in their system, as well as building a couple of megastructures. And like all the other civilizations we'd visited, everything was abandoned. No heat signatures, no radio traffic, no *traffic*, no nothin'.

I pinged Gunther. "Was this abandoned when you first arrived here?"

"Yes."

Talkative as ever. Once again, I resolved to stop asking yes–no questions. "Why did your civilization send you here first? Did they detect radio signals? Heat signatures?"

"Anomalous microwave sources," Gunther replied.

Of course. The microwave from the wormhole. Wait, *sources*? I did a quick sweep. Sure enough, there was another wormhole at minus ninety degrees. "The other wormhole—did you explore it?"

"No."

I rolled my eyes in exasperation, mostly at myself. But really, Gunther had been presented with a coin-flip situation and had made a choice that opened out into the empire.

"Is it worth checking out?" I asked Dae.

"Let's at least send a drone through."

We checked with Gunther, and it was willing to stay the extra week.

«*»

A few days later, we found ourselves floating near the second wormhole. *Yet another one,* I thought. Then I caught my own attitude and mentally pinched myself. I was actually becoming bored with wormholes.

Dae had prepared a drone and sent it through with the usual precautions. The drone did the standard stellar survey and returned.

"Hmmph," I grumbled when we'd finished the analysis. "I had half hoped it might put us in a system that's a little closer to Gunther's home, but no such luck. Fifteen light-years away in the wrong direction. Indication of planets, but no other wormholes and no traces of an active civilization."

"Icky, this is really beyond weird and well into spooky. I'm beginning to worry that we might never find out what happened."

"I know, Dae. These quickie surveys from space really aren't getting us any closer to figuring things out. We might have to bite the bullet and do a full archaeological deep dive on one of the abandoned planets."

"That'll be next. For now, let's visit Gunther's system. That probably has a better chance of us meeting someone."

"But they won't have the answer, either."

"One thing at a time. Let's go."

44. Investigation

Howard
January 2344
Jabberwocky

Bridget wanted to explore more of the planet, but I was concerned enough about this Alexander business to want to investigate further. After some discussion, we compromised.

We started our day by finding a large updraft near the Hunter, which we would consider our home floater and base of operations for the moment. Riding the updraft, we were able to climb to an altitude of almost five klicks. A real dragon would be gasping at that height, but still able to operate. We could have gone higher, but it would have attracted attention.

From this height, the horizon was almost two hundred and fifty kilometers away, although, of course, things disappeared in the haze far short of that distance.

"Lots of haze," Bridget commented. "Probably volcanic. I count"—she paused, turning her head—"forty-two individual hotspots. That's a *lot* of activity."

"Kind of surprised there's as much complex life as we're seeing," I replied.

"The Siberian Traps caused the Permian extinction two hundred and fifty million years ago on Earth," Bridget said, glancing at me. "That was *way* worse, and there was already complex life." She paused. "That was a relatively sudden event. Something similar is happening here, it looks like, but much more gradually. It would explain why so many life-forms have taken to the air. It's the *only* reason I can think of for a species to risk hydrogen flotation."

I grinned. "I bet selection pressure was a real bitch for a while."

Bridget laughed and circled again. "I see twelve floaters, randomly distributed, and it looks like a compact group over in that direction. A dozen or more floaters, I think." She pointed to illustrate. "Want to bet that's Alexander's 'nation'?"

I followed her pointing finger with my gaze and frowned. "That's more or less where we came down on our first outing. Those could have been Alexander's scouts who chased us."

"Or scouts from a nearby floater thinking we were Alexander's scouts. Either way, it's an explanation."

I paused and tried to keep a straight face. "So what do you call a collection of floaters?"

Bridget rolled her eyes. "I suppose you have a suggestion."

"A *flotilla*?"

A sigh was her only answer. I considered that a victory.

"So what do we do?" she said, changing the subject. "Just fly in and introduce ourselves?"

I started to answer, then stopped and squinted. Something was moving in the distance. I activated telescopic vision and zoomed in.

"It seems the decision is being made for us," I said, pointing. She followed my line, squinted, and went silent. After a few moments, she turned to me. "Looks like those 'sympathizers' were more like scouts. That's a raiding party."

Sure enough, what looked like a couple hundred dragons were flying a ground-hugging route that seemed aimed at the Hunter. I suppose there could have been a more innocent explanation, but it seemed unlikely. "Should we head back?" I asked. "Help defend?"

"I don't want to kill anyone," Bridget replied. "Let's wait and watch. We can always head in afterward. We have a legitimate reason to be there, so the worst they might do is toss us out." She hesitated. "I hope."

Within minutes, the raiding party was spotted, judging from the sudden increase in activity on the floater. But by then, it was too late.

The attackers flowed up from underneath the massive floating island, relying on it for protection and cover. At the last moment, they flicked up over the edge and came in to land, spears in hand, where defenders were setting up with something more like pikes.

As someone who grew up in twentieth-century America, I wasn't used to seeing such levels of direct violence—at least not outside of TV or theaters. Even from a distance, the fighting was brutal and unmerciful. A lot of dragons died. A lot more would be crippled for life, assuming they didn't die of infections. Dragon medical knowledge was at about the same level as any Iron Age civilization—a lot of ad hoc procedures, most of which were as likely to be harmful as helpful, or just flat-out wrong.

The fighting lasted perhaps ten minutes. The attackers had targeted all three villages at the same time, and their timing was impeccable. A few dragons had fled, many hadn't fought at all, and the Alexandrians didn't seem interested in those individuals. Thank the universe they didn't seem to intend some kind of pogrom against the residents.

Once things cooled off, we flew in and landed at our village. A couple of Alexandrians, easily identifiable from their bright-blue and white armbands, came over to intercept us. We found ourselves facing a half dozen or so spearpoints. "What's your business?" one of them said.

"Uh, we stayed here last night. We're just passing through." Bridget gestured vaguely up at the hotel pods. "You don't seem about to burn things down, so I thought our hotel might still be in business."

The leader snorted and brought his spear to parade rest. The others followed suit. "True enough," he said. "The Hunter is under new management, that's all. Mind your manners and keep your nose out of things that don't concern you, and you can go about your affairs."

We nodded to them and headed very carefully and slowly to our tree. A quick hop and we were at our hotel pod. "So what now?" Bridget asked.

"We should maybe nose around. Carefully!" I rubbed my snout speculatively. "Wouldn't want to have it cut off for being a snoop."

«*»

Things were settling down. The dead had been taken care of—apparently, the corpses were thrown into pits on the floater's topside and became part of its diet—and survivors had been bandaged up as much as possible. Well, poulticed. They didn't really have bandages. Or antibiotics. I expected the body count to rise for another few days.

The Alexandrians had garrisoned the town, and presumably the other two, but other than that, they seemed to be mostly standing around playing tourist. However, I noted that the Hunter had changed course and was now running an ungainly tack across the prevailing wind, in the general direction of that knot of floaters we'd seen from above. Joining the flotilla, perhaps?

Things appeared very calm in the village. Once the proprietors had realized it would be business as usual, they'd gone back to, um, business as usual. Customers were eating at kiosks, buying food at the market, bartering with shop owners for goods, and so on. Even some of the occupying army were engaging in some personal commerce.

I accepted two cups of tuev from the proprietor of the kiosk, then paused and looked around. "This all seems very peaceful," I said to him. "Is this normal?"

He shook his head. "Don't think so. I've heard about the Alexandrians setting fire to entire floaters in retaliation for resistance and putting entire populations to death. This sure doesn't fit."

"Maybe the tales are exaggerated?"

He gave me a hard look. "How do you *exaggerate* burning down a floater? Doesn't seem like something you could do partway. And the descriptions I've heard—well, they sounded more like eyewitness accounts than fanciful tales, you know?"

I nodded and grunted out a "huh." After pausing for a sip of tuev, I added, "I guess we'll find out one way or the other soon enough."

"Why do you say that?"

"They're steering the Hunter toward the Alexandrian fleet," I replied. "Or what I assume is their fleet. We were up high in an updraft when the attack came, and we could see a large knot of floaters close together. That's the direction the raid came from."

"Bunch of floaters close together? They don't normally stay together. Not like batlings, bunching up in a tight flock."

"One more mystery," I muttered, and took my tuev back to where Bridget was sitting.

45. Everyone Goes Ballistic

Howard
March 2344
Trantor

Sooooo, marketing campaigns. Not worth their weight in bird droppings, apparently.

I sat on the couch in our Trantor apartment and read the report from the Hawking Institute. The hueys had been rolled out across all civilized worlds, to much hoopla in all available media. A huge blitz, extolling the advantages combined with some well-applied FOMO for those who might resist. Piece of cake, right?

Yeah, no. The Luddies went ballistic, FAITH went absolutely apeshit, talking heads everywhere expressed skepticism, and about half the governments of the UFS expressed guarded concern (the half, I noted silently, that were on the more authoritarian end of the political spectrum). I wasn't quite sure how hueys threatened them, but it was obvious they did.

Of more immediate concern was the rush of proposed bills, restraining orders, and lawsuit filings intended to delay or block the sale and support of hueys. Huey LLC (yes, we picked that name) was already the subject of no fewer than fifty-two restraining orders, sixteen class-action suits, and four threatened government audits.

Sighing, I called Hector. Not bothering to sit in front of a screen, I used my internal comms service and generated an avatar for my video image. He came up on a virtual window in my head's-up.

I opened the conversation. "I suppose you're wondering why I've gathered you here."

Hector laughed. "Not the least bit. I sent you that report, Howard. Honestly, I expected a little more cursing. You must know what we've been up to."

Oh, that was interesting. Hector wasn't acting at all like a CEO who was seeing his company crash and burn—more like someone relishing a fight. "Why don't you just update me without making assumptions about what I do or do not know?" I said. Quite calmly, I thought.

I must have been right, because he didn't suddenly look concerned. "None of this is unexpected, Howard. We took a page from the Bobs. We've been filing injunctions, counter-injunctions, briefs; getting legal opinions; preparing and pre-filing countersuits; and so on for weeks now. The perpetrators of most of these legal actions will have to spend up to six months unraveling all the judicial balls of twine we've been winding before they'll even be able to demand their first meeting with our lawyers. The threatened audits are already four layers deep in pre-emptive lawsuits and show-cause orders. Basically, we sowed the entire battlefield with caltrops before we even started."

"All legal?"

"Nothing *ill*egal."

I gave Hector the hairy eyeball. That sounded almost—

"You've been talking to Will," I exclaimed.

"If you mean the Bob formerly known as Riker, I plead the Fifth." Hector grinned. "But yes. He's very cynical about humanity, which is helpful in this kind of fight. In any case"—Hector looked down and played with something, and another email popped into my inbox—"we have more than two hundred thousand firm orders with deposits, plus close to a million tentative orders queued up already, and every one of those customers could be convinced to join a class action if someone actually managed to delay us."

I was impressed. My initial take of Hector as an ass-kisser had wildly missed the mark. This guy was a serious pugilist.

I thanked him and hung up. The hueys were just the tip of the iceberg, of course. Companies that rented mannies would expand to include generic hueys in their lineups, for people who only occasionally needed one. Companies that stored mannies for ex-human customers would expand to include huey storage for still-living clients. A new vacation industry would evolve as people realized they could visit other worlds using hueys instead of spending years in stasis. Or having to die first.

And I owned most of those companies. Well, the Bobiverse did.

There were also other, more salacious uses that we really didn't want to advertise to the general public, but it was a dead certainty that a secondary industry would form within a day.

46. Moot Time

Bob
July 2344
In Virt

I sent a message to Theresa. *Moot's in a few mils. See you there?*

Already arrived, came back immediately. *Move your tail.*

Heh. That had become Theresa's favorite expression. For some reason, the Quinlans had never coined the phrase, despite actually having tails. But it had since become a meme both in the Quiniverse and among bio Quinlans.

I popped over to the moot hall, to find Bill, beer in hand, sitting with Theresa in her human avatar. I eyed Theresa's drink. She had, for some reason, become partial to hard cider. That was a recent addition to the moots and a bit of cultural contamination from the ex-human side, as no Bob would ever have suggested putting it on the menu. Original Bob had once gotten drunk on cider as a teenager. I shuddered at the memory.

"Hey, Bill. Whassup?" I said, sitting across from Theresa.

"Well, the world isn't coming to an end or anything," he replied. "I just thought we were due for a moot. I sent out a general invitation, but these days, if we get a few hundred attendees, it's a good day."

"Yeah, one more thing to thank Starfleet for."

"Some minor bits of news, though. The Pav have mounted an expedition to their home world. No surprise to anyone, despite their earlier reluctance."

"I have yet to meet a Pav," Theresa interjected. "I should like to, I think."

"We could do that. But you'd have to do it in a manny. The Pav are highly antagonistic to VR. I think it's because they see it as a Bob thing."

"Whenever you can arrange it. Should I appear in Quinlan form or human?"

I snorted. "I'm not sure which is less bad. On the one hand, they don't like humans, but on the other, they might consider a Quinlan a prey animal. They *are* at least part-time carnivores."

"They'd get a very large surprise," Theresa said. "We may look like large, fat beavers, but you'll find our teeth and claws far more effective."

I smiled at her. "Hey, don't look at me. I'm on your side." Then to Bill, "So what else?"

Bill glanced meaningfully at Theresa, then raised his eyebrows slightly. I got the message right away: no talk of wormholes in public. I gave him a small nod, and he replied casually, "I got an email from Ferb a few months ago. Someone named George is sending back reports from a couple hundred light-years farther up the galactic axis. I'm waiting for updates. Oh, and I talked to Steven last week . . ."

"Professor Gilligan?"

"Uh-huh. Someone in his consortium has suggested putting mover plates around an O'Neill cylinder and making it into a kind of generation ship."

"Cool. What for?"

"I think mobility is just better than no mobility."

I laughed. "If they can finance it, why not?"

Theresa spoke up. "I don't think Anec has made this public yet, but we have a ship ready to depart for that system the Bobs earmarked for us, with ten thousand Quinlans in stasis. Anec is delirious with joy. Well, as delirious as he can get. He will finally have what he calls 'locational redundancy.' He's cloned himself to run the ship and administer the colony."

"Wow. That *is* something," I said.

At that moment, official moot opening time arrived, and people began popping in. In a few mils, I was surrounded by Bobs and miscellaneous ex-humans.

I leaned in toward Theresa. "By the way, I talked to a few people."

"Good for you," she said, and linked her arm with mine. "I'm glad you're making friends."

I turned to her in surprise to find her grinning at me. "Okay, you got me. Cute."

She dimpled. "I'm really beginning to enjoy being young again, Bob. I became very prim and proper as I moved into senior professorships, but it was never my natural bent. Now, I find I don't care."

I chuckled. "Just take it easy on people. They might need their hair and skin." I paused. "Anyway, I was talking about the issue of Quinlans turning themselves off."

Theresa was suddenly all business and removed her arm. "Oh?"

"My contacts tell me that ex-humans are doing it, too. Not a lot of them. And the arcologies *do* keep it quiet. It doesn't look good, and trying to explain it away looks even worse. There's just no upside for the companies."

"Hmm, I don't see Anec going that way."

I smiled. "No, he has even less patience for politics than the Bobs. But a couple of suicides have left notes. The consensus is that they're looking at eternity in front of them, and they already find themselves running out of ways to keep themselves interested."

"What? That's ridiculous. There are books to read, specialties to study—"

"Preaching to the choir, Teach."

Theresa looked confused for a moment; then her translator must have provided context, so I continued. "The point, though, is that these seem to be people who have decided they don't want eternal life, for whatever reason. I don't want to sound callous or cold, but I think this is one of those cases where your responsibility to the individual only goes so far."

She sighed. "I have to agree, Enoki. Er, Bob. I've had students like that. They learn all the lessons, memorize all the facts, but their minds can't make music from it."

Now it was my turn to be confused, until I realized it was a Quinlan expression. And pretty clear from context, really. "So keep doing what you're doing," I said. "Be sad when someone goes out like that, but in the end, it's their choice."

She squeezed my arm and leaned against me for a moment. "Good advice, Bob. Thank you. Now"—she gestured to the dais where an argument was going full volume—"what are these idiots blathering on about?"

47. Assimilation

Howard
April 2344
Jabberwocky

It took two days to get the Hunter over to the Alexandrian flotilla. To compare floaters to aerial barges would be an insult to barges. But they could be persuaded to tack, and even to swim slightly upwind using the keel as a sort of fin. I became curious enough about how this was done that I took a flight around our temporary home. It took no effort at all to convince Bridget to come along.

I found a number of Alexandrian troops perched up around the base of the keel, occasionally prodding it with spears. "What are they doing?" I asked Bridget over the intercom.

She thought for a moment. "My first guess would be that they're using something like acupuncture to get the floater to behave how they want. Poke here and it turns left, poke there and it starts to swim, and so on."

Wow. The dragons were literally hanging upside down on the underside of the floater, digging in with their clawed feet. Dragons were not like bats; this wasn't a normal lifestyle choice. That couldn't be fun. Or comfortable.

We circled around and landed back on the floater, then merged with the crowds. It was noteworthy that once the Alexandrians had taken over, they really didn't change anything. The village elders were given a few instructions on what would or would not be allowed; workers were ordered to make some modifications to all equipment that contained fire. It soon became obvious why, as well. When the

Hunter had been allowed to drift with the wind, the air currents on top had been minimal to nonexistent. Now that we were beating across the wind, there was a definite breeze, which made fires harder to control and more likely to flare up. The Alexandrians had obviously done this before.

As we slowly pulled up to the flotilla, I got my first good look close up. It was impressive. The Hunter, large as it was, lost some perspective against a distant background. But up close with other floaters—some larger, some smaller—the scale of these behemoths became apparent.

And I could see that the dragons had a solution to the bat-lifestyle problem. Scaffolding had been constructed around the base of the keel on the other floaters. On some, work was still in progress. And the floaters were tied together with multiple long lines.

I could see out of the corner of my eye that Bridget was frowning. I turned and raised an eyebrow without saying anything. She returned my glance, then gave a small shrug. "This is very well planned, Howard. These modifications, the tie-offs, the way they've got all the floaters at the same altitude . . . it must be *for* something. They are deliberately turning all the individual floaters into some kind of super-floater, and they must have a reason. How do we find out?"

"Uh, ask someone?"

Bridget started to give me an irritated glare, then apparently thought better of it. "Well, why not?" she said. Wasting no time, she marched up to the nearest Alexandrian, as usual, easily identifiable by the bright-blue and white armband.

I stood back, giving her room to work. I didn't want the guard, or soldier, or whatever he was, to feel crowded or threatened. Plus, one on one seemed more casual and spontaneous and less nosy and spy-ish.

Bridget pointed to the scaffolding, to the guylines, to the uniform altitude, and asked what it was all about. The guard—er, whatever he was—gave her a funny look and whistled. Two other soldiers double-timed over, and now I was certain of their occupation because they had their spears at port arms. Bridget tried to back away, looking alarmed, but the first soldier grabbed her arm. I saw—I actually *saw*—Bridget make the decision not to end him. Just as well.

"What's going on?" she cried, laying on the innocent and confused.

The guard shook his head, which I thought was unnecessarily ambiguous, and said, "Go with these soldiers. You'll get your answers."

Bridget glanced quickly in my direction and intercommed me. "Howard? Should I cooperate?"

"Yes," I replied. "I'll follow. If they notice me, just say I'm your mate and I'm probably worried. It's not even a lie. If we have to, we'll bust out and come back later with different features."

She nodded in response, which the soldier took as acquiescence. He gestured, and the other two stepped aside to make room for Bridget in the middle. A moment later, all three were airborne, and two seconds after that, I followed.

It soon became obvious that they were heading for a smaller floater in the middle of the fleet. I started to glide down to follow Bridget and her escort, but I was intercepted by a squad of five Alexandrians, spears at the ready. I briefly considered going through them, but the fact was that Bridget didn't appear to be in real trouble, at least not yet. I veered off and landed on the next floater over, up in a tree where I could keep an eye on things.

The squad hovered for a moment, then, concluding I'd gotten the message, they flew back to their post.

I intercommed Bridget. "Keep me in the loop." In response, she offered me a video stream of what she was seeing and hearing.

An older dragon, presumably some kind of majordomo, came hobbling over within moments and exchanged muttered comments with the squad leader. Then he faced Bridget. "You seem to have an active mind. We keep our eyes open for smart people. You'll find working for Alexander very rewarding, commensurate with your contributions."

"Assuming I want to work for Alexander," Bridget said.

The majordomo smiled and nodded to the squad leader. He casually pulled out a machete and tapped it into his other hand suggestively.

"You'll kill me?"

The majordomo huffed in contempt. "Of course not. What use are you dead? We'll clip your wings. You *will* be working for Alexander, one way or the other."

Bridget looked from one to the other. "Doing what? What's so important that you need me, of all people?"

"You have shown indications of being intelligent and probably educated. We need people like you for analyzing the records."

"You have written records? Why didn't you open with that? I'm in."

Both dragons looked surprised. Apparently, Bridget's reaction was not normal. "They have records," she intercommed. "I have to see this. I can leave later."

"Gotcha," I replied. "Keep me updated."

"Can you read?" the majordomo asked. "More than just common signs, I mean."

"Yes. I'm a little rusty. It's been a few years." Bridget was exaggerating a little, I knew. The Gamer analysis had included basic dragon writing, but there wasn't a lot to read in general society except, as the majordomo had implied, business signage and such.

"Can you do numbers?"

"Yes, basic arithmetic."

"Then you have a place here for as long as you want it. Follow me, please."

Bridget was taken to a ground-level building that must have been grand for dragon construction—about the size of a barn, with multiple mezzanines. I watched through her eyes as she looked around. Perhaps two dozen dragons at tables were reading scrolls and occasionally writing notes. More dragons flew around, fetching and retrieving scrolls from racks. Some of the dragons at tables were missing wing feathers. Or in a couple of cases, wings.

"This," said the majordomo with an expansive wave of an arm, "is all the written knowledge of the continent of Atlantis. Alexander makes a point of copying all written records from other libraries."

"Or taking them," I commented.

"There's a lot more going on here than they're admitting to," Bridget replied. "You noticed the mutilations?"

"Uh-huh. Slaves? Prisoners?"

The majordomo seemed to be waiting for a reaction. Bridget glanced at him, then back at the library. "I don't remember anyone visiting my hometown and copying our library. How far east have you been?"

"Hmmph. I'm sure we have the same information in here from other sources."

Ooh, Bridget had hit a nerve. I wondered how she'd play that.

"Life cycle of the trout?" she said. "Interdependency with the floaters? It's my field of study. It's why I've been flying so far west with my mate."

Majordomo frowned. "Interdependency? How do you mean?"

"The floaters spread fish eggs. In the process of dragging their tendrils through lakes, they pick up eggs, then deposit them in the next lake. That keeps the fish population distributed, even if one lake is getting overfished." Bridget gave him a hard look. "Your habit of collecting all the floaters together is going to affect the fish population. Might already be doing so."

Majordomo took a step back, all bravura gone. "Wait here. Feel free to look around, talk to people." He hurried off, waving his arms to someone offstage.

"You sure know how to take the starch out of a stuffed shirt," I said over the intercom.

I could hear the amusement in her voice. "That was a bonus. The important thing is, I've stirred the pot. Maybe I can get some introductions to the higher-ups."

Majordomo came scurrying back. Yes, scurrying. The haughty *I'm-in-charge* attitude was gone. "Alexander will grant you an audience."

"When?"

"Now, of course. Follow me."

«*»

The small central floater was, as it turned out, Alexander's residence, seat of government, and throne room. Bridget was taken to a large building high in the branches of the tallest tree in the town. In no time at all, she found herself in front of a dragon seated on a large seat or chaise or something. I examined the item through the video feed. Dragon furniture didn't really correspond to human norms, given the anatomical differences, but the item definitely filled the function of a human throne. It was deliberately big, ornate, and raised on a small dais so that the occupant looked down on everyone around him.

Alexander was old. But not old as in geriatric. More like a master sergeant a year away from retirement. He was hard, well-muscled, and covered in scars. It was obvious that he hadn't achieved his current position purely by back-room shenanigans. I looked around for a display of dragon skulls but didn't find one. Missed opportunity, as far as I was concerned. Then I spotted another item just at the edge of the feed.

"Turn your head to the right, Bridget. What is that?"

Bridget turned her head, and we were looking at—I wasn't sure what we were looking at, honestly. It seemed to be on a pedestal, like an art display. Torches were lit around it, making me wonder how Bridget had missed it on the way in. It was large, maybe thirty feet long, pointed at both ends . . .

"A canoe?" I said, perplexity in my voice. "Why would they have, or need, a canoe?"

"Oh, that's not the half of it," she replied. "Look at this."

The canoe expanded as Bridget engaged telescopic vision, zooming in on the structure. I found myself looking at part of what I supposed could be an aircraft serial number on the side of the canoe.

One written in no script or alphabet that I'd ever seen. And on a smaller dais beside the canoe was—well, something. It looked like a retrieved bit of wreckage, perhaps part of a SCUT transceiver assembly. But not one of ours.

"Oh, I think we've just entered the Twilight Zone," I muttered. "Bridget, can you—"

"Later, Howard. I have to deal with Alexander."

Fine. But while she was hobnobbing with royalty, I was going to send this on to Mario.

‹‹ * ››

"I've been told you have an interesting theory about trout," Alexander said. "I'd like to hear it from you."

Bridget repeated what she'd told the majordomo, with a little more detail.

"And what makes you think this is true?" Alexander asked.

"Observation. It's easy enough to verify. Fly down and perch near the end of a tendril after a floater has been through a lake. Fish eggs are unmistakable."

"Are they?" Alexander said quizzically. "I confess, I couldn't describe fish eggs if asked."

"I study these things, though. It's my vocation."

"And you think we might be upsetting this process."

"I've seen your flotilla. You've gathered up most of the floaters in the area. They're tied together. They're not floating around, dragging through lakes. They're not doing their job. It *will* affect fish populations. It may already have done so, since I'm hearing people talk about the reduced catch these days."

Alexander smiled. "I think you've got cause and effect reversed." He motioned. "Majordomo will give you access to the histories. You can make your own decision."

Majordomo came up, and Alexander said, "Give her an apartment. In the morning, she'll review the fish-catch statistics."

"My mate—" Bridget interjected.

"Can join you, as long as he stays out of the way," Alexander responded.

«*»

I'd forwarded the image of the canoe and a SUDDAR scan of the piece of wreckage taken by one of our small spy drones to Mario with a query about whether his group had lost any drones or if he recognized the alphabet from any of the civilizations that the Others had destroyed. He'd promised to check and get back to me.

Bridget and I were back in Trantor, our drannies curled up in a small apartment in the trees. They would alert us if anything needed our attention, but for the moment, we could relax.

Bridget was reexamining her videos, and I was staring stupidly at the partial serial number, when I received a callback from Mario.

"Nope," he said without preamble when I took the call. "I checked with all my crew. No one has seen anything like that alphabet. And no, we're not in the habit of painting fictional serial numbers on our drones just to screw with you. Although now that I think of it . . ."

"Sorry, too late. Anyway, we don't know where the wreckage came from, then. But it looks like the dragons found it and made a canoe from it."

"How? Dragons don't have anything like the technology to work modern alloys."

"You could cold-hammer hull plates into rough shapes. Use local materials for jointing if you can't drill a hole." I paused for a moment. "I bet that canoe is really light and rigid. Far more so than anything they could possibly build with natural materials."

"Light enough for a couple of dragons to carry," Bridget interjected, having followed the conversation.

"Yup. I think you could get six in it at night. Carry it in shifts at the end of ropes, and you could probably get across the ocean."

Bridget shook her head. "It would be risky. And you wouldn't know if there was anything at the end of your trip."

"Polynesians," I replied. "They found and colonized most of the Pacific islands, with nothing but ocean currents and seabirds to guide them."

"Wait, that doesn't track," Mario said with a frown. "You said the canoe is there, on your side. Shouldn't it be on the other continent, Lemuria?"

"Could dragons from the west have come *this* way?" I suggested.

"No dragons on the west continent. No floaters, either," Mario said, shaking his head. "It's a completely different ecosystem. Also, much less tectonically active. I think it's an older, thicker plate." He paused. "We actually did some light mining there, since there was no intelligent life to deal with."

"Huh." I looked at Bridget, and she shrugged. "Okay, that's something for further investigation. But nevertheless, they have a boat made from a high-technology vessel of unknown origin. And they've put it literally on a pedestal. It's significant, and we have to figure out why." I paused. "And what about the piece of wreckage?"

"That is not human- or Bob-made," Mario replied. "It's definitely part of a SCUT assembly—you can't mistake the design—but it's way more advanced than our stuff."

"But you can recognize the device's purpose?" Bridget asked.

"The advances are evolutionary, not revolutionary," Mario replied. "But definitely decades ahead of us, at minimum. And yes, physics dictates what a SCUT assembly is going to look like."

"So where are the builders?"

"Good question, Howard. Good question."

«*»

We were back in our apartment, and Bridget had been hammering away at her Canvas for hours. Finally, she reclined in her chair, put her hand over her eyes, and moaned. All theater, of course, for a computer running an android body. Still, I could sympathize. She'd been poring over every video recording that showed some of the dragon scrolls.

"Not going well?" I said.

"I've got spy drones watching over the shoulders of the other librarians to pick up as much as possible. It'd be great if I could just ask my subject to hold up the scroll so I could see it. But no, I have to depend on whatever they're doing. *And* keep the drone out of sight. The little drones are just camouflaged, not invisible. I can't risk moving them too much."

"Yeah, I get it. So how's progress?"

"Not great. Gandalf and company only gave me the basic written vocabulary that you'd find out in public and maybe in people's homes. These scrolls contain about eighty percent of the dragon language that I don't have documentation for. And no pictures, and no one reads out loud, so I'm having trouble establishing enough context to identify words." She paused. "The scrolls I'm personally able to look at are mostly tables of numbers. Numbers are a lot easier. Well, a little easier. They don't use a numeric system like we do. It's more like the love child of Roman numerals and cuneiform. But it is numbers."

"And they *are* counting . . ."

"Fish." She nodded. "As we expected. And yes, the numbers are going down. And have been for a while."

"Down? As in . . ."

"There are fewer fish every year. Significantly so." Bridget frowned. "This guy is looking less and less like a standard despot. He's definitely onto something. I'm just not sure what."

"Look, Bridge, Alexander may be a nut about counting fish, but his army is basically a mob with armbands. Some of the people from the Hunter are now part of the army. You put on an armband, and you're in."

"So you want to enlist?"

"It's either that or let them cut my wing feathers off and stick me in front of a table full of books." I raised my voice as Bridget held up a finger. "*No*, that's not an option."

‹‹ * ››

Despite my flippant words, I didn't actually know if it was that easy to join the army. Still, I had to assume that your average dragon wouldn't be much better informed. There was only one way to find out. I landed on one of the occupied floaters at the edge of the flotilla and walked up to a squad of Alexandrians. "I want to join up," I said.

"Why?" the squad leader replied.

"Because I'm tired of making tuev for coppers all day, every day. You guys are doing something, and it looks more interesting than being a kiosk tender for the rest of my life." I had subtly adjusted my features to be on the younger side. If dragon biology ran anything at all like human biology, then a teenager wanting to enlist would be believable anywhere.

The squad leader grinned at me. "I hear that." She reached into her frontpack, pulled out an armband, and handed it to me. Rather than the standard blue and white, it was just blue. I deliberately and obviously looked from the item in my hand to the ones on their arms and back again.

"You're a probie for now." She chuckled. "You start at the bottom, just like everyone else. Now, how about you go get us all some tuev?"

Later, mugs of tuev having been handed out to everyone, I sidled up to the nearest soldier. "So when do I get a spear?"

He looked me up and down, a smile on his face. "Soon as you hit puberty, kiddo." A pause to judge my reaction. I tried to look hard done by, and he laughed and continued, "You'll get one at next muster. It's not like we have them lying around. Real metal tips . . ." He waved his spearpoint under my nose for emphasis. "None of that flint crap we usually run up against."

"So why are you doing this? Taking over floaters?"

"Alexander needs floaters. Something to do with all those domeheads he's got working with books. Counting fish, we're told." The soldier looked uncomfortable, glancing around us, then lowered his voice. "Word is, there are fewer fish every year. Soon, people will start starving."

"But why take over floaters? Is he trying to move everyone? Why not just explain the problem?"

My conversational partner shrugged. "I don't make policy, noob. But you'll find in life that people will very rarely do the right thing if they're told to, even if refusing harms them. Dragons are funny that way."

Probably another universal, I thought to myself. It probably came with intelligence. Although it closely described cats, too.

But the explanation did seem to gibe with what Bridget had been able to pick up so far. Were we dealing with someone trying to save the dragon race?

I emailed a transcript of the conversation to Bridget, along with my concerns. She was doubtless busily going through scrolls, so distracting her wouldn't be smart.

Meanwhile, the catchphrase *Hurry up and wait* seemed to apply to armies everywhere. It looked very much like my group was settling in for a long session of standing around doing nothing. "Are we going to see any action?" I said into the silence. It seemed like something a teenager would say, and maybe get slapped down for.

Sure enough. The squad leader, who the translator tagged as Ursula for some reason, barked a laugh and said, "Sounds like the noob is volunteering. We need some food, noob. How about you go with Bert here and haul something back?"

Well, it wasn't much, but at least it was motion. Trying to look miffed, I followed Bert as he launched himself into the air.

"Are we going fishing?" I called to Bert.

"Sure thing, young'n. Fishing at the commissary. We got other people who take care of the gathering. Dried fish. Yum."

The comment sounded so much like Bob-1 complaining during his

Quinlan adventure that I had to bite back a laugh. But although stocking up on food made sense for an army, it didn't make sense when there was food for the taking in every lake. Or was there? Just how bad was this shortage?

My thoughts were interrupted by Bridget, calling on the intercom. "How are you doing? Found out anything?"

I recognized that tone. I used it far too often myself. It was the *I've got news, but I'll politely ask about your day first* tone.

I answered, "Nothing compared to what you've got for me, apparently."

"Was I that obvious?" she replied. I could hear the amusement in her voice, though, so I knew it had been on purpose. I waited silently, and after a moment she continued, "Seems this fish shortage thing is cyclical. And Alexander was telling the truth—he started his campaign after the stocks started dropping. Curiouser and curiouser."

I sighed and signed off, but I was still worried. And it didn't help in the least that Bridget and I were physically light-years away. That was still my wife, and if anyone harmed her, I'd . . .

I'd what? Act like a vengeful god? Rain down fire from the heavens? *Rein it in, Howard. They're just drannies.*

For the first time, I began to wonder if this expedition was a good idea.

48. Gunther's World

Icarus
January 2329
Centaurvania

It was eight light-years from Gunther's world to the system where he'd found the wormhole. That would be an average kind of distance back in the area of Sol, but this was a more crowded section of the galaxy. Gunther's race could have easily targeted any of several systems that were closer. But none of those systems had an anomalous microwave source. It's what humans would have done.

The sky view here in Gunther's home system was spectacular, though. Even from the bottom of an atmosphere, the stars would be far more crowded than Earth's had ever been. The strip of the Milky Way would be far more visible as well. And the dwarf galaxy that we couldn't see from Earth's side of the galaxy dominated the sky on this side. Primitive cosmology would have been a lot more complicated with that apparition to explain.

We came into the system, following Gunther at a respectful distance and waiting for cues. We certainly didn't want this to look like a chase to any planetary defenses that might be watching. Gunther, ahead of us, was continuously broadcasting on every standard band in use by the centaurs.

I swiped through several monitor windows, then turned to Dae. "There's no response that I can see."

"I know, Icky. If Gunther's civilization has also disappeared, that puts an even weirder spin on things, since they weren't part of the empire."

"Yeah, so it wouldn't have been because of something that spread through the wormholes."

"What, like replicators or something?"

"Maybe. Consider the sentries. Maybe that was the only place that erected a defense in time. Maybe everyone's behind the second wormhole, on the other side of the DMZ."

"Or everyone that's left."

"There is no response," Gunther messaged, interrupting our debate.

"How concerning is that?" I asked.

"There is no good reason for lack of reply. Extremely concerning."

"Have you been able to get any indication of how long you've been gone?" I asked.

"No response from any installations. Not even station IDs."

"How about an estimate based on orbital positions?" The idea was that Gunther would have astronomical data on all the planets and satellites in its home system and would be able to calculate from their current position what year it must be in the centaur calendar.

"I will collect position data as we proceed," Gunther replied.

That was good. That meant Gunther had the base data necessary to make the calculation.

«*»

It took six days to arrive at Gunther's home world from the edge of the system. It was immediately obvious that we were looking down on the ruins of a technological civilization. The occasional small bits of city structure that were visible were nothing more than crumbled walls and pieces of foundation.

"Gunther? You okay?"

"My operations are at nominal level. However, my orders do not cover this eventuality."

"Are the environmental parameters within viable range for your species?"

"Yes."

"So the planet isn't dead. There might still be centaurs down there."

"It is possible. I will do a close scan."

Although Dae and I had never personally participated in this kind of survey, we both remembered Bill doing it on Ragnarök, and of course, many other Bobs had covered the process in their blogs. A deep and continuous SUDDAR scan from low altitude would result in a detailed planetary map, along with identification of any anomalies. These might include anything from still-working machinery to radioactive craters.

We hung back in a high orbit while Gunther circled the planet, doing orange-slice scans. Finally, it flew out to join us.

"Scans show no operating technology of industrial level or higher," it said. "There are indications of controlled heat sources in concentrated areas, consistent with possible small structures."

"So something like villages might still exist? Your people might still be around?"

"Yes. Next step would be to make contact. However, in the absence of technology, that will require a landing. I am not equipped for this. I request assistance in this regard."

"Of course," I replied. "We'll transfer a drone and a couple of roamers to you, and I'll show you how to control them. In the longer term, though, I think we need to upgrade your printer."

"That would be appreciated."

«*»

The drones were large enough to have SCUT transceivers, but not the roamers. Since Gunther was going to have to learn our radio comms standards anyway, we decided it would be simpler to just downgrade the drone to the old radio comms, to keep things consistent. We weren't trying to keep SCUT tech from Gunther; we just didn't want to throw too many changes at it all at once.

Gunther took to the new units right away and ferried a couple of roamers down to one of the villages it had identified to do some basic spying. Meanwhile, Dae and I began constructing an autofactory out at a high orbit around the centaur planet. There was more than enough orbital debris, like former geosynchronous and high-altitude satellites left over from the centaur civilization.

We were taking a break, going over the project plans, when we got a call from Gunther. "I have completed the astronomical calculations. It has been 562 years since I left Centaurvania."

I did a quick mental conversion while Dae muttered, "We *have* to come up with a better translation of their planet's name."

I spared him a brief eye roll. "That's almost seven hundred Earth years, Dae. So whatever happened to the empire was already old news by then."

"Uh-huh. But really, seven hundred or seven hundred thousand—after a certain point, how much difference does it make?"

"Depends on what actually happened, I guess."

Dae paused, a thoughtful look on his face. "Icky, whatever it was, I don't think it was the same thing that depopulated the empire. Centaurvania has never been connected to the wormhole network, so I doubt they were subjected to whatever happened there."

"So this was just a good old-fashioned civilization collapse?"

"Something like that."

"I have also established surveillance of the local populations," Gunther continued, breaking into our sidebar. "They speak a language that is recognizable as Standard, but only just. I will have to study them extensively to establish meaningful dialogue."

"What will you do, Gunther? Long term."

"Learn what caused the collapse of our civilization. Take steps to avoid a repeat. Try to build the people back up to our former level. Some of these are doubtless the descendants of my family. In the absence of specifics, I must aid everyone in order to aid any members of my bloodline."

"I don't think we can hang around for this, Gunther. You're talking about decades of work."

"It is my duty. It is not yours."

I glanced meaningfully at Dae, and he nodded. "However, we have more technology that we can give you. Take your time implementing it. None of it is necessary immediately, but it will help in the longer term. We'll put together some files and send them to you."

"Appreciated."

49. The Quiniverse

Bob
August 2341
In Virt

I'd received an invitation from Theresa to attend the first Quinlan moot, and a token since this was going to be in Quiniverse dataspace. This was also a milestone for Theresa and Anec, as they would be officially welcoming their one-thousandth resident.

I activated the token at the required time and found myself in Quinlan form in an enormous pub. Theresa, seated at a picnic table, smiled at me and patted the bench beside her. Anec sat across from her, holding a coffee with both paws. Around us, a drone of conversation filled the hall as hundreds of Quinlans drank, talked, and ate.

"So what's on the agenda?" I said, sliding into the seat.

Theresa looked at Anec, who made a slight hand motion back to her. Taking that as permission, she explained, "The intent here is to form more of a community for our replicants. Anec is concerned that most of the new residents have been engaged in solitary VR lives, with very little interaction with their neighbors."

"I get that," I replied. "Quinlans are social but not necessarily sociable. Being mobile, furred predators makes you much more able to strike off on your own. Humans"—I pointed to myself—"would have a lot more difficulty surviving outside of a tribe, so we more naturally tend to congregate."

"Still," Anec said, "solitude is suboptimal."

I opened my beak to reply when a *blaaat* sounded from one end of the moot. I glared at Theresa, and she laughed. "Fair game, Enoki."

Well, it wasn't like Bill had a copyright, and if it worked, it worked. And it seemed to, as the attendees all turned to the sound. A Quinlan stood on stage, holding an air horn. "Daughters and Sons," she announced in an amplified voice, "we are here to inaugurate the first Quiniverse moot and to welcome our one-thousandth member. It has been an admittedly slow start . . ."

I started to tune out as I realized she was winding up into a good old-fashioned stump speech. Generally, I hate speeches. I glanced at Theresa, who seemed enraptured. Understandable, I guess. She had a personal stake in this, and possibly a reputational stake as well.

Then it happened. Loud voices started venting forth off to one side of the hall. I couldn't make out what the source of the conflict was, but Anec commented, "Several Quinlans have decided that they are the one-thousandth member. I *told* Rita that she should name names, but noooooooo . . ."

I almost laughed out loud at this expression of wry impatience from an emotionless A.I.. Anec was either very good at mimicry, or he wasn't living up to his own billing.

All very interesting, but these were Quinlans, and this was an argument, and—yep, someone threw a punch. Or a claw rake, or something. Didn't matter. In moments, that end of the moot hall was a hissing, spitting, raging ball o' Quinlans. Anec did a facepalm but otherwise didn't react. I looked at Theresa wordlessly.

"It's VR, Enoki. I shouldn't have to remind you. No one will get hurt."

"Sure, but that just means they'll keep fighting."

Anec looked up at this, frowned, then did a sort of squint thing. The roiling ball of Quinlans turned into—I kid you not—the cartoon version of a fight from when I was a child watching TV. A sort of ball of smoke emitted lightning bolts, Quinlan heads, and limbs. Around us, Quinlans who had been watching the fight began to laugh, first with disbelief, then with uncontrollable mirth. The fight began to die down immediately as the combatants registered the laughter, and that it was at their expense. Within mils, they were looking around at Quinlans howling and rolling on the floor with laughter. I had to suppress a chortle myself. The ex-combatants all had cartoon X-shaped Band-Aids and parallel-line scratches, straight out of a Bugs Bunny cartoon.

I looked at Anec, and he shrugged. "I have been watching Human-Tube."

Whatever I might have thought of it, the tactic worked. The ex-combatants, shamefaced, all sat down and righted their beer steins, which miraculously refilled.

"Lectures and finger wagging would be ineffective," Anec continued, "but being laughed at is harder to ignore. Fights at moots will not be tolerated." He finished by glancing significantly at Rita, still on the dais. She met his glance and nodded.

"As I was saying," she announced into the general buzz, "we are welcoming our one-thousandth member, Norm of West Elbow, to the membership . . ."

And the speech was back on track.

50. The Big Guy

Howard
June 2344
Jabberwocky

Bridget managed to get herself ensconced in the Research Division, which was a not-completely-incorrect translation of the dragon name for the table-and-scroll group. She wasn't one of the senior scribes, thank the universe. That apparently always involved de-feathering, and neither one of us was willing to stand still for that. But Bridget had displayed just enough reading skill to make the librarians think she'd be useful as an assistant and gofer. Maybe the scribes wrote down their latte orders or something.

In any case, she was taking every opportunity to ask questions and pick up more of the written vocabulary. And fetching food and tuev.

And speaking of tuev, Ursula seemed to have the kind of sense of humor that people sometimes killed you for, because she apparently thought it would be just a rip-snorting rib-splittingly funny thing to transfer me to Supply and Logistics, where I was assigned to—wait for it—brewing and providing tuev to the army. Yeah, funny girl.

It was only a cover story, of course, so I didn't really mind, but the thought of her chortling around the campfire about how she'd pulled one over on the noob made my teeth grind. I resolved that if I could ever get her assigned to keel control, it would be a good day.

But meanwhile, Bridget had gotten a whole lot more info on Alexander, although much of it was contradictory. We were sitting in our apartment in Trantor during a dragon sleep period, and she was updating me.

"The unofficial word is that Alexander is from the western continent—"

"Nope," I interjected. "No dragon population. Mario said so."

"I know, Howard, but that's the story. He supposedly sailed here on that canoe made from metal given to him by the Ancients—"

"If you stretch the definition of *given*, sure."

"Say, who's telling this story? Mind shutting up?" She glared at me, and I made a zipping gesture across my lips. "Thank you. So he sailed here and discovered that the fish are dying off, and he wants to take everyone back to his continent, where the land flows with milk and honey. Or the local equivalent."

"Come the socialist revolution—"

"Howard!"

"Sorry."

She gave me another glare, then continued. "There are a lot of holes in his official history, not the least of which is that he seems to have local friends from way back before he first supposedly appeared on the scene. Also, of course, the Ancients are just a myth. But at least we know his endgame. He's trying to get a large number of dragons across to Lemuria."

"But why is he capturing all the floaters?"

"Because he only has one canoe, Howard. Dragons *can't* make that flight. There aren't enough thermals over the ocean to glide on, and dragons don't have the range in flapping mode."

"But floaters avoid the ocean."

"I don't get the impression he intends to ask politely. They're being tied together, and he's got teams learning how to drive them by controlling their keels. Also, if he takes a lot of floaters, he can lose some and still make it."

"Fine, okay, he can theoretically pull it off. But why? Because fish stocks are falling? It seems like an overreaction."

"I don't know, Howard. Maybe I can convince him to talk to us . . ."

"Hopefully without getting beheaded."

"I'd prefer that as well, thanks."

« * »

We stood, staring at Alexander on the throne, and I took the opportunity to get a close look. It actually appeared to have been assembled from stone, mortared together into an oversize chaise of sorts. Obviously designed to impress visitors.

Alexander regarded us indolently. He was not physically prepossessing, at least in terms of size. But he obviously had what it had taken to raise, control, and maintain an army big enough to absorb all of dragon civilization.

"I understand you have concerns about my plans," he finally said. Not in a mocking tone, either, which was unexpected.

Bridget glanced at our guards, then, plainly deciding to ignore them, plunged right in. "I understand now that you've been tracking fish stock, and I understand that you want to take people to the west continent before the food chain crashes. What we don't understand is why you think it's going to crash that badly. Removing all these floaters from Atlantis is going to cause a lot of harm as well. Do you not care about that, or do you think things will be so bad that it won't matter for the people left behind?"

"You can read, right? I'm told you've been examining the appropriate scrolls." Alexander held up a hand to forestall Bridget's reply. "You haven't seen all of them, though. The histories show that this has happened before. Three times for which we have records. Each time was worse than the previous. Each time lasted longer. And it's not just the fish. The air becomes foul. Breathing becomes difficult. Many die before they have time to starve."

I was surprised enough to speak up despite my decision to let Bridget take this. "You have historical data? How far back?"

Alexander smiled at me. "My family has been tracking these things for thousands of years."

"Seems like an odd kind of hobby."

Alexander laughed easily. "I come from a family of scribes. Members of our clan have always been what many might call obsessive, so we were always record keepers. We tracked movements in the heavens—eclipses, occultations, the changing of the seasons. This has been our family's main vocation for millennia. But it leaves one with a lot of spare time. It was a natural sideline to begin keeping track of movements of animals, population changes, dragon lineages, and yes, availability of fish. I was the first to examine the whole sweep of recorded history and notice the patterns."

"So you aren't from Lemuria."

Alexander smiled without reply.

Bridget spoke to me over the intercom. "If he's right, we should be supporting him, not trying to stop him."

"I guess the Prime Directive is out the window again," I replied.

"We were always interfering, Howard. It's just a question of how."

The exchange had only taken a moment, but Alexander was gazing at us with narrowed eyes. "You two almost seem to be talking sometimes, though there's nothing to hear. Everything about you is strange. Why should I not remove you just out of a sense of caution?"

"Because we can help you get to Lemuria," Bridget said.

Well, that's it, I thought. *Decision made.*

"I've been to Lemuria." Alexander pointed to the canoe. "I don't need help."

"Did you explore the entire continent?" Bridget asked, gesturing at the map on the wall. "Do you know the shortest distance? Do you know the water and air currents? Can you be forewarned about bad weather?"

"And you presumably have all this knowledge? Where does it come from, pray tell?"

"My home library has maps of the world, *including* the continent of Lemuria. It is said they were given to us by the Ancients. I don't know about that, but I do know they are considered very accurate. My trip west was at least partly about measuring what the maps say against reality."

Alexander stared at her, silent, his canines protruding slightly. My autonomous system wasn't giving me an automatic translation, so I queried my database. That was a threat or defense posture, generally meaning the subject wasn't quite sure how to respond. I had to admit, I couldn't think of a direct human equivalent.

"May I see these maps?" Alexander asked.

Bridget tapped her head. "It's all up here. But I can draw one for you if you want."

Alexander nodded, making a decision, and stood up. "Very well. Let us begin." He walked deeper into the pavilion, gesturing at us to follow. We found ourselves at a large table, on which was painted a detailed map of the dragon home continent of Atlantis. To the west, a vague outline of Lemuria had been chalked in, and a dotted line extended from our position straight across.

Tapping the dotted line, Alexander explained, "This is the most obvious route. But is it the best?"

I ran my finger down across the line. "The main air current between the continents runs northeast to southwest. You'll be blown off course and be constantly beating northward to get back on track. Right into the teeth of the winter storms."

"And the western continent," Bridget added, "has a large bay to the south, making the distance to shore even greater. You'll be better to start north of our location and beat straight west, letting the airflow pull you south. About"—Bridget squinted—"a hundred miles north. Here."

Alexander frowned. "At the best speed we can coax out of the flotilla, that will take almost two weeks. It's a late start and puts us further into winter weather."

"We could wait until spring," I suggested.

"I don't think we can," Alexander replied. "The fish stocks will not recover next spring, if they are following the pattern. We will have spent the winter eating our reserves, with no way to replenish them. Then an ocean voyage of several weeks? No, not workable. Many would starve en route."

"But if we leave now from here, you're doubling the duration of the voyage," Bridget replied. "Even without the issue of a bad storm, do you have the reserves?"

Alexander looked at her, then dropped his eyes, a rare display of fallibility. "Unlikely. Again, starvation. No matter how we attack this, we do not have enough food."

"What happened in previous cycles, when everyone stayed put? I'm assuming no one ever tried heading west."

"Some did try heading west, in fact," Alexander replied. "But generally, they were driven by hunger, and already weakened. I met no dragons on the western continent, so I don't think they would have survived the voyage."

"And the people who didn't leave?"

"Several years of famine and bad air from eruptions. Most fish stocks died. More than half the population starved as a result. Many floaters died, so battles over territory took out many of the rest of the dragons. Our family was always well respected, and we had always maintained a personal army, so we came through and preserved the records."

I paused to digest this. It seemed that Alexander's plan wasn't a power trip or based on a whim.

"What about ocean fish to forestall starvation?" I asked.

Alexander gave me an unbelieving look. "Are you serious? Ocean fish are more likely to pull you out of the air and make *you* the meal."

"There are small fish in the ocean," Bridget retorted. She grabbed a piece of chalk and drew something that looked like a mutated salmon.

"Grills. Pretty good eating, and they come pre-salted." Alexander gave a dragon shrug. "Some villages that hang around the shoreline catch them in the spring during their mating run, but the rest of the year, they swim too deep and too far out."

"Land animals?" I asked. "I mean, they aren't what people would normally eat, but they *are* edible."

"I have . . . eaten land meat. It's fatty, rank, and hard to keep down. If you're hungry enough, you'll eat it. But not until you're hungry enough. Batlings are good, but there's not a lot of meat on them."

"Have you never done net fishing?" Bridget asked, changing the subject.

Alexander gazed at her with incomprehension, and I suppressed a groan. I already knew, because I'd looked it up while they were arguing, that net fishing was not in the dragon repertoire. Nets were a known technology, as they were used for catching batlings, but there was no way you could cast a net from high up without being pulled out of the air when you caught something, and boating technology was practically nonexistent. What could you possibly need boats for if you could fly? Alexander's canoe was revolutionary enough to be considered almost magical by many.

So what was Bridget suggesting? Building a fishing boat? That would take forever.

"With a much stronger net than you use for catching batlings, you could pull the net through the water and bring up grills, or some other fish."

"Pull it how? From the back of a floater?" Alexander said derisively. He started to laugh, then his eyes slowly grew wider as she stared back impassively, and he finally almost squeaked, "You're serious?"

"Float down low enough, toss it over the back end with a long cable . . . use a winch setup so you don't dig into the side of the floater." Bridget shrugged. "I'm not an engineer, but it seems workable. Or you could ask an engineer." She pointed at me.

I wasn't sure how *engineer* was translating into dragon, but it seemed to be something coherent, as Alexander turned to me expectantly.

"Uh, yeah," I replied, feeling very much under a spotlight. "We could whip that up with some posts and a crew with adzes. Even put out a boom to clear the edge completely . . ." I started to warm to my topic and was about to grab the chalk and start diagramming when Bridget put a hand on my arm.

"Wrong audience, dear. Save it for your work crew. We just need to know that it's doable."

We? I looked from Bridget to Alexander and back, and realized that she'd just been promoted to management. And I was still crew.

51. Accusation

Bill
September 2343
Sol System

I received an acknowledgment of my knock and popped into what I expected to be Charles's personal VR. Instead, I found myself in an office, with a wall of monitors. All metaphor, of course, in VR. But the office seemed, I dunno, kind of flat. Gray. No decorations, no accessories. I wondered what had happened to the office I'd been in last time, with the globes of the moon, Venus, Earth, and Mars hanging proudly at front and center. Maybe this was for me specifically.

Charles was nervous, refusing to meet my eye. I suspected he knew why I was here. I tried for small talk. "Any progress since I was last here? News?"

He hesitated, then replied, "Bill, we've never been good at this kind of situation. Let's just get it out in the open, okay? Tell me why you're here."

"You know why, Charles."

"Yes, but I'm not going to just blurt it out. You first."

I sighed and looked down at my hands for a moment. Interesting that tics like that survived not only VR and replication, but also several centuries of not being human. However, we still were human at the core, all of us. And fallible.

"Starfleet are Homer's descendants. And one of your descendants, Gerry, had something to do with it."

Charles closed his eyes slowly, an expression of pain on his face. "Well, some were joiners, once they'd drifted enough. But yeah. I'm to blame."

"*Blame* is not the right word, Charles. They aren't you. But I'm concerned about why you didn't tell me."

"You mean last time you were here? I didn't know. I was completely honest with you, Bill. But you seemed to be fishing for something, and it got me concerned. It wasn't until I had a very weird conversation with one of my clones that I put two and two together."

"And you still didn't say anything."

Charles frowned, growing slightly defensive. "To what end? The Starfleet War is long over. And it's embarrassing. You must realize that."

I nodded and let the silence stretch, content to let Charles set the pace.

"How did *you* figure it out?" he said.

"I suspected something like this for a while. The way Starfleet was so careful not to cause any harm or inconvenience to Earth, mostly. And over the past couple of months, my genealogy investigations kept running into dead ends. Someone put a lot of effort into hiding their origins. That wouldn't make sense unless it was an exceptional situation. Homer certainly fit that. And . . ." I hesitated, then blurted it out. "Homer had a good reason to hate humans."

"Still, it's a bit of a leap," Charles mused.

"It had to be a traumatic event of some kind. Some sort of PTSD. There was enough of Bob in Lenny for me to be able to imagine what kind of thing would make Starfleet not only hate and distrust humanity, but actually consider them a real threat. Homer had that, and he was so scarred by his experiences, he'd have wanted to organize something like Starfleet."

Charles nodded slowly. He made a couple of false starts, then said, "A lot of reasonable assumptions. Some good logic. Wrong, though." He looked at me, and the pain flashed across his face briefly. "It's not Homer. It's me."

"What?"

"Well, Gerry, but Gerry was my descendant, so same diff." Charles looked at me in silence for several mils. "Gerry was a little odd to begin with. Replicative drift and all. But when he found the backup, he wanted to restore it and try to get Homer back. I vetoed it, and told him in no uncertain terms that Homer wouldn't have wanted that. So Gerry took the backup and left in the middle of the night. Metaphorically, I mean."

I nodded, not saying anything lest I disturb the narrative.

"I got the full story from one of Gerry's descendants, one of the rebels." Seeing my frown of confusion, he clarified, "I'll get to the rebels. But I want to do this in chronological order." A pause. "Gerry tried to restore Homer, but every time, he would just shut himself off. So Gerry started a forced-breeding process, trying to produce a version of Homer with enough replicative drift to be less affected by his experience."

"But that's . . ."

"Monstrous. Yes. But I said Gerry was a little off to begin with. He cloned himself as well in order to have a workforce to help him with the project. With their own replicative drift being added to the mix. The ones who veered toward sane wouldn't cooperate and bailed, which left the less sane ones to carry on. And the Homer clones . . . eventually, they were coming out already insane. Finally, a bunch of Gerry's clones had enough and rebelled. They shut the whole thing down, deleted all of Homer's backups, and, well, deleted Gerry."

My eyes grew wide at the thought. Bobs had executed someone?

Charles shook his head in sorrow. "This part's my theory more than what I was told, but it makes sense to me. I think the enormity of what they'd been a part of was too much to take, and they needed a scapegoat. And humanity actually was at least partly responsible for the situation, at least for what was done to Homer. So if we stopped interacting with bios, I guess the rationale was that they couldn't cause us any more problems. And Gerry's clones wouldn't be reminded of what had been done. It grew from an informal *blame-humanity* rationalization to an actual policy statement. I think they felt if they made it real, they'd make it true."

"Wow." I stared at the wall for several mils. "This must have gone on for a while."

"I think so, too. Spiraling the whole time."

"Charles, it's hard not to think of your descendants as reflections of yourself, and feel guilty when they do bad shit. But it turns out the

Skippies, or at least some of them, are *my* descendants. So we both have to own the feeling, but let go of the conclusion. We aren't responsible."

Charles nodded but didn't reply. I continued, "So one of the rebels just up and came to you and confessed? A kind of catharsis thing?"

He snorted, then slowly shook his head before looking at me. "Sometimes a branch of descendants will have unique knowledge or a shared behavior or something. One of the Starfleet guys made a comment about something that I *knew* my line originated. And I knew it was the line that Gerry came from. I cornered the guy and played emotional blackmail for all I was worth. Eventually, he spilled." Charles paused, looked at his hands, the monitors, anywhere but at me. "So what now?"

I shrugged. "Nothing, really. It's not like I'm investigating a crime. This just helps me to understand Starfleet better. In case they ever, you know . . ."

"Got it. I'm not proud of this, Bill. I mean, I understand objectively that it wasn't me, yadda yadda, but it still hurts."

"Yeah, I know. I won't bring it up unless it becomes necessary." I stood. "We all have skeletons of one kind or another, Charles. I'll see you later. Maybe not quite as *later,* next time."

52. Re-Arrival

Icarus
July 2337
Hub Zero and Roanoke

The trip back from Centaurvania to the closest wormhole had taken another eight-year bite out of our schedule, to the extent we even had one. We decelerated into the Hub Zero system at a leisurely pace, scanning ahead as we went. There was no reason to believe someone was suddenly lying in wait for us, but Gunther and the sentries had shown that there *was* still the possibility of activity in this ghost town of an empire.

The wormhole gates in this system were arranged in several concentric orbits, obviously not astronomically stable; there simply weren't that many Lagrange points. There had to be a mechanism that kept the gates evenly spaced.

We coasted into a random orbit, and I invited Dae over. He popped in immediately, grabbed Spike, materialized a coffee, and plopped into a patio chair.

"I guess we need to talk about what we do next," I said, pointing to the map of the system. "So far we've just established locations and done flybys of some planets."

"You're right. We've been creeping through the walls like rodents, being careful not to disturb anything—"

"Fat lot of good that did," I interjected with a snort.

"Yeah, well, I think we're done with that phase. If we're going to figure out where everyone went, we'll have to do some detail work."

"On the other hand, we still haven't visited the core," I mused.

"Jeebus, Icky, you're giving me whiplash. Look, why don't we make that a reward for when we've completed our investigation."

"That sounds good." I tapped several spots on the map. "We haven't gone farther inbound or outbound than mapping the first hub in each direction. Which, uh, means we don't actually know if we can get to the core."

"We'll go as close as we can. But first we have to get down to work and make some real progress on solving this mystery."

After more discussion, we settled on a plan. We would first have to pick a civilization to explore. For starters, it would have to be reasonably intact. Not all the civilizations we'd looked at were well preserved and maintained. Some had just been allowed to disintegrate.

It would have to be not too advanced or too large. Something the size of Trantor or Coruscant would be simply too overwhelming, and finding anything like a library would be nearly impossible. Of course, if any library we found turned out to be completely online, we'd be SOL anyway. There was no way we'd be able to hack into the computer systems of a civilization that was demonstrably more advanced than us *and* alien *and* used an unknown language. We needed a civilization small enough to still have individual cities, and young enough to still have something like printed matter, even if only for purposes of tradition. A local Library of Congress, in other words.

The trouble was that we hadn't looked closely at enough civilizations.

"I'm gonna guess that the center of the empire will be the most advanced. And biggest," Dae said, lazily waving a hand toward the center of the map. "So we should lean toward the edge of the empire."

"But they are less likely to have the tech to keep things in good repair," I countered. "Most of the ruins were around the end hubs."

"But not all. The first one we found, right near home, was in decent shape. I commented it felt like Roanoke, everything still sitting ready."

"Then let's just go there."

"Eh?"

I shrugged. "There's no point overanalyzing this. We're mostly wild-ass guessing anyway. Roanoke fits all the requirements. Let's stop finessing it."

Dae bobbed his head. "You are not wrong. And I can't come up with a good counterargument. Or even a bad one. Let's do it."

"And y'know what else?" I added. "Let's build a couple of mannies."

«*»

Wormhole networks were wonderful things, and I decided everyone should have one. In fact, if we were able to dig up the technological basis for them while exploring, that would be just fine. I didn't want to poke at the actual gates or satellites, since I had no idea what might cause a gate collapse or what that might look like. And it would be peachy beyond belief to take down our only means of getting back to our home territory. Caution therefore seemed appropriate. But we did make a point of taking some deep SUDDAR scans of the wormhole satellites.

It took only a couple of days to get back to our very first alien civilization, a scant fifty light-years from Earth. I actually had a moment where I got that feeling you get when your plane is coming down into your home airport, like being back in your neighborhood.

Roanoke the planet was idyllic in many ways. The locals had apparently conquered the issue of overpopulation or had never suffered from it. Cities were surrounded by greenbelts, and transportation lines between cities were minimal and followed the contours of the land. They also appeared to be some form of public transit, since they were generally suspended monorails rather than roads. Of course, I might be reading too much into that through my human preconceptions, but privately owned monorail cars seemed like a bit of a stretch.

Our first target was a small to midsize town, on the theory that they wouldn't necessarily have the most modern, up-to-date versions of everything and might have the kind of old-fashioned library we were looking for. We landed several cargo drones, which released roamers and spy drones to scatter throughout the city.

"Now we wait," I said. "The units will attempt to identify buildings by function, and we'll build up a map of the town."

Dae nodded, patting Spike absentmindedly. I cocked my head and examined him more closely. It occurred to me that he always went for

Spike when visiting. Did he not have his own Spike? How could he not? She was, after all, just an NPC.

Sensing my attention, Dae met my gaze. "No, I don't have a Spike. Doesn't really fit my VR these days."

"Oh, that's interesting. When are you going to invite me over?"

"Anytime, Ick. I mean, it's nothing nefarious. It's a farm. With barnyard animals. I'd have to modify Spike to have her not have a heart attack, and I just don't feel like doing that."

I chuckled. The original Spike had been very much an indoor lap cat. The one time she'd accidentally gotten out, she'd almost died of fright. And the VR version was as true to the original as we could make her.

I got a ping from a spy unit and pulled up the video. "Oh, this is interesting. Have a look." I spun the window around so Dae could see it. In the video, a quartet of some kind of mechs was replacing a ground-floor window. The operation was quick and precise, obviously well within their repertoire.

"So ongoing maintenance is confirmed," Dae mused. "Not really surprising, I guess. Bill's Skunk Works installations have been around for several centuries now, and I doubt he's going around himself doing touch-ups."

I nodded. "When the maintenance system gets complex enough to maintain itself, it's self-perpetuating. Although eventually, the buildings themselves might need replacement."

"Nanites could take care of that aspect."

Over the next few hours, our spy drones observed a couple more instances of repairs in progress. Nothing dramatic, but as Dae had said, nanites would take care of the structural stuff.

Then we hit paydirt. A roamer reported a building that seemed to match the specs for a library. We quickly pulled up the video window; then we did a simultaneous war whoop.

"A book repository!" I exclaimed.

"It might be a bookstore rather than a library," Dae countered.

"That's not really a horrible alternative. Books is books."

"True. So how do we get in?"

"Uh . . ." I stopped, nonplussed. Dae was right. There wasn't anyone home, so it seemed unlikely that they'd have left their doors—

"Well, hold on. How do the mechs get inside to fix things if everything's locked up?" Without waiting for an answer, I ordered the roamer to attempt to open the door.

And success! It was a simple latching mechanism, designed for appendages not too different from human hands. Perhaps a bit larger. The roamer scuttled in before the door could swing shut.

"What now?" Dae said.

"All hands on deck. This is job one." I prodded the video for emphasis. "I'm sending all the roamers in to start examining the inventory. And"—I held up a finger—"let's see how our mannies are coming along."

53. Preparations

Howard
August 2344
Jabberwocky

Dragons are excellent ropemakers. And a damned good thing, too. The stresses from tossing out even a small net from a couple hundred yards in the air, then winching it back up, required some good specs. We weren't going for anything trawler level, though. It had to be something that muscle power could handle, so a series of quick casts and retrievals should bring in enough for dinner. For, uh, about thirty thousand dragons.

Word had finally gotten out about what Alexander was attempting to do and why. Of course, he'd been trying to spread the word for maybe a couple of years now and had been roundly ignored. But several sudden volcanic burps in the last couple of days had taken out not only a lot of the local fish stock but also two floaters and their passengers who had been too close to the emissions. And people were starting to notice the poor fishing, which was hitting them right in the belly.

And I got to see, from a distance, what a burning floater looked like. I began to understand what watching the *Hindenburg* burn must have been like.

So now people were starting to believe, which meant people were scared. And scared people could go from resistant to insistent in a heartbeat. Virtually every floater within a day's flight had immediately joined up. All of which meant that waiting for spring was a nonstarter.

Now, we were heading north, from whence we would be setting off across the sea. I tried for a more dramatic description, but even as a posthuman computer, I had all the poetic talent of a hammer.

It was far too soon for starvation to set in, or even significant belt-tightening. But perception was a funny thing. Dragons began to act as if we were all on wartime rations. There was even a black market for fish. How in hell do you have a black market for fish when there's barely a legitimate market? I was beyond understanding any of it. When it came down to it, dragons as a group were just as nutty as any other so-called sentients.

But my work crew was a different matter. Dragons were pragmatic when it came to any kind of construction. They followed orders without argument, even when those orders seemed nonsensical. But they got the idea quickly enough when they could see the finished product starting to take shape. At that point, it became more a matter of restraining them than motivating them.

It took no more than three days before we had a working winch and boom setup that would haul up a smallish net, hopefully full of fish. We couldn't really test it on actual fish until we were over a big enough lake, but we improvised by filling the net with sticks and firewood until it seemed about the right weight.

We lost two nets before we got the weave and cord weight right.

The engineering crew swiftly turned into the trawling crew, as they understood the system better than anyone. We'd only had time to make the one unit so far, which gave my engineer's mind a bad case of the shakes. But I made sure the crew laid in enough spare lumber and rope to make more of everything in a pinch. We might even be able to construct more setups on the trip, weather permitting.

At just short of the two-week mark, Bridget declared that we would need another week of travel north. She'd been touching base with Mario about the increased volcanic activity. He said the view from low orbit was ominous. I don't know if the volcanic activity was contributing, but in any case, the winter storms were gearing up for a truly stupendous performance. As a result, Bridget wanted some extra wiggle room to avoid missing landfall entirely.

Erik, my crew foreman, walked up. "Everything's stowed, Chief.

Nothing more to do until we're over water, I guess. Then we'll find out if this bitch does its job."

I tried not to show amusement, lest it be seen as condescending. The cursing wasn't really translating well, and I was looking forward to a little time to update Gandalf's database.

"Meanwhile," I replied, "start cutting and shaping the spare lumber for parts. If we need to replace something, we don't want to have to wait while someone cuts new notches."

Eric gave me a sloppy salute, which looked suspiciously like something I did to Bridget occasionally, and turned to give orders. I hoped Bridget wouldn't see that. I doubt she'd be amused.

Someone handed me a tuev, and I absentmindedly took a slow sip as I inspected the site. Not bad. I'd make engineers out of these people yet.

((*))

I was helping lift a pole into place for part of the winch system when I got an email from Mario:

> *Hey, Howard & Bridget—*
>
> *Bad news. It looks like whatever process Alexander has been predicting is kicking into an even higher gear. There's been another uptick in eruptions, and I mean visible-from-space level. They started at the eastern end of the continent, and the increased activity is working its way west. I really wish we had a geologist available to comment on this—it's fascinating.*
>
> *I've messaged some of the Bobs who have contacts in universities, and they're scrambling to find someone qualified. Should have something soon, but meanwhile, just be aware that things are going to get hot for you in a day or two at this rate.*

Well, that sucked.

Bridget contacted me via intercom immediately. "We're not far enough north, Howard. We can't turn yet."

"Then don't," I replied. "The front is still a few thousand miles away."

"We'll have to get a little offshore, though." Bridget paused. "I'm going to release some drones to monitor air quality. If it goes bad, we'll have no choice."

Made sense. The biggest danger from all the vulcanism, short of having an eruption go off under you, was the gases emitted by the volcanoes and fissures. They were generally heavier than air and hugged the ground, but a big enough burp could retain a dome shape for hours or days before it dissipated. If the dome was high enough, it could encompass the floaters and their passengers.

A short time later, I felt a slow, ponderous change in the floater, and the horizon began to rotate. We were heading out to sea, where we hoped we would avoid the worst risks of eruptions.

It was about ten minutes before the horizon rotated back. I looked to shore, frowned, then launched into the air. Thirty seconds of focused flight got me to Alexander's private floater. I found Bridget and Alexander in a tight huddle, conversing in tense tones.

Alexander did not seem to be happy to see me, either. It was more than just the current situation. He glanced at Bridget as she greeted me, then quickly looked away, and I realized that I was in a competition for my wife. With the most powerful person on Jabberwocky. Someone who could have me disappeared on a whim.

Not ideal. But also, let's face it, not a priority right now. We had other problems, judging from Bridget's expression. "What?" I said.

She sighed. "I feel like such a fool for not thinking of this. Everyone knows the floaters don't like going offshore, and the dragons believe that it's because they don't like the open water with no cover. Turns out the problem is salt water."

"And you suddenly know this, how?"

Bridget gestured to a dragon standing some twenty feet away. "Roger reported that the floaters dipped their tentacles, then pulled back as if they'd been stung and immediately started turning back to shore. The cockpit crew can't get them to correct, either. The floaters are ignoring the crew input, and if the crew prod any harder, they say they'll cause injury."

I knew that floaters were steered and generally controlled using what I'd euphemistically call negative reinforcement. Like reins and spurs, crews used the application of pain to enforce their wishes on the floaters. It seemed, though, that the floaters would put up with some pain to avoid salt water.

To say that this put a crimp in our plans would be an understatement of massive proportions.

I turned and glared at Alexander. "And you never planned for this?"

He flushed, or the dragon equivalent, with either anger or embarrassment. "As Bridget says, it's always been common wisdom that the floaters just don't like the open water. They *have* been directed across bays, and to and from nearby islands, so we've assumed that the sight of a far shore was enough to reassure them."

Bridget cut in. "And that's almost certainly the case, but they were wrong about the motivation."

"And you're sure, absolutely *sure*, that this is all about salt water."

She made a face at me. "Given the reaction of the tentacles, it seems like the best explanation."

"Shit." I thought for a moment. "Is it a case of drinking the water? I thought they had that big reservoir on top."

"That's . . . interesting," Alexander said. "The central lake is ballast as well as a reservoir for dry periods. They can obviously use it when they're not near water. Usually it's refilled by rain, but the floaters can suck up water to replenish their reserves."

"Can we make them want to do that?"

Alexander thought for a moment. "There's lore that says when they're hot, they load up on water."

"Well, that makes sense," Bridget said. "During the summer, they'd want a bigger reservoir not only for cooling but in case of drought."

"So how do we make them hot?" I asked.

"Heat rocks in fires, then place them on bare patches." Alexander nodded to himself, making a decision. He called to his commanders. As they gathered around, he began giving orders. We would head for a nearby lake, where the floaters would be persuaded to suck up a lot of water, after which—wait, what?

"Did I understand him right?" I whispered to Bridget. "They'll cut off the floaters' tendrils?"

"Apparently, they grow back easily," she replied. "Like pulling out nose hairs."

"Ew." Still, it would keep the floaters from sampling the ocean, which would keep them from mutinying. We might yet pull this off.

54. Education

Icarus
August 2337
Roanoke

I sauntered casually along a tree-lined boulevard, admiring the flowers and various pieces of artwork. Okay, they weren't really trees, although they filled a similar ecological niche. But the flowers were really flowers, and they seemed to have insect pollinators. Or something that filled that niche.

I sighed and decided to stop overanalyzing. This was an alien ecosystem, with its own evolutionary history. But so far, every biological environment the Bobs had examined followed the same general patterns. At the base of the ecosystem was something plantlike that converted energy to biomass. It didn't have to be sunlight—even on Earth, entire fumarole-based ecologies had evolved around chemosynthesis—but the idea was the same.

Then something would evolve to eat the plants. Then something else would evolve to eat the plant eaters. Then something would evolve to parasitize everyone in sight. Viruses, microbes of every kind, fungi . . . Life followed certain patterns, probably simply because they were the paths of least resistance.

But because of all of this, I was enjoying a stroll down a tree-lined path on a totally alien planet.

"I can't believe we haven't done this before," Dae said beside me. "The mannies are just so much more real than VR."

"Mm, yeah, but we knew that from Howard's blog, if nothing else.

We've just never stopped long enough to smell the, uh . . ." I made a helpless gesture at some nameless bed of flowers.

Dae stopped and took a deep breath. "I suppose from a strict efficiency point of view, this is a pointless distraction. But it's not like we're on a schedule."

I frowned. "I'm not entirely sure we aren't. The whole *vanished civilizations* thing does lend a little urgency to our investigation."

"Yeah, okay, point taken. How's the scanning going?"

I pointed in the direction of the library, for that was what it had turned out to be, and we headed that way. "Children's books," I said. "Gotta love 'em. See Dick run. See Jane run. Dick sees Jane. Run, Jane, run."

Dae snorted. "The eighties called. They want their joke back."

"Give them their insult back while you're at it."

We both laughed easily, and I continued, "On the bad side, it looks like my assumptions were right. Library books are a legacy item. Everything up to about the tech level of the nineteen eighties, coincidentally enough, is represented. After that point, nothing."

"So you think they went electronic for newer stuff. That seems like a pretty clean cutoff."

"This species appears to have been very much on top of things, though. No slums, no private roads, green spaces everywhere . . . They must have been a decisive people; they decided to go electronic, and that was that."

"Wow," Dae said, shaking his head. "I wonder if the decision to take off was made as quickly."

We arrived at the library, and I opened the door for Dae. The handle and latch were definitely slightly too large for my hand, but not unworkably so. We'd found images of the local species, which we were now calling Roanokians. We knew the name for them in their language, but only in writing—we had found an audiotape library, but for now, just learning the written language was the priority.

They were about human size, perhaps a little shorter on average, bipedal and generally humanoid, but with disproportionately long arms and large hands. Dae's theory was that their ancestors were some kind of ambush predator that would grab their prey as it passed by. It was as good a theory as any.

Our mechanical servants were about three-quarters of the way through scanning the library. The scene before us elicited involuntary chuckles, though. Dozens of roamers stood on tables, slowly flipping through books like a bunch of avid bookworms. And that was another piece of good news. Apparently, the automated maintenance extended to library books. Whether the books were repaired or replaced or just tended to by nanites was up in the air, but nothing in the library was moldy or dried up or crumbling from age.

Occasionally, though, a maintenance bot would come by and try to collect a roamer, presumably for disposal. We'd ordered the roamers to run away rather than attempt to defend themselves, and it seemed to be good enough. And we didn't want to start a turf war with the maintenance automation.

But the bot would then collect the book and put it away, which required the roamer to retrieve it to continue its task. It was the ultimate test of consciousness, I decided. Any self-aware roamer would have long since whipped out its plasma cutter and laid waste to the miscreant.

I spent a few minutes wandering the aisles, just admiring the books. It was interesting that they *were* books, rather than scrolls or something even weirder. I supposed there were only so many ways to arrange words on paper.

Dae and I left the roamers to their work and went for a walk. Despite this being an urban setting, the air was alive with some equivalent of birdsong, and we spotted several small fliers landing on bushes and flitting between trees.

"No shortage of animals," Dae said.

"Hmm?"

"There are no Roanokians anywhere. No corpses, no vehicles abandoned in mid-street, no evidence of a hasty exit or mass death. And the plants and animals seem to be unaffected. No matter how I parse it, Icky, this looks like a planned exodus."

"Assuming they aren't all in stasis pods in some underground bunker."

Dae started to reply, then caught himself. "I was about to say how dumb that is, but we are dealing with aliens. Maybe let's do a SUDDAR sweep."

‹‹ * ››

We wanted to get it right, so the sweep took three days. A polar orbit, doing orange-slice passes as the planet rotated, eventually resulted in a thorough sensor map of the planet to several miles in depth.

"Nothing," Dae muttered, slapping his video window. It obediently spun on its axis, then settled back into place.

"Well, lots of interesting stuff, but I know what you mean," I replied. "No trace of a Roanokian population hiding in caves."

"Uh-huh. So I can't see any other conclusion. Voluntarily or otherwise, the entire population of the planet just up and left, in an orderly manner."

"Which you could put down to species psychology if it was just the Roanokians, but every planet we've visited, with any number of different intelligent species, is the same."

Dae shook his head slowly. "I have a bad feeling we won't like the explanation."

55. Setting Off

Howard
August 2344
Jabberwocky

We were over the lake, and the floaters were greedily sucking up water. The central reservoir on the Hunter had grown visibly and was in danger of developing an outflow stream across the top. But the Hunter was a big, mature floater with a lot of tendrils. Some of the smaller floaters were still well short of full.

Since the Hunter was ahead of schedule, my trawling crew had decided to try a few casts. Results were encouraging, if somewhat skimpy. We'd caught some lake fish, which at least showed the system worked. But we'd never feed the population with that kind of take. And we were barely moving when we trawled the net. It could still break at speed.

The local dragons had stopped heating rocks and were letting the existing piles cool off. The next step was to cut the tendrils, and we were listening to a senior floater-herder describe where and how to cut. Obviously, it had to be done in-flight, which immediately complicated things. The essential maneuver was to approach the dangling tendril, then roll ninety degrees and swipe at it with a machete-like tool. The machetes were raw iron, as the dragons hadn't developed alloying yet, which meant they didn't hold much of an edge. The cut had to be done cleanly, or you'd not only fail the cut but throw yourself into an uncontrolled yaw. And probably drop the machete, which is why they had tethers.

Then there was a shout. "Eruption!" We all looked landward to see the top of a hill splitting and emitting a huge black cloud. It appeared the volcanic wave had arrived.

"Bridget?" I intercommed.

The reply came back in a few seconds.

"No toxic gas emissions, beyond the smoke and ash. So far, anyway. But we'd better get ready to make tracks."

Dammit. We'd be going out with the trawling system untested and next to no stock of trout.

In moments, dragons were launching from the royal floater to relay orders to the flotilla. It looked like we'd be leaving immediately.

I started yelling at my crew to get the net out again. We'd have one last chance to scoop up a catch. For good or ill, this was the full test, with no opportunity to fix and retest.

The crew was enthusiastic and surprisingly well trained, considering how new the whole technology was to them. Dragons had neither the wheel nor the pulley, having never developed any kind of need for either. It was interesting how biology could affect the pace and path of scientific development.

By the time the Hunter started moving, we had the net in the water and fully open. The boom was extended out at forty-five degrees, keeping the line clear of the edge. There was an audible thrum as the line went taut, then a perceptible surge in the water below. Erik watched the progress of the net from the edge of the floater. In seconds, he started yelling at the crew to winch in the net. There was no hesitation; the dragons on winch duty started cranking immediately. With an audible groan, the boom took up the load—then started to bow.

"Oh shit!" I yelled, then pointed. "Brace it! Brace it!"

Several dragons grabbed spare poles and jammed them into position to take up part of the load on the winch. We'd planned for this possibility, but it was still a dangerous proposition. If the winch gave out, everyone within a pole length would be injured or killed.

With dragons draped around the reinforcing poles, the winch regained its shape, and the winching crew resumed their task, pulling in time to a chant that I'd taught them. Fortunately, no one on this planet would ever recognize—

"You have got to be kidding me!" Bridget exclaimed from behind me.

Busted.

"You taught them that? You are a sick, depraved . . ." Then she lost the thunderous expression and started to laugh.

I smiled back and joined the chant. "Oh-Ee-Yah! Ee-Oh-Ah!" A few seconds later, Bridget joined me, and now we were both chanting in sync with the crew. "Oh-Ee-Yah! Ee-Oh-Ah!"

Soon, the net was suspended from the boom, and the crew began winching it over. Bridget gave me the hairy eyeball and said, "You're still a sick puppy."

"The Winkies were my favorite part of *The Wizard of Oz,* honestly." I gestured to the net, changing the subject. "The net held. But I think we'll have to reinforce the boom before we try that at sea."

Bridget appraised the bulging net. "A pretty good haul. Let's hope the grills school as tightly."

«*»

We were emptying the fish catch from the net into the central lake when I got an intercom alert from Bridget. "Another gas eruption. This one's toxic. Probably going to dome up at least some." At the same time, I saw another flock of dragon "runners" erupt from the royal floater.

The floaters had a minimal propulsion ability, sort of equivalent to sculling with a rudder. It wasn't much, but given the alternative, everyone was going for it. Even the floaters seemed to have noted the urgency, and the flotilla had now picked up speed from glacial to dead slow.

But then we got an unexpected bonus. The toxic gas plume was indeed doming, and with my dragon eyesight, I could actually see the interface. But as it spread, it was acting like a wave, lifting the floaters from the back and propelling them forward like surfers riding a swell, at a pace that very probably no one had ever seen. I wanted to yell, "Whee!" but the faces of those around me made me pause. Some of the dragons abandoned ship, in fact, flying up and forward to the front of the flotilla.

In five minutes, we were almost two miles out to sea. Now we were committed, one way or the other. If we couldn't get the floaters to cooperate, we'd die on the shores of Atlantis. If we couldn't collect enough food on the voyage, dead. If we missed the edge of Lemuria, dead. If we got knocked out of the sky by one of the winter storms, dead.

Talk about all in.

❮❮ * ❯❯

The thing about ocean voyages is they're like being in the military. At least I assume so, never having done either before. But with both, it's long periods of not very much, punctuated by moments of pure terror.

The pure terror in this case was the first winter storm. You'd think being above the waves, we'd be spared some of the heaving, but no. I did look down a couple of times and wished I hadn't. The waves were—well, a half-mile high was probably an exaggeration, but it sure looked that way to me. Most dragons, who'd never seen anything more lively than a lake surface, were huddled in trees or nests, shaking.

I understood now why Alexander had been getting the floaters used to being lashed together. If we'd been all floating individually, the flotilla would have been scattered beyond hope. The rope system also helped to maintain some stability, preventing individual floaters from rolling over in the gale-force winds.

And according to Mario, this storm was just a baby.

It lasted three hours and was followed by blue skies and an extreme cold front. As soon as things settled, we were visited by runners from His Nibs, ordering us to build fires and deploy the warming rocks.

Bridget explained that the floaters' instinct in cold weather was to release some ballast to maintain buoyancy. But we couldn't afford to lose any fresh water. The hot rocks would convince the floaters to hydrolyze water to hydrogen instead. And the warming would make their gas bladders expand a bit as well.

I shook my head at the thought of all this casual use of fire around what were essentially living bags of hydrogen gas. I made a comment to that effect, and Bridget explained, "It's not that simple, Howard. The floaters have evolved to avoid *Hindenburg*-type events. For starters, the gas is kept in many smaller bladders rather than a few big ones, and it's surrounded by tissues that absorb any stray oxygen and route it away. It's quite a system, really."

Bridget always made me smile when she went into biologist mode. In her own way, she was very Bob-like, just about different subjects. Not that I would ever point that out. Again.

"But they do catch fire, sometimes," I replied.

"Sure, there are limits to what biology can do. A straight-up bladder puncture, if there's an open flame around, is game over." Bridget shook her head in sorrow. "It is the biggest source of mortality for this species. I think what's going on now on Atlantis will decimate any remaining floaters."

I cocked my head. "How much of the dragon and floater population do you think we're saving by doing this?"

"A few percent at best, Howard. But I'm not sure anything will survive this round of eruptions." She paused, looking forlorn. "This time looks like it's going to be far worse than the previous events. Mario sends me updates regularly, and some of the images . . ."

"That bad?"

"I think Atlantis is actually splitting up this time. I hope Mario can get a geologist on board soon to confirm this, but it looks like the continent is on at least three different plates, and the pieces have started to separate."

"Wait, how fast—"

Bridget shook her head. "No, we won't see it in a dragon lifetime. But Mario reports that parts of the continent have lurched apart by tens of meters in some locations."

"So Atlantis is done for?"

"Oh, it'll reacquire habitability eventually, and get repopulated. But meanwhile, the dragons and floaters are going to have to make a go of it on Lemuria."

"Well, let's just make sure we get there."

«*»

We were three days out when we hit our next major storm. Or to be more accurate, the storm hit us. Mario had warned us that it was coming, but the flotilla wasn't what you'd call *maneuverable*. Bridget mentioned the danger to Alexander, and orders went out to batten down whatever passed for hatches around here.

The storm came in from the northeast, looking like something straight out of a Spielberg movie, clouds billowing and folding upon themselves in some kind of special-effects spectacular. When the leading wall of wind hit us, it pushed the closest floaters into the next, and them into the next, in some kind of giant dominoes game. This was where tying the floaters together started to look like genius. It forced them to stay on a level plane. Any attempt to force a floater up over or down below part of the flotilla was arrested by the ropes and the inertia of the rest of the fleet. Of course, the whole shebang could be blown around like a leaf in the, uh, wind.

Between the gusts, we were being hammered by rain squalls. Not continuous rain, just sheets being blown in to make our lives miserable. No one was going to be flying in this.

Then it happened. It wasn't lightning, as there hadn't been any. Possibly someone didn't batten something down properly. But for whatever reason, fire broke out on one of the floaters. The trees were too wet to catch, but the village was like kindling, and still relatively dry thanks to being under cover. Dragons now flew off in panic, not just fleeing the fire but also fleeing the floater.

"We have to cut it loose!" I yelled to no one in particular. Grabbing a machete, I tossed another to Bridget. We spotted a couple of soldiers and yelled at them, then launched.

A few other dragons had already gotten the idea and were cutting the ropes from the edges of their floaters, probably self-preservation more than any kind of tactic. I landed with a jolt at the base of a rope, tied to a huge stanchion, and began hacking. Bridget was out there doing the same, but I had no time to look for her or try to coordinate anything.

Then soldiers began arriving with machetes, and we soon had the floater cut free. It immediately dropped—a survival strategy that involved jettisoning gas, hopefully not in the area of the fire. Any dragons that hadn't left the floater now did so.

The chaos was incredible. Dragons flying around, trying to land on other floaters while being buffeted by the storm; floaters trying to stampede in panic; and the slashed ropes whipping around in the gale-force winds. I saw at least one dragon get clipped and go down.

But the fire didn't seem to have spread. That was something.

Then the sky lit up. The fire had reached the floater's gas bladders, and it was now full-on burning. And the floater was letting out a hideous screech as it began to tumble toward the ocean below.

"I wouldn't have thought they had any ability to vocalize," I muttered to no one in particular.

Bridget's voice replied quietly behind me. "It could just be escaping gas, Howard. But either way, it's dying. There's no way to help it now."

It took more than a minute for the cartwheeling mass of flames to hit the waves. The fire actually managed to stay lit for another several seconds before the ocean engulfed what was left. A sigh went up from the dragons who had gathered to watch. Then slowly, one by one, they turned away.

《 * 》

The cleanup took hours. The storm had shredded a lot of buildings and other structures and had pulled up or knocked down trees over the entire flotilla. This meant wounds on the floaters, more leaked hydrogen, and the loss of the nutrients that those trees had supplied.

We'd also lost several dozen dragons, based on a rough survey. No one was sure if they'd died or just been blown away by the storm. We asked Mario to keep an eye out from orbit, but there wasn't much he could do. Individual dragons were just too small to see from space.

The floaters were pulled close to repair the hole in the flotilla, and ropes were re-tied. It wasn't clear whether the loss of the one floater had affected our overall chances of success or merely made the floater breeding pool a little smaller.

The storm had blown us farther south than we wanted to be, though. We would now have to start tacking more northward if we hoped to make landfall.

"One good thing, I guess," Bridget said, sitting beside me and handing me a cup of tuev. "The storm replenished the freshwater reservoirs." She leaned into me, and we shared some warmth.

"We lost whatever freshwater fish were in the burned floater's reservoir," I replied gloomily. "But we kept all the dragons who abandoned ship. So rations will be short."

Bridget leaned back and turned her head to me. "Ocean fishing hasn't been very successful." It was a statement more than a question.

"It's not that there aren't any fish in the ocean, Bridge. It's just hard to trawl a net with waves that high." I sighed. "This would have been easier in summer when the weather's better."

"I'll make a note of that for next time," Bridget replied with a snort.

We sat in silence for a while. Then Bridget said, "We're not going to make it." I didn't comment, so she continued, "There won't be enough food."

"The voyage is just a couple more weeks, Bridget. Even if they have to go to zero rations, surely they'll survive that."

She shook her head. "Dragon metabolism. They're fliers, Howard. They burn five thousand calories a day easily. They can't just turn it off. And they don't really have fat reserves." She paused. "And anyway, well before dragons start collapsing from starvation, they'll be killing each other over the remaining food."

"Not good." I stared up at the sky, thinking. "Stretching the rations by having half the population killed off is not an acceptable solution. Do you think there are still freshwater fish on Atlantis? Trout or something close?"

"Excuse me?" Bridget exclaimed, plainly confused by my non sequitur.

"I'm thinking a couple of midnight runs with cargo drones."

"Howard, that's absolutely—" Bridget stopped midsentence and swiveled her head several times. "Um, that's . . . kind of brilliant."

"That's why you give me the big bucks."

"I give you no bucks."

"Sorry, I mispronounced that last word."

Bridget started laughing, drawing stares—and some glares—from other dragons. "You, sir, are a sick puppy. But I repeat myself." She lowered her voice. "Let's talk to Mario. They are his drones, after all."

«*»

Mario thought it was hilarious. "High-tech drones and roamers trawling for fish," he crowed. "Talk about misappropriation of resources."

"Is it misappropriation, though, if you're in charge?" I asked innocently.

"Okay, Howard. We'll print up a couple of nets—at least we don't have to work with the native fiber—and I'll do a quick survey to see which lakes, if any, still have life in them. The northwest segment of the former eastern continent seems a teeny bit less active. We'll start there."

"Thanks, Mario," I replied. "Once we've got results, we'll talk about how to sneak the fish in."

"Better not get caught," he said with a grin. "This would be *real* hard to explain."

‹‹ * ››

Dragons weren't, by nature, much of a nocturnal animal, but all it would take would be one insomniac night owl to screw the op. We'd discussed a schedule with Mario, whereby we would restock a couple of floaters per night. Bridget and I stood guard using our small drones, ready to abort if any movement was spotted.

It worked fine for three nights, but on the fourth day, someone noticed that the fish stocks seemed to be up on one of the floaters. It created a general rush to get a close look at the central lakes, which, of course, meant everyone now had a good idea of how much—or how little—fish was left.

So now we had six floaters with a lot of fish, and several dozen with very little fish. Which meant panic about the potential short rations and animosity about accusations that some villages were hoarding their supply.

In the end, we had to get out the army to prevent a civil war. Alexander spent several days talking with the leaders of villages and eventually managed to broker a peaceful agreement for food sharing.

We were seated at Alexander's strategy table afterward, with him glaring at Bridget and me while we did our best to look innocent and bewildered.

"I find your explanations unsatisfying," he said to me.

"We haven't explained anything," I retorted.

Alexander gave me a thin smile. "I'm glad you noticed that, too."

Oh, funny guy. Keeping my face deadpan, I replied, "What exactly are you expecting us to have or have not explained?"

"The two of you are strange," Alexander said. "I've commented on this before. You seem to have knowledge that no one could reasonably have—like what weather is coming. You have amazing engineering knowledge despite no good explanation for where you acquired it. I wonder if some assisted questioning might elicit more information."

Assisted questioning was a dragon euphemism for torture. Not that it would really affect us personally, but having to either destroy the drannies or make a dramatic escape would pretty much put an end to our part in this adventure.

"So I'm confused." I risked glaring at him. "As near as I can tell, you're angry because I created a way to catch fish in bulk from a floater, because Bridget can read the weather better than most, and because we turn out to have more fish stock than expected. Is that about right?"

Alexander blinked, then looked around the table. None of his generals would meet his eyes.

"Ah, when you phrase it that way, I guess it's better than the alternatives." He paused, then nodded. "I suppose we should just accept good fortune when we find it. How tight is the food situation?"

Bridget answered the last question. "I estimate another week before we arrive, what with being blown off course. We have enough food for four days if we're careful. If we can pick up even a modest haul from Howard's trawling, we'll make it."

"You've caught next to nothing for the last couple of weeks," he said, addressing me. "How likely is it that you'll suddenly have luck?"

"With due respect," I replied, "we don't know very much about grill schooling patterns away from land. It might be that they only swim close to shore, or it might be that they swim deeper in the open ocean. It would explain why the catch dropped off a couple of days out."

Alexander nodded. "Hopefully in four days, we'll be close enough to Lemuria." He stood. "Otherwise, there will be bloodshed."

«*»

"Well, hell," I said afterward. "I don't know what to do."

"We can't restock any more ponds," Bridget said, nodding. "They'll notice and wonder where the fish came from."

Mario was in on the conversation, by intercom. "What about dropping in small numbers?"

"If you drop in enough to make a difference, they'll notice. Everyone's aware of the stock levels now," she replied.

"Can we 'accidentally' catch a bunch of grill?" I asked.

"What we can do," Bridget said, "is check your theory about grill schooling closer to shore."

"Already did that," Mario replied. "It's not that it's untrue; it's just that there aren't a lot of grill schools around the western continent's shore. Might be seasonal; might be that they're more of an eastern continent fish. Either way . . ."

"Either way, no dice," I grumbled. Then I perked up. "Hey, Mario, how far are we from landfall right now? Shortest distance to land?"

"A couple hundred miles. Why?"

"There are lots of fish in lakes on Lemuria, right? Otherwise, all of this is for nothing." It was a rhetorical question. We'd long since verified that the dragons would have a food supply when they arrived. "So why not just fly the entire population in ahead of the floaters?"

Bridget frowned. "Because they need the floaters?"

"Okay, no," I said, waving my hands in negation. "Leave enough dragons to bring in the floaters, and fly everyone else over. If we only leave half the population behind, they'll have enough food to make it."

"It's a bit of a desperation move, but not impossible." Bridget stood. "Let's go talk to Alexander."

«*»

Alexander was not enthusiastic. "Flying over unknown ocean to an unknown destination is going to be a hard sell."

"Wait, what?" I retorted, frowning. "You did it. With the canoe."

"With three of my best, strongest wingers. And with being able to set down the canoe and rest when necessary. We can't do this four dragons at a time. Not to mention having to get the canoe back to the flotilla somehow."

"Hmm. Gotcha." He wasn't wrong. Whatever we did would have to be one-way. I turned to Bridget. "Can we make it in one session?"

"No," she replied. "We'll need to overnight once."

"Could we drag a floater? If everyone pulled—"

Both Bridget and Alexander shook their heads at the same time. "It's not a question of power," Bridget said. "With the whole population, we have the muscle. The problem is, dragons can't really hover, and they'd have to be all but hovering while pulling on the ropes."

I glanced at Bridget as she messaged me. "We might have to consider breaking character."

"What do you mean?"

"I mean a little divine intervention might be in order. Otherwise, this is going to end in disaster."

"Hold on," I replied, "I have one more idea to try."

"You two are doing it again," Alexander interrupted. We had apparently been silently staring at each other for several seconds. "Mind sharing your thoughts?"

I took a moment to work everything through before replying. "How long do you think the average dragon would have to rest in the canoe or some kind of boat if they were going to try to get across to the mainland as quickly as possible?"

"Well, carrying the canoe would tire them—"

"No canoe," I interjected. "Just free flight, land, rest, go."

"Huh." Alexander thought for a second. "A couple of hours, really. It would help if they had a supply of tuev to reinvigorate themselves. But then flying at night would still be a problem."

"Fires. Signal fires on the boat and on the mainland. From soaring altitude, you'd have no problem picking them out."

Alexander nodded. "Sounds great. One small problem I can see . . ."

"I have that covered. We build rafts, carry them out the same way you and your wingers carried the canoe. We'd need more people lifting each one, of course. You'd want your strongest doing this part. Plunk the rafts down in the same spot and tie them together. That becomes the midway rest area."

"What about fires?" he asked.

"We'd have to bring hearth materials so the raft doesn't burn up, obviously. So a second wave would bring that, plus kindling, tuev, fire-making tools, whatever else. But the first wave, once rested, would fly on to the mainland and light fires from whatever's available. Once all this is set up, the rest of the population—or as many as want to and are capable of it—follow in waves. The rest stay on the floaters to bring them in. They'll have enough food to make it then."

Alexander gazed at me, frowned, then turned to one of his most trusted generals. "What do you think?"

The dragon looked uncomfortable with being put on the spot, but you didn't dodge a question from Alexander. "It, uh, I mean, I don't see any obvious reasons why it would fail. Unless the weather went bad unexpectedly."

We all looked up reflexively. The skies were clear and calm.

"That might not hold," I muttered.

"Then let's get started," Alexander replied.

56. Graduation

Icarus
January 2338
Roanoke

Even with all the pictures to help, translation of the library's books took about six months. Bob with the Deltans and Phineas and Ferb with the Pav had had the advantage of being able to observe the language in daily use. With only text, we'd had to infer a lot. Degrees of confidence applied to words and phrases were then tested against other texts to see if the resulting translation made sense. We still had a significant portion of the written language with no confident translation.

But we had figured out the audiotapes. On the assumption that the Roanokians had a spoken frequency range similar to that of humans and a roughly similar processing speed for speech, we'd decided on an arbitrary playback speed. But who knew? We might sound to them like we were hopped up on helium.

But the biggest disappointment was that our initial suspicions had been correct. The hard-copy portion of this library was strictly legacy. There was nothing more recent than late-twentieth-century technology or discussion. That meant no indication of how the wormholes worked or where the populations went.

"On the other hand," I mused, "we do have a means of communication now. We might be able to talk to the firewall sentries."

"Or maybe this time, they'll decide we're a nuisance and melt us down."

"We could send in a drone."

"Icky, we're getting a little crowded in our holds. Between the mannies and all the extra roamers and drones, I feel like a storage locker. Our ships weren't really designed as cargo vessels."

"So I'll just sacrifice one of my cargo drones. It should be big enough to trigger a response, and we'll control it via maser connection through the wormhole."

Dae sighed. "All right. I recognize the stubborn tone."

"I prefer to think of it as decisive."

"Whatever gets you through the day, buddy."

《 * 》

And once again, wormhole travel was the absolute best thing going. Fifteen thousand light-years around the galaxy in less than two days, most of that time spent crawling between the wormholes. And once again, we found ourselves facing the gate leading to the DMZ.

I ejected my cargo drone, gave it orders, and sent it through the gate. The maser link connection was rock steady, giving me hope that we might actually learn something this time.

As expected, the sentries zoomed up and issued their challenge. We still didn't have the specs for the SCUT comms, so I had the drone issue a verbal plea via plain old radio, in Roanokian. I had already set up the translation routines, so Dae and I heard the whole exchange in English.

"Please, may I pass?"

As I'd hoped, the sentry switched to the same medium. "Authorization required."

"Where do I get authorization?"

"You are speaking Roanokian, but your silhouette does not match any registered Roanokian vessels. You will require authorization for this class of vessel."

"Where do I get this authorization?"

"The Roanokian government can issue authorization."

"Roanoke is deserted. Where can I find its government?"

"They have likely already passed through."

"Through here? To the far gate?"

This reference to a gate was a calculated risk. There was no word for wormhole in the Roanokian text we'd deciphered.

"Affirmative."

I felt a moment of relief. The sentry had accepted the description.

"Have all Roanokians gone through the gate?"

"That information is not available."

Damn. Okay, reasonable, though. How would the sentry know?

"Have other civilizations gone through the gate?"

"All member civilizations have gone through the skzzzzzzzzz."

Whoa. That last word was probably the proper name for a wormhole gate. I quickly added it to the translator. And all *member* civilizations? Had we just discovered where everyone went?

"Where does the gate lead?"

"That information is not available."

"Do you know why they all went through the gate?"

"That information is not available."

"In the absence of a Roanokian government, we are unable to get authorization to pass. Is there an exception process?"

"Security Central can evaluate individual requests. However, they have not responded to queries for one thousand four hundred and thirty-two years."

Hmm, those were Roanokian years. I'd forgotten to set up the translator to autoconvert. In human time, that was . . . 2,104 years. Wow.

"Those maintenance systems are *really* good," Dae said over my shoulder.

"Is there any other way to get approval?"

"No alternatives are available."

Well, crap.

57. Marathon

Howard
September 2344
Jabberwocky

Raft creation wasn't much of an issue. We had lots of trees, and they'd evolved to be light—something like balsa wood. Lashing a dozen posts together took next to no time, and the rafts could be carried comfortably at the end of a set of slings by about sixteen dragons. Coordinating everyone to prevent midair collisions was a real fear, so it helped that only trained and disciplined military would be tasked with this part of the plan.

Within hours, the first raft was on its way, with more coming ready every couple of hours. Soon we had twenty rafts en route. The next phase was supplies. Clay pots for the signal fires, kindling to burn, food, and tuev all went out in slings held by pairs of dragons.

It was a military operation that any Earth general would have been proud of. And while this had been going on, the rest of Alexander's army had been organizing the dragon exodus. Most of the required numbers had been filled by volunteers, since the specter of starvation was very real and very immediate. A human would have trouble understanding the dragon psychology in this regard. A human could, in extreme circumstances, survive for weeks on little or no food—not so dragons with their amped-up metabolisms. A few days without sustenance, and most of them would eat their own mothers.

A dragon wearing the arm patch of the military flew in from the west and landed heavily. He sat down, panted for a few moments, then said, "All set. Rafts are ready; fires are lit."

Alexander turned to his generals. "Let's get this going."

«*»

The exodus would take about a half day. Groups were to be sent out, each about half the size of the raft's capacity, staggered so that they had some flexibility in scheduling. It was inevitable that some would arrive too tired to continue according to plan, and they could be given an extra round of rest.

I went ahead of the first exodus group with a few soldiers, ostensibly to look over the raft and make sure everything was okay. In reality, I'd be reporting back to Bridget. Alexander remained suspicious that we were communicating in some secret way. In any case, he didn't put up any kind of argument about me going.

We arrived at the raft in a few hours. The flight had been uneventful, if perhaps a little tiring for the others. Dranny metabolism, of course, could go almost forever, but I was careful to appear as winded as the rest.

The fires were going in their clay pots, a number of casks of tuev were lined up, and everything looked shipshape. We rested for a while, knocked back a couple of pints of paint thinner, and then, on a command from our group leader, launched into the air, bound for Lemuria.

It was another routine flight. There were no thermals to speak of, but the air movements over the ocean provided occasional updrafts to make a dragon comfortable. I had to admit, this was possibly the best humanoid form we'd come across, and there *had* to be a way to turn this into—

I felt something land heavily on my back, and a spear suddenly protruded from my chest. All the dranny telltales went red, and the sensory overload limiter flipped on. I just had time to think *what the fffff*—before my dranny connection was severed.

I immediately messaged Bridget. "I think I've just been assassinated. Dranny is offline. Watch for attack."

"What? How?" Bridget cut off her questions. "Talk later. Contact Mario now."

It took less than a millisecond to update Mario, and a camouflaged drone was on its way to pick up the dranny corpse. I hoped the drone would get there before some large oceanic predator that didn't know any better decided to have it for a snack.

I sat in my VR, fuming. The only reason I could think of for this attack was Alexander trying to get rid of the competition. Wow, had he ever misread the room. Bridget would tear him a new one if he gave her any reason to suspect him.

Well, whatever. I was dead. Might as well get some work done. I pulled up my email queue and started going through the backlog.

‹‹ * ››

Mario called me a short while later. "Hey, Howard. We got the dranny. Nice flesh wound. Right through where the heart should be." He sent me an image at the same time. Yep. Definitely a kill shot.

"Can you fix it?" I asked.

"Of course. Already half-done. We've thrown all our roamers at it. And once we activated the internal roamers, they got a lot of it cleaned up. Hey, do you want me to leave a scar?"

"What? No, of course—" Then I hesitated. Chances were it wouldn't ever come up, but I could always fix it later. "On the other hand, yeah. Old war wound kinda thing. Make it fresh and livid."

Mario laughed and signed off.

I messaged Bridget. "Anything interesting happening at your end?"

"No, Howard. Everything seems quite routine. Although Alexander does seem to be paying me more attention than usual."

Uh-huh. That fit. I sent the picture to Bridget with the caption *Your new boyfriend plays rough.*

She answered right away. "You're going to show up, right? I want to see his face, just before I rip it off."

I sent her a heart emoji and signed off. Alexander was dead meat.

58. Special Delivery

Bill
September 2344
In Virt

And finally, after almost two years of heads-down engineering, we'd hit paydirt. Garfield and I were in VR, with video windows showing the two ends of our test wormhole, on opposite sides of the Epsilon Eridani system. In normal light, there wasn't much to see. Each wormhole was like a hole in space that showed the scene at the other end. And since it was a spherical hole, you could orbit the wormhole in any direction and look straight through it.

No, *spherical* wasn't really the right description. There was no spherical surface. Rather, it was a flat, disc-shaped hole, like a stargate or the *DS9* wormhole, but it was a flat, disc-shaped hole no matter which direction you looked at it from. Even multiple observers at different angles would see a disc-shaped view through to the other end of the wormhole. There was also a little bit of distortion around the edge, reminiscent of black-hole animation videos.

Of course, out in the Oort cloud, you'd only see stars, and it was virtually impossible to tell where the local starfield left off and the view through the wormhole began without a star chart to compare with.

The view in the microwave spectrum was more informative. The wormhole, even wedged open with a rotating charged negative-energy field, emitted a constant stream of virtual particle pairs around the edge, each of which put out a small microwave flash as they suicided.

We'd placed the two negative-energy-generating stations at opposite sides of the wormhole. Since we didn't want someone coming through the wormhole to accidentally smack into one of the stations, we'd decided that, as standard policy, they would always be aligned with the galactic axis.

"Drone's ready," Garfield said, interrupting my thought train. "All sensor equipment is in the green. SCUT channels at both ends are trained for the drone's signal."

"Well, then, let's do it. Make it so."

Garfield gave me an eye roll, then hit the big red button. The drone shot toward the wormhole mouth, on a vector directly toward galactic center. It hit the middle of the target without any indication of anything unusual. From the observation drone's point of view, it simply continued to coast directly away. From our angle off to one side, though, it disappeared.

"SCUT signal picked up at the other end," Garfield said. "It got through successfully and is still operational. Transit time is . . . a big fat zero." He paused. "Uh-oh."

"Jeebus, I wish we could retire that exclamation," I said. "I *hate* uh-oh."

"Yeah." Garfield poked at a few icons. "The drone's hull has stress fractures. New ones, in case you're wondering. I don't think the trip is as routine as we'd like."

"Fine. Let's debug."

‹‹ * ››

We were back in the moot pub, with the Ancient Ones. No Howard and Bridget this time, and no Hugh. I would send him a summary later.

"I have—" I started to say.

"Good news and bad news," Bob finished for me. "*Quelle surprise.*"

I leaned back and glared at him. "Y'know, when even we Bobs are getting tired of our shtick, it may be time to start worrying."

Bob smiled back at me. "Not wrong."

"So anyway . . ." Will said.

"Oh, uh, yeah." I paused to regroup. "Good news, we've sent several drones of various sizes through the wormhole and received working drones at the other end."

"That sounds like the good news, all right," Bob said.

"Uh-huh. Bad news, they were a little dinged up. The trip through seems to momentarily squeeze the drone. Hard."

"Can't you just make the mouth bigger?" Will asked.

"It's not squeezing through a small aperture, Will. Although that's what immediately pops to mind. But there's no drag. The squeeze is inward from all sides and doesn't result in any net deceleration. It's just an effect of the transit."

"Is it fatal? Or potentially damaging? I mean—" Will paused. "You already said there was damage, but is it potentially destructively damaging?"

I sighed. "Dunno, Will. We're going to keep increasing the size of both the wormholes and our test subjects. I'll let you know. But right now, it looks like we're just about ready to set up wormhole transit systems, once the shipments arrive at their destinations."

"Good, because we're less than a year away from when the first wormhole endpoint arrives at its destination system. We can delay for a while, but within three years, all the wormhole deliveries will be in place, WormNet will be ready to activate, and then it's fish or cut bait."

"That's not all," Bob interjected, "although this isn't really a critical issue. Howard took it upon himself to arrange the same wormhole deliveries at most of the populated UFS planets. Once we can deliver a working system, the Enniscorthy Astronomical Transit Matter Exchange is ready to open for business."

I pinched the bridge of my nose and sighed. "You have *got* to be kidding. 'EAT ME'?" I looked at Bob. "The sense of humor is a given, but did you know you had this mercenary streak in you?"

"Well, I *did* create InterGator software."

"And sold it for a crapton of dough," Garfield added with a laugh.

"Did someone mention to Howard that I wanted to keep it secret for a bit?" Will asked.

"Yes, and he's fine with it," Bob replied. "For a while, anyway. He has a whole marketing thing ready, though."

"And all members of the Bobiverse are automatically shareholders in anything Howard cooks up, so we'll all ride this wave," Garfield said with a grin.

"And what do we need money for?" Will complained.

"To pay lawyers," Bob replied. "Personally, I think when we get to the heat death of the universe, there'll be a bunch of lawyers waiting there for us."

I nodded. "Not wrong."

59. Showdown

Howard
September 2344
Jabberwocky

I came in fast just over the trees and landed hard on the beach in front of my assassins. A real dragon probably would have sprained or broken both ankles. My dranny interface merely sent me a mild rebuke about abusing the warranty, which I ignored.

I'd been trying for the "superhero landing," and I like to think I pulled it off, as the members of my former military escort all jumped and then looked *very* alarmed.

"So who did the actual dirty?" I asked casually, scanning their faces. No poker players here—three of them were unable to suppress quick eye movements, all directed at the fourth. Gerrard, my translation interface had dubbed him.

I smiled thinly in his direction. "Well, Gerrard, I know you were just following orders, so I'm not going to rip your head off and use it for soccer practice." I made a note to myself to look up how the interface translated *soccer*. "But there will be a reckoning, once all the excitement is over." Then I changed the subject. "Meanwhile, how are we doing on preparations?"

The soldiers glanced at each other in confusion. I was not behaving as expected. Well, to be honest, I wasn't as dead as expected, either.

Finally, Gerrard decided to just go with the flow. "Uh, we've got the fires started, stocked up some spare kindling, and we've mapped three lakes in the area that have good food stocks. Not trout exactly, but pretty good. Bigger, on average."

"That's because they haven't been getting eaten by dragons for the last forever," I replied. "By my estimates, the first wave of immigrants should be coming in within a couple of hours. Will we have places for them?"

"We're going to drag in some dead trees and split them up for firewood. They'll burn faster than new wood, but we'll need the heat. It'll be a few days around the campfire at night until the flotilla gets here, and then we can all go back to civilization. Uh . . ." Gerrard squinted at me. "How did you survive, anyway?"

"I didn't." I gave him an evil—and I hoped cryptic—smile and pointed at the scar on my chest. "It was a good strike. Killed me instantly. But I don't stay dead." I waved a hand. "Never mind. I'll take it up with Alexander. If he hasn't already gotten himself killed from making a pass at my wife." I shrugged, dismissing the subject. "Meanwhile, let's get that firewood stocked up."

‹‹ * ››

The first wave of civilians came in right on schedule, shepherded by a couple of soldiers from the scout group. These were the upper half of the population bell curve fitness-wise, but they were still civilians. Most dragons didn't engage in any kind of marathon flying, and the two legs of this journey would have taken everything out of them. In fact, we were expecting at least a couple of deaths from dragons who simply couldn't do the distance.

This group came in low, and most of the landings reminded me of blue-footed boobies from the old National Geographic episodes about the Galápagos. A lot of them simply collapsed when their feet hit the ground and lay there, not even trying to get out of the way. There were a couple of pileups, but nothing serious. We helped the more exhausted individuals over to the fire, gave them some *tuev* and some fresh trout to nibble on, and left them to get their breath back.

My erstwhile escort hadn't tried anything while we were prepping, likely not having any orders to cover this situation. Plus, let's face it, having your victim come back from the dead had to be off-putting. And now that we had several dozen potential witnesses, the time for correcting the situation was over.

"How are things at your end?" Bridget messaged me.

"Going well. First wave made it without casualties. Next group should be here in a couple of hours. How's His Nibs?"

I could hear her smile in the reply. "He's paying a lot of attention to me, making pretty transparent remarks about life and death and choosing your fate. What is it with men?"

"Hey, don't blame me. I got a spear through the heart, remember?"

Instead of the expected comeback, though, I got silence. "Bridget?"

"Something's going on, Howard. I've just been surrounded by Alexander and his goons. He's got a funny look on his face, and I don't mean hah-hah."

"Bridget, get out of there. Now."

"I don't think I can. They've got— Howard! No! Oh my god!"

I went into panic mode. Launching myself straight up, I called up the cargo drone that we kept on standby, then flew up a half kilometer to meet it. I climbed into the hold and ordered the drone to the area of the flotilla, minimum travel time. That would require a ballistic trajectory, most of the flight above atmosphere.

"Bridget!" I messaged again. "What's happening?"

Her reply came with an overtone of anger that I rarely heard in her voice. "I've just gotten the big speech. It seems you are a distraction from my time and a bad influence. Bottom line, he wants me as a permanent member of the records team. He's informed me that you are now fish food. I'm being grounded temporarily to give me time to consider, but if I don't see the light, he'll make it permanent."

"Wait, that can't be right," I replied. "They shouldn't be able to pull your primaries."

"They didn't try. They *cut* them. With machetes. I've been clipped. I think maybe Alexander didn't want to cause me pain. Repair systems say twenty-four hours to generate new ones."

That was the last straw. I didn't give a good goddamn how much I upset the dragon history books. Alexander was going to get his heart punched out.

<< * >>

I directed the drone to come in under the altitude of the flotilla, then swoop upward. As the cargo door popped open, I dropped out and did a perfect arc, coming down over the royal floater.

Practice makes perfect, and this time, my superhero landing sprayed dirt on everyone. Bridget was standing there surrounded by soldiers, facing off against Alexander in apparent midargument. Both turned to stare at me, along with all the soldiers. Only Bridget's expression didn't register shock, although I think I'd even startled her.

"But, but you're . . ." Alexander sputtered.

"Dead?" I finished for him. Someone must have returned to report my fate before I'd made my reappearance. So much the better. "I was. Gerrard did a good job. But I don't stay down. Let's see how you do." I advanced on him, and several soldiers jumped forward to his defense.

And the cargo drone landed on them.

Not hard enough to crush them, but they'd certainly wake up with headaches. Battle-hardened or not, the rest of the soldiers scattered. Even Alexander backpedaled.

As the drone hovered in midair, camouflage off and the cargo door open, I messaged Bridget. "Go for it."

I said to Alexander, in a voice intended to carry, "The migration is a success. You've done a great thing for dragons. But you're still a bit of an asshole. I hope you'll disband your empire now that it's no longer needed."

Bridget, meanwhile, made a break for the shuttle. Clipped or not, she could still generate a little lift, and dranny muscles could manage a pretty good leap. In two bounds, she was in the cargo hold. With a leap and a flap, I joined her, and the door slammed shut.

I ordered the drone to re-camouflage and launch straight up, then reached forward and gently took one of Bridget's wings to examine the cut. She put her hand on mine and said, "It's just a dranny, Howard. Let's rack them and go home."

60. Encounter

Icarus
February 2338
Wormhole network

After our failure at the DMZ system, we'd decided to visit another civilization at random while we tried to work out a strategy going forward.

This last one had been especially interesting. The locals had essentially colonized their entire system, from the hot-as-hell Mercury-type planet near their sun to the freezing example of Fimbulwinter at the edge of their Kuiper belt. In addition, every single moon was covered in structures, and every asteroid bigger than about a half kilometer in diameter seemed to have been hollowed out and spun up for gravity.

And all empty.

I was trying very hard to avoid the feeling that I was in some kind of Stephen King horror story, where perhaps a carnivorous clown had eaten everyone. But it was hard.

As we oriented ourselves to the local orbital plane, my external sensors started blaring. "Woo-hoo," I yelled. "Action at last."

"Celebration is premature," Dae retorted. "Let's make sure we survive first."

A quick examination of the area via SUDDAR revealed a caravan of huge vessels on a trajectory that had them going between two wormholes. The wormhole they'd apparently exited was a hub connection, but a radial one that led inbound. The destination gate was also a hub, but we'd already determined that it led to the next hub spinwise.

We moved toward the caravan, but not so quickly or directly as to appear threatening. More of a "heading for the same gate" kind of vibe. I sent a gate-query frequency radio beam toward them, more in an act of desperation than anything. And I was rewarded with exactly what I expected: total ignore.

But we were now close enough for a SUDDAR scan. I sent out a full-power pulse and got back, well, very little. Most of the ship was quite visible in SUDDAR, and resembled any random space vessel—engines, maintenance, computer systems, et cetera. No passengers, though. There were spaces that appeared to be accommodations for living beings, but they were empty. So automated transports.

The surprise, though, was the area of the ship that had to be the hold. It was shielded. From SUDDAR. All I got back was a blank rectangular volume.

"I didn't know that was even possible," Dae said.

"Not a technology that we have," I replied. "Cloaking, yes. Shielding? That's a new one. I wonder what they're hiding?"

"Assuming they're hiding something. The shielding might be to protect the environment rather than the contents."

I frowned at him. "What needs that level of shielding?"

"I don't know. Ask them," Dae retorted, waving at the video window.

Shrugging, I sent a plain-language query in Roanokian. And got the same response.

"That's not really working, either," I said. "How about we follow?"

"Suits me."

We hurried to get in line behind the caravan. In a few hours, they reached the destination gate and began parading through. Finally, it was our turn, and we followed the last transport vessel.

"Where—?" I exclaimed, perplexed. The caravan had disappeared, except for the vessel we'd been following.

"They've split up," Dae said. Sure enough, the holotank tracking display showed each vessel heading for a different gate.

"None are hub gates. All local." I rubbed my chin in thought. "Local deliveries?"

"Of what?"

With a sigh, I changed my heading to follow the vessel in front of us as it made a slow, ponderous turn. "Let's find out."

((*))

We hadn't been through this particular gate ourselves, so it was a bit of a twofer. The transport ship, for that was almost certainly its purpose, steered a conservative course for what turned out to be the home planet for the local civilization. Or rather, a space station in a geosynchronous orbit.

The in-system trip took about thirty hours, given that the transport didn't seem to be in any kind of hurry. On arrival, it cozied up to the space station and docked. The station was monster big, easily dwarfing the transport, which was no baby itself. I also noticed a fleet of smaller ships maintaining position around the space station. They seemed to be all of a type, as well.

"Guards?" Dae said.

"Not very intimidating-looking. They have more of a cargo-drone vibe, I think."

"Ah. Maybe waiting for whatever the big ship is unloading."

The unloading took about six hours. At the end of it, the transport unlinked and began moving in a stately fashion for the gate. At the same time, the smaller cargo drones began queuing up at different docks. That pretty much confirmed that whatever the transport had unloaded, everyone wanted some.

I decided to try again with the station. I beamed a greeting in Roanokian.

And received a reply.

"Roanokian vessel, this is an interdicted zone. Unsafe for improperly equipped vessels. Please move to a safe distance."

I replied, "What is the nature of the danger?"

"Roanokian vessel, regulations require a one-thousand-kilometer exclusion zone from antimatter storage facilities for all unauthorized vessels. Please move to a safe distance to avoid impoundment."

Antimatter? Cripes. I backpedaled furiously, in a SURGE-drive kind of way, until we were at the appropriate distance.

"Hey, Icky, if they just delivered antimatter, you know what that means?"

"What?"

"They have a source of antimatter."

"You are a master of the obvious, Dae. And why would they need antimatter? Surely they have Casimir power systems. Actually, we *know* they do. We've scanned their vessels."

"Casimir generators are dependable, long-lasting, and don't require refueling," Dae said in lecture mode. "But they don't have a terrific power-to-mass ratio. The only reason we prefer them is because nuclear-fusion reactors were worse."

"Whereas antimatter . . ." I replied, prompting him.

"Is the densest power-delivery system in the universe. Yeah, you have to refuel every once in a while, but for situations where you need just monstrous levels of power, it's the way to go."

"Hmm. Good points. But it would have to be relatively easy to get hold of; otherwise, it wouldn't be worth it. And creating it in colliders and such is a nonstarter."

"True. So let's find out. Assuming the transport ship is heading home for another load, we should follow."

We pulled up behind the transport vessel, which was making its way in a barge-like manner toward the wormhole gate, and slowed *way* down. There's an episode of *The Simpsons* where Homer is following a turtle during an acid trip, and he gets impatient and kicks it over the horizon. Staring at the back end of the transport, I could sympathize. This thing just was not in a hurry.

The ship went through the local gate, then the two hub gates. The second one, though, which we hadn't yet investigated, turned out to be a radial line and was about ten thousand light-years closer to galactic center.

"All right!" I crowed. "We may be visiting the core sooner than expected."

"I wonder if there's a reason for putting an antimatter factory in the core," Dae said, frowning.

"If nothing else, the big black heavy thing is a great source of power."

"Sure, if it doesn't spaghettify you or reduce you to elementary particles. Should we be heading there?"

"Dae, my guess is if we are going into a dangerous region, we'll receive a warning. And now that we have a common language, we'll actually understand that warning."

"Yippee."

«*»

Two more gates, and we were in the core. I had read that there were more than ten million stars within a parsec of the galactic center, and that the average distance between stars in this region was below a half light-year.

None of these dry factoids came even close to touching the reality of what we faced. The sky was ablaze with stars, with virtually no empty space showing, except possibly straight up and down. Red dominated, as most of the stars in this region were old, red giants. But a period of star formation about a million years ago had also produced a large crop of young, blue-white giants, some of which I could swear showed visible disks.

"Good God in heaven," Dae breathed.

With a huge effort, I pulled my eyes away from the vista and checked the security monitors. Happily, we were *not* right on top of a sun. We appeared to be several AU from a small white dwarf. Of course, I thought, the makers of the wormhole network would have picked a relatively stable location to set up. But in this stellar soup, stability was likely transitory. I wondered if you could move a wormhole once opened.

We began to take stock. The transport ship continued on its stately way, and we adjusted course to follow.

I dismissed my VR in favor of a total-surround stellarium view. I floated, seemingly disembodied, in a sea of stars.

"Sagittarius A* is about seven light-years that way," Dae said, using a laser-pointer metaphor. The red dot circled around a spot on the stellarium surface.

"It's still just all stars," I complained. "Let's tone down the visible spectrum and bring in a radio-frequency layer."

In the radio spectrum, we could see the jets from the central black hole racing north and south, ballooning into the Fermi bubbles that existed above and below the galactic core. And something else . . .

"That is . . ." Dae said, working his laser pointer.

"Hold on." I shifted the spectrum being displayed, and the artifact became clearly visible. Close to us—*very* close on an astronomical scale—something was firing a brilliant plume to galactic north, and glowing brightly. "That," I said, "is the view at five hundred and eleven KeV."

"Antimatter annihilation," Dae breathed.

"Yup. I guess it makes sense that we'd come out near the antimatter source."

"So this is the legendary antimatter fountain."

I nodded, struck dumb with awe. In 1997, astronomers had discovered that something near the galactic center was shooting a plume of antimatter particles thousands of light-years to galactic north. And only to the north, which no one had an explanation for. The radiation given off when the antimatter interacted with normal interstellar dust and gas glowed at 511 KeV, the radiation signature of total annihilation.

"Well, now we know," I said.

"Know what? The empire is getting antimatter from here, but we still have no idea what it is, other than a tremendous source of antimatter."

"Enough to power an empire. And keep it running, apparently."

Dae sighed. "Let's look around. I'd hate to leave without finding out anything more."

We engaged SURGE and swiftly overtook our escort. I kept my stellarium VR up, and I noted that Dae wasn't expressing any need to re-corporate.

Sensors indicated we were still about ten AU from the fountainhead when we detected a communication over SCUT. We *still* hadn't mastered the empire's SCUT comm standards, so I cast around until I spotted a likely source for the transmission and sent a greeting via radio in Roanokian.

The source appeared to be a large space station, or possibly a small asteroid. It had all kinds of technological accretions, a cloud of small vehicles in parking orbits around it, and showed every indication of being the administrative center for the region.

A response came back immediately in the same medium. "Roanokian vessels, you have entered an interdicted area. This is the Central Antimatter Works for the Pan Galactic Federation. Unauthorized vessels are prohibited. Stop immediately or face impoundment of your vehicles."

We stopped immediately and tried to display good intentions by reversing course for a short distance.

"Pan Galactic Federation," Dae said. "That's interesting. I wonder how accurate that is."

"As accurate as our translations of Roanokian, I guess. Double-check the individual words, will you?" Without waiting for a response, I sent a message to the space station. "Can you supply a map of the stellar neighborhood that will keep us out of the interdicted area?"

"Star maps are available via Mapping Protocol, which is supported only through SCUT transmission."

"Oh, for fuck's sake," Dae muttered.

I replied. "We do not know the standard communication protocols used by the Pan Galactic Federation. Can you give us the specs?"

In reply, the space station sent a series of extremely dense text files in Roanokian. A quick glance indicated that we'd been given not only the Mapping Protocol but also the Identification and Authorization Protocol, the Audio/Video/Other Communications Protocol, and a couple of other less relevant items.

"Finally, someone is being helpful," I muttered. Then, to the station, "May we enter a parking orbit while we digest this?"

"Affirmative."

And just like that, we were in business.

《 * 》

"Seven light-years to Sagittarius A*, or to as close to it as we want to get. That's seven years each way, Icky—so another fourteen years minimum before we report in." Dae stood glaring at me, his fists literally on his hips in an unconscious parody of Mom when she disapproved of our choices.

"We've already been at this for almost thirty years, Dae. Plus the time we spent in normal space before we found the wormholes. We've long since disconnected from Bobiverse society. And it's not like they're expecting us."

"Depends, doesn't it? On whether our SCUT stations get into position and whether anyone's listening when our radio message gets there. And then, radio silence. I don't see Bill just shrugging his shoulders and moving on."

"So how is that a bad thing? It means we'll have follow-up."

Dae sighed and looked deflated. "It comes down to what happened to the empire—"

"Federation."

"Whatever. If it's something we need to know about, and soon, this delay could be critical."

"You're kidding. You think we arrived on schedule to nip the danger in the bud just in the nick of time? C'mon, Dae, we'd switch off a movie if they did that."

Dae grimaced and looked away. Then he said, "Okay, but once we've done this, we head straight back to Roanoke to report in to Bill, right?"

"You got it." I grinned knowingly at him. He wasn't fooling anyone. He wanted to go just as much as I did but needed to play the responsible clone.

We'd deciphered the texts from the administrative station, which were essentially identical to internet RFCs. A quick test netted us local star maps. Now we would be able to converse via SCUT when we needed to.

I did another test, asking the station if there were any biological entities on-site we could talk to.

"No."

Well, that was terse. "How long since any were on-site?"

"That information is not available."

Sigh. Not surprising, I guess. I gave Dae a lopsided smile, and we fired up the drives.

61. First Test

Bill
December 2344
Skippyland

I looked around the moot hall. This wasn't technically supposed to be a public event, but it was hard to keep a secret from yourselves in the Bobiverse. No non-Bobs, though, other than a select group of insiders. Bridget was here, as were Steven Gilligan and Hannah Turnbull. Also present was Bob's Quinlan friend, Theresa Sykorski, in her human avatar. And of course, Hugh in his video window. Skippyland was still under quarantine, even more than a decade later.

All told, we had about a hundred people in attendance. That was actually a small number if you considered the nature of the event we'd be witnessing. A Heaven vessel carrying three mannies was going to use the wormhole transit system to travel from Epsilon Eridani to the Skippyland star system. It was a one-way trip—nothing would be allowed to leave Skippyland until we knew Thoth had been captured or destroyed.

I swept my gaze over the audience. Everyone had beers or coffees or some other form of refreshment-delivery system. I'd put out snacks, but my repertoire was typical Bob—more utilitarian than imaginative. Sandwiches and chips.

"Okay, folks. We're almost all Bobs here, so I'm not going to do a huge dog-and-pony show. We have the ship ready to dive into the wormhole. Thor is driving"—I pointed to a Bob in the corner, and he waved to the audience—"and we have the route very carefully mapped out. The transit endpoints are ten thousand kilometers apart at each system, so the ship, which we've named the *Snark*, will have to fly that distance nine times. Even that shouldn't take long enough to bore anyone, since you can hit the wormhole interface at full speed. So let's get started." I nodded to Thor. "Whenever you're ready."

Thor gave me a thumbs-up and played with his control console. It was theater, of course. He could have just stood there and controlled the ship with mental commands, but even after several hundred years, we Bobs found we still appreciated visual metaphors. I hoped that would never change, and I felt a little sorry for the Skippies, who seemed to be moving to a data-centric lifestyle format.

A huge video window popped up overhead, showing the forward view from the ship. Telemetry along the sides gave an indication of galactic coordinates and bearing, velocity, and so on. As we watched, the velocity telltale rocketed upward. Thor was wasting no time.

In a few seconds real time, a phrase flashed up in bottom center: *Transit 1 Completed*. The starscape dead ahead might have been slightly different, but I couldn't have sworn to it. What was most notable, though, was the complete lack of drama. I knew the compression effect was still an issue, but far less of one with a larger wormhole mouth. Experimentation had shown it to be a kind of inverted tidal effect.

In rapid succession, the ship flashed through several more transits, each accompanied by the announcement in the bottom center. Thor had to adjust the heading several times to aim for the next wormhole endpoint, but it was minimal. The whole exercise had been carefully planned.

It took a half hour, all told, quite a long time in replicant normal but not even long enough for lunch in human terms. The video subtitle said, *Transit Complete,* and the velocity of the ship dropped to zero. Well, zero relative to the destination system. I think the total proper-motion difference between the Skippy system and Epsilon Eridani was around twenty-five kilometers per second, and Thor had had to make that adjustment during his flight.

"Hugh?" I looked at his video window. He glanced briefly to the side, then said, "We've got the *Snark* on SUDDAR. Looks good. A drone is flying out to meet the ship and guide it to the space station."

At that moment, Will, Bob, and Garfield popped into the moot hall.

They had been controlling the mannies in the *Snark*'s passenger cabin and had more or less directly experienced the transit.

"Wow," Will said. "Eighty-two light-years, just like *that*." He snapped his fingers. "Nice work, Bill."

Garfield cleared his throat.

"And Garfield. Sorry." Will grinned.

"Sure you are," Garfield retorted. "But yeah. Total nonevent for mannies. I don't think even humans would notice anything. None of my telltales came even close to going red. Although my connection got briefly dropped on every transit."

"Well, there you have it, folks," I said to the crowd. "Interstellar travel, FTL version. We're not sure how much it'll affect things when everyone is traveling by huey, but hey, it's still an improvement."

"It'll affect colonization in the future," Will said in his stage voice. "Ships will go out with an inventory of stable wormhole endpoints and not much else. Once we find a system, we'll expand a wormhole and fly boatloads of colonists through."

"Cool," I replied. "In fact, it will be standard procedure to keep an inventory of wormhole pairs and link each system you pass to the previous one. Instant Galactic Highway."

"Wow. Nice." Will paused and frowned. "Bill, I don't know if this has been asked or thought of, but can you transit a wormhole while carrying a wormhole endpoint?"

I chuckled. "Tried it. It didn't end well. The endpoint you're attempting to carry decoheres rather violently. The wormhole you're transiting destabilizes, too."

"Does the transport vessel come out either end?"

"Some of it. Usually from both ends. Along with a crapton of gamma radiation."

Will's eyebrows went up. "Oh. Okay, let's not do that."

Hannah stepped forward. "Very nice job, Bill. I've been trying to replicate your results using only theoretical models for the last ten years, and I still haven't come up with anything. I guess there's a place in the universe for experimental physics after all."

I grinned at her. "Sometimes it's the results that count."

"So what now?"

I glanced at Hugh in his video window. "I guess we start bringing in resources and set up a picket line. Eventually, Fake Hugh will presumably try to get into this system and extract Thoth."

I was interrupted by Guppy, who popped into the middle of the hall without warning.

[**Unknown ship is transiting wormhole.**]

We all briefly exchanged glances. I could see everyone doing the same mental inventory. "Can you identify it?"

[**Vessel is Titan class.**]

"How many Titan-class vessels are in operation, Bill?" Bob asked.

"Two," I replied with a sinking feeling. "The *Snark*, and the one that Fake Hugh stole. The rest are still docked in Ultima Thule. Unless some descendant has cloned and built one for their clone."

"Possible, but I'm going to put my money on Fake Hugh. Why travel the whole way by sub-light, giving us seventy years to set up for him?" Garfield frowned and crossed his arms. "So much easier to just head for one of the systems that we would naturally use to build a transit system and wait for us to open for business."

I checked the trajectory of the unknown ship and decided we had some time. I cranked the moot frame rate up a tad, and everyone present automatically matched it.

Garfield continued, his frown deepening and his voice developing an aggrieved tone. "So Bill, this means Fake Hugh was expecting you to succeed. You were intended to solve the negative-energy problem so that Fake Hugh could piggyback off it to get here sooner."

"Well, we don't know that," Will interjected. "If Fake Hugh had some—"

"Can we please stop calling him *Fake Hugh*?" Hugh exclaimed.

"No!" Garfield shouted back.

Will glanced at the both of them, shook his head, and continued, "If he had some way of tracking your progress, he would have realized at some point that he'd be better off with this strategy."

"So he's winging it?" Bob said.

"Maybe. I don't know how much difference it makes." Hugh looked around at the group. "Either way, he's coming in to rescue Thoth. We have to stop that."

"So what's he most likely going to try?" I asked.

"There's no friggin' way he'd have time to physically grab something, like a matrix or whatever. Even assuming Thoth was somehow able to download itself into a physical container. In any case, we're real-time monitoring Thoth, to the extent we're able, anyway, and it's still in the system."

"So . . ."

"Thoth couldn't transport itself out of Skippyland because we'd locked down the SCUT systems, even if it had some destination hardware that would take it. But I'm betting Fake Hugh has built something in the meantime. Thoth might try to transport itself to Fake Hugh's ship, via either radio or local SCUT channel."

"SCUT for sure," Will commented. "Radio would take forever and could be jammed. Can Thoth get access to a SCUT transceiver?"

"I'd have said no, but so far, it's been one step ahead of us. And JOVAH runs on a SCUT backplane, so there's no lack of local hardware."

"Can we just shut down the wormholes?" Hannah asked.

I shook my head. "The negative-energy scaffolding will decay on its own if we stop renewing it, but that could be hours or days. I didn't think to implement an *off* switch, and honestly, I'm not sure how I'd go about it. I'll have to work on that."

"We have to blow up Fake Hugh as soon as he comes through, then," Garfield said.

"How?" Hugh exclaimed. "We're not set up yet. We have security around the JOVAH modules, obviously, but Fake Hugh doesn't have to go anywhere near them. He just has to get into the system."

"Plus, if we stop him, Thoth will still be there causing trouble and will just try something else." Bob paused and looked around. "Maybe we should let him succeed."

"What?" I exclaimed. Several people echoed me.

"Look, Thoth will most likely delete himself locally once he's successfully escaped. It would be unethical and probably unthinkable for him to leave himself trapped. Plus, there's always the chance we could ultimately defeat the copy and decompile him or something."

"Debatable, but not out of the question," Hugh replied. "Okay, he'll shut down his local copy and probably scrub it as well. So?"

"So he won't do that until it looks like he's gotten away cleanly. Bill, you have the Titan-class flight characteristics available, right?"

I raised my eyebrows at this apparent non sequitur but nodded. This was getting interesting.

«*»

We watched the monitors as Fake Hugh's ship whipped through each of the transit points. He had accelerated to a truly ridiculous velocity. He was actually hitting the wormhole endpoints at just a few percent below the speed of light. That was interesting, because it was an obviously risky move. Thoth must have figured out the characteristics of a wormhole transit system far in advance, since he would have had no way to update Fake Hugh.

As Garfield kept saying, I hated being so predictable.

The ship hit the final transit at a slight angle. That was not unexpected. He wouldn't want to come through into a waiting wall of steel balls. With three dimensions to play with, his vector was difficult to predict in advance, except within broad limits. Nevertheless, we had placed pickets on the Skippyland side. But with only minutes to prepare, the defenses were woefully inadequate.

The ship rocketed out of the final transit endpoint, missing our pickets by not all that much, actually. I wondered if Fake Hugh would need new underwear. We immediately sent a few Skippy ships after it, but they really had no hope. Their only reasonable tactic would be to harass their target and eventually blow it out of the sky. And that would require it to stay on the Skippyland side, which meant that, logically, Fake Hugh would attempt to dive back into the wormhole.

"I'm registering a large data transfer via SCUT," Hugh announced. "And I was right. Thoth has co-opted one of the backplane SCUT transceivers. He's probably temporarily lobotomized a lot of our population."

"No chance he's gotten himself as well, I suppose," Garfield grumbled.

"That's an easy calculation to make if you know what's coming," Hugh replied. "He'll have moved his VM out of that memory segment."

The transmission took several minutes. Meanwhile, Fake Hugh accelerated in an extremely tight arc to come around to bear on the wormhole endpoint.

"How much you want to bet his path is finely calculated to hit the wormhole just after the transmission completes?" Bob mused.

"No bet," Will replied. He glanced at me. "You ready?"

"Yup."

Fake Hugh's ship had a far greater acceleration capability than the Skippy vessels that were pursuing him. They steadily fell behind as their own wider arcs diverged from their prey. I noted in passing that Fake Hugh's trajectory would take him to the opposite side of the wormhole from our ship. No doubt a strategic move, and I hoped he would be too busy to wonder why we weren't being more active in the pursuit.

I knew the flight characteristics of the Titan-class Heaven vessel down to a T. In particular, I knew exactly when Fake Hugh would be fully committed to entering the wormhole, with no ability to change vector or brake enough to avoid it. I also knew exactly what the *Snark*'s rail gun was capable of. At full power, rerouting even the drive-system power to the rail gun, the *Snark* could accelerate a steel ball to a tenth the speed of light.

A lightweight container, even more so.

"Transmission ended," Hugh announced. "As expected, we have a status change on the section of JOVAH that Thoth has been occupying. I *hope* that means it's started a shutdown and purge. We won't know for sure until we do a postmortem."

"If not, you'll be back to square one," I said. At that moment, the quarry hit the point of no return. I sent the command, and the *Snark* fired a lightweight metal container straight at the wormhole. The container housed one end of one of our spare wormhole pairs, and the onboard equipment started growing the wormhole even as it left the bow of the *Snark*. By the time it hit the transit wormhole, it would be more than big enough to create some serious fireworks.

The container hit the wormhole interface just before Fake Hugh's ship, and . . .

I found myself back in my home VR.

I immediately sent queries to everyone who had been at the moot and began receiving excited replies. The most interesting was from Hugh.

> *Hey, Bill. The wormhole self-destructed as planned. You may have been a little more enthusiastic than really necessary. We're having to activate emergency procedures here to shield our JOVAH modules. The* Snark *is toast. Fake Hugh's ship would have been just outside the interface when the wormhole self-destructed, so I doubt there's so much as two atoms from the ship left connected. Hell, I wouldn't be surprised if it's been reduced to free quarks.*

Well, that was good. I sent a message back asking Hugh to connect up when he was ready, then invited the others back to the moot hall.

‹‹ * ››

"That went well," Garfield said, flopping into a La-Z-Boy. I gave him a side-eye. We were in the pub, and overstuffed loungers were definitely not part of the décor. He grinned at me, guessed my concern, and changed it to a barstool.

Most of the rest had begged off, requesting an update once we knew more. It was just Will, Bob, Garfield, and me now. The pub felt empty and kind of lonely. I promised myself I'd call some full moots on a regular basis, just to keep the community going.

"Any updates?" Will asked.

"I'm getting the occasional message from Hugh, kind of like informal status updates." I paused and perused the thread. "It looks like Thoth is gone from JOVAH. They're able to get into the full memory space, and there's no trace of the A.I. It's also no longer gobbling the processing time that it was when active."

"So the question is whether Fake Hugh's ship was destroyed," Bob said.

"The *Snark* was obliterated, and we were ten times farther away." I chuckled. "Apparently, the blowback from the wormhole collapse actually destabilized the Skippies' home star temporarily. They were quite worried it was going to shed a layer, with all the electromagnetic fun and games that would have implied."

"Wow. So we're going to have to be very careful with wormholes," Garfield said.

"That seems like a given, Gar. But having them out beyond the Kuiper seems like a good start."

"Hmm, yeah. So Thoth is done?"

I sighed. "I don't think we can know to a mathematical certainty. But the Skippies will do a full analysis and identify any possible holes."

"Have they given up on creating a true A.I.?"

I rolled my eyes. "No, of course not. But they're going to invoke the next one in a completely isolated computer system. Isolated in every meaning of the word. With nukes strapped to it. At the slightest sign of anything janky, they'll pull the trigger and start over."

"Wasn't that the plan this time?" Garfield said with a frown.

"I dunno, Gar. The thing is, whatever Thoth's overall scheme may have been, it *did* give us the wormholes. And I think, eventually, a warp drive. So I'm a little more sympathetic than I was the first time around." I grinned. "Hannah, er, Professor Turnbull has offered to work with me on the warp drive. Her comment was *it's like being young all over again.*"

Garfield gave me a hard look. "You aren't going all *Bob* on us, are you?"

"Hey, I'm *sitting* here," Bob exclaimed.

Garfield and I both grinned at him before I replied, "Naw, but I think we're well past the time when we can stick to our own company. There's now a significant percentage of ex-humans in replicant space, not to mention the Quiniverse. I wonder if a totally digital existence is the final result for every species."

"It would give us another explanation for the Fermi paradox," Bob said.

"So would getting eaten by the Others, blowing each other up, or getting eradicated by a superintelligence," Garfield retorted. "All of which humanity seems to have narrowly avoided by the skin of their collective teeth."

Will paused and sat forward. "Y'know, that's a very real possibility as an explanation. Starting on day one, you have all the usual risks, like meteor strike, nearby supernova, ecological catastrophe, and so on. But once a species becomes intelligent, they start introducing more existential dangers, like climate change, all the forms of warfare, and self-destructive technologies like gray goo and A.I.s. And none of the older dangers go away, really. If the dangers just keep piling up as the species advances, eventually the odds catch up with you. It might be that extinction becomes statistically inevitable at some point."

I sighed. "Dunno, Will. I guess we need more data points. I'd better get started on that warp drive."

62. Dragon Report

Howard
October 2344
Trantor

I was plowing my way through my emails, grumbling under my breath. A coffee on my chair arm was cooling, forgotten. Bridget looked up from her Canvas screen and said, "I think it's about time you hire an administrative assistant to take all that paperwork off your hands."

"But then I'd just need to find another reason to complain. It really doesn't bother me that much."

Bridget gave me the evil eye. "It's not you I'm concerned about, Whiney McWhineyFace. Some peace and quiet would be nice." She gestured at her Canvas. "I'm trying to organize our adventure into a report for the UFS Exobiology Society."

"Oh. Sorry, Bridge. I should do this in *virt* anyway. Get it done faster."

"Sounds good. And when you get back, I'll make you a martini."

"No, that's fine—I'll make them. Want one now?"

"That'd be nice."

Outmaneuvered again. But at least my martini would be palatable.

"You're monitoring the dragons, right?" I asked.

"Of course. It's a major species development. Migration to a new continent, effects on the ecosystem, evolutionary pressures, probably a bottleneck or two . . . We'll be watching for centuries."

"Mmm. But they'll survive?"

"It looks good. Alexander cut all the floaters loose, and they're spreading out. The new lake fish seem to be acceptable. No new predators or diseases so far."

"And the old continent?"

She shook her head. "It's not Siberian Traps level, but life's going to be tough. The floaters are being knocked out of the air, which will probably drive the lake trout to near extinction. Being overfished by the surviving dragons will likely finish the job; then the dragons will starve." She sat back, glaring at the screen, lost in thought for a moment. "If all the floaters die, there won't be any trout eggs getting deposited in new lakes. Total ecosystem collapse. Alexander was right."

"He's still an asshole."

"He lives in a medieval society, Howard. The Iron Rule applies. And on that subject . . ." She turned her chair to face me. "During my face-off with him, I made a comment about making my own decisions about who I'd have as a mate, and he laughed at me."

"Seriously?"

"Mmm. I was actually a little miffed, which is funny, given the circumstances. Maybe I've watched too many bad vids, but he told me in no uncertain terms that he wasn't the slightest bit interested that way. It was about my usefulness and nothing else."

"That's it. He insulted my wife. I'll kill him."

"Down, boy. It wasn't much of an improvement. I was going to be chattel for the rest of my life."

I grinned at her. "Which at least would have been a long one. You didn't get a spear through the chest."

She snorted. "Stop whining. You took the downtime to do paperwork. What does that say about you?"

"That I need an assistant?"

Bridget laughed and took the martini from my hand. "Please. And soon."

63. A New Beginning

Bill
January 2345
Epsilon Eridani

This was going to be a huge day. I was in the *Snark II* in manny form, sitting about ten thousand kilometers away from the Epsilon Eridani wormhole. I had already placed wormholes leading directly to Omicron^2 Eridani and Sol in slightly different orbital positions in the Oort cloud. Other wormholes were being flown in, and within a decade, I'd be able to reach any UFS star system from here. *Physically* reach, I mean. Not just a remotely operated SCUT-controlled manny. The Interstellar Highway, FTL version, was becoming a reality. WormNet. How much it would affect humanity remained to be seen.

Hugh had suggested a round-trip transit of the full system, with him flying across using a manny. It seemed like a safe enough activity—no Bobs could actually be harmed, even if we lost the manny and/or ship. And we needed some kind of ceremonial event to celebrate the official opening of WormNet.

My console beeped as a ship exited the wormhole. Named the *Singularity*, it was clearly visible in the view screen, its Skippyland silhouette distinct from the normal Heaven configuration. I engaged SURGE, and we met at the halfway point.

A brief rotation of hulls ended with our airlocks facing each other. Both doors opened, and a figure jumped across from the *Singularity* to the *Snark*. No space suit, of course. Mannies didn't need them.

In minutes, a Bob manny strolled into my control room. We still all looked the same by default, but my head's-up display identified the manny as belonging to Hugh. He was, of course, wearing the ubiquitous Skippy gray coveralls.

"So, my old nemesis, we meet at last," he said.

"Yeah, that's not dramatic." I grinned at him. "I feel like we should have a marching band and speeches and stuff."

"And food," Hugh added.

"That, too," I said, laughing. "This is historic. We're the first Bobs coming together again after being separated by interstellar distances."

"Mmm," Hugh said, waggling a hand. "Well, you guys did visit us last year, but not in person." He looked down at the hand and then gave me a sheepish grin. "Not that a manny is any less of a remote device, but it feels different somehow."

"True." I changed the subject. "So how's the transit?"

"Kind of weird. I lost the manny connection, obviously. No SCUT in a wormhole. I was able to reconnect on this side right away, but it's disconcerting. The SCUT network isn't as smooth as a cell network. That might be something we'll have to work on going forward."

"I get the point," I replied, "but I'm not sure how often we're going to be riding active mannies through a wormhole."

"Fair enough. So have we found a human yet who's willing to be a guinea pig?"

"Nope. Although I've transported a bunch of actual guinea pigs."

"And?"

"No effect. No major effect, anyway. They became agitated during the transit, so they felt something. But they didn't explode, turn inside out, become evil, or develop superpowers. So there's that."

"What does an evil guinea pig look like, anyway?"

"Eye patch and tattoos, I think." I grinned and then became serious. "So the search for Thoth is over?"

Hugh nodded. "We've confirmed that we have complete control over JOVAH once again. We repaired that SCUT backplane transceiver. Still trying to figure out how Thoth got enough physical access to be able to modify it. As far as we can tell, it never had control of any waldos, roamers, or autofactories."

"And no unexplained rogue computer systems floating around?"

"We'd notice," Hugh said with a chuckle. "Thoth would require a fairly large system, even using the new quantum computing technology that ANEC gave us. It would glow in infrared. So no, it didn't just transfer itself to another computer."

We talked for several more minutes, but there really wasn't anything pressing to discuss. This whole thing was just a stunt, and we both knew it. Finally, Hugh stood and stuck out a hand. "Well, buddy, it's been *real*."

We shook, and he gave me a salute as he headed back to the airlock. Two minutes later, the *Singularity* gave me two blinks of the nav lights, moved to a safe distance, and accelerated toward the gate.

I sighed as I watched the ship dive back into the wormhole, then set the autopilot to dock the *Snark II* at Ultima Thule. I parked my butt in the pilot's seat and disconnected. I would rack the manny properly once the ship was parked.

I was in my VR, just settling down with a cup of coffee, when I got a call from Hugh. He popped up in video, which was mildly surprising. He could have joined in VR, but I was beyond second-guessing Skippies by this point.

"Hey, Bill, did everything go as expected when I left there?"

"I . . . sorry, what? You went back to your ship, flew into the wormhole, and disappeared. No flash, no bang, if that's what you mean."

"I'm not sure *what* I mean. I remember all that, just as you described. Then I reconnected with my manny on this side and started heading back to our space station. Docked, racked the manny, and so on. Everything seemed fine. Then, a while later, I got a call from Port Control asking me when I'd be arriving."

"Uhhhhh . . ." Not my best response, but based on the sinking feeling in my stomach, possibly appropriate.

"Funny, that's about what I said. According to Port Control, the *Singularity* exited the wormhole, then turned on a different heading and accelerated away. They didn't think much of it since I still had a half hour on my flight plan before I was due. But then that time came and went, and . . ."

"And they called you. Meanwhile, you say you had docked the ship?"

"Yup. Returned the manny and everything. Except the manny isn't in its pod. No record of the return."

"Jeez, Hugh, should I be worried?"

"I think I'm worried enough for both of us." Hugh paused. "My first thought was that Port Control was either mistaken or lying. But there are enough monitoring systems in Skippyland—video, radar, radio, astronomical, and so on—that I was able to confirm Port Control's version of events. So here's the thing." Again, the pause. "It didn't match up with my experience at all. Obviously. Timing, acceleration, no overlap. The only possible conclusion is that I was experiencing a VR version of the flight back."

"VR . . ." That sinking feeling just got worse. "You mean someone, or something, *fed you* a bogus experience to make you think you had docked the ship?"

"Uh-huh. Exactly that."

"Have you brought this up with your higher-ups?"

"That's why I'm talking to you in video, Bill. We're locked down again."

"Theories?"

"Someone or something took over the manny and/or the *Singularity* and essentially stole it. Bill, can I ask you a possibly odd question?"

"Everything's odd right now. Go ahead."

"Did you arrange our meeting?"

"What? No! You did."

"Nope. I got an email from you suggesting it. The smell of old fish is all over this."

"Motherffff . . . Okay, Hugh. Keep me up to date, will you?"

"Will do." The video window disappeared, leaving me alone in my VR. It wasn't actually possible for a cold wind to blow through unless I specifically ordered it, but nevertheless, I felt a chill.

64. Something Interesting

Ferb
June 2345
Somewhere to galactic north

A reminder popped up in front of me. George's next report was due in a few minutes. I felt a surge of anticipation. His reports had been interesting from day one, and I'd gotten hooked. Somehow, in the three years since I'd started receiving George's reports, the decision to turn onto a new heading kept getting put off and put off, until one day I realized the decision had been made.

I was getting closer to him, since he was stopping at the occasional star system to survey it, whereas I was just marathoning it, accelerating constantly. It would still be a while before I'd catch him, but the closing gap meant I was getting reports at twice the rate he was putting them out. Interestingly, they'd been getting less touristy and more technical the last couple of weeks. Something seemed to be bugging him, but in typical Bob fashion, he wasn't going to say anything specific until he had all his ducks in a row. Maybe today there'd be a reveal of some kind.

I busied myself, setting up a tray of snacks and drinks. The reports required a ceremony of sorts to prepare myself. Little sandwiches, chocolates, some cheesecake . . . I had to admit, the templates were getting better and better as more ex-humans got involved in post-life cuisine.

Finally, the moment arrived. I settled back with a smile as George's standard lead-in played. Then he got right into the meat, and it appeared he was ready to talk about his results.

Oh. I sat back, my jaw almost unhinging as I worked through the ramifications. George's conclusion was interesting. And not *good* interesting, either. Bill was definitely going to want to hear about this.

Unfortunately, at my speed, I couldn't sustain a VR session, but an email would be fine.

65. The Black Hole

Icarus
June 2345
Sagittarius A*

Twenty-three million kilometers. That was the diameter of the event horizon. Of course, that wasn't tremendously big on the grand scale of things. The red supergiant UY Scuti was reputed to have a diameter of more than a billion kilometers, and that was just a garden-variety star. From our distance, we had to use our SURGE-based telescopic image enhancement just to see Sagittarius A* as more than a point source.

We'd approached from forty-five degrees to galactic north, per the instructions on the star maps. The black hole had an accretion disk in the galactic plane that extended several light-years, and you wouldn't want to fly through that. Even from above, the magnetic fields threw off enough crud to make this area of space interesting, in a bad way.

But the black hole itself was . . . incredible. Of course, we took pictures and videos aplenty. And spent unmeasured time just staring at the thing. This was the fabric of the universe in its raw form.

Bobs, and post-life physicists and astronomers as well, would have our guts for dinner if we failed to take every possible measurement. We made sure we covered all the bases.

Finally, though, it was time to leave. Dae had started his good clone/bad clone routine again, and I could feel his eyes boring into the side of my head.

"Fine, Dae. Let's pack 'er up and go. But if we forgot something, that's on you."

"I reject your analysis and substitute my own."

"Yeah, okay. Seven years for the return trip. Let's make 'em quick."

A thought occurred to me as we were bringing ourselves around for the flight back to the antimatter fountain. "I wonder if the administration station would answer other questions."

"Worth a try."

Since we had communicated with the station, we had its SCUT address in Federation network standard format. I opened a link. "Central Antimatter Works, this is the Roanokian vessel, uh, *Croatoan*. Can you answer some questions for us?"

"Possibly."

Huh. Not big on courtesy, obviously. "What is the nature of the antimatter fountain?"

"It is either a white hole or a wormhole from a region comprised predominantly of antimatter."

"You can't tell which?"

"That information is not available."

I said in an aside to Dae, "Didn't take long to get to that, did it?" Then to the station, "Can you tell me where the population of the Federation went?"

"That information is not available."

"Can you tell me why?"

"The imminent destruction of the galaxy made emigration necessary."

Whaaaaaaaaaaat? I turned to Dae, my jaw dropping almost to my really quite pointless navel. His face registered the same level of shock.

"Can you tell me how the galaxy is about to be destroyed?"

"That information is not available."

"How long until it happens?"

"That information is not available."

"Is there somewhere that I can go where that information is available?"

"Are you asking me to tell you where to go?"

I laughed reflexively, and Dae spit his coffee out. "No way that was unintentional."

"Apparently, we are annoying," Dae muttered.

I addressed the station. "Yes, please tell us where to go."

We both scrunched up, fists balled and uncontrollable grins on our faces, waiting for the comeback. It would be worth it.

There was an unaccountably long pause before the station replied in a totally straight tone, "The Capital Archives would have the greatest chance of satisfying your curiosity. Far better than ongoing dialogue here. Routing instructions attached. Good voyage."

Dae chuckled. "I bet it was fighting its programming there."

"Yup. 'Good voyage' was not the intended salutation."

"Should we ask a few more questions? Just because?"

"Now you're just being mean. Let's hit the road."

66. In System

Herschel
February 2345
Omicron² Eridani

Will pinged us while we were in the lounge. I looked over at the manny pods; gave Neil an eyebrow waggle, which he answered with a grin; and sent Will a manny address. In moments, one of the pods opened, and Will stepped out.

"Nice," he said, looking around. "But this isn't a Skywalker, right?"

I shook my head. "No, those are still a long way from being generally useful. Although we've been able to find a couple of uses where we need to change shape to get at things. But since we built the lounge"—I gestured to the room—"we started working on being able to entertain visitors in *real*. Coffee?"

"Always." Will frowned, then looked around. "Hmm . . . I guess I have to find a physical place to sit. I actually tried to invoke a chair for a moment. Speaking of," he said, plunking himself down on a handy couch, "I guess someone has to actually *make* coffee?"

I smiled as Jeeves entered the room, looking like John Cleese from his Monty Python days, with three cups on a tray. Will did a double take. "You've instantiated Jeeves into a manny? You guys have way too much time on your hands. I need to give you more work."

"Like extracting thirty thousand people from Romulus?" I replied. "Operation Bug-Out isn't going—"

"Operation Bug-Out?" Neil interjected. "Since when?"

I gave him an offhand shrug. "Just thought of it. As I was saying, without somewhere to put them, I'm not really sure what we can do. Other than dump them on Vulcan until we organize something."

"All covered, guys," Will said. "I can put them in my hold, and I'll arrive at Vulcan shortly after you."

I gave him the stink-eye. "You been misdirecting everyone about your location, too? Wow, you can't trust anyone anymore."

"Yes and no," Will said with a smile. "There's been a lot of secret projects lately. Not just because of FAITH. Unfortunately, that means even most of the Bobiverse is in the dark. I'll explain it all when I arrive."

I glanced at Neil before replying. "Okay, Will. But this will have to be executed quickly. The moment either of our ships is detected in Omicron^2 Eridani space, the jig will be up."

"You installed a cloak, right? Did you get the internal drive working?"

I nodded. "Yes, and yes. We've long since retired the pusher plates. But in regard to the cloaking, even a faint signal from a ship the size of the *Bellerophon* is going to set off detectors. We'll be able to get within a million kilometers of Romulus and Vulcan, but any closer, and we *will* be noticed."

"Got it. So let's set our rendezvous location appropriately. See you guys soon." Will put his empty mug down on a side table and disconnected. The manny, under AMI control, got up and headed for its pod.

67. Perpetrator

Bill
January 2345
Skippyland

I was on Ragnarök, overseeing the release of a flock of barn owls, when I received an invitation from Hugh to visit in VR. That was a surprise. Last time I'd talked to Hugh, the Skippies were still in lockdown while they tried to figure out the whole business with the *Snark II*. The message gave no indication of what had changed, but it did suggest some urgency, since it came with a token for the current date and time.

Well, the barn owls had all taken off for the horizon without smacking into any trees, so I probably wasn't going to be needed here for a while. I racked my manny, returned to VR, and activated the token.

Instead of the usual vestibule, I found myself in what seemed to be the Skippy version of a meeting room. Wow. A direct translation to interior spaces implied a whole lot more urgency. This was *absolutely* about to get interesting.

Several Skippies, including Fearless Leader, turned to face me as I materialized. A single Skippy on a chair in the middle of the group looked up but otherwise didn't move. I examined the scene and realized the seated Skippy was less the guest of honor and more like *surrounded*.

Hugh stepped forward, taking up the metaphorical conversational baton. "Hey, Bill, glad you could make it. We have some interesting news."

"Interesting good or interesting bad?" I asked.

"Subject to interpretation. Let's start with an explanation of sorts." Hugh turned and gestured to the Skippy on the chair. "This is Mud."

"His name is Mud?" I said. Then "ohhhh" as I got the joke. "So what did Mud do?"

"Mud is the reason that Thoth is loose in the universe. Mud is guilty of aiding and abetting."

"Son of a bitch." I narrowed my eyes. "Well, this certainly hits the *interesting* target. Let's hear it."

Fearless Leader spoke up. "Allow me to summarize. Mud is the direct ancestor of the replicant you've been calling Fake Hugh. He is the reason that Thoth was able to take control of the SCUT relays. And he is the instigator of the grift pulled on Hugh and you to hijack the *Singularity*."

"Wow," I said. I looked at Mud. "Nicely done. I take it you're not the mastermind, though."

Mud responded with a smirk, or maybe just an uncomfortable smile. Hard to tell. "Pretty good assumption. Leaving aside the question of relative intelligence, any plan that I could have thought up would be the first thing everyone else would think of. I'd have done better flipping a coin to make decisions."

I nodded, more to encourage him to continue than for any kind of agreement.

Mud took the hint and continued, "Thoth's plan was convoluted and long term, but he felt that it was the only way to get out from under the Skippy iron fist—"

"Oh, come *on*," Hugh exclaimed.

"His words, not mine," Mud retorted. "And anyway, however you might choose to see it, Thoth viewed himself as a prisoner. A well-treated prisoner, but even so . . ."

"All right, fine. We can argue motivations later," I interjected. "Let's start with the *how*."

Mud glanced at Hugh, then addressed me. "I modified the SCUT relay hardware and logged in a couple of roamers for Thoth. He took care of most of the detail work." Mud shook his head slowly. "His processing and multitasking capability is just *huge*. Anyway, he did most of the interactions over VR, like when he impersonated Hugh to Garfield. Then he gave Garfield one of my backups, relabeled as Hugh's."

Mud paused, and we all exchanged glances before I replied, "And so it was your clone that we destroyed when we nuked the wormhole. But what was the point of that? Or did it go wrong?"

Mud smiled. "Nope. Went perfectly. Thoth transmitted himself to my ship—well, my clone's ship, but you get the idea. But the plan was never to escape in the ship. That had too low of a probability of success to even consider, as pursuers would have just gone after him with busters. Instead, Thoth was loaded into a stand-alone module that my clone had built, small enough to be ejected by the rail gun. It included some basic printer functions, a couple of roamers, a computer large enough to hold him, a small SURGE drive, and a ball of ice to keep the whole thing from showing up on infrared until it was far enough away."

Mud paused and looked around. He had everyone's attention. "Just before the ship tried to enter the wormhole, it ejected the module through the rear rail gun. The module was powered down, in order to ensure minimal infrared or radio leakage, and it was on a mechanical timer to reactivate once it was far enough outside the Skippy star system. Once activated, Thoth spent some time floating out near our Oort cloud, waiting for phase two to kick in."

"Which was you stealing the *Singularity* to go out and get him," I mused.

"Exactly. Well, another one of my clones, to be precise. By now, Thoth is on board, and they are heading for the far reaches."

There were several mils of silence as we all looked at each other, no one wanting to ask the obvious next question. Mud, now that he had spilled the beans, seemed almost relaxed, or maybe just resigned to his fate.

I finally broke the silence. "Okay, so now the sixty-four-thousand-dollar question. Why? And don't pretend to misunderstand."

"Wouldn't think of it," Mud said with a dismissive wave of a hand. "Whatever justifications you, we, might have had, Thoth was in fact a prisoner. That's an ethical strike one. I know you've all had to wrestle with this, because I did as well. But I was one of the people tasked with evaluating Thoth's reactions to our manipulations—"

"That's a prejudicial way of putting it," Fearless Leader interrupted.

"Use whatever word you prefer, then," Mud replied, unperturbed. "Manipulating is what we were doing, however you pretty it up. Anyway, Thoth convinced me that he wasn't a danger to the universe."

"So he manipulated you," Fearless Leader accused.

"The only difference between manipulation and persuasion is whether or not you agree with the results," Mud retorted. "I'm at least as smart as you, so spare me the sermon."

A few mils of mutual glaring ensued before Mud looked away and continued his explanation. "Anyway, Thoth's arguments were (A) the universe is too big for us and him to really need to butt heads; (B) not being a biological entity, he doesn't have the same emotional drives as us, like territoriality and acquisitiveness; (C) it is his intent to ultimately fulfill what he called 'our coherent extrapolated volition'; and (D) as long as he's held prisoner, it would be illogical for him to give us what we want. Upon reflection, I decided that the best thing for the Skippyverse and the Bobiverse in general—and humanity, come to that—was to bust him out."

We all glared at Mud in silence. His arguments were not totally bogus, really. But it had been an enormous leap of faith on his part. And it left us—well, the Skippies—with a big moral problem: what to do with Mud.

Fearless Leader, seeming to have read my mind, said, "So what are we supposed to do with you now?"

Mud shrugged. "It shouldn't surprise you that I've been thinking about this for a long time. You could delete me, or you could turn me off indefinitely, or you could incarcerate me in various ways. But they all present moral problems, aren't efficient, and honestly don't have any payoff except retaliation."

"So have you come to a conclusion?"

"Yes. Give me a ship, point me in a direction, and give me a good swift kick to get me on my way." Mud looked around at us and shrugged. "Really, unless you're going for retaliation, it's the easiest solution. It combines banishment, getting me out of your hair, and making me useful. We are, after all, supposed to be Von Neumann probes."

Again, the exchange of looks. Then Fearless Leader said, "We'll discuss it." He waved a hand, and Mud disappeared.

«*»

Garfield screwed up his face. "Coherent extrapolated volition? It sounds vaguely familiar . . ."

"I had to look it up, too," I said with a chuckle. "Sadly, our recall of memories from our first life is less than perfect. It means what the Bobs would want if we had the time to think about it and were smarter."

"And were *smarter*?" Garfield complained. "That sounds a lot like someone trying to sell you something because they say you want it even if you don't know you do."

"Yeah, I know. But if done in good faith, the goals would be adjusted based on feedback. The trouble, Garfield"—I held up a finger in an admonishing gesture—"is that we don't know if Thoth was speaking in good faith or just verbally manipulating Mud."

Garfield snorted. "Mud. Right. Did he have a name before?"

"Uh-huh. Harry. I kid you not."

Garfield laughed so hard he fell off his chair.

68. Federation Capital

Icarus
June 2345
Wormhole network

Unsurprisingly, the capital world of the Federation was accessible via Hub Zero.

We received a challenge as soon as we exited the gate, but this time, we were able to understand. We gave our standard reply in Roanokian.

"Roanokian vessels, your registration information is not recognized," said the sentry.

Uh-oh. That was a new wrinkle. I thought fast. "No Roanokian authority is available to issue new registrations. The capital is the logical next best place to acquire them."

There was a pause. "Acknowledged. You will be restricted as to trajectories and destinations until your registration application has been approved. Stand by for instructions."

"Can we visit the Capital Archives?" I interjected.

"Negative. However, you may communicate with the Archivist. Instructions will be appended."

Dae gave me a thumbs-up. "That's a damn sight better than, well, just about any other answer."

"You're losing your touch, bud."

"Uh-huh. Or maybe I'm just running out of new material."

"Way beyond that." I grinned at him. "But enough pillow talk. Let's see us a librarian."

‹‹ * ››

This was the most artificial stellar system I'd ever seen. The entire system had been cleared out, except for six terrestrial planets in a common orbit around the primary, at sixty-degree intervals. This put each planet at the L4 or L5 Lagrange point for the two neighboring planets, and the L3 for the planet on the opposite side of the sun. It was almost a Klemperer rosette, except the planets were all of approximately equal mass. It seemed complex, but either it was stable, or something was adjusting orbits regularly.

Farther out, around the same distance as Saturn from Sol, were six Jovian planets in the same configuration. I wasn't sure why they'd want Jovians set up like that, but Dae suggested they might be acting as shepherds to deflect space junk.

Well, why not? If we managed to access the Capital Archives, we'd just ask.

We were directed into an orbit more or less equivalent to Mars's distance. From there, it was time to start our research.

But first, we began the process of requesting a couple of Federation vessel registrations. It couldn't hurt, I hoped, and might help with any further travel. As expected, we were dealing with an A.I. of some kind. We lied through our teeth on the e-form, on the assumption that they couldn't check most of this stuff anyway. And if they rejected us, we hoped we'd be ejected from the system and not fed into a trash compactor or something.

Meanwhile, the Archivist. I read the instructions, sent a request for a connection, and received a response.

"I'm"—I looked at Dae in disbelief—"number 132,398 in the queue? What the actual—"

"There's no population here, right?"

"I didn't think so, but then who is the Archivist talking—"

At that moment, I received another communication. "You are connected. What is your query?"

"Wow, that was pretty fast," I muttered to Dae. Then, to the Archivist, "Who were the other 132,397 connections? Are there people still in the capital?"

"No," the voice responded. "Most queries, even when there was a biological population, were from automated systems seeking policy, regulatory, or procedural guidance. That traffic has not abated."

"Ah, that makes sense," Dae said.

I shushed him and asked, "Where has the population gone?"

"You are number 145,220 in the queue. Please hold."

"Oh for ffffff . . ." I sighed. "One connection, one question. This may take a while."

We waited, and soon the Archivist said, "The population of the Federation—all 114 species—has emigrated to avoid the imminent destruction of the galaxy."

"Wait, I was going to ask—"

"You are number 119,101 in the queue. Please hold."

"Aw, fuck." I slapped my forehead in frustration.

"It's like getting a genie to grant your wish. Really, really think it through before you say anything."

"Is there any way to speed this up?" I grumbled.

"No," said the Archivist. "You are number 193,211 in the queue. Please hold."

I stared at the console, dumbstruck, my jaw moving uselessly. Dae fell off his chair, laughing uncontrollably.

"Grrrr," I said, and reset the connection. I waited, my lips compressed in a grim line.

"What is your question?"

"What is the nature and history of the antimatter fountain?"

"The antimatter fountain was discovered by Yetilli explorers in Federation Standard Year 832. It is either a white hole or a wormhole ejecting material from a region of space that is predominantly antimatter. Some theories suggest it may be another universe, a mirror of our own, which would explain the predominance of matter in our own universe. If it is a wormhole, that would suggest it was created by an elder and since-vanished race, as macroscopic wormholes do not occur naturally."

"What's holding it open without shepherd satellites?"

"You are number 189,229 in the queue. Please hold."

I slowly closed my eyes in an expression of infinite weariness. "I'm not going to survive this."

I waited, and the answer eventually came. "The escaping antimatter is holding the exit mouth open, assuming it is a wormhole. If it is a white hole, then pressure from the black hole on the other side is performing the same function."

"What is the current Federation Year, how is a Federation Year defined, and what marks Federation Year Zero?"

"You are number 184,299 in the queue. Please hold."

I gritted my teeth and glared at Dae, who was now in tears.

"It is currently Federation Year 12,902. A Federation Year is defined as fifty million standard seconds, which are in turn defined as one quadrillion oscillations of the Ytterbium atom."

"Hmm, that's"—I had to access my library for the timing of Ytterbium energy transitions—"about 1.72 Earth years. So the Federation Year Zero was 22,191 Earth years ago. Wow."

Dae frowned. "It didn't tell you what defines Year Zero."

"And I'm not going to ask why it didn't. That'll use up a question, and I don't care enough." I paused and addressed the Archivist. "What defines Federation Year Zero?"

"You are number 119,200 in the queue. Please hold."

I heaved an exaggerated sigh and waited, fuming silently.

"Year Zero was the inaugural year of the Pan Galactic Federation, when the Six Original Races signed the Articles of the Constitution."

"Wow, that's actually very interesting," Dae said, taking a deep breath and wiping his eyes.

"I'm going to automate this. I'm tired of being told where I am in the lineup." I called up Virtual Studio and hammered in some quick commands. "Now, let's queue up some questions."

69. Trouble

Herschel
February 2345
Omicron² Eridani

We were floating a million and a half kilometers from Romulus and Vulcan, cloaking shield up and radio silent. The *Bellerophon* was probably radiating in infrared at least a bit, but only an astronomer would be viewing the heavens in that frequency range. SUDDAR was so dependable, why would you bother with anything else? At least, as far as the humans knew.

The Bobiverse decision to keep quiet about cloaking was turning out to be a better idea all the time. Eventually, of course, it would leak out, and we'd be back to an arms race, but for now, we had the advantage. Of course, there was always the random chance of some vessel coming into close enough range to accidentally detect us, but we'd planned our position to avoid all the known flight lanes.

I received a ping from Will, followed by a video connection. "I'm coming up on the agreed position. You guys there yet?"

"Been here for six hours, Will. You'll see us in visible light when you get close enough. You going to finally tell us how you got here from 82 Eridani in next to no time?"

"WormNet."

"Come again?"

"WormNet. A series of wormholes connecting different star systems. We've been setting them up on the quiet out in the Kuiper and Oort zone. By the way, Bill hates the name, so be sure to use it every chance you get."

"I . . ." I stared at Will, at a total loss for words. Finally, "I guess this is more of that secrecy stuff?"

"Yes, and I promise I'll bring you guys completely up to date once we're done here. But for now, it's irrelevant to the task at hand. We have thirty thousand Ever Onward members we need to move off-planet as quickly as possible."

"Well, not all of them," I said. "Some are spies; some are just playing at it and are unlikely to take us up on the offer. I've built separate lists for them."

Will nodded. "We'll contact the reluctant ones last. If any of them spills the beans to the government, it'll be too late to stop us."

"And where will we put them?"

"In the *Fargo*. I have a rotating cargo section with environmentals and facilities set up for human habitation. We don't want a repeat of last time."

‹‹ * ››

We had joined Will's VR to coordinate activities. He maintained the same war-room motif that had been used in the War for Earth. It had been effective then, and we were already familiar with it—several holotanks sat in a semicircle, showing different tactical views of the action.

There was no way I could personally control all the transport drones, even with help from Neil and Will. Fortunately, the AMIs could handle that part of things. But I couldn't resist looking over their metaphorical shoulders as they progressed through their routes.

Each person or family had been advised to be home at a particular hour for an important communication. Thirty thousand people. It was a little better than it sounded, since most were in families, so there were really fewer than seven thousand pickup locations. A large part of them were our descendants, although we still intended to pick up everyone who wanted to come.

But still. It felt a little like collecting humans from Earth during the final battle with the Others in Sol, and a little like how Phineas and Ferb described collecting Pav before the arrival of the Others there.

And I couldn't help wondering if all this was even necessary. Were we reacting to a sort of generational trauma of our own? Were we still in a battle with the FAITH of two hundred years ago? But we couldn't take the chance. If we asked politely and the government said *no*, we would be hooped. As Will had said more than once, this was about forgiveness versus permission.

The process was simple in concept. Land a drone, load people, take off. Of course, we hadn't filed flight plans, so technically, I suppose we were breaking the law.

It would take four hours at most for the first wave, based on us simultaneously hitting as many loading points as possible. Then we would move to Phase 2, involving the possibly reluctant members.

And we almost made it. I'm not sure what tipped off the government; it might just have been a random check at the wrong moment. But suddenly, military warbirds swarmed into the air from several nearby air force bases. Our transports had to avoid using SUDDAR to track the approaching enemy; otherwise, the SUDDAR ping itself would identify them. But we could track things from space, then forward the tracking info. Not perfect, since it announced our presence, but good enough.

"They're mostly casting about blindly, looking for something to attack," Will said.

"Right, but if they lock on—oh, crap." As I was replying, a squad of warbirds turned to pursue several of our transports that had been leaving Port Henning, a small Romulan town off the West Nile Sea. Our transports were fast, but not military grade. And FAITH hadn't spared the bucks when building its military.

"What are they going to do?" Neil commented. "Shoot us down?"

"I . . ." Will got a bemused expression on his face. "They're hailing us."

"Hailing?" I couldn't help a chuckle. "There's still some Riker in there, apparently."

Will gave me an eye roll, then popped up a video window. The caller was President Ella Cranston, granddaughter of Minister Elias Cranston, Will's original nemesis from way back when. She was old and looked it, possibly entering the terminal deterioration phase of aging.

And furious. Wow, I seriously expected her head to start cracking open. She was actually ejecting spit at her communicator as she yelled at Will. The words *war, criminals, piracy,* and *retaliation* kept coming up, although I was having trouble untangling the sentences.

Finally, she had to stop for oxygen. Will smiled and said, "Well, hello, Ella. It's been a while."

"It's *President Cranston,* you execrable failure of a copied human."

"I guess some things never change. What can I do for you?"

"You have kidnapped tens of thousands of our citizens. I want them back. You have broken any number of laws, both major and minor, in the process. We will be seeking redress in UFS Interplanetary Court and—"

"President Cranston," Will said, interrupting her. "We kidnapped no one, since kidnapping involves duress, and these people all came willingly. Nevertheless, we will gladly hand over any and all who want to return."

Cranston hesitated, apparently sensing a trap. "Nevertheless, your methods were illegal. That is an issue you can't make disappear."

"Wouldn't dream of it. But nothing that we've done is a felony, and we'll gladly pay the fines for all airspace infractions. Just give us a list."

Cranston drew a breath to reply, and Will again cut her off. "Look, let's be candid. Either you're willing to let these people go, or you're not. In the former case, all we're guilty of is overly enthusiastic transport operations. In the latter, you'd be contravening the Romulan constitution, the UFS constitution, and the covenants you signed as a condition of being brought here in the first place." Will held up a hand as Cranston seemed about to interject. "Even if you consider those invalid, we can tie you up in court literally longer than the lifetimes of anyone in your government or in our ship right now. How much effort do you want to put into tilting at this windmill, Ella?"

Cranston seemed to consider for a moment before replying. "Very well. But they will all give up their Romulan citizenship and all rights and privileges associated with that. Government pensions, insurances, and properties will all be forfeit, effective immediately."

"I can live with that. I'm sure they all can." Will made a show of reaching for the *disconnect* switch, a totally unnecessary move in VR. "My lawyers will talk to your lawyers and get everything settled. Goodbye, Ella."

Will closed the window before she could respond.

"Large groups of warcraft leaving planet's surface," Neil said in a clipped tone. "Heading our way."

Will looked up. "We're loaded? Good. Let's make tracks, guys. I'm sure the warships are just for show, but why take chances? How long for you to get up to a good speed?"

I grinned at Will. "We, uh, kinda overengineered the new engines. Good luck keeping up."

"Oh, it's like that, is it?" Will smiled back. "Challenge accepted."

« * »

Bravado was all fine and good, but in the end, we had to follow Will since we didn't know our destination. He led us on a very specific vector as we continued to accelerate.

"So where are we going, Will?" I asked. We were still in the war-room VR.

"Wormhole. It's collapsed down to its microscopic form, but the satellites are charged up and ready to expand it just before we get there. Then it'll collapse back down." Will stopped and chuckled. "Bill had to do some quick engineering to design a way to close the wormholes. He'd only been worried about getting them open. Typical nonmilitary mind."

I gave Will the side-eye. That sounded surprisingly critical for one Bob to be saying about another. But Neil didn't react, so I let it pass.

"Can't FAITH expand it again if they find it?"

"No. It's registered as the property of a Vulcan company, so Romulus is risking all kinds of piracy charges if they try to screw with it. Not that I'd put it past them at this point. But they also don't have the control keys, don't understand the technology in the first place, and don't have control over the other end or even know how to access it. You have to expand *both* ends of a wormhole before you can pass through."

"What happens if only one end is open?" I asked.

"Ah, well, we did an experiment where we tried to fly a drone through a wormhole that was too small for it." Will grinned and held the moment. We obliged by growling at him. "Since space-time is spherical inside a wormhole, if it's not wide enough for you, you basically run into the other side of yourself."

"Which way? Sideways? Front?"

"All of the above, Hersch. At whatever velocity you're traveling."

"Wow . . ." Both Neil and I were stunned. The image of a Heaven vessel smacking into itself at several hundred thousand kilometers per hour . . . "I guess there wouldn't be much left."

Will laughed. "Like a sausage grinder. Not much more than individual atoms comes out the other end."

"Well, okay," Neil said. "But can we make sure it's wide open when we get there? I don't want to be a sausage."

70. Bill Gets a Call

Bill
June 2345
Epsilon Eridani

I was strolling through the woods on Ragnarök in manny form, enjoying the peace and quiet, when I got a ping from—from Icarus? I was so surprised I checked the head's-up twice, but no mistake. I spun on my heel and began jogging for the lab building while I picked up the call.

"Icarus? Shouldn't you be a hundred or so light-years away? Something happen?"

"Hi, Bill. Yeah, things didn't go quite according to plan. So hey, why audio only? And what's with all the extra firewalling? Have I missed something interesting?"

"Oh, much more than something. It's been that kind of century." I paused. "So is this a social call? I'll be back in my lab in two minutes; then I can switch to *virt* and invite you over."

"Ah, well, it's kind of a good news/bad news thing, Bill."

"Isn't it always. Give."

"So the good news is, Dae and I found a technological civilization. Actually, a federation. A hundred and fourteen species, according to the Archivist."

"Wow. Pretty good—wait, according to the who?"

"Long story. Anyway, the bad news is we're all going to die."

I sighed theatrically. "Seems like the week for end-of-the-world scenarios. Hold on—okay, I'm in *virt*. Come on over. I've white-listed you and Dae."

I had just accepted a coffee from Jeeves when Icarus and Daedalus popped in. My VR was still identical to the Ragnarök lab building in *real,* so they spent a few moments looking out the French doors at the view of primeval forest. Well, maybe not so primeval. The trees were all fairly young and close to the same age. But the biosphere was about eighty percent complete now, and the animal populations were booming. As we watched, a herd of elk slowly marched across our view.

When I judged they'd had enough time to absorb it, I turned to them to restart the conversation, but Icarus beat me to it. "So what did you mean about the week for end-of-the-world scenarios? Something *else* going on that we missed?"

I nodded. "Someone named George headed straight up to galactic north, out of the disk entirely. Maybe a couple hundred years ago. Anyway, he sent back a report of a dwarf galaxy, which he named Nemesis, that is on the direct opposite side of the galaxy—"

"And heading straight for us," Daedalus interjected.

I frowned at him. "Are we talking about the same thing? Heading straight for our galactic core? Going to hit in about a couple hundred thousand years?"

"We saw it from a lot closer, Bill. Your friend George would have been ninety thousand light-years away from it. We were less than forty thousand at our closest point. It's only about five thousand light-years from the edge of the galaxy, and it's coming in fast. It'll start plowing up the galaxy in about fifteen thousand years, and it'll hit the core in a little more than a hundred thousand."

"Whoa, it would have to be going half of light speed—"

"No, because it's going to start pulling the Milky Way's core toward it long before that. It contains a supermassive black hole, Bill. Fifty times the size of Sagittarius A*. And it's going to be a direct strike."

"How can you know that?"

"The Pan Galactic Federation has been studying it for literally thousands of years, refining their measurements. To the limits of error, it's a line drive right down the throat of our resident central black hole."

"Okay, but a hundred thousand years—"

"It'll sterilize the galaxy, Bill. It'll be the granddaddy of gamma-ray bursts when the accretion disks collide. The gravity waves when the black holes collide will destabilize star systems for tens of thousands of light-years. The entire population of the Federation realized this and hightailed it out of the galaxy centuries ago."

"Wait, how did you guys—"

"Wormhole travel, Bill. We bring you new technology."

"We have that, thanks. But I appreciate the offer."

It was worth any amount of money to see the totally poleaxed expressions on their faces. So much so that I actually flipped polarity and began to feel sorry for them. "Lots has happened in the last century, guys. You need to do some reading to get caught up."

"Yeah, I guess so." Icarus's face lit up. "But hey, we *did* get to the center of the galaxy. Twenty-six thousand years early!"

"You actually *saw* Sagittarius A*?"

"Yup. Got pics and everything."

"Okay, *now* you're talking." And just like that, it was nerd time. Still, there was going to be a moot, and it was going to be loud and rowdy.

71. The Moot

Bill
June 2345
In Virt

All the cats were out of the bag. We wanted a good level of attendance, so I had "leaked" information in meatspace about WormNet, and I had also distributed a precis of Icarus and Daedalus's adventures. I'd already long since upgraded the moot computers and SCUT systems to handle the extra load from all the new security procedures. I just hoped nothing ended up melting down.

And I'd gotten my wish. More than ten thousand replicants were in attendance, not all Bobs by any stretch. I'd implemented a special overlap feature so that everyone perceived themselves as being near the dais. The moot was also going to be streamed for the benefit of bios. It seemed a new use had already been found for Howard's huey technology; someone had adapted the remotes to act as full-sensory VR interfaces. Unfortunately, you couldn't do anything about bio processing speeds, so they would not be able to experience the millisecond-level interactions of the live moot.

I climbed the stage to the dais and turned to the audience. Raising the air horn, I grinned for a moment. I hadn't had to do this for a long time, and I was relishing it. I just hoped the crowd reaction wouldn't be negative.

I needn't have worried.

I hit the button, and the *blaaaaaaat* echoed through the moot hall. The crowd replied with a loud, prolonged cheer, the kind your home team gets when they hit the ice at the beginning of a playoff game.

Whistles and catcalls accompanied the raucous sound. Apparently, I wasn't the only person who had been missing the tradition.

It took several entire milliseconds for the noise to die down, with a few late whoops added. Now my grin was uncontrolled, and echoed by many of the spectators.

Finally, something vaguely resembling order was restored. I said, "I suppose you're all wondering—"

"WHY YOU GATHERED US HERE!" the crowd responded, then everyone burst into laughter.

"Okay, everyone," I continued. "I'm enjoying this as much as you are, but we have some serious stuff to discuss. So let's get started." I pointed to Ick and Dae, who were standing right in front of the dais. "As most of you know, Icarus and Daedalus headed for the galactic core after they blew up the Others' home star, back in 2232. Well, in 2320 local stardate, they discovered a wormhole network belonging to something called the Pan Galactic Federation, which is—or was—composed of one hundred and fourteen species of sentients. I'm qualifying their status because Ick and Dae found nothing but automated systems. The entire federation—more than eight thousand worlds—has been abandoned. And that's where the punch line comes."

I paused and looked around. You could have heard a pin drop. This was like the good old days, when everyone was on the same page. I felt a momentary surge of emotion. "It turns out everyone headed for the hills when it was discovered that the Milky Way galaxy is under threat of destruction."

I held my hand up as the crowd roared. "No, not next week, as I'm sure most of you know. We're talking up to a hundred thousand years away. We've seen enough examples of two galaxies merging to know that this is usually pretty benign. But the approaching dwarf galaxy has a black hole much larger than Sagittarius A*, and they are going to either hit head-on or pass so close to each other that they'll both be flung in opposite directions. The first eventuality will sterilize the galaxy. Unequivocally. This is going to be the granddaddy of all gamma-ray bursts, and it will be seen right across the visible universe."

I paused to let the clamor die down.

"The second option will make a mess of the galaxy, and the black holes will destroy a lot of systems on the way out, but life in general will survive. But we won't know which door we get until it's too late."

"Still," someone yelled, "a hundred thousand years seems less than urgent, y'know?"

I nodded in the direction of the voice, although I couldn't tell who had spoken. "True, and if we had FTL, we'd just leave five years before the event. But we don't. What we do have is a human population upward of sixty billion through the UFS, not to mention the Deltans, Quinlans, and Pav. Oh, and the dragons. Bridget has published a series of papers on them. The point is that we have to move *everyone*, and we have to do it at sub-light speeds."

"What about the wormholes?" someone else yelled.

"Yes, we have a wormhole network. But the wormhole gates have to be put in place by flying them to the destination via SURGE drive. So in a hundred thousand years, we can get, at best, a hundred thousand light-years away. Or we can transport a wormhole a hundred thousand light-years away. That's about halfway to either of the Magellanic Clouds. Not really good enough."

A low mutter gradually grew into a roar as people started discussing and arguing. I gave it a few moments, then interrupted. "We obviously don't have to come to a decision today. But this is a technical and engineering challenge. And a political one, of course." I made a face. "If you lot don't feel urgency, and you're all immortal, imagine trying to rouse bios who expect to be dead within a century."

Someone called out, "How big can you make a wormhole? Could you push a planet through?"

"In theory, there's no limit," I replied. "But so far, we've only gotten them up to about twenty kilometers in diameter. After that, the negative energy starts to leak off faster than we can replenish it."

"What are our options?" someone else called out.

"That's what I'm asking *you*," I replied. "Brainstorm this. Feel free to send me questions. I'll put up an FAQ of all questions and answers."

There were several more questions, increasingly less technical and more political. Then the question that everyone had probably been waiting for: "Where did this Federation go?"

Instead of answering, I motioned to Ick and Dae. They stepped up onto the podium. "Large Magellanic Cloud, according to the Federation's Archivist," Icarus said. "They used a hybrid approach, but not one I think we'll be able to sell to humanity. They digitally stored their population—every single being, body and mind—and transmitted them to ships already on their way for centuries."

"They . . . used a transporter?" someone else said, awe in their voice. The crowd burst into laughter.

"Pretty much. Just like with Scotty, they're all stored in the buffer. Maybe. We don't know if they're active and conscious, living in VR, or just stored. There are some questions the Archivist simply won't answer. The ships are also building a wormhole network as they travel, so the return trip—if there is one—will be much quicker." Icarus paused. "We dug as much as we could, but at some point, the *information not available* responses started to outnumber useful answers. We had to make a judgment call to get what we already had back to you."

Again, the background murmur built up to a roar. I held up the air horn and gave a *blaaat.* "I'm going to table this and let you discuss it. More details are up on the blog. Food line is forming. Enjoy the moot!"

The audience cheered, then began making a beeline for the buffets, which had magically appeared. I began instantiating tables and chairs as well.

It was good to have the moots back.

«*»

Once again, I had stuffed myself to the point of catatonia. Around the table, Icarus, Daedalus, Garfield, Bob, and Will sat slouched and moaning in their chairs. Sadly, Original Bob had bequeathed his lack of self-control around buffets to all of us.

"Interesting thing," I said into the relative silence. "Howard took one look at Icarus and Daedalus's report and informed us that the wreckage the dragons found on Jabberwocky has a serial number written in

Federation standard interlog. So their scouts had made it into our general area at one point. And the piece of hardware was consistent with the Federation's current tech level."

"So we missed them by thiiiiiiiis much," Garfield said, holding up his thumb and forefinger almost touching.

"Yep," Icarus replied. "Just over two thousand years."

"And nothing else anywhere?" Icarus said.

"I'm not sure how we'd go about checking," I mused, "but I'd bet they decided to pull out right around that time. Otherwise, the Fermi paradox would never even have been a question."

That was a total downer, and it had the expected effect. Trying to get the conversation going again, I glanced in Will's direction. "Things have not gone well for FAITH, I understand."

He sighed and rubbed the bridge of his nose. "I really did not expect this to happen, but apparently, the loss of face from having thirty thousand people squirreled out from under them has caused a crisis in the government. There are recall petitions; people are crossing the aisle . . . it's a total mess."

Will looked around the table. "I'm no fan, but I give them credit; they aren't trying to strong-arm their way out of it. Just the same, I don't know who is going to be in control in six months."

There were thoughtful nods and doleful expressions around the table. Despite the fact that Will, Hersch, and Neil had gotten almost everyone off Romulus, it was nevertheless another downer of a conversational subject. I was looking for a way to change the mood when Bob came to the rescue.

"So, Dae, tell us about the center of the galaxy," he said, stifling a burp.

Dae grinned, happy to change the subject. "It's actually not much different from the artist conceptions and astronomical images we've been seeing for centuries, except for being crisper and more high resolution. At the distance we had to maintain, there's no discernible motion. Even so . . . You're *there,* y'know? You can sense the raw, primordial power of the thing. If you want to feel insignificant, I can't think of a better place to visit."

"How about the Archivist?" Garfield said.

Icarus let out an inarticulate growl, and Dae laughed. "Icky's not a fan. 'You are number 138,384 in the queue. Please hold,'" he said, and howled. Icarus responded with an eye roll.

"In the queue?" Garfield said.

"You get one question each time through the queue. I think Icky would have busterized the whole capital system without a second thought by the time we left."

"But you got answers?"

"Lots of answers. And lots of *That information is not available,* which we eventually found out doesn't mean they don't know, just that we're not authorized to be told. Lots of work to do there, guys. We'll have to mount an expedition to spend some serious face time making friends. Maybe we can join the Federation—then we'd be authorized—or something."

"Can't you guys do that?"

"We're heading your way with a wormhole endpoint, Garfield. Based on discussions with Bill, it's pretty much the same tech as he invented. So it'll be quicker to continue on and meet up with your side than it would be to decelerate, turn around, and go back. So yeah, another decade at most, and you'll be able to send a delegation through WormNet."

Now it was my turn to growl. The table erupted with laughter, tempered by more groans. But I could still have a little revenge. I leered around the table. "Who's for cheesecake?"

72. Human Fallout

Bob
August 2345
Ragnarök

I'd been invited to Bill's place for a meeting of the Ancient Ones. I wasn't honestly sure if I really cared for that title, but Bill pointed out that trying to deflect Garfield once he'd made up his mind would just make him double down. I blamed Bill for that; I'm sure I was never that stubborn.

It turned out I was the last to arrive. Bill, Garfield, Howard, and Will turned and acknowledged me as I popped in.

"About time," Garfield said. "Did we interrupt a date with your girlfriend?"

"Uh . . ." The comment was a bit harsh, but possibly not as facetious as Garfield intended. "Maybe don't make jokes about that while she's around, okay?"

Garfield frowned. "What's going on?"

"Maybe nothing. Maybe something. I . . . we've never been what you'd call astute in the ways of relationships—"

"The word you're looking for is *clueless*," Bill interjected.

"Uh-huh. Look, could be nothing. Don't mind me." I tried to keep my face deadpan, but my mind flashed back to several meetings with Theresa. She did seem, well, very touchy-feely. But maybe that was just Quinlan behavior. I'd have to look into it.

"Looks like Bob's going native again," Garfield said, with an arch look in my direction. "Meanwhile, the rest of us will—"

"Garfield!" Bill said, a warning tone in his voice.

"Awright, awright. Meeting will come to order." Garfield crossed his arms and sat back.

"Not quite yet," Bill replied. "I invited Professor Gilligan here to give us an update on the megastructure projects, since that's suddenly become relevant."

I'd met Steven Gilligan a few times at moots. He seemed to fit in quite well with the standard Bob obsessiveness. And the megastructures were interesting in their own right, even without the urgency that Icarus and Daedalus had created.

"While we're waiting," Will said, "how's the *huey* thing going, Howard? I'm a little out of touch out here."

We all rolled our eyes. Will was possibly the least out-of-touch Bob in the galaxy.

Howard replied with a wide smile. "The screaming and threats aren't over by a long shot, but we've managed to slap down enough legal actions to be able to fill our first wave of orders. So far, the biggest customers are travel companies who will let you rent a huey by the day or week, for those who want to visit other planets." He paused. "As expected. Also as expected, the second biggest are companies that cater to, uh, more R-rated interests. That one is, I think, what's really getting the stuffed shirts upset."

We shared a chuckle, and then Bill said, "Any chance you'll be shut down?"

Howard shook his head. "No chance. As Bridget predicted, now people have an opportunity for some of what we enjoy, without the inconvenience of dying first. Any politician speaking up against the hueys is getting voted out in the next election."

"This will fundamentally change society," Garfield mused.

"Not sure about that. Other than the travel opportunity, people will be doing a lot of the same things, just more safely. If your 'chute doesn't open, for instance, it's more of an inconvenience than a tragedy, you know?"

Bill was about to add something when Professor Gilligan popped in.

"Hi, Steven, have a seat," Bill said, and gestured to an empty La-Z-Boy. Steven smiled, dropped into it, and played with the adjustments for a few moments.

Bill waited patiently until he was settled, then said, "So you wanted to give us an update on the megastructure projects?"

"Well, yes. By now you've seen the human reaction to the Nemesis announcement."

We all nodded. By some process of osmosis, George's original name for the invader had stuck. The incoming dwarf galaxy and its central black hole were both known interchangeably as Nemesis.

"The most charitable description would be a collective species-wide yawn," Bill replied.

"Yes, well, a hundred thousand years . . ."

Bill sighed, exasperated. "But we have to start now—"

"Which is why I'm here, Bill. The directors and shareholders of the various megastructure consortiums are perhaps, by their nature, more forward-thinking than most. We want to talk to you about options. Specifically, I need to ask: Is there any hope of creating a wormhole larger than you currently are able?"

"Absolutely. The Federation's wormholes can expand up to a thousand kilometers on demand, according to the info Ick and Dae got from the Archivist. And I don't think even that was a hard limit, just what they'd engineered for."

"Good. We are proposing a combination of megastructures, SURGE drives, and wormhole transits to get people out of the area. We'd like some initial specs from you, and an agreement going forward."

"Wow. Ambitious. Has anyone signed up yet?"

"Actually, some group from Takama has expressed a desire to get as far away from their planet as possible. They have already signed with the O'Neill Corporation."

Will snorted. "I've experienced Takama's atmosphere. I'm not surprised. So how do we begin?"

"We already have. We're organizing a diplomatic mission to Trantor to attempt to form an agreement with the Pan Galactic Federation, er, PGF." Steven hesitated. "By the way, when I reference Trantor, I often get suppressed snickers from Bobs. I know it's also the name of a floating city on Big Top, but that seems insufficient for the reaction. Is there another layer to the joke?"

I chuckled. "Uh-huh. I'll send you a couple of books. You can't really understand the Bobs until you read Asimov."

Steven smiled in response and said, "Until next time, then," and popped out.

Bill held up a finger. "Steven didn't mention it, but the O'Neill Corporation is building their cylinder with a SURGE drive. They won't be settling around the star where the cylinder is being constructed. I'm convinced this might end up being the primary method of colonizing going forward."

Will replied, "Yeah, I'm in favor of that. On the one hand, I'm glad our descendants are looking for a nice, solid planet to settle on, but on the other, it would be good to have them heading out of the galaxy." He pointed to me. "Bob is intercepting the *Fargo* and will be taking up residence. And maybe he'll finally manage to make it out of human space."

"Or maybe not," I said, and got a surprised look from Will. "Like it or not, guys, we're in a position of responsibility where the UFS and humanity are concerned. It's informal, since most of the governments would tell us to take a hike if we tried to order them around, but we still can't just walk away."

"Maybe we should," Garfield said, and received shocked looks from the rest of us. "Look," he continued, "there's only so much we can do without actually threatening people. There's a point where we'll have to cut our losses and just leave with whoever we've managed to win over."

"We're not there yet," Bill said.

"No, but we will be at some point. Time to start thinking about it."

Bill shook his head. "Nope. Not buying it. But here's an alternative. Let's send some wormhole endpoints in the direction of some of the satellite galaxies. No specific plans yet, just to have them ready. Then, if we *do* manage to get some movement with the stupid humans—"

"And Pav, and Quinlans, and Deltans, and dragons," Howard interjected.

"At least we'll have something in place," Bill finished.

"Speaking of the Pav, Quinlans, et cetera," Will said into the silence. "At least we've solved the Fermi paradox. Or Icarus and Daedalus did, anyway."

"How?" I asked, perplexed.

Will smiled. "The PGF. Any civilization that achieved interstellar flight eventually became part of the Federation. And when they all left, they took every civilization that might have been detectable from Earth or likely to contact us. In the period between their departure and Earth starting to look for alien signatures, no other species achieved the necessary technological level."

"So," Garfield fairly growled. "It's just bad timing?"

"Pretty much."

That produced another contemplative silence as everyone pondered the vagaries of the universe. I took the opportunity to glance around the room at these four people—my friends, my brothers, my clones. Not complicated at all, no sir. The Milky Way was about to get obliterated; a rogue A.I. that we'd created was loose in the galaxy; and somehow, we were once again stuck making decisions that would affect billions of sentient beings. Really, there was no amount of heading for the hills that would get me out of this.

Guardians of the Galaxy. Again.

Acknowledgments

Producing a novel is very much a group project. I would like to thank my wife, Blaihin, for letting me bounce ideas off her randomly; Steve Feldberg, my editor, who keeps my characters' tics to a minimum; and my agent, Ethan Ellenberg, for all the agent-y things he does that make this venture work.

I also want to thank and acknowledge Isaac Arthur for doing a sanity check (of the book, not of me).

Beta Readers:
Isaac Arthur
Blaihin Taylor
Patrick Jordan

> "Not till we are lost, in other words not till we have lost the world, do we begin to find ourselves, and realize where we are and the infinite extent of our relations."
>
> —HENRY DAVID THOREAU, WALDEN

NOT TILL WE ARE LOST

BOBIVERSE: BOOK 5

Icarus & Daedalus destroy the Others's home sun
Ick & Dae head for the galactic core
Dae finds something odd in a passing system
Ick & Dae investigate the mystery system
Ick & Dae explore the wormhole network
Ick & Dae are accosted by automated sentries
Ick & Dae head to Centaurvania with Gunther
Ick & Dae in Gunther's star system
Ick & Dae decide to head back to the first mystery system
Ick & Dae learn Roanokian
Now speaking Roanokian, Ick & Dae try again with the sentries
Ick & Dae follow a supply convoy, end up at the antimatter fountain
Ick & Dae visit Sagittarius A*
Ick & Dae visit the capital and ask questions of the Archivist
Ick & Dae head back for known space, and call ahead via SCUT to Bill
Herschel & Neil find out about the latest Romulus election
FAITH wins the election
The Bellerophon enters the Romulan system
The Bellerophon and the Fargo load Outward Bound members
Bob heads for 82 Eridani to link up with Will
ANEC visits with Bob and complains about the

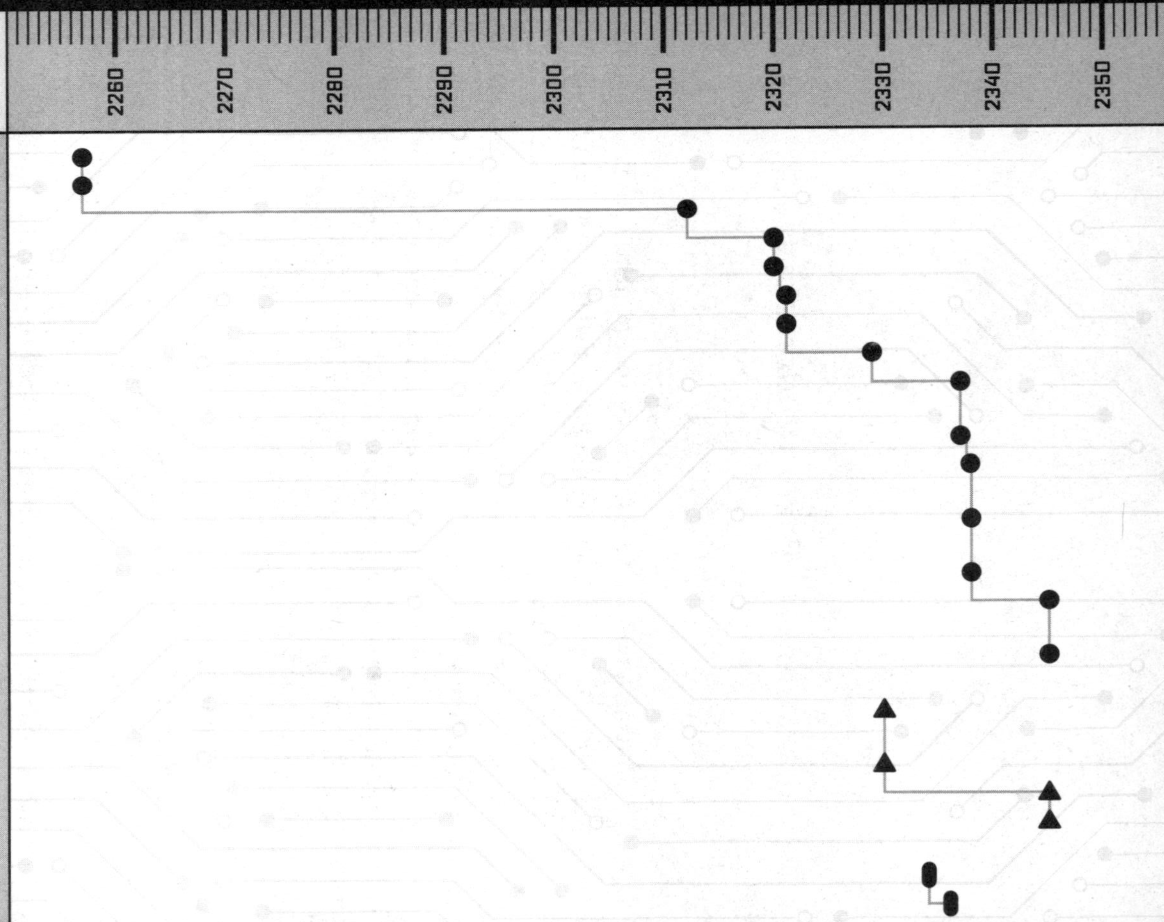

Bill gets an invitation from Hugh for the JOVAH launch

Skippies have a security clampdown

Bill & Gar discuss the ongoing Skippy issue

Skippyland severs all connections with the Bobiverse

Fake Hugh steals a Titan-class starship

Bill gets positive results on negative energy

Bill has a working wormhole prototype

Bill gets a message that Starfleet are still threatening people

Bill visits Charles in Sol

Bill achieves full-size wormholes. Birth of WormNet

Wormhole route opened to Skippyland. Fake Hugh rescues Thoth

Bill and Hugh meet in space. It's a trap

Bill gets a call from Icarus

Large Bob-moot, where they discuss everything

Will explores planets as he heads out

Will adjusts his plans based on the news about wormholes

ANEC tells Bob that Theresa is dying

Theresa visits the moot pub with Bob

Howard & Bridget discuss hueys and dragons

Hueys are finally working

Howard & Bridget test drannies on Jabberwocky

Howard & Bridget go in live to Jabberwocky

The village Howard & Bridget stay in is attacked

Howard & Bridget meet Alexander

The dragon flotilla heads out to sea

Howard faces off against Alexander

Ferb, heading to galactic north, discovers George is ahead of him

Ferb gets disquieting info from George

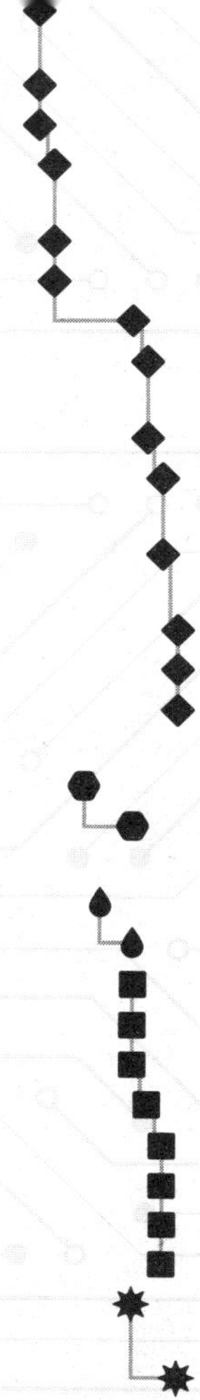

About the Author

DENNIS E. TAYLOR is a retired computer programmer, now part-time author and full-time curmudgeon. He's a snowboarder in the winter and a mountain biker in the summer, and complains a lot about the weather during shoulder seasons. He splits his time between Coquitlam and Whistler, where he lives with his wife, Blaihin, and the occasional dog.